The Borg cube loomed like a nightmare on the main viewer.

Worf longed for the raw physicality of the great Klingon battles of old, fought on fields of honor where warriors faced one another with blades to test both prowess and courage. *War was more glorious then,* he brooded. *But death remains the same.*

"The Borg cube is arming weapons," Choudhury declared.

Three shots struck the *Enterprise.* Deafening concussions rocked the ship, and consoles along the starboard bulkhead crackled with sparks, belched acrid smoke, and went dark.

Captain Picard glanced at Worf. "Now, Number One."

"Fire at will," Worf said. "Helm, execute attack pattern!"

Streaks like blue fire blazed away from the *Enterprise* and ripped into the towering black grids of dense machinery that served as the outer hull of the Borg cube. Large segments of the Borg ship disintegrated as the torpedoes exploded, and a cobalt-colored conflagration began to consume the cube from within.

Then it returned fire.

STAR TREK®

D E S T I N Y

BOOK I
GODS OF NIGHT

DAVID MACK

Based upon

STAR TREK and

STAR TREK: THE NEXT GENERATION®
created by Gene Roddenberry

STAR TREK: DEEP SPACE NINE®
created by Rick Berman & Michael Piller

STAR TREK: VOYAGER®
created by Rick Berman & Michael Piller & Jeri Taylor

STAR TREK: ENTERPRISE®
created by Rick Berman & Brannon Braga

POCKET BOOKS
New York   London   Toronto   Sydney   Erigol

Pocket Books
A Division of Simon & Schuster, Inc.
1230 Avenue of the Americas
New York, NY 10020

This book is a work of fiction. Names, characters, places, and incidents either are products of the author's imagination or are used fictitiously. Any resemblance to actual events or locales or persons, living or dead, is entirely coincidental.

First Pocket Books paperback edition October 2008

POCKET and colophon are registered trademarks of Simon & Schuster, Inc.

For information about special discounts for bulk purchases, please contact Simon & Schuster Special Sales at 1-800-456-6798 or business@simonandschuster.com

Cover art by Cliff Nielsen. Cover design by Alan Dingman.

Manufactured in the United States of America

10 9 8 7 6 5 4 3 2 1

ISBN-13: 978-1-4165-5171-3
ISBN-10:   1-4165-5171-9

*For Mom and Dad, who gave me
more than I can ever repay*

HISTORIAN'S NOTE

The prologue takes place in 2373 (Old Calendar), roughly one week after the events of the *Star Trek: Deep Space Nine* episode "Children of Time." The main narrative of *Gods of Night* takes place in February of 2381, approximately sixteen months after the movie *Star Trek Nemesis*. The flashback portions begin in 2156 and continue through 2168.

Der krieg findet immer einen Ausweg.
(War always finds a way.)

—Bertolt Brecht, *Mother Courage
and Her Children,* sc. 6

2373

PROLOGUE

It was a lifeless husk—its back broken, its skin rent, its mammoth form half buried in the shifting sands of a mountainous dune—and it was even more beautiful than Jadzia Dax remembered.

Her second host, Tobin Dax, had watched the Earth starship *Columbia* NX-02 leave its spacedock more than two hundred years earlier, on what no one then had realized would be its final mission; Tobin had directed the calibration of its starboard warp coils. A pang of sad nostalgia colored Jadzia's thoughts as she stood on the grounded vessel's bow and gazed at its shattered starboard nacelle, which had buckled at its midpoint and lay partially reclaimed by the dry waves of the desert.

Engineers from *Defiant* swarmed over the primary hull of the *Columbia*. They took tricorder readings in between shielding their faces from the scouring lash of a sand-laced sirocco. Behind them lay the delicate peaks of a desolate landscape, a vista of wheat-colored dunes shaped by an unceasing tide of anabatic winds, barren and lonely beneath a blanched sky.

Jadzia counted herself lucky that Captain Sisko had been willing to approve another planetary survey so soon after she had accidentally led them into peril on Gaia, where eight thousand lives had since been erased from history on a lover's capricious whim. Though the crew was eager to return to Deep Space 9 as quickly as possible, Dax's curiosity was always insatiable once aroused, and a flicker of a sensor reading had drawn her to this unnamed, uninhabited planet.

A sudden gust whipped her long, dark ponytail over her shoulder. She swatted it away from her face as she squinted into the blinding crimson flare of the rising suns. Adding to the brightness was a shimmer of light with a humanoid shape, a few meters away from her. The high-pitched drone of the transporter beam was drowned out by a wailing of wind in minor chords. As the sound and shine faded away, the silhouette of Benjamin Sisko strode toward her across the buckled hull plates.

"Quite a find, Old Man," he said, his mood subdued. Under normal circumstances he would have been elated by a discovery such as this, but the sting of recent events was too fresh and the threat of war too imminent for any of them to take much joy in it. He looked around and then asked, "How're things going?"

"Slowly," Dax said. "Our loadout was for recon, not salvage." She started walking and nodded for him to follow her. "We're seeing some unusual subatomic damage in the hull. Not sure what it means yet. All we know for sure is the *Columbia*'s been here for about two hundred years." They reached the forward edge of the primary hull, where the force of impact had peeled back the metallic skin of the starship to reveal its duranium spaceframe. There *Defiant*'s engineers had installed a broad ramp on a shallow incline, because the ship's original personnel hatches were all choked with centuries of windblown sand.

As they descended into the ship, Sisko asked, "Have you been able to identify any of the crew?" Echoes of their footfalls were muffled, trapped in the hollow beneath the ramp.

"We haven't found any bodies," Dax said, talking over the atonal cries of wind snaking through the *Columbia*'s corridors. "No remains of any kind." Her footsteps scraped across grit-covered deck plates as she led him toward the ship's core.

A dusty haze in the air was penetrated at irregular angles by narrow beams of sunlight that found their way through the dark wreckage. As they moved farther from the sparse light and deeper into the murky shadows of D Deck, Dax thought she saw brief flashes of bluish light, moving behind the bent bulkheads at the edges of her vision. When she turned her head to look for them, however, she found only darkness, and she dismissed the flickers as residual images fooling her retinas, as her eyes adapted to the darkness near the ship's core.

"Is it possible," Sisko asked, stepping over the curved obstacle of a collapsed bulkhead brace, "they abandoned ship and settled somewhere on the planet?"

"Maybe," Dax said. "But most of their gear is still on board." She pushed past a tangle of fallen cables and held it aside for Sisko as he followed her. "This desert goes on for nine hundred kilometers in every direction," she continued. "Between you and me, I don't think they'd have gotten very far with just the clothes on their backs."

"That's a good point, but I think it's moot," Sisko said as they rounded a curve into a length of corridor draped with cobwebs, and disturbed a thick brood of small but lethal-looking indigenous arthropods. The ten-legged creatures rapidly scurried into the cracks between the bulkheads and the deck. He and Dax continued walking. "I don't expect to find survivors from a two-hundred-year-old wreck, but I *would* like to know what an old Warp 5 Earth ship is doing in the Gamma Quadrant."

"That makes two of us," Dax said as they turned another corner toward a dead end, where Miles O'Brien hunched beneath a low-hanging tangle of wires and antiquated circuit boards—the remains of a control panel for the *Columbia*'s main computer. "Chief," Dax called out, announcing their approach. "Any luck?"

"Not yet," said the stout engineer. His tightly cut, curly fair hair was matted with sweat and dust. The two officers stepped up behind him as he continued in his gruff Irish brogue, "It's a damned museum piece is what it is. Our tricorders can't talk to it, and I can't find an adapter in *Defiant*'s databases that'll fit these inputs."

Sisko leaned in beside O'Brien, supporting himself with his right hand on the chief's left shoulder. Dax hovered behind O'Brien's right side. The captain stroked his wiry goatee once and said, "Are the memory banks intact?"

O'Brien started to chortle, then caught himself. "Well, they're here," he said. "Whether they work, who knows? I can't even power them up with the parts we have on hand."

Dax asked, "How long will it take to make an adapter?"

"Just for power?" O'Brien said. "Three hours, maybe four. I'd have to do some research to make it work with our EPS grid." He turned away from the Gordian knot of electronics to face Dax and Sisko. "Getting at its data's gonna be the real challenge. Nobody's worked with a core like this in over a century."

"Give me a number, Chief," Sisko said. "How long?"

O'Brien shrugged. "A couple days, at least."

Sisko's jaw tightened, and the worry lines on his brown forehead grew deeper as he expressed his disapproval with a frown. "That's not the answer I was looking for," he said.

"Best I can do," O'Brien said.

With a heavy sigh and a slump of his shoulders, Sisko seemed to surrender to the inevitable. "Fine," he said. "Keep at it, Chief. Let us know if you make any progress."

"Aye, sir," O'Brien said, and he turned back to his work.

Dax and Sisko returned the way they'd come, and they were met at the intersection by Major Kira. The Bajoran woman had been in charge of the search teams looking for the crew's remains. Her rose-colored militia uniform was streaked with dark gray smears of dirt and grime, and a faint speckling of dust clung to her short, close-cropped red hair. "We finished our sweep," she said, her eyes darting nervously back down the corridor. "There's no sign of the crew, or anyone else."

"What about combat damage?" asked Sisko. "Maybe they were boarded and captured."

Kira shook her head quickly. "I don't think so. All the damage I saw fits with a crash-landing. There are no blast effects on the internal bulkheads, no marks from weapons fire. Whatever happened here, it *wasn't* a firefight." Nodding forward toward the route to the exit, she added, "Can we get out of here now?"

"What's wrong, Major?" asked Sisko, whose attention had sharpened in response to Kira's apparent agitation.

The Bajoran woman cast another fearful look down the corridor behind her and frowned as she turned back toward Sisko and Dax. "There's something in here," she said. "I can't explain it, but I can *feel* it." Glaring suspiciously at the overhead, she added, "There's a *borhyas* watching us."

Sisko protested, "A ghost?" As tolerant as he tried to be of Kira's religious convictions, he sometimes grew exasperated with her willingness to embrace superstition. "Are you really telling me you think this ship is haunted?"

"I don't know," Kira said, seemingly frustrated at having to justify her instincts to her friends. "But I heard things, and I felt the hairs on my neck stand up, and I keep seeing blinks of light in the dark—"

Dax cut in, "Blue flashes?"

"Yes!" Kira said, sounding excited by Dax's confirmation.

Sisko shook his head and resumed walking forward. "I've heard enough," he said. "Let's get back to *Defiant*."

Kira and Dax fell into step behind him, and they walked back into the compartment through which they had entered the *Columbia*. Sisko moved at a quickstep, and Dax had to work to keep pace with him as he headed for the ramp topside.

"Benjamin," Dax said, "I think we need to make a more detailed study of this ship. If I had a little more time, maybe the chief and I could find a way to use *Defiant*'s tractor beams to lift the *Columbia* back to orbit and—" She was cut off by a chirping from Sisko's combadge, followed by Worf's voice.

"*Defiant to Captain Sisko,*" Worf said over the comm.

Sisko answered without breaking stride. "Go ahead."

"*Long-range sensors have detected two Jem'Hadar warships approaching this system,*" Worf said. "*ETA nine minutes.*"

"Sound Yellow Alert and start beaming up the engineers," Sisko said as he climbed the ramp into the blaze of daylight. "Wait for my order to beam up the command team."

"*Acknowledged,*" Worf replied. "*Defiant out.*"

Back atop the crash-deformed hull, Sisko stopped and turned toward Dax. "Sorry, Old Man. The salvage has to wait."

Kira asked, "Should we plant demolitions?" Dax and Sisko reacted with confused expressions, prompting Kira to elaborate, "To prevent the Jem'Hadar from capturing the ship."

"I doubt they'll find much more than we did," Sisko said. "*Columbia*'s over two hundred years old, Major—and technically, it's not even a Federation vessel." He lifted his arm to shade his eyes from the morning suns. "Besides, it's kept its secrets this long. I think we can leave it be."

Dax watched him walk away toward the apex of the primary hull. All around him, in groups of four or five, teams of engineers faded away in luminescent shimmers, transported back to the orbiting *Defiant*. The outline of Sisko's body dissolved in the suns' glare until the captain was just a stick figure in front of a sky of fire. Kira walked beside him on his right, as familiar and comfortable as someone who had always been there.

Sisko's voice emanated from Dax's combadge. *"Command team, stand by to beam up."*

The broken gray majesty of the *Columbia* lay beneath Dax's feet, an empty tomb harboring secrets untold. It pained her to abandon its mysteries before she'd had time to unravel them . . . but the Dominion was on the move, and war made its own demands.

2381

1

—◆—

Captain Ezri Dax stood on the bow of the *Columbia* and made a silent wish that returning to the wreck wouldn't prove to be a mistake, at a time when Starfleet couldn't afford any.

Engineers and science specialists from her crew swarmed over the derelict Warp 5 vessel. Its husk was half interred by the tireless shifting of the desert, much as she had remembered it from her last visit, as Jadzia Dax, more than seven years earlier. The afternoon suns beat down with an almost palpable force, and shimmering waves of heat distortion rippled above the wreck's sand-scoured hull, which coruscated with reflected light. Dax's hands, normally cold like those of other joined Trill, were warm and slick with perspiration.

Lieutenant Gruhn Helkara, Dax's senior science officer on the *Starship Aventine,* ascended the ramp through the rent in the hull and approached her with a smile. It was an expression not often seen on the skinny Zakdorn's droop-ridged face.

"Good news, Captain," he said as soon as he was within polite conversational distance. "The converter's working. Leishman's powering up the *Columbia*'s computer now. I thought you might want to come down and have a look."

"No thanks, Gruhn," Dax said. "I'd prefer to stay topside."

One of the advantages of being a captain was that Ezri no longer had to explain herself to her shipmates if she didn't want to. It spared her the potential embarrassment of admitting that her walk-through of the *Columbia* earlier that day had left her profoundly creeped out. While touring D Deck, she'd been all but certain that she saw the same spectral blue flashes that had lurked along the edges of her vision seven years earlier.

To her silent chagrin, multiple sensor sweeps and tricorder checks had detected nothing out of the ordinary on the *Columbia*. Maybe it had been just her imagination or a trick of the light, but she'd felt the same galvanic tingle on her skin that Kira had described, and she'd been overcome by a desire to get out of the wreck's stygian corridors as quickly as possible.

She'd doubled the security detail on the planet but had said nothing about thinking the ship might be haunted. One of the drawbacks of being a captain was the constant need to maintain a semblance of rationality, and seeing ghosts didn't fit the bill—not one bit.

Helkara squinted at the scorched-white sky and palmed a sheen of sweat from his high forehead, up through his thatch of black hair. "By the gods," he said, breaking their long, awkward silence, "did it actually get *hotter* out here?"

"Yes," Dax said, "it did." She nodded toward the

bulge of the ship's bridge module. "Walk with me." The duo strolled up the gentle slope of the *Columbia*'s hull as she continued. "Where are you with the metallurgical analysis?"

"Almost done, sir. You were—" He caught himself. "Sorry. *Jadzia* Dax was right. We've detected molecular distortion in the spaceframe consistent with intense subspatial stress."

Dax was anxious for details. "What was the cause?"

"Hard to be sure," Helkara said.

She frowned. "In other words, you don't know."

"Well, I'm not prepared to make *that* admission yet. I may not have enough data to form a hypothesis, but my tests have ruled out several obvious answers."

"Such as?"

"Extreme warp velocities," Helkara said as they detoured around a large crevasse where two adjacent hull plates had buckled violently inward. "Wormholes. Quantum slipstream vortices. Iconian gateways. Time travel. Oh, and the Q."

She sighed. "Doesn't leave us much to go on."

"No, it doesn't," he said. "But I love a challenge."

Dax could tell that he was struggling not to outpace her. His legs were longer than hers, and he tended to walk briskly. She quickened her step. "Keep at it, Gruhn," she said as they reached the top of the saucer. "Something moved this ship clear across the galaxy. I need to know what it was, and I need to know soon."

"Understood, Captain." Helkara continued aft, toward a gaggle of engineers who were assembling a bulky assortment of machinery that would conduct a more thorough analysis of the *Columbia*'s bizarrely distressed subatomic structures.

Memories drifted through Ezri's thoughts like sand devils over the dunes. Jadzia had detailed the profound oddities that the *Defiant*'s sensors had found in the *Columbia*'s hull, and she had informed Starfleet of her theory that the readings might be a clue to a new kind of subspatial phenomenon. Admiral Howe at Starfleet Research and Development had assured her that her report would be investigated, but when the Dominion War erupted less than two months later, her call for the salvage of the *Columbia* had been side-lined—relegated to a virtual dustbin of defunct projects at Starfleet Command.

And it stayed there, forgotten for almost eight years, until Ezri Dax gave Starfleet a reason to remember it. The salvage of the *Columbia* had just become a priority for the same reason that it had been scuttled: there was a war on. Seven years ago the enemy had been the Dominion. This time it was the Borg.

Five weeks earlier the attacks had begun, bypassing all of the Federation's elaborate perimeter defenses and early warning networks. Without any sign of transwarp activity, wormholes, or gateways, Borg cubes had appeared in the heart of Federation· space and launched surprise attacks on several worlds. The *Aventine* had found itself in its first-ever battle, defending the Acamar system from eradication by the Borg. When the fighting was over, more than a third of the ship's crew—including its captain and first officer—had perished, leaving second officer Lieutenant Commander Ezri Dax in command.

One week and three Borg attacks later, Starfleet made Ezri captain of the *Aventine*. By then she'd remembered Jadzia's hypothesis about the *Columbia,* and she reminded Starfleet of her seven-year-old report that a Warp 5 ship had, in the roughly ten years after it had disappeared, somehow journeyed more than seventy-five thousand light-years—a distance that it would have taken the *Columbia* more than three hundred fifty years to traverse under its own power.

Ezri had assured Starfleet Command that solving the mystery of how the *Columbia* had crossed the galaxy without using any of the known propulsion methods could shed some light on how the Borg had begun doing the same thing. It had been a bit of an exaggeration on her part. She couldn't promise that her crew would be able to make a conclusive determination of how the *Columbia* had found its way to this remote, desolate resting place, or that there would be any link whatsoever to the latest series of Borg incursions of Federation space. It had apparently taken the *Columbia* years to get here, while the Borg seemed to be making nearly instantaneous transits from their home territory in the Delta Quadrant. The connection was tenuous at best.

All Dax had was a hunch, and she was following it. If she was right, it would be a brilliant beginning for her first command. If she was wrong, this would probably be her last command.

Her moment of introspection was broken by a soft vibration and a melodious double tone from her combadge. "Aventine *to Captain Dax,*" said her first officer, Commander Sam Bowers.

"Go ahead, Sam," she said.

He sounded tired. *"We just got another priority message from Starfleet Command,"* he said. *"I think you might want to take this one. It's Admiral Nechayev, and she wants a reply."*

And the axe falls, Dax brooded. "All right, Sam, beam me up. I'll take it in my ready room."

"Aye, sir. Stand by for transport."

Dax turned back to face the bow of the *Columbia* and suppressed the dread she felt at hearing of Nechayev's message. It could be anything: a tactical briefing, new information from Starfleet Research and Development about the *Columbia,* updated specifications for the *Aventine*'s experimental slipstream drive . . . but Dax knew better than to expect good news.

As she felt herself enfolded by the transporter beam, she feared that once again she would have to abandon the *Columbia* before making its secrets her own.

Commander Sam Bowers hadn't been aboard the *Aventine* long enough to know the names of more than a handful of its more than seven hundred fifty personnel, so he was grateful that Ezri had recruited a number of its senior officers from among her former crewmates on Deep Space 9. He had already accepted Dax's invitation to serve as her first officer when he'd learned that Dr. Simon Tarses would be coming aboard with him, as the ship's new chief medical officer, and that Lieutenant Mikaela Leishman would be transferring from *Defiant* to become the *Aventine*'s new chief engineer.

He tried not to dwell on the fact that their prede-
cessors had all recently been killed in fierce battles
with the Borg. Better to focus, he decided, on the
remarkable opportunity this transfer represented.

The *Aventine* was one of seven new, experimental
Vesta-class starships. It had been designed as a multi-
mission explorer, and its state-of-the-art weaponry
made it one of the few ships in the fleet able to mount
even a moderate defense against the Borg. Its sister
ships were defending the Federation's core systems—
Sol, Vulcan, Andor, and Tellar—while the *Aventine*
made its jaunt through the Bajoran wormhole to this
uninhabited world in the Gamma Quadrant, for what
Bowers couldn't help but think of as a desperate long
shot of a mission.

He turned a corner, expecting to find a turbolift,
only to arrive at a dead end. *It's not just the crew you
don't know,* he chided himself as he turned back and
continued looking for the nearest turbolift junction.
*Three weeks aboard and you're still getting turned
around on the lower decks. Snap out of it, man.*

The sound of muted conversation led Bowers farther down the corridor. A pair of junior officers, a
brown-bearded male Tellarite and an auburn-haired
human woman, chatted in somber tones in front of a
turbolift portal. The Tellarite glanced at Bowers and
stopped talking. His companion peeked past him, saw
the reason for his silence, and followed suit. Bowers
halted behind the duo, who tried to appear casual and
relaxed while also avoiding all eye contact with him.

Bowers didn't take it personally. He had seen this
kind of behavior before, during the Dominion War.
These two officers had served on the *Aventine* during

its battle at Acamar five weeks earlier; more than two hundred and fifty of their shipmates had died in that brief engagement. Now, even though Bowers was the new first officer and a seasoned veteran with nearly twenty-five years of experience in Starfleet, in their eyes he was, before all else, merely one of "the replacements."

Respect has to be earned, he reminded himself. *Just be patient.* He caught a fleeting sidelong glance by the Tellarite. "Good morning," Bowers said, trying not to sound too chipper.

The Tellarite ensign was dour. "It's afternoon, sir."

Well, it's a start, Bowers told himself. Then the turbolift door opened, and he followed the two junior officers inside. The woman called for a numbered deck in the engineering section, and then Bowers said simply, "Bridge." He felt a bit of guilt for inconveniencing them; he and the two engineers were headed in essentially opposite directions, but because of his rank, billet, and destination, the turbolift hurtled directly to the bridge, with the two younger officers along for the ride.

He glanced back at the young woman and offered her a sheepish grin. "Sorry," he said.

"It's okay, sir, it happens," she replied. The same thing had happened to Bowers countless times when he had been a junior officer. It was just one of many petty irritations that everyone had to learn to cope with while living on a starship.

The doors parted with a soft hiss, and Bowers stepped onto the bridge of the *Aventine,* his demeanor one of pure confidence and authority. The beta-shift bridge officers were at their posts. Soft, semimusical feedback·tones from their consoles punctuated the low thrumming of the engines through the deck.

Lieutenant Lonnoc Kedair, the ship's chief of security, occupied the center seat at the aft quarter of the bridge. The statuesque Takaran woman stood and relinquished the chair as Bowers approached from her left. "Sir."

He nodded. "I'm ready to relieve you, Lieutenant." A more formal approach to bridge protocol had been one of Bowers's conditions for accepting the job, and Captain Dax had agreed.

"I'm ready to be relieved, sir," Kedair replied, following the old-fashioned protocol for a changing of the watch. She picked up a padd from the arm of the command seat and handed the slim device to Bowers. "Salvage operations for the *Columbia* are proceeding on schedule," she continued. "No contacts in sensor range and all systems nominal, though there have been some reports from the planet's surface that I want to check out."

Bowers looked up from the padd. "What kind of reports?"

A pained grin creased her scaly face. "The kind that make me think our teams are more fatigued than they're letting on."

He grinned and tabbed through a few screens of data on the padd to find the communication logs from the away teams on the planet. "What gives you that impression?"

"A pair of incident reports, filed eleven hours apart, each by a different engineer." She seemed embarrassed to continue. "They claim the wreck of the *Columbia* is haunted, sir."

"Maybe it is," Bowers said with a straight face. "Lord knows I've seen stranger things than that."

Kedair's face turned a darker shade of green. "I don't plan to indulge the crew's belief in the supernatural. I just want to make certain none of our engineers have become delusional."

"Fair enough," Bowers said. He glanced backward over his shoulder. "Is the captain in her ready room?"

"Aye, sir," Kedair said. "She's been on the comm with Admiral Nechayev for the better part of the last half hour."

That doesn't bode well, Bowers realized. "Very good," he said to Kedair. "Lieutenant, I relieve you."

"I stand relieved," Kedair said. "Permission to go ashore, sir?"

"Granted. But keep it brief, we might need you back on the watch for gamma shift."

She nodded. "Understood, sir." Then she turned and moved in quick, lanky strides to the turbolift.

No sooner had Bowers settled into the center seat than a double chirrup from the overhead speaker preceded Captain Dax's voice: *"Dax to Commander Bowers. Please report to my ready room."* The channel clicked off. Bowers stood and straightened his tunic before he turned to the beta-shift tactical officer, a Deltan woman who had caught his eye every day since he had come aboard. "Lieutenant Kandel," he said in a dry, professional tone, "you have the conn."

"Aye, sir," Kandel replied. She nodded to a junior officer at the auxiliary tactical station. The young man moved to take over Kandel's post as she crossed the bridge to occupy the center seat. It all transpired with smooth, quiet efficiency.

Like clockwork, Bowers mused with satisfaction.

He walked toward Dax's ready room. The portal slid open as he neared, and it closed behind him after he'd entered. Captain Dax stood behind her desk and gazed through a panoramic window of transparent aluminum at the dusky sphere of the planet below.

Though he'd known Dax for years, Bowers still marveled at how young she looked. Ezri was more than a dozen years his junior, and he had to remind himself sometimes that the Dax symbiont living inside her—whose consciousness was united with hers—gave her the resources of several lifetimes, the benefit of hundreds of years of experience.

Since they were alone, Bowers dropped the air of formality that he maintained in front of the crew. "What's goin' on? Is Starfleet pulling the plug on us?"

"They might as well be," Dax said. She sighed and turned to face him. She sounded annoyed. "We have twenty-four hours to finish our salvage and head back to the wormhole. Admiral Jellico wants us to be part of the fleet defending Trill."

"Why the change of plans?"

Dax entered commands into her desktop's virtual interface with a few gentle taps. A holographic projection appeared above the desk. According to the identification tags along its bottom, it was a visual sensor log from the Starfleet vessel *U.S.S. Amargosa.* There wasn't much to see—just a brief, colorful volley of weapons fire with a Borg cube followed by a flash of light, a flurry of gray static, and then nothing.

"The *Amargosa* is one of five ships lost in the last sixteen hours," Dax said. "All in the Onias Sector, and all to the Borg. No one knows if the same Borg cube destroyed all five ships."

"If it was the work of one cube, it might be another scout," Bowers said. "Another test of our defenses."

"And if it wasn't," Ezri said, "then the invasion just started—and we're out here, playing in the dirt." She shook her head in frustration and sat down at her desk. "Either way, we have to break orbit by tomorrow, so we can forget about raising the *Columbia*. We need a new mission profile."

Bowers crossed his arms and ruminated aloud, "Our main objective is to figure out how the *Columbia* got here, and our best chance of doing that is to analyze its computer core. We could beam it up, but then we'd have to re-create its command interfaces here, and that could take days, since it wasn't what we'd planned on. But if Leishman and Helkara's adapters work, we can leave it in situ and download its memory banks by morning."

"And then we can parse the data on our way back," Dax said, finishing his thought. "Not my first choice, but it'll have to do." She looked up at him. "Let's get on it. Before we leave this planet, I want to know what happened to that ship."

In the darkness, there was a hunger.

The need was a silent pain in the blank haze of awareness—a yearning for heat, for life, for solidity.

Mind and presence, the very essence of itself lay trapped in stone, its freedom a dream surrendered and forgotten along with its name and memory.

It was nothing but the unslaked thirst of that moment, unburdened by identity or the obligations of a past. All it knew were paths of least resistance, the push and pull of primal forces, and the icy void at its own core—the all-consuming maw.

For so long there had been nothing but the cold of empty spaces, the weak sustenance of photons. A momentary surge of energy had roused it from a deathly repose and then slipped away, untasted. Now, in a dreamlike blink, it had returned.

At long last it was time.

After aeons of being denied, the hunger would be fed.

2156

2

—◆—

"Sensor contacts, bearing one-eight-one, mark seven!"

Captain Erika Hernandez snapped her attention from the line of ships on the main viewer to her alarmed senior tactical officer, Lieutenant Kiona Thayer. "Polarize the hull plating," Hernandez ordered. She was taking no chances. The *Columbia* was a long way from home, escorting a mining convoy home from the Onias Sector, which was the site of the hotly contested intersection of the Romulan Star Empire, the Klingon Empire, and the farthest extremity of Earth-explored space.

A single whoop of the alert klaxon sounded throughout the ship as Hernandez rose from her chair. She took a single step forward, toward the helmsman, Lieutenant Reiko Akagi. "Bring us about," Hernandez said. "Intercept course." She glanced left at her senior communications officer, Ensign Sidra Valerian. "Hail the convoy, tell them to take evasive action."

Thayer looked up from her console. "We can't get a lock on the enemy vessels, Captain. They're jamming our sensors."

"I can't raise the convoy," added Valerian, who turned her desperate stare toward the ships on the viewscreen. Anxiety sharpened her Scottish accent. "Ship-to-ship comms are blocked."

Lieutenant Kalil el-Rashad, the ship's second officer and sciences expert, intensified his efforts at his own console. "I'll try to help you break through it," he said.

"Tactical alert," Hernandez said. She returned to her seat as the turbolift door opened and her first officer, Commander Veronica Fletcher, stepped onto the bridge. The blond New Zealander nodded to Hernandez as she walked past and took over at the unoccupied engineering console directly to Hernandez's right. "Tactical," Hernandez said, "report."

"Signal clearing," Thayer replied. "Six ships, closing at high warp." She looked over her shoulder at the captain. "Romulans."

Valerian made fine adjustments at her panel's controls as she said, "Breaking the scrambler code, Captain. We're intercepting one of their ship-to-ship transmissions." Fear overcame the young woman's training, and her voice wavered as she informed the bridge, "All vessels are being ordered to target us first."

"Arm phase cannons, load torpedoes," Hernandez said. "Number One, tell Major Foyle and his MACOs to lock and load. Helm, all ahead full. Tactical, target the lead Romulan—"

Catastrophic deceleration hurled Hernandez to the deck, pinned her officers to their consoles, and wracked the ship with a groaning crash. Consoles dimmed, and the overhead lights went dark. The throbbing of the engines became a low, falling moan. On the main viewscreen, the long pulls of starlight resolved to a slowly turning starfield, indicating the ship had dropped out of warp and was drifting at sub-light.

"Report!" Hernandez shouted as she picked herself up off the deck.

"Command systems aren't responding, Captain," Fletcher said, making futile jabs at her console.

"Valerian," said Hernandez, "patch in the emergency line to engineering, put it on speakers."

A few seconds later, Valerian replied, "Channel open."

"Bridge to engineering," Hernandez said. "Report."

After a few moments of sputtering static on the line, Lieutenant Karl Graylock, the Austrian-born chief engineer, responded, *"Minor damage down here, Captain. Main power's still online, but I don't have any working controls."*

Hernandez sharpened the edge in her voice to mask her deepening concern. "What hit us, Karl?"

"Nothing from outside," Graylock said. *"The last set of readings I saw before we went dark looked like a cascade failure, starting in the communication systems."*

Fletcher cut in, "The intercepted message, Captain. It could've been a Trojan horse, a way to slip a computer virus past our defenses."

"If it was," Hernandez said, "how long to fix it?"

"We'll have to shut down the whole ship," Graylock said. *"Power up the main computer with a portable generator, wipe its command protocols, and restore from the protected backup."*

"I didn't ask for a checklist, Karl, I asked *how long.*"

His disgruntled sigh carried clearly over the comm. *"Three, maybe four hours if we—"*

The overhead lights snapped back to full brightness, and every console on the bridge surged back to life. The thrumming of the impulse engines resounded through the bulkheads and deck plates. The bridge officers all checked their consoles.

Fletcher looked more confused than she had before. "We have full power, Captain, but still no command inputs."

Turning in a circle, Hernandez asked, "Is anyone's console responding?" The officers all shook their heads in dismay. Then the resonant pulsing of the engines returned, and the starscape on the main viewer stretched into a tunnel of drifting streaks. "Engineering," Hernandez snapped, "what's going on?"

"No idea, sir," Graylock shouted back, sounding profoundly disturbed by the situation. *"Speed increasing. Warp three . . . warp four . . . warp five, Captain!"*

Thayer recoiled from her console as if it were demonically possessed. "Torpedo launchers powering up, sir!" Staring in horror at the panel, she added, "We're targeting the convoy!"

"Karl, shut down main power!" Hernandez shouted. "Hurry!"

From the helm, Akagi called out, "We're on an intercept course for the convoy, Captain."

Hernandez sensed what was happening, felt it like a cold twist in her gut. It was all unfolding so quickly, and she felt as if she was drugged, too slow to do anything to stop it.

Thayer was pressed against the bulkhead behind her console, mute with shock. Fletcher scrambled over from the engineering station to monitor the tactical console. Her voice trembled with dismay. "Weapons locked, Captain."

Cut off from the ship's command systems, Hernandez didn't have the option of overloading the *Columbia*'s warp reactor—not that it would have changed the outcome of this one-sided slaughter. It would have denied the Romulans the pleasure of using her ship as their weapon, but then there would be nothing to stop them from destroying the convoy anyway.

This was the Romulans' way of rubbing salt in the wound of the *Columbia*'s defeat. The insult added to the injury.

Fletcher's voice was flat and emotionless. "We're firing."

The shrieks of electromagnetically propelled torpedoes leaving the ship reverberated in the deathly silence of the bridge. On the main viewscreen, images of the defenseless civilian vessels in the convoy were replaced by the spreading red-orange fire blossoms of antimatter-fueled explosions. In less than ten seconds, the entire convoy was destroyed, reduced to a cloud of sparking debris and superheated gases.

Then the lights flickered again and went dark, followed by the bridge consoles. The ship became as quiet as the grave. Hernandez choked back the urge to vomit. Anger and adrenaline left her shaking with impotent fury. Hundreds of men and women had been lost in the convoy, and the last thing they had known before they died was that it was the *Columbia* that killed them.

"I don't get it," Valerian murmured. "We were disabled. The Romulans could've destroyed the convoy. Why use us to do it?"

"Because they could, Sidra," Fletcher said to Valerian. "This is a trial run for how they'll attack the rest of the fleet. We're just the guinea pigs."

Graylock's voice crackled over the intraship emergency comm. *"Engineering to bridge!"*

"Go ahead," Hernandez said.

"Captain, I think we've got a shot at getting out of this with our skins, but it'll be tight."

Hernandez forced herself into a semblance of composure and looked around at the rest of the bridge crew. "Stations." Everyone stepped quickly and quietly to their consoles. She returned to her chair. "What's the plan, Karl?"

"When the Romulans powered us up for the attack on the convoy, they left a residual charge in the warp nacelles. We can trigger a manual release and make a half-second warp jump."

El-Rashad sounded dubious. "I think they'd notice that."

"I've got Biggs and Pierce venting plasma through the impulse manifold, and the MACOs are pushing a photonic warhead out of the launch bay. If we detonate the warhead and trigger the jump at exactly the same moment, it should look like we self-destructed."

"If anyone has a better plan," Hernandez announced, "let's hear it." Silence reigned. "Make it fast, Karl. It won't be long before th—" Explosions hammered the

Columbia. The deck pitched wildly as sparks fountained from behind bridge panels. A sharp tang of smoke from burnt wiring filled the air. Within seconds, the only light on the bridge came from the irregular flashes of EPS-powered displays bursting into flames and showering the crew with stinging motes of shattered glass.

Then a bone-jarring concussion launched Hernandez up and backward through the shadows. She hit the aft bulkhead like dead weight and felt as if her consciousness had been knocked free of her body. Sinking into a different, deeper kind of darkness, she could only hope that the last explosion she'd heard was the one meant to save the *Columbia* and not one sent to destroy it.

2381

3

———◆———

Commander Christine Vale sat in the captain's chair of the *Starship Titan,* stared at the main viewer, and let her thoughts drift in the endless darkness beyond the stars.

A soft murmur of daily routines surrounded her, enveloped her in its familiar cadence of synthetic tones and hushed voices. *Titan* was more than two thousand light-years past the Vela OB2 Association, a dense cluster of new stars that had proved rich in spaceborne life-forms and other wonders. Now the ship was deep into a vast expanse of space that was unmapped and appeared to be unpopulated and untraveled, as well. For the past few weeks, intensive scans for subspace signal traffic had turned up naught but the scratch of cosmic background radiation. This far from the Vela cluster, cosmozoan activity was sparse, and there had been no sign of other starships within a range of twenty-five light-years since leaving the OB2 Association.

Vale saw a certain majesty in that lonely space; it was like a mirror for her soul. Several months earlier, she and a handful of her shipmates had become stranded during a mission to a planet called Orisha. Experiments conducted by the planet's denizens had produced dangerous temporal anomalies that destroyed the *U.S.S. Charon,* a *Luna*-class vessel like *Titan,* and they had almost claimed *Titan,* as well.

Jaza Najem, *Titan*'s senior science officer—and, for a brief time, Vale's lover—had sacrificed himself to protect the ship and its crew; as a result, he had been forced to live out his life in Orisha's past, permanently exiled to history.

It was still hard for Vale to believe that Najem, a man she'd once loved, and who then became her trusted friend, had been dead now for centuries. *He was dead when I met him.*

Months had passed, and her grief still cut like a sword in her side. She had resisted talking with the counselors at first, but she'd consented to a handful of sessions with Dr. Huilan after the captain had made it an order. Not that any of it had done any good. She had been "unwilling to commit to therapy," according to Huilan. Vale chose to think of it in simpler terms: She just didn't want to talk about it.

Shaking off the torpor of her maudlin brooding, she got up from the center seat and made a slow tour of the bridge. She took light steps, and the carpeting on the deck muffled her footfalls. A peek over flight controller Aili Lavena's shoulder confirmed that *Titan* was continuing on its last course while Lieutenant Commander Melora Pazlar—who had succeeded Jaza as *Titan*'s senior science officer—continued a detailed star-mapping operation.

A glance at the console of senior operations officer Sariel Rager showed a steady stream of astrocartographic data flooding in and being steadily processed, logged, and filed.

All was quiet at the engineering station, which was manned by Ensign Torvig Bu-kar-nguv, a cybernetically enhanced Choblik. His narrow head was barely visible above the console. The meter-tall biped—to Vale, he resembled a cross between a large, flightless bird and a shorn sheep—used his bionic arms and hands to work the console's controls with delicate precision. At the same time, he made adjustments on the wall panel behind him by means of the bionic manus at the end of his long, agile tail.

Vale quickly lost track of the dozens of systems that Torvig was modifying. "What has you so busy, Ensign?"

The expression on his ovine face switched from one of focused curiosity to petrified innocence. "I'm upgrading the power-distribution efficiency of the internal EPS network."

As usual, the specificity of his answer left Vale very little room to insert any small talk. This time, she decided not to try. "Very well," she said. "Carry on, Ensign."

"Thank you, sir," Torvig replied. His face became a mask of contentment as he resumed working. Vale admired his singularity of focus. He had come aboard the previous year to complete his senior-year work study for Starfleet Academy, and along with fellow cadet Zurin Dakal, had stayed on after his long-distance graduation, as a regular member of *Titan*'s crew.

Ranul Keru, the chief of security, was next on Vale's circuit of the bridge. A bear of a man, the dark-bearded Trill loomed quietly over his console. He looked up and favored Vale with a half smirk as she obtrusively leaned over to see what was on his screen. It was a plan for an unannounced security-division drill, a simulated intruder alert. Looking closer, she noted its details with amusement. "A dikironium cloud creature?" She accused him with a raised eyebrow. "That's just mean, Keru."

"It's my job," he said, flashing a devilish grin.

"Let me know if any of us survive," she said, moving on.

Commander Tuvok didn't look up as Vale neared the tactical console, but there was something about his demeanor that felt unusual to her. Her curiosity aroused, she stepped behind him and eyed his console readouts. All she saw was a series of long-range sensor reports, all saying the same thing: no contacts. It was the most placid tactical profile she had seen in decades.

She turned to the brown-skinned Vulcan and lowered her voice to a discreet whisper. "Want to show me what you were really working on?"

He didn't say anything at first. Then he responded with a hesitant glance from the corner of his eye, coupled with a tired grimace. He tapped a few commands into his console, and the serene lineup of empty scans was replaced by a complex set of fleet-deployment grids and battle scenarios.

Vale paged through them and asked, "Core system defenses?"

"Yes," Tuvok said, keeping his own voice hushed like hers.

He had prepared dozens of tactical profiles analyzing the recent attacks by the Borg into Federation space. In some of the scenarios, he was assessing strategic and tactical flaws in Starfleet's responses; in others, he had focused on isolating possible breaches in the Federation's perimeter defenses that the Borg might be exploiting.

She singled out one of interest. "Projecting possible next targets?"

"Unfortunately . . . no," Tuvok said.

It took her a moment to infer his meaning. "There have been more attacks."

"Yes," Tuvok said. Then he called up a recent, classified news dispatch from Starfleet Command. "This arrived ten minutes ago. Five ships destroyed by the Borg in the Onias Sector, in separate engagements." Tuvok lowered his eyes. "I did not wish to alarm the crew, so I refrained from announcing its arrival. I had intended to finish my analysis and brief you in writing a few minutes from now, for the sake of discretion."

"Probably for the best," Vale said. Messages from home had become less frequent since *Titan* left the Vela cluster, and the horrifying news of recent weeks had left many of its crew fearful for their families and loved ones in the Federation. She nodded once. "Carry on."

Vale returned to work, but over the relaxed air of her daily routine had been cast a pall of unspoken anxiety. It was the first time since *Titan*'s departure from known space that she wished she could suspend its mission of galactic exploration. Though *Titan* was devoted to peaceful scientific inquiry, it was also a state-of-the-art Federation starship, and its captain was a formidable combatant.

Starfleet doesn't need another map of another empty sector, Vale brooded as she slumped back into the captain's chair. *It needs every ship it can get, on the front line, right now.* But there was no way *Titan*'s crew could be there. It would take them months to get home—and if the Borg threat was as serious as it appeared, *Titan*'s return would come far too late to make any difference. *So let's just keep running into the night,* Vale fumed. *And hope we still have homes to go back to when it's over.* She stared at the viewscreen and struggled to bury her ire and frustration in that cold, endless void beyond the stars.

Xin Ra-Havreii stood on the narrow platform inside the stellar cartography holotank and admired Melora Pazlar from afar. The slender, blond Elaysian woman hovered in the center of the zero-gravity environment, several meters from the end of the platform, manipulating holographic constructs with easy grace.

"You should come up," she said to Ra-Havreii.

He smiled. "I like the view just fine from here."

Pazlar reached out with her left hand, palm open, and selected the floating image of a geology department report that detailed the results of the ship's most recent planetary survey. Bending her arm, she pulled the image toward her, enlarging it in the process. "The new interface is a blast," she said as she paged through the report with small flicks of her fingers.

"I'm glad you like it," Ra-Havreii said. He had designed a sweeping upgrade to the holotank's user interface after Pazlar's promotion to senior science officer. Her uniform had been modified with a complex network of embedded nanosensors, which extended from the soles of her boots to the tips of a pair of tight-fitting black gloves. A clear liquid matrix applied directly to her eyes enabled her to trigger functions inside the holotank with a mere glance. He had transformed this high-tech chamber from a work-space into Pazlar's personal sanctum sanctorum.

She paused in her labors and tossed another flustered grin at the white-haired Efrosian chief engineer. "So, what brings you up from engineering? Worried I'd broken it already?"

"No, I just wanted to see how it works, now that we're out of the test phase," he said. "Trial runs and normal operations can be very different experiences." With a note of melancholy, he added, "A lesson I learned the hard way."

In fact, the reason he was there was that he'd wanted to see her in action. Watching her use the new system was a delight for Ra-Havreii, who envisioned the fetching science officer as a conductor directing a symphony of data and light.

A sweep of her arm whirled the room's rings of data screens in one direction and spun its backdrop of nebulae and stars in another. "Everything's so easy in here," she said. "It makes me hate to leave." In a more conspiratorial tone she added, "Between you and me, I cringe every time the captain calls a staff meeting, because it means putting the armor back on."

Outside the stellar cartography lab, Pazlar, a native of a low-gravity planet, had to wear a custom-made pow-ered exoskeleton in order to walk or stand in *Titan*'s standard one-*g* environment. Her armature worked well enough, but it was cumbersome, and when its power reserves dwindled she was forced to use a mechanized wheelchair instead. Even with those devices, her body was exceptionally fragile, in any environment.

At first, Ra-Havreii had pondered ways to improve Pazlar's ability to move through the ship. Then he'd decided that a more elegant solution would be to bring the ship to her.

"What would you say," he remarked with a dramatic flair, "if I told you that you could go anywhere on the ship, any time you want, without ever putting that pile of metal on again?"

With a languid flourish, she dispelled all her work screens and left herself surrounded by a vista of stars. Crossing her arms with deliberate slowness, she turned in place until she had fixed all her attention on Ra-Havreii. "This, I have to hear."

He waved his hand casually at the galactic panorama. "Am I still welcome in your weightless domain?" She responded with a mock glare that he took as an invitation. In a carefree motion he stepped onto the flat, circular platform at the end of the ramp, and then with a gentle push he launched himself into the zero-gravity area. Having spent years as a starship designer and construction manager, he knew from experience exactly how much force to apply to position himself beside Pazlar. His long white hair and snowy moustache, however, drifted around his face like seaweed buffeted by deep currents.

"Computer," he said, "integrate Ra-Havreii interface modification Melora Four."

"Modification ready," the feminine computer voice said.

He glanced sideways at Pazlar. "I hope you won't think it too forward of me to have named it in your honor."

"I'll let you know when I see what it is," she said.

Ra-Havreii shrugged. "Reasonable. Computer, activate holopresence module. Location: Deck One, conference room." The all-encompassing sphere of outer space was replaced in a gentle, fading transition by a holographic representation of the conference room located behind *Titan*'s main bridge.

The simulacrum was perfect in every detail, down to the scent of the fabric on the chairs and the scratches that Pazlar's armature had made in the table's veneer the last time she had attended a meeting there. Outside its tall windows, warp-distorted stars streaked past.

A subtle change in the environment's gravity enabled Pazlar and Ra-Havreii to stand on the deck rather than float above it.

"Cute trick," Pazlar said.

Ra-Havreii chuckled and held up his index finger. "Wait," he said. "There's more." He tapped his combadge. "Ra-Havreii to Commander Vale."

"Vale here. Go ahead, Commander."

"Commander, could I ask you to have one of your bridge personnel step into the Deck One conference room for a moment?"

Vale sounded confused. *"Anyone in particular?"*

"No," Ra-Havreii said. "Whoever can spare a moment."

"All right," Vale said, suspicion coloring her tone. *"Ensign Vennoss is on her way."*

"Thank you, Commander. Ra-Havreii out." He smirked at Pazlar and lifted his thick white eyebrows. "This, I expect, will be the fun part."

A portal that led to a corridor that linked the conference room and the bridge opened with a soft hiss, and Ensign Vennoss, an attractive young Kriosian woman, entered carrying a padd. She stopped short and recoiled in mild surprise from Pazlar.

"Sorry, sir," Vennoss said. "I was expecting to meet Commander Ra-Havreii." Then she eyed Pazlar more closely. "Pardon me if this is none of my business, but don't you normally use a motor-assist armature outside of stellar cartography?"

Pazlar's mute, slack-jawed stare of surprise was an even richer reward than Ra-Havreii had hoped for. He tapped his combadge again. "Ra-Havreii to Ensign Vennoss."

Half a second after he'd finished speaking, his call was repeated from the overhead speaker inside the simulacrum. As Vennoss spoke, he heard her reply both "in person" and echoing from his combadge. "Vennoss here. Go ahead, Commander."

"Lieutenant Commander Pazlar and I are conducting a test of some new holopresence equipment in the stellar cartography lab. Can you bear with us a moment while we make a few adjustments?"

Vennoss gave a single nod. "Yes, sir. My pleasure."

"Thank you." He looked from Vennoss to Pazlar and said in a gentle but prodding way, "Go ahead—talk with her."

It took a second for Pazlar to compose herself, then she straightened her posture to carry herself like a proper officer. "Ensign," she said, and she stopped, apparently uncertain what to say next. Then she continued, "Have there been any new sensor contacts since your last report?"

"No, sir," Vennoss said. "I may have detected a Kerr loop in a nearby star cluster, but I'm still crunching the numbers to confirm it before I put it in the log."

"Ensign," Ra-Havreii said, pausing as he heard his voice emanate from Vennoss's combadge. "Is your analysis on that padd you're carrying?"

The Kriosian blinked. "Yes, sir."

"Would you let Commander Pazlar look at it a moment?"

"Yes, sir," Vennoss said, and she walked up to Pazlar and offered her the padd.

Pazlar stared at it for a second before she accepted it from the ensign. She paged through some of the ensign's facts and figures, and then she handed the padd back to Vennoss. "Thanks, Ensign. I look forward to reading your report."

"Aye, sir."

Ra-Havreii was satisfied with the test. "Thank you, Ensign," he said. "You can return to the bridge now."

Vennoss nodded, gave a small grin of relief, and exited the way she had come in. As soon as she was gone, Pazlar turned and beamed at Ra-Havreii. "Did you mean what you said? About this being able to go anywhere on the ship?"

"Indeed, I did." He strolled closer to her. "It took weeks," he continued, "but I'm fairly certain the holopresence system is fully integrated in all compartments and on all decks. Your holographic avatar is a

completely faithful stand-in for you, and your shipmates' avatars in here should be able to represent
them with near-perfect fidelity."

Teasing him every so slightly, she asked, "*Near*-
perfect?"

"Well, all but perfect," he said. "But only to a point."

Perhaps because his reputation had preceded him
once again, she asked, "And what, pray tell, might
that point be?"

He was standing very near to her, close enough to
be captivated by the delicate fragrance of her perfume.
"I would say the simulation loses its value at precisely the point where the real thing would be emi-
nently preferable."

She seemed quite amused. "That's a very discreet
way of phrasing it."

"Well, yes," he said, flashing a grin. "Discretion is a
virtue, I'm told." He leaned toward her, a prelude to a
kiss—

She pulled away and stepped back. "I'm sorry," she
said, avoiding eye contact with him. "I was just kidding around." She turned her back. "I hope I didn't
lead you on."

He inhaled to sigh, then held his breath a moment.
"No," he said, with as much tact and aplomb as he
could muster. "I guess I just got carried away. If there
was any error to be found here, it was mine, and I
apologize."

"No apology needed," she said, half turning back
toward him. "But thank you, anyway."

He bowed his head and showed his open palms
next to his legs, a polite gesture of contrition and
humility. Inside, however, he felt deeply ashamed.

Seeing her empowered and happy had made him forget, just for a moment, that her emotions could be just as fragile as her physique.

Many months had passed since Commander Tuvok, while temporarily under the telepathic influence of a spaceborne entity, had assaulted Pazlar in the ship's main science lab. Not only had he harmed Pazlar physically, breaking some of her bones, he had forced critical information from her memory with a Vulcan mind-meld, a grotesque personal invasion. Since then, she had bravely confronted her fears by working with Tuvok to learn ways of defending herself, in spite of her physical limitations.

But there was no denying that the attack had changed her. She could be warm at times, even jovial—but since the attack she had become more distant, a little bit harder to reach. In a very real sense, she seemed even more isolated than she had before.

Ra-Havreii knew about emotional scars, unforgiven sins, and lingering pain. He still blamed himself for a fatal accident years earlier, in the engine room of *Titan*'s class-prototype ship, the *Luna*. Everyone who had been there, and many others who hadn't, had tried to console him with empty platitudes:

It wasn't your fault, Xin.

There's no way you could have known what would happen.

You have to move on.

He knew better. As the designer of the *Luna* class, it had been his job to know what would happen. It *had* been his fault.

Some wounds, he had learned, could not be left behind. His past stayed with him, haunted him, reminded him always of his limitations. He saw shades of that same pain in Melora.

Efrosians often attuned themselves to one another's emotional needs; it was considered a foundation for intimacy, which in turn strengthened social bonds. So it came as no surprise to Ra-Havreii that Pazlar's profound physical and emotional vulnerabilities had awakened a protective side of his nature. That had, no doubt, been a subconscious factor in his tireless efforts to rebuild the stellar cartography interface and create the holopresence network for her.

He let his gaze linger a moment on her profile. Though he had enjoyed the attention of a wide range of female companions over the years, including a few on *Titan,* such pleasures had always been fleeting. He sometimes suspected that his serial seductions were really little more than feeble distractions from his suppressed melancholy.

Faced with the emptiness of it all, he breathed a quiet sigh and watched Melora out of the corner of his eye.

I should ease up before I make myself fall in love with her. Besides, what would I do if she fell in love with me? A shadow of self-reproach darkened his mood. *Don't be stupid, Xin. You don't deserve to be that lucky . . . not in this life or the next.*

Deanna Troi had begun tuning out Dr. Ree's voice the moment he said, "I'm sorry."

He was still talking, but she was only half listening to him now, as she sank into a black pit of grief and fury. *Not again,* she raged inside. *I can't go through this again. Not now.*

Will Riker—her *Imzadi,* her husband, her friend— stood beside her and gripped her left hand in both of his as she sat on the edge of the biobed. She shut her eyes against the cold light of sickbay while Dr. Ree continued delivering bad news.

"I ran the test several times," he said. "There was no mistake." He bowed his long, reptilian head and looked at the padd in his clawed, scaly hand. "The genetic abnormalities are irreparable. And I fear they will only become worse."

It was so unfair. Burning tears welled in Troi's eyes, and her throat seized shut on a knot of sorrow and anger. A suffocating tightness in her chest made it hard to breathe.

Will, sensing that she was unable to speak for herself, asked the Pahkwa-thanh physician, "Do you know *why* it happened? Can you tell us if it'll happen again?"

"Not yet," said the dinosaur-like doctor. Troi fixed him with a sullen glower. It didn't seem to faze him. "I need to make a detailed analysis before I can offer a prognosis."

Troi's empathic senses felt protective indignation pulsing in waves from her *Imzadi* before he snapped at Dr. Ree, "Why didn't you do that the *last time,* five months ago?"

"Because a first miscarriage in a humanoid normally isn't cause for long-term concern," Ree said. "The likelihood of a miscarriage for a woman who has already had *one* is the same as for a woman who hasn't. But a *second* event greatly increases the risk of future complications." Once again he spoke to Troi instead of to Will. "Betazoid women your age often have successful pregnancies, but your half-human ancestry introduces some hormonal factors that muddy the picture a bit. That's why I need to run more tests. With your permission."

Numb, torn between a desire to scream and the impulse to retreat to someplace dark and quiet and simply hide for weeks on end, all Troi could muster in response was a tiny nod of her chin. Then she cast her forlorn gaze at the floor, desperate to be done with this hideous day. The doctor finished entering his notes on the padd, looked up, and said, "Unless you have more questions, we should probably get you prepped."

Will turned his body in a way that interposed his shoulder between Troi and the doctor. "Prepped? For what?"

"To remove the fetus," he said.

Troi covered her abdomen with her right arm, and her response was sharp and instantaneous. "Absolutely not."

A rasp rattled behind Ree's fangs before he said, "Commander, please—I'm recommending this procedure because it's in your best interest medically."

"I don't agree," Troi said, sliding forward off the biobed and onto her feet. She inched closer to Will.

Ree sidestepped to block Will and Troi's path, leaving them cornered between two biobeds. "My dear counselor, forgive me for being blunt, but your fetus will not survive to term. It will die in utero—and unlike your last miscarriage, this one poses a serious risk to your own health, and perhaps your life."

He had made a logical, reasonable argument, but Troi didn't care. Her child, however flawed, was bound to her by slender threads of breath and blood, depended upon her for everything from food to antibodies. So tiny, so defenseless, her fragile scion was an innocent vessel, one in which she and Will had invested all their hopes and dreams. She couldn't bring herself to do what Dr. Ree asked, not even to save herself.

She hardened her resolve. "The answer is no, Doctor."

"As the chief medical officer, I could insist," Ree said. To Will, he added, "As I'm sure you well know, Captain."

Ree's challenge made Will bristle with anger. "My wife said the answer is no, Doctor. I'd advise you to think twice before you try to force the issue." He stretched one arm across Troi's shoulders and nudged her forward toward Ree, who held his ground. Will glared at him. "We're *leaving now,* Doctor."

The hulking Pahkwa-thanh, Troi knew, could easily snap off both their heads with a casual bite of his massive jaws. His frustration and irritation were radiant to Troi's empathic mind, and even more vibrant than her *Imzadi*'s fearless resolve. She expected Ree, as a predator by nature, to relish confrontation. Instead, he turned away and plodded toward his office, his mood a leaden shadow of resentful disappointment.

Will guided her out of sickbay. In the corridor he took her hand, and they walked together in mournful silence toward their quarters. As always, he wore a brave face and played the part of the stoic, but his heartbreak was as palpable to her as her own. She sensed a deeper unease in him, one that he refused to express—a profound inner conflict mixed with fear. There had been undertones of this in his emotions in sickbay, as well. Probing his thoughts, she realized he had strongly disagreed with her decision to refuse Dr. Ree's advice, yet he had backed her choice without hesitation.

As his wife, she was grateful that he had supported her wishes over his own. As a mother, she hated him for being willing to sacrifice their child in her name.

It had been several months since their initial attempt at having a child had ended in tragedy. Her first miscarriage had occurred with no warning, just a surge of pain in the night. Until that moment, they had thought that conception alone would be their greatest hurdle.

They had both been subjected to lengthy, invasive fertility treatments to overcome what Dr. Ree had politely described as "genetic incompatibilities" in their DNA. Several failed attempts at conception had strained her relationship with Will to a degree they'd never endured before, and the hormonal changes she had undergone for the fertility enhancements had weakened her psionic defenses, causing her to project her emotions on others in unexpected and sometimes dangerous ways.

Everything had seemed so much easier when they'd thought that the only things their family-to-be had to fear were "out there," far away and unnamed. Now the greatest threat to their dreams lay within themselves—a flaw, some monstrous defect that had rendered them unfit for the roles they most desired.

Their second attempt at conceiving a child had been an act of hope, a refusal to succumb to despair. Through all of Troi's nights of bitter tears and black moods, Will had never faltered, never given up hope that they would persevere. "I have faith in you," he'd said one night, months earlier. "Faith in us. I have to believe that we'll get through this. I have to believe that."

Until tonight, he had.

Something in Will had changed when Dr. Ree had delivered his diagnosis. She had felt it, an icy resignation in his mind. It lasted only a moment, but it had happened: He'd lost hope.

Lost in her thoughts, she didn't notice that they had been in a turbolift until they stepped out onto the deck where their quarters were located. A few paces into the corridor, she stopped. Will continued for a step until he felt the resistance in her hand, and he turned back, concerned and solicitous. "What's wrong?"

"I don't know," she lied. "I'm just feeling a need to walk for a while. Maybe in the holodeck."

He nodded. "All right. Anywhere you want."

As he started back toward the turbolift, she let go of his hand. "I meant . . . that I'm feeling a need to walk by myself."

His face slackened and paled, and he lowered his chin. "I see," he said in a voice of quiet defeat.

Troi didn't need empathy to know how deeply she had wounded him. All his body language signaled his withdrawal, and his anguish was overwhelming, too intense for her to tune out. She was desperate to comfort him, but her thoughts were awash in her own toxic brew of dark emotions. Twice in less than half a year, their hope of starting a family had turned to ashes, and she didn't know why. She couldn't accept it.

"I'm sorry," she said. "It's just . . . I . . ."

"I understand," he said, and she knew it was true, he did. He was her *Imzadi,* and their emotional bond, normally a comfort, now was an amplifier of their shared grief. It was too much.

"I'm sorry," she said again. Then she walked away, knowing how badly Will wanted to stop her, and hoping that he wouldn't. She hated herself for abandoning him, and she both loved him and hated him for letting her go.

She stepped into a turbolift, and the doors closed behind her. "Holodeck One," she said, and the lift hummed as it accelerated away, circuiting the primary hull.

As the turbolift sped her through the ship, she thought of her older sister, Kestra, who had drowned at the age of seven, shortly after Troi had been born. Their mother, Lwaxana, had caused herself severe psychological trauma by repressing all her memories of Kestra for decades, until the submerged grief all but destroyed her from within.

At the time, Troi had felt sympathy for her mother, even though she had been horrified that Lwaxana could erase her own child from her memory. Now, faced with her own, imminent second miscarriage, Troi no longer felt revulsion at the thought of her mother's self-inflicted amnesia. She felt envy.

Captain William Riker crossed from the turbolift to his ready room in quick strides, making only fleeting eye contact with his first officer, Christine Vale, who had command of the bridge during beta shift. He made a brief nod as she got up from the center seat. "As you were," Riker said, and he kept walking, trying to raise as minor a wake with his passage as possible. As soon as the ready room's door closed behind him, he slowed his pace and moved in heavy, tired steps to his desk.

Circling behind it to his chair felt like too much effort, so he turned and perched himself on its edge. His head drooped with fatigue. For Deanna's sake he had maintained a façade of placid control, but his emotions felt like a storm battering the empty shores of his psyche. Depression, anger, guilt, and denial followed one another in crushing waves.

Removing himself from Deanna was only an illusion, he knew. The bond he shared with his *Imzadi* transcended distance and physical barriers. Their emotions were so tangible to each other, so present, that when one of them was in the throes of a powerful experience, both of them felt it. Ever since they had first fallen in love, their bond had been so strong that they sometimes were able to communicate telepathically. Such moments were rare, but they had made him feel so connected to her.

And now she felt so distant.

His door chime sounded. He pushed himself up from the desk to a standing posture, turned, and tugged the front of his uniform smooth before he said, "Come in."

The portal slid aside, briefly admitting the ambient sounds of the bridge. Christine Vale stepped inside his ready room and stopped just outside the range of the door's sensor. It shut behind her. Her gaze was level and concerned. "Sir."

"Chris," he said with a forced nonchalance, and he circled behind his desk. "What can I do for you?"

She flashed a weary smile. "I was gonna ask you the same thing." Turning a bit more serious, she asked, "Are you all right? You haven't seemed like yourself for a while now."

He pulled out his chair. "Define 'a while.'"

All traces of jocularity left her tone. "A few months, at least," she said. "Don't get me wrong, you mask it well. But something's changed. You just seem . . . disengaged."

Riker sat down with a tired sigh. "How so?"

"Can we drop the ranks and speak freely, sir?"

Her accusatory tone caught Riker off guard. "Of course," he said. "Always, you know that."

"Will," she said, "what's wrong?"

Instinct impelled him to denial. "Nothing. I'm fine."

"No, Will, you're not." She stepped to his desk and sat down across from him. The concern in her voice grew more pronounced as she continued, "You and I served through some rough times on the *Enterprise,* and I've been your XO for almost a year. And I have *never* seen you act like this. Please talk to me. What's going on?"

He reclined his chair and pulled his hand over his face. It was a reflexive action; he thought he'd done it to massage the fatigue from his head and neck. Only as he prolonged the gesture did he admit to himself that it was a delaying tactic, a way to avoid eye contact and postpone his reply. He hated feeling so exposed, so easily read. Denial was no longer an option, but he still found himself reluctant to confide in her. Finally, he lowered his hand and said, "It's complicated."

"Simplify it," Vale replied.

A heavy breath did nothing to relax him. "I could invoke rank and tell you to leave this alone."

Vale nodded. "Is that what you *want* to do?"

"What, are you a counselor, now?" He swiveled his chair away from her, showing her his profile. "Sometimes, captains have to keep barriers between themselves and their crews."

"And that's fine, up to a point," Vale said. "But right now it seems like your ability to do your job is being impaired by whatever it is you're going through. And seeing as it's my job to make sure this ship and its crew are kept in a state of full readiness, that makes *your* problem *my* problem."

Riker frowned. "I'm still not sure I—"

"Especially since it involves your wife, who's also part of the command staff," Vale added.

He swiveled back to face her, his temper aroused. "How did you know that?"

Vale hesitated before answering, and then she spoke with tact. "Will, I know that you and Deanna had problems conceiving a child. She told me all about it on Orisha. The treatments, the strain it put on the two of you. I noticed you having the same kind of problems then that I'm seeing now. But for a while, the two of you seemed happy, so I'm wondering what's happened."

Denying the obvious was tiring, and he felt his guard slipping; he wondered if it might be a relief to let it down entirely. "You understand," he said, "that what we talk about stays in here. You don't discuss it with anyone—not the crew, not the counselors. . . . *Especially* not the counselors."

"Of course," Vale said.

Riker took another deep breath and let it go slowly as he composed his thoughts and steeled his resolve. "The past few months *have* been hard for me and Deanna," he confided. "You know that we were working with Dr. Ree on fertility treatments—"

"All too well," Vale said, referring to the effect that Troi's empathic projections had had on her personally.

"We thought we'd succeeded," Riker said. He found it difficult to go on. "It hasn't gone as we'd hoped."

As he'd feared, a grim silence fell between himself and Vale, whose expression softened. She leaned forward and folded her hands atop his desk. "How bad is it?"

He couldn't name it. "Bad."

Vale asked in an apprehensive whisper, "A miscarriage?"

Hearing the words spoken in sympathy, rather than in Dr. Ree's cold and clinical rasp, was even more terrible than Riker had imagined. Grief surged upward inside his chest, and he barely nodded his confirmation before tears overflowed his eyes. He covered his mouth for a moment and struggled to contain the sorrow he had been swallowing for so long. "I've been carrying this for months," he said, fighting to talk through halting gasps for air. "Piling one thing on another. Feeling like I'd failed Deanna."

"You didn't fail her," Vale said. "I know you didn't."

"Maybe not, but I feel like I did." He palmed the tears from one cheek and then the other. "She's part Betazoid, so it's hard to know where my desires end and hers begin. It makes me wonder if maybe her wish to have kids was really *mine,* and I led her into this." He got up from his chair, turned away from Vale, and walked to the window behind his desk. "We just found out it's happening again. We're losing another pregnancy. And this time, if she doesn't do something about it . . . it could kill her."

"I'm sure Dr. Ree could—"

"He offered," Riker said. "He almost insisted, actually. Deanna won't have it. She knows she's in danger, and she just won't do it. And instead of arguing with her, I let her refuse treatment and walked her out of sickbay."

Vale's reflection was semitransparent against the backdrop of drifting starlight. "Even so," she said, "that doesn't make any of this your fault."

"It doesn't really matter," Riker said. "It's starting to feel like the damage is done, either way."

He watched Vale's mirror image as she stood and circled behind his desk to stand with him. "What damage?"

"That barrier I was talking about," he said, "the one between me and the crew? It's starting to feel like it's between me and Deanna. We can hear each other's thoughts, but it feels like we don't know how to talk about this." Now he regarded his own ragged reflection in the window. "It's never been easy being such a visible couple on a starship. Even harder now that I'm the captain and this crew is so small, compared to what I was used to on the *Enterprise*."

"I know what you mean," Vale said. Her own muted grief reminded Riker of the loss of Jaza Najem just months earlier.

"Yeah," Riker said. "I guess you do." He turned to face her. "After the first . . ." The word was so hard for him to say. "After the first miscarriage, I did everything I could to keep Deanna's spirits up. The odds were on our side, Ree told us. But I could tell Deanna wasn't ready to try again, so I waited. I know that losing the baby had to be worse for her. For me it was an idea, but for her it was part of her body—it was *physical*. There's no way I can understand how that *feels* for her."

"But it's good that you know where the difference is," Vale said, trying to reassure him. "That you know *why* her experience is different from yours."

More tears burned Riker's eyes. "But I still don't know how to help her," he admitted. "She's in so much pain, and I feel cut off, and I don't know what to do." Now that he had opened the gates to his grief, he didn't know how to close them again.

Vale pulled him to her, and she closed her arms around him in a sisterly embrace. He hesitated to return the gesture, and then he reluctantly surrendered to it. "It'll be okay, Will," she said, her voice breaking slightly, echoing his sorrow. "You'll be okay, and so will Deanna. You're not alone."

Riker felt embarrassed to have shown such vulnerability to his first officer. *Captain Picard would never have bared his feelings like this,* he thought. He reminded himself that Vale was not just his first officer; she was his friend. Maybe a captain more obsessed with strict protocol and formality would have been stalwart in hiding his feelings, but Riker didn't subscribe to such emotionally stunted ideals of manhood. He didn't believe that expressing emotions made him weak, and he was grateful that he had chosen a first officer who seemed to feel the same way.

As he lingered in Vale's embrace, Riker brooded over the emotional wedge that he felt had been driven between him and Deanna by their recent tragedies. At a time when he most needed comfort, Deanna seemed to recoil from his touch. Her rejection and abandonment of him in the corridor made him all the more grateful now for Vale's compassion.

That was when he began to wonder if perhaps this moment was continuing a shade too long. Vale's head was resting against his chest, her hair color du jour a rich auburn that contrasted with his predominantly black uniform. Riker eased Vale away from him, and as she lifted her face to look at him, he thought he caught a glimpse of a less than platonic emotion in her eyes.

Then they both pushed away from each other and averted their eyes as they composed themselves. "Anyway," Vale said as she backpedaled and smoothed her uniform jacket, "if you need me, or if there's anything I can do to help, just let me know."

"I will," Riker said, and he sat down at his desk and tapped a few keys on his computer's interface. "Thank you, Chris."

"My pleasure, Captain," Vale said, continuing to back away to the other side of Riker's desk. Her hands seemed to be in constant motion—waving, clenching, opening, weaving together at the fingers and flexing. "If there's nothing else?"

"No, thank you," Riker said, pretending to be engrossed in whatever it was on his computer monitor. "Dismissed."

"Aye, sir." She turned and walked quickly out the door, back to duty on the bridge.

Riker watched the door close behind her, and then he ran a hand through his thatch of graying hair. *Did I just imagine that?* he wondered. *Am I wrong, or was that kind of . . .* awkward?

Suddenly, being emotionally unavailable to his crew didn't seem like such a bad idea after all.

"You're obviously looking for someone to blame," said Pral glasch Haaj. "The question is, would you rather it be you or your husband?"

As usual, the Tellarite counselor had chosen to take the most confrontational possible tack in addressing his patient's issues, and Deanna Troi, being a trained counselor and his supervising officer, didn't appreciate it. "This isn't about blame," she said, surprised at how defensive her manner seemed.

"Of course not," he said, his cultured voice tuned to a perfect timbre of derision. "It's just a coincidence, yes?"

The rank insensitivity of his remarks sparked Troi's fury, which she found easier to face than the smothering sorrow of sympathy she'd expected from the ship's other counselor, Dr. Huilan. "We didn't choose this. It's not our fault."

"I see. So it's random chance and not some defect in your respective biologies that's put you on a course for your second miscarriage in half a year."

Troi sprang from the couch, turned her back on the slender Tellarite, and paced toward the far bulkhead of his office. At the wall she turned and began walking back toward him. He watched her with expressionless black eyes, which gave his face a cipherlike quality. "You're just trying to provoke me," she said with a note of resentment.

"Provoke you? Into doing what?"

She stopped and glowered at him. "Now you're trying to make me name my own dysfunction and outline my own needs. Are you this transparent with all your patients?"

"Yes, but most of my patients don't hold doctorates in psychology." He grinned. "Tell me what I'll do next."

"You'll try to shock me by saying something rude."

He shook his head. "I tried that. And I followed it with the echoed remark and the leading question, all of which got me nowhere. So guess what my next trick will be."

It amazed her that even as he was admitting to the failure of his manipulations, he still sounded smug. "I don't know," she confessed. "Reciting old Tellarite parables?"

"No." Haaj reclined and folded his hands behind his head. "Just an honest question: Why are you wasting my time?"

At first, Troi recoiled from the hostility in his voice. Then she replied, "Is this another example of your patented Tellarite argument therapy?"

"I'm serious, Counselor. You're my supervising officer, so I'm expected to show you a certain degree of deference, even in a therapeutic setting—but I don't have time for this. You're clearly not ready for therapy, and you're taking away valuable session time from my patients who are."

She called upon her empathic senses to try and sense whether he was dissembling in order to draw her out. He wore an intense aura of bitter dudgeon. If he was merely pretending to be annoyed with her, he was doing a very convincing job of it, inside and out. "Why do you say I'm not ready for therapy?"

"Are you kidding?" He leaned forward, elbows on his knees. "All you've done since you got here is obstruct the process. You've dissected my method instead of answering my questions, and you'd rather criticize me than examine yourself." He leaned back and folded his hands in his lap. "Therapy only works when the patient is willing to participate."

All his accusations were true, and Troi was ashamed of herself for indulging her appetite for denial. "You're right," she said. "I have been sabotaging the session. I'm sorry."

"Don't apologize to me," he said. "Apologize to Crewman Liryok. This was supposed to be *his* hour."

Troi stared out a window at the wash of starlight streaking past the ship and felt the subtle vibrations of warp flight in the deck under her feet. "I don't know why I'm having so much trouble surrendering to the process."

"Yes, you do," Haaj said, barely disguising his contempt.

She fixed him with a scathing glare. "No, I don't."

"Do."

He was the most exasperating therapist she'd ever met. "Is this your idea of therapy? Contradiction?"

"You're critiquing me again, Counselor. Why is that?"

She didn't mean to shout, but she did anyway. "I told you, I don't know!"

"And I'm calling you a liar," he said.

The more she felt herself losing control, the calmer he became. There were a thousand things she wanted to yell at him, and they were slamming together inside her mind, a logjam of epithets. Her face and ears felt hot, and her fists clenched while she struggled to put words to her fury.

Then he asked, "What are you feeling right now?" She stared at him, dumbstruck. He continued, "Would you call it rage?"

"Yes," she said, paralyzed by her emotions.

His voice took on a calming tenor. "Breathe, Deanna. Clear your mind, just for a few seconds. Remember your training: What's the difference between anger and rage?"

It was hard for her to pull air into her chest, even harder to hold it there. *I'm hyperventilating,* she realized. With effort, she did as Haaj asked, and then she closed her eyes.

"Ready?" he said. She nodded. He asked, "What's anger?"

"An emotional cue that something is wrong, that we have been injured or mistreated, or that values we consider important are being challenged or disregarded."

He harrumphed. "I imagine you did very well on the essay portions of your exams. . . . Now, tell me what rage is."

"A shame-based expression of anger," she said. "And a reaction to powerlessness."

"Powerlessness," Haaj repeated, tapping his index finger against his upper lip. "Impotence. Helplessness." He wagged his finger at her. "You don't like feeling out of control, do you?"

She crossed her arms over her chest. "I don't know many people who do."

"I do," Haaj said. "There are plenty of folks who like not having to make decisions or take responsibility. They're happy to go along and believe what they're told, because it's easier than thinking for themselves."

Troi drummed her fingers on her bicep. "And what does that have to do with me?"

"Nothing," the wiry Tellarite said. "It was just a tangent. Those happen sometimes in conversation." Feigning embarrassment, he added, "I'm sorry, I forget. What are we talking about?"

"Control," Troi said, feeling a new tide of rage swell inside her chest.

He clapped his hands. "Ah, yes! Control." He let the words linger between them for a moment before he added, "You've been feeling out of control lately."

She shook her head. "I don't recall saying that."

"But you've certainly been at the mercy of events," Haaj said. "Not much recourse when a tragedy like yours happens."

"No, there isn't."

The Tellarite nodded. "It's too bad Dr. Ree isn't skilled enough to correct the problem."

"It's not his fault," Troi said. "Medicine isn't magic. There's only so much he can do."

"True," Haaj said. "I mean, he can't be expected to compensate for your husband's genetic shortcomings. After all, the captain is, as they say, 'only human.'"

Troi cast a reproachful stare at Haaj. "You're repeating yourself. I already told you it's not about blame."

"Oh, but it most certainly is," he replied. "You're blaming yourself."

She recoiled from his accusation. "I'm not!"

"You're cursing your poisoned womb," Haaj declared, as if it were a piece of gossip everyone else already knew. "To paraphrase Shakespeare, you know the fault lies not in your stars but in yourself."

"There's a difference between an argument and an insult, Doctor," Troi said in her most threatening tone.

Uncowed, he replied, "Do you really expect me to believe you don't blame yourself for back-to-back miscarriages?"

"I don't."

"Then where is all this *shame* coming from?" He continued as if he was scolding a child. "You said it yourself: You're filled with rage, and rage finds its roots in powerlessness and shame."

Denial had Troi shaking her head as a reflex. "Rage comes from being ashamed of our anger," she said.

"So, you're ashamed of your anger?"

"No!"

"You just said you were! Who are you angry at? Yourself? Your husband? Some higher power that's betrayed your trust?"

His relentless, vicious badgering forced her to turn away, because her fury had become swamped in the rising waters of her grief. Her chest felt crushed, and her throat was as tight as a tourniquet. All her bitter emotions were bleeding into one for which she had no name. She closed her eyes to avoid seeing her dark reflection in the compartment window. Then she heard footfalls behind her, followed by Haaj's voice, somber and soft.

"You're angry at the baby," he said.

It was the sharpest truth that had ever cut her.

Her hands covered her face as deep, funereal bellows of grief roared from some dark chasm inside her. Tears were hot against her face as she doubled over, robbed of her composure by her wailing cries. Haaj's hands found her shoulders and steadied her. He guided her to a chair and eased her into it.

She stared at her tear-moistened palms. "I don't understand it," she said between choking gasps.

"You and William invested this child with your hopes and dreams," Haaj said. "You wanted it to be your future. But now joy has turned to sorrow, and you resent your baby for failing you, when you've already given it so much."

Troi looked up through a blurry veil of tears at Haaj. "But it's so unfair. It's not the baby's fault . . . it's no one's fault."

"You're right," Haaj said. "It's not fair. But when we're wronged, our instinct is to assign blame. Even if it means hurting someone we love—someone who doesn't deserve it."

Dragging her feelings into the open was a hideous sensation and not at all as cathartic as she had hoped. Worse still, it was forcing her to confront other torments and terrors she would have preferred to ignore for a while longer. "Dr. Ree wants me to terminate my pregnancy," she said. "I told him no."

"The good doctor doesn't make such suggestions lightly," Haaj said. "I presume his concern is for your safety?"

Troi shrugged. "So he said."

"And you think he's wrong?"

"No," Troi said. "I know he's probably right. But I can't do it. I won't."

Waggling his index finger, Haaj said, "No, no, Counselor. I'm afraid you need to choose a verb there. Either you *can't* terminate your pregnancy, or you *won't*. 'Can't' implies that you have no choice in the matter, no capacity to make an affirmative decision. 'Won't' suggests a defiant exercise of your free will. So which is it? Can't? Or won't?"

She wrestled with the semantics of his question for several seconds before she answered, "Won't. I won't do it."

"Even though it puts your life in danger?"

A calmness filled her. "It's not important."

Haaj looked deeply worried. "Counselor, are you saying you want to die?"

"No," she said. "I don't."

"But you seem ready to risk your life for a pregnancy that's already failed. Why is that?"

Her calm feeling became an emotional numbness, and in a dull monotone she told him the simple truth: "I don't know."

4

———

The voice of the Borg Collective lurked at the edge of Captain Jean-Luc Picard's awareness, taunting him with inhuman whispers.

It was a susurrus of thoughts—omnipresent, elusive, and inaccessible. Picard had been able to hear them for weeks now, lurking on the periphery of his consciousness, ever since the first wave of unexplained Borg attacks deep inside the protected core systems of the Federation. When he was caught up in the business of command, he could shut them out, but when he tried to relax or sleep, when his mind was idle . . . those were the times when the voice of the Collective smothered him from within. With his eyes closed, he could almost hear the name that continued to stab icy fear into his heart: *Locutus*.

Beverly Crusher's voice pulled him sharply back into the moment. "Look at him, Jean-Luc—isn't he amazing?"

Here-and-now returned in a flood of sensation. He blinked his eyes back into focus on the details. A delicate cup of hot Earl Grey tea in his hand, its subtle aroma soothing his frayed nerves. His wife, Beverly, warm beside him as they sat together on the sofa in their quarters. The murky bluish image on the display of her medical tricorder, which she had thrust in front of him, as if for inspection. He stared at it; awestruck.

Our son, he had to remind himself. *That's our son.*

"Words cannot do him justice," Picard said, aglow with a moment of quiet, paternal pride.

Then the soulless voice of the Collective returned and intruded on his moment of reflection to remind him: Pride was irrelevant. Hope was irrelevant. Resistance was futile.

Months earlier, to stop a new Borg queen from rising in the Alpha Quadrant, he'd dared to let himself be transformed once more into Locutus. Hubris had led him to think he could fool the Collective, walk into the largest cube it had ever spawned, and kill its nascent queen with impunity. He had even believed that his mind was strong enough to open itself to the Collective and behold all its secrets at once. Only when it had been too late to turn back had he realized how foolish he'd been.

One mind could not grasp the Collective. It was too great, too complex. It had reminded him of his true stature in the universe: small, weak, fallible, and insignificant.

And now the voice of the Collective thundered in his mind, louder and more intimate than ever before.

His brow grew heavy and furrowed with concern while he gazed down at the sensor image of the child growing inside of Beverly. His jaw tightened, not in anger but in remorse. *You've always known something like this would happen,* he upbraided himself. *You knew it. How could you have been so foolish?*

He had confided in Beverly after the first new wave of Borg attacks. Drowning in the merciless depths of the Collective's devouring group mind, he had needed her strength and passion to anchor him. She'd kept him grounded in all that he loved: her, his life, and their family-to-be.

She turned off the tricorder and set it aside. "You're hearing them again, aren't you?"

Picard nodded. "It's hard not to," he said. "They're always there, just waiting for me to let my guard down."

"Sounds like what I had to do," she said with a teasing smirk, trying to cheer him up.

He was smart enough to grab a lifeline when it was offered. He smiled back. "There were definite similarities in strategy."

"Jean-Luc," she said with mock umbrage, "are you saying I wore you down?" She pressed closer against him and stroked his smooth pate. He extended his arm across her shoulders and rested his head against her silky, fiery red hair.

"I'm just saying that I could tell resistance was futile."

"If you call a few pathetic excuses 'resistance,'" she said, obviously enjoying the opportunity to needle him.

It had been nearly three months since the *Enterprise* crew had succeeded in its mission to hunt down and destroy the Borg-assimilated Federation science vessel *U.S.S. Einstein*. At the end of that mission, Beverly had sensed and taken advantage of an opportunity to cajole Picard into the most hopeful undertaking of his life: starting a family with her.

There had been no denying that, on some level, he had wanted this for a long time. The need had been awakened in him nearly ten years earlier, when his older brother, Robert, and young nephew, René, had been killed in a tragic fire at the family's vineyard home in Labarre, France.

Beverly's reason for wanting a family was just as poignant to Picard. Her only child, Wesley—whom she had treasured not only as a son but as the last surviving remnant of her late husband, Jack Crusher—had evolved many years earlier into a Traveler, a wondrous being capable of moving freely through time and space . . . but he also was no longer fully human. The more Wesley had grown into his powers as a Traveler, the less frequently he had returned to visit with Beverly. He had appeared at their hastily arranged, low-key wedding a few months earlier, but there was no telling when he might return—or if he ever would.

After the *Einstein* was destroyed, Picard had thought they'd earned a chance to seize their dream. After all, *Voyager* had destroyed the Borg's transwarp hub to Federation space a few years earlier. The *Enterprise* and her crew had stopped the most fearsome Borg cube ever encountered. And the last rogue Borg element in Federation space seemed to have been eliminated.

For a moment, Picard had dared to hope. He and Beverly had started their family. And less than a month later, as they were still marveling at their newly conceived son, the Borg had begun their blitzkrieg into Federation space.

You should've known. You've always known.

There was no going back now. He and Beverly had committed themselves, and they were going to see this through, to whatever end awaited them. Even as they huddled in the dim light of their quarters and shut themselves away from the gathering storm, he knew that this interlude of happy domesticity had never been fated to last. It was doomed to end in tragedy, like every other moment of joy he'd known in his life.

"It's time," he said with a glance at a chrono set on the end table beside him. He extricated himself from her embrace and stood. Then he picked up the tricorder from the sofa and turned it back on, to admire the image of his son again, even if just for a moment. "You're right. He's amazing. In every way."

He switched off the tricorder and set it on a table as Beverly stood beside him. She laid her warm hands on either side of his neck and kissed him tenderly. Resting her forehead against his, she said, "I'll be in sickbay if you need me."

"Meet you back here when it's over."

She nodded somberly, her demeanor calm. They let their hands fall away from each other, and she stayed behind as he left, to avoid the awkward ritual of another farewell in the corridor. Sharpening his mind for battle, he left their quarters at a brisk step and headed for the turbolift, which would bring him to the bridge.

In less than an hour, the *Enterprise* would arrive at the Federation world of Ramatis, near the Klingon border. If Picard and his crew had responded quickly enough to the planet's distress signal, the *Enterprise* might arrive only a few minutes later than the Borg cube that was on its way to the planet.

Picard knew that the time for diplomacy was past.

It was time to go to war.

From his first glimpse of the scorched and glowing northern hemisphere of Ramatis on the *Enterprise*'s main viewer, Worf knew that every living being on the planet's surface was dead—and that the Borg cube in orbit was responsible.

"No life signs on the planet," said Commander Miranda Kadohata, the ship's second officer. "It's been cooked down to the mantle." She swiveled her seat away from the ops console to add, "The Borg cube is sweeping up all the satellites and defense-platform debris in orbit, probably for raw materials."

Disgust churned up bile in Worf's throat. An enemy that would conquer a world to possess it could be hated and still be respected as an adversary. The Borg, however, had undertaken a campaign of slaughter without even the pretense of assimilating the people of the Federation. Their mission had been defined in stark terms by their actions at Acamar, Barolia, and now this ill-fated world. The Borg agenda was nothing less than genocide.

Captain Picard's voice snapped orders through the grim hush of the bridge. "Helm, intercept course, full impulse." The captain looked at Worf. "Destroy the Borg ship."

"Aye, sir."

Worf moved to stand beside the ship's chief of security and senior tactical officer, Lieutenant Jasminder Choudhury. The lithe, fortyish human woman's unruly mane of raven hair was tied in a tightly bound ponytail much like Worf's own.

"Prepare to execute attack pattern Tango-Red," Worf said. He discreetly pointed out a reading on her console to her. Dropping his voice to a coaching whisper, he added, "Increase the frequency of the transphasic shielding's nutation."

"Aye, sir," Choudhury said with a polite nod as she made the adjustment. She was highly skilled and a quick learner, Worf had observed. When they had first met, he had been concerned that her philosophy regarding security matters—which she shared with her deputy chief, a Betazoid man named Rennan Konya—might be too pacifistic. After seeing them both in action during the mission to stop the Borg-assimilated science vessel *U.S.S. Einstein,* however, Worf no longer had any doubts about their competence, or their ability to wield force when necessary.

As the captain rose from his chair, Worf said, "Arm torpedoes and target the Borg vessel."

He noted with approval how deftly Choudhury found the Borg vessel's known vulnerable points. "Locked," she replied.

Confident that she had no further need of his oversight, he moved to an aft station and configured it to gather damage and casualty reports.

Around the bridge, he saw hunched shoulders and clenched jaws, people tensed for action in a battle that would require little more than pressing buttons. Kadohata was the exception. Her countenance of mixed Asian and European ancestry was the very portrait of calm, and her British-sounding accent conveyed the same unflappability that Worf had come to expect from the captain. "Borg vessel in firing range in ten seconds," she reported.

The Borg cube loomed like a nightmare on the main viewer.

Worf longed for the raw physicality of the great Klingon battles of old, fought on fields of honor where warriors faced one another with blades to test both prowess and courage. *War was more glorious then,* he brooded. *But death remains the same.*

"The Borg cube is arming weapons," Choudhury declared.

Three shots struck the *Enterprise.* Deafening concussions rocked the ship, and consoles along the starboard bulkhead crackled with sparks, belched acrid smoke, and went dark.

Captain Picard glanced at Worf. "Now, Number One."

"Fire at will," Worf said. "Helm, execute attack pattern!"

Streaks like blue fire blazed away from the *Enterprise* and ripped into the towering black grids of dense machinery that served as the outer hull of the Borg cube. Large segments of the Borg ship disintegrated as the torpedoes exploded, and a cobalt-colored conflagration began to consume the cube from within.

Then it returned fire.

The bridge crew was thrown like rag dolls rolling in a drum as the *Enterprise*'s inertial dampers overloaded. Everyone was hurled to port, and they plummeted as the ship kept rolling. In the span of just a few seconds, they struck the consoles along the port bulkhead, tumbled across the overhead, and dropped

DAVID MACK

hard back to the deck as the ship's artificial gravity and inertial compensators reset themselves.

Worf's nose caught the scent of blood, which mingled with smoke and sharpened his focus. He pushed himself up to his hands and knees and looked first to the captain—who was bruised and had suffered a scrape on his forehead, but was not seriously hurt—and then to the main viewer, on which he saw the Borg cube consumed from within by an indigo fury. The cube collapsed into itself. Its core of blue fire turned blinding white . . . and then the ship was just a cloud of carbon dust and superheated gas.

If we could arm all of Starfleet with these weapons, Worf imagined, *we could end this war with the Borg on our own terms.*

He finished a cursory review of the damage and casualty reports and moved to the captain's side to help him up.

"Thank you, Mister Worf," the captain said once he was back on his feet. "Damage report."

"Hull breaches on decks twenty-six through twenty-nine, and the ventral shield generators are offline."

Picard nodded once. "Casualties?"

"Several on the lower decks," Worf said. "Mostly blunt-force trauma. No fatalities."

"Good," Picard said. "Are the sensors still operational?"

Worf stole a quick look at Kadohata, who wobbled her hand in a gesture that meant *sort of.* Worf looked at the captain. "Their function is limited."

"Focus our repairs on the sensors. We need them to trace the Borg ship's arrival trajectory."

"Aye, sir."

The captain palmed a sheen of sweat from his forehead and regarded the smoldering planet on the main viewer with a frown. "I'll be in my ready room, Commander. You have the bridge."

The battered and shaken crew remained at their posts and focused on their jobs as Picard left the bridge. Worf could tell that despite their swift victory over the Borg cube, the jarring blow the ship had taken had rattled the nerves of a few of the younger officers. Figuring that the crew would benefit from a bit of encouragement, Worf made a slow tour of the bridge stations and offered quiet, low-key compliments. It did not have the effect he'd hoped for. By the time he reached the tactical station, he noticed sly, questioning looks passing from one junior officer to another.

Choudhury confided to him, "I think you confused them."

He didn't mean to glare at her, it was just a habit. To her credit, she didn't flinch from his withering stare. "I was only trying to improve morale," he said, relaxing his expression.

"*That's* what confused them," she said.

That drew another glare from Worf, which, in turn, provoked a wan smile from Choudhury. *She is teasing me,* Worf realized, and he smirked. "You also did well."

"Stop," she joked. "You're confusing me."

He exhaled heavily in mock frustration. They stood together for a few moments. She stared at the image of Ramatis on the screen. Worf surveyed the bridge and was about to return to the center seat when Choudhury said, "That was home to nearly a billion people. An entire civilization. And it's gone forever." She looked at Worf. "If the rest of the fleet had transphasic torpedoes, we might be able to stop this from happening again."

"Perhaps," Worf said. "But those decisions are made by the admiralty, and we must respect the chain of command." Choudhury clenched her jaw as if she were struggling not to say something. He found her intensity unusual; she was a tranquil person by nature, and not one to evince strong emotions. "You disagree?"

She returned his inquiring stare with a fiery gaze. "I just wonder sometimes . . . what if the admiralty is wrong?"

Worf smirked. "Good question." He left her to brood on that and returned to the center seat to monitor the repair efforts.

In fact, Worf shared Choudhury's sentiments more than he could say. The admiralty, in Worf's opinion, were making a grave error by not distributing the new weapon design, which had been reverse-engineered from prototypes acquired from an alternate future by the late Kathryn Janeway of the *Starship Voyager*. Transphasic warheads were quickly proving to be the best defense against the renewed Borg onslaught. The admiralty, however, remained concerned that the Borg would eventually adapt to this seemingly unstoppable weapon, thereby robbing Starfleet of its last effective defense. Consequently, the *Enterprise* was the only ship in Starfleet that was armed with the warheads. That meant it was up to its crew to find out how the Borg were bypassing the Federation's defenses—and to do so while there was still a Federation left to defend.

With each passing week, the number of Borg attacks had been rising, and Worf had detected a pattern in their targets and frequency. The Borg's invasion was building to what he suspected was some kind of critical mass, and when it was reached, it would be too late to stop it.

Worf glowered at the burning planet on the main viewer. *For a billion people on Ramatis III,* he reminded himself bitterly, *it is* already *too late*.

5

———

Dax entered the *Aventine*'s Deck One conference room to find several of her senior officers waiting for her. She took her seat at the head of the polished, synthetic black granite conference table and nodded to the others.

Bowers sat to her immediate left, and Lieutenant Leishman was seated next to him. Across the table from Leishman was the senior operations officer, Lieutenant Oliana Mirren, a pale and reed-thin woman of Slavic ancestry who wore her blond hair short and closely cropped. Helkara sat between Mirren and Dax. The three humans at the table, Dax noted with quiet amusement, each had a cup of coffee in front of them.

As soon as Dax was settled, she said, "Let's get started."

Helkara leaned forward. "The salvage of the *Columbia*'s logs is under way, Captain. Ensign Riordan is helping its computer talk to ours, and they seem to be getting on splendidly."

Leishman cut in, "I'd just like to commend Ensign Riordan for his work on this project, Captain. If it weren't for the schematics he found in Earth's archives,

I doubt we could've made a successful connection to the *Columbia*'s memory banks."

"I'll note it in my log," Dax said. She asked Helkara, "How much of their data have you translated so far?"

The Zakdorn inflated his lower lip while he pondered his answer. It gave him an unflattering resemblance to a Terran bullfrog. "About thirty-five percent, I'd say," he responded at last. "We're dividing our time between downloading the sensor logs and the flight records."

Dax turned her attention toward Mirren. "Have you made any progress in analyzing their data?"

"Some," Mirren said. "By cross-referencing the two sources, we're developing a simulation of the *Columbia*'s crash landing and its approach to the planet. We're starting from the last synchronous data points and working backward from there."

Bowers nodded and then asked, "How far along is the sim?"

"We've locked down roughly the last forty seconds before the *Columbia* impacted the surface," Mirren said. "It looks as if the ship had been on autopilot as it—" A dry crinkling sound stopped her in mid-sentence. She glowered across the table.

Leishman unwrapped a bite-size piece of chocolate, which Dax suspected was from the chief engineer's jealously guarded personal stash of sweets. Years earlier, on *Defiant,* her colleagues had routinely raided her hidden candy cache, and Dax suspected that history would soon be repeated. Leishman popped the morsel into her mouth and started to chew. She froze as she realized that everyone else was staring at her. Through half-masticated chocolate, she asked in a defensive tone, "What?"

With the ire of an interrupted elementary-school teacher, Mirren replied, "Do you mind?"

"I get low blood sugar," Leishman said with guile-less sincerity through cocoa-colored teeth. "Makes me cranky."

Dax smirked at Sam Bowers's put-upon expression, because she knew from experience that what her XO really wanted to do was laugh. He and Dax both appreciated Leishman's knack for finding out what annoyed high-strung people and then exploiting it for her own clandestine amusement. Apparently, Leishman had decided that Mirren was going to be her latest victim.

Bowers glossed over the interruption. "Mirren, you said the *Columbia*'s autopilot had been engaged?"

"Aye, sir."

"Any idea by whom?"

Mirren shook her head. "Not yet. We're not even sure *when* it was activated. It might have been online for minutes, or it could've been flying the ship for years."

"All right," Dax said. "We still have twenty-one hours to work on this before we have to pull up stakes. Sam, I want all our resources focused on this. Understood?"

"Yes, sir," Bowers replied.

She planted her palms on the tabletop. "Thank you, everyone. Dismissed." The others stood half a second after Dax, and they moved in a ragged line toward the door to the aft corridor. Leishman fell into step a couple of paces behind Mirren and began whistling a soft and erratic melody. It took only a few seconds for Mirren to look back at Leishman and fume through clenched teeth, "Must you?"

"Sorry," Leishman said. "Helps me think."

As the group exited the conference room, Dax hoped that Mirren developed a sense of humor soon—because if she didn't, she was going to be on the receiving end of Leishman's subtle but deliberate irritations for a long, long time.

"This place gives me the creeps," said engineering crewman Yott, his voice echoing down the *Columbia*'s empty D Deck corridor.

Chief Celia Komer looked up from the antiquated power-distribution node she was dismantling, brushed a sweaty lock of hair from her face, and scowled teasingly at the fidgety young Bolian man. "Don't tell me you're seeing ghosts, too?"

His eyes darted one way, then another. "Not ghosts," he said. "But something's been following us since we came up from E Deck." A low, reedy moan of wind disturbed the dusting of fine-particle sand they had tracked down from the surface.

Komer sighed. She pointed her palm beacon aft, down one round-ribbed stretch of passageway. Then she turned it forward to light up another before aiming it squarely into Yott's face. "Who's following us? The invisible man?"

"Chief, I'm serious. There's something here."

"Fine." Komer hated to humor superstitious behavior, but it seemed to her that the only way to get Yott back to work would be to take him seriously for a few moments. She set down her coil spanner, stood up, turned, and lifted her tricorder from its holster on her hip. "This'll just take a few seconds," she explained. "I'm running a full-spectrum scan for life-forms and energy readings. Anything special you want me to look for?"

Yott shook his head and continued to shift his gaze every few seconds, as if he expected something to try and ambush him.

"Y'know, you ought to lay off the *raktajino*," Komer said with a grin, hoping to lighten the mood. "It makes you jumpy."

To her dismay, Yott seemed immune to humor. "I don't drink *raktajino*," he said. His eyes scanned the ceiling. "Can't you feel it? Like a charge in the air? It smells like ozone."

Komer wondered uncharitably, *How'd this kid ever make it through basic training?* "I'm not reading anything unusual," she said, hoping her matter-of-fact tone would calm him. She pivoted as her scan continued. "No bio signs in this section but us."

"There are things tricorders can't read," Yott said. "Trace elements, exotic energy patterns, extradimensional phenomena—"

"And paranoia," she interrupted. "I can't believe I really have to tell you there's no such thing as—" A flicker of blue light behind a bulkhead caught her eye, and Yott's as well.

He cried out, "You saw that! You saw it!"

Taking a breath to suppress her irritation, she focused the tricorder in the direction of the flash. "Residual energy," she said, her tone one of mild rebuke. "Just a surge in the lines. Makes sense when you think about how much juice we're pumping into this old wreck."

"Not down here," Yott replied, and he lifted his tricorder to show her a schematic on its screen. "The main power relay was severed in the crash, and both the backups are slagged. There's *no power* on this deck." He pointed at the nearby bulkhead. "So where did *that* come from?"

Another groan of hot, dry wind pushed through fractures in the bulkheads. Crackles of noise echoed off the metal interiors of the passageway, growing closer and sharper. Then a light fixture on the overhead stuttered momentarily to life and flared brightly enough to force Komer to shut her eyes. Its afterimage pulsed in myriad hues on her retina.

"Chief!" shouted Yott. He tugged on her sleeve. "Come on!"

Shielding her eyes with her forearm, she backed away from the glare and tapped her combadge. "Komer to—"

Twisted forks of green lightning exploded from the light, in a storm of shining phosphors and searing-hot polymer shards. The synthetic shrapnel overpowered Komer and Yott, peppering their faces with bits of burning debris as the bolts of electricity slammed into their torsos and hurled them hard to the deck.

A steady, high-pitched tone rang in Komer's ears. Spasms wracked her body, but she barely felt them— she was numb from the chest down. Her mouth was dry, and her tongue tasted like copper. As the last of the light's glowing debris fell to the deck and faded away, darkness settled upon her and Yott.

Then a spectral shape formed in the blackness, as pale and silent as a gathering fog. It descended like a heavy liquid sinking into the sea—spreading, dispersing, enveloping the two downed Starfleet personnel on the deck.

For a moment, Komer told herself that she was imagining it, that it was nothing more than a trauma-induced hallucination, another afterimage on her overtaxed retinas.

Then Yott screamed—and as the ghostly motes pierced Komer's body like a million needles of fire, she did, too.

Lieutenant Lonnoc Kedair strode quickly through the sepulchral darkness of the corridor, toward the cluster of downward-pointed palm-beacon beams. A charnel odor thickened the sultry air.

Four *Aventine* security officers stood with their phaser rifles slung at their sides, facing one another in a circle. Kedair nudged past them and stopped as she saw the two bodies at their feet. Both corpses were contorted in poses of agony and riddled with deep, smoldering cavities. In some places, the two engineers' wounds tunneled clear through their bodies, giving Kedair a view of the deck, which was slick with greasy pools of liquefied biomass.

Kedair turned to Lieutenant Naomi Darrow, the away team's security supervisor. "Who were they?"

"Yott and Komer, sir," Darrow said. "They were collecting evidence for analysis."

Kedair squatted low next to the dead Bolian and examined his wounds more closely. "What killed them?"

"We're not sure," said Darrow. "We picked up some

residual energy traces, but nothing that matches any known weapons."

Pointing at a smoking divot in Komer's abdomen, Kedair said, "These look like thermal effects."

"Partly," Darrow said as she pushed a handful of her flaxen hair from her face. "But we think those are secondary. The cause of death looks like molecular disruption."

The security chief shook her head. "I've never seen a disruptor do this. Did you check for biochemical agents?"

"Yes, sir. No biochem signatures of any kind."

It was a genuine mystery—exactly what Kedair hated most.

Everyone on the *Columbia* had heard the bloodcurdling shrieks emanate from the ship's lower decks and echo through its open turbolift shafts, but Kedair was determined to contain and compartmentalize as much information about this incident as she could. She asked Darrow, "Who's been down here?"

Darrow swept the beam of her palm beacon over the other security officers on the scene: Englehorn, T'Prel, and ch'Maras. "Just us," she said.

"Keep it that way," Kedair said. "Have these bodies beamed to sickbay on the *Aventine*. I want Dr. Tarses to start the autopsies immediately."

"Aye, sir," Darrow said.

"And not a word of this to anyone," Kedair said, making eye contact with the four officers in succession. "If anyone asks—"

Englehorn interrupted, "*If?*"

Correcting herself, Kedair continued, "*When* you are asked about what happened, the only thing I want you to say is that there was an incident, and that it's under investigation. Don't mention fatalities, injuries, or anything else. Do not mention Yott or Komer by name. Is that understood?" The four junior officers nodded. "Good. I want you four to secure this deck. Move in pairs and maintain an open channel to the *Aventine*." She looked down at the bodies. "If you encounter anything that might be capable of this, fall back and call for backup. Clear?" Another round of heads bobbing in unison. "Make it happen."

Darrow pointed at the other security officers as she issued their orders. "Englehorn, sweep aft with T'Prel. ch'Maras, forward with me." She looked at Kedair. "Sir, I suggest you beam up to *Aventine* and track our search from there." To the others she added, "Move out."

The four security officers split up and walked away in opposite directions, with one member of each pair monitoring a tricorder's sensor readings while the other kept a phaser rifle leveled and ready. Kedair remained with the bodies as her team continued moving away. Their shadows spread and then vanished beyond circular section bulkheads in the curved corridor. In less than a minute Kedair was alone, her solitary palm beacon casting a harsh blue glow over the dead.

I was so focused on not fueling their fears that I failed to protect their lives. Bitter regrets festered in her thoughts. *I should have kept an open mind, no matter what they told me.*

Kedair still didn't believe that the two-hundred-year-old wrecked starship was haunted—but the twisted, horrific corpses in front of her left her no doubt that she, and her away team, were definitely not alone on the *Columbia*.

2156–2157

6

—•—

Stygian darkness pressed in on Erika Hernandez as she made her slow descent into the frigid abyss of the *Columbia*'s aft turbolift. Her breath misted as it passed over the plastic-sheathed chemical flare clenched in her teeth.

She had underestimated the effort involved in climbing from the bridge portal on A Deck to the entrance of main engineering on D Deck. The blue glow of the flare was fading slowly after having burned for more than an hour. It was still bright enough to let her see the rungs under her hands, but her feet probed the cold blackness for each new, unseen foothold.

Above her, and attached to her by a safety line that was secured on the bridge, was Lieutenant Vincenzo Yacavino, the second-in-command of the ship's MACO detachment. At the request of Commander Fletcher—who, like most first officers, was quite protective of her captain—he had climbed up from the MACOs' berthing area on C Deck to escort Hernandez safely belowdecks. A necklace of variously colored emergency flares was strung around his neck. He called down to her, "Are you all right, *signora*?"

DAVID MACK

"Mm-hmm," Hernandez mumble-hummed past the flare in her teeth. Then, a few meters below, she saw flickers of light.

She quickened her pace and reached the open turbolift portal of D Deck. Using handholds and a narrow lip of metal that protruded from the shaft bulkhead beside the opening, she eased her way off the ladder and onto the catwalk at the forward end of main engineering. As soon as Yacavino had joined her on the platform, she unfastened the safety line that he had looped in a crisscross pattern around her torso. She would rather have borrowed one of the MACOs' tactical harnesses, which were designed and reinforced for rappelling, but most of the spares had been lost in the same blast that had crippled her ship.

Almost every available emergency light on the *Columbia* had been brought to bear in its engineering compartment, but because most of the lights were focused on specific areas of interest, the majority of the deck remained steeped in smoky shadows. An acrid pall of scorched metal put a sharp tang in the air.

Karl Graylock, the chief engineer, stood with warp-drive specialist Daria Pierce at a control console on the elevated platform behind the warp reactor. The surface panel of the console had been removed, exposing half-melted circuit boards and blackened wiring. On the lower deck, more than a dozen engineers removed heavy plates from the reactor housing, decoupled enormous plasma relays, and sifted through a dusty pile of crystal shards and debris.

No one paid much attention to Hernandez as she walked down the stairs from the catwalk and continued toward Graylock.

"Try cross-circuiting to A," he said to Pierce as he made a minor adjustment to something inside the console. He watched Pierce make a few changes of her own. They both stared intently into the mangled workings of the console, then shook their heads in shared frustration. "Nothing," Graylock said, his shoulders sagging in defeat.

"Karl," Hernandez said. Normally, he snapped-to at the sound of her voice. This time he sat back against the railing opposite the control panel and looked down at the captain with a weary expression. "*Ja*, Captain?"

"Good news," she said with a tired grin. "Looks like your plan worked. If the Romulans had figured it out, we'd probably all be dead by now."

Graylock's dour frown was steady. "Is that your idea of cheering us up, Captain? Because if it is, you suck at it."

"I take it things aren't going well down here?"

"You could say that," Graylock replied. He climbed down from the platform and led Hernandez on a slow stroll down the length of the reactor. "The warp drive is irreparable," he said. "All that's left of the crystal matrix is dust and splinters. At least half the coils in each nacelle are ruptured, maybe more. And the ventral plasma relays were all severed in the last explosion."

Hernandez glanced inside the reactor through a gap left by a detached pylon conduit. She could see for herself that Graylock wasn't exaggerating. The damage was extensive.

"So what are we looking at? Do we need the *Enterprise* to bring us a whole new warp drive?"

The stocky chief engineer turned and folded his arms over his chest. "*Ja,* that would help." He leaned back against the oblong reactor housing. "And if you can think of a way to ask them, or anyone else, I will be most impressed, Captain."

It took her a moment to deduce his implication. "Subspace communications?"

"*Kaput,*" he said. "The virus corrupted our software and firmware, and the explosion that covered our escape destroyed both our shuttlepods and the transceiver array. We can send and receive light-speed signals, if you don't mind waiting the rest of your life for a reply."

"Wonderful," Hernandez muttered. "Isn't there something we can raid for parts to fix the subspace antenna?"

Graylock gestured vaguely around the compartment. "We don't have enough working parts to keep the lights on, and you want me to reinvent subspace radio?"

Hernandez sighed. "Since you brought it up, when *can* we expect to have the lights back?"

"It depends." He looked back at his engineers, who were tinkering with an assortment of broken or deformed components that looked more like scrap metal bound for reclamation than like the essential components of a starship's warp propulsion system. "If we can all stay awake, maybe ten hours."

"Make it six," Hernandez said. "I want the turbolifts running before alpha shift goes to their racks."

"*Jawohl,* Captain," Graylock said with a nod. "I'll keep Commander Fletcher informed of our efforts."

She returned his nod. "Carry on."

None of the engineers looked up from their tasks as she walked back to the catwalk staircase and rejoined Lieutenant Yacavino at the open portal to the turbolift shaft. "Time to head back up to A Deck," she said to the fit, dark-haired MACO. "Let's get ready to climb." He picked up the safety line and started paying out slack to wrap around her. As he reached behind her back to loop the end of the tether around her thigh, she gave him a teasing grin. "And watch your hands this time, Mister. I want to keep our relationship professional."

Commander Veronica Fletcher waited until the door of the captain's ready room closed before she said, "It's worse than we thought."

Captain Hernandez pushed her chair back from the small desk tucked into the corner of the compartment. She crossed her legs and nodded to another chair. "Have a seat."

Fletcher pulled out the chair and sat down. She handed a small clipboard to Hernandez. "We lost more than half the crew in the attack, and most of the MACOs were killed setting off the diversionary blast."

"Damn it," Hernandez whispered. "Where'd the jump take us?"

"Kalil plotted our position against the known shipping lanes," she explained as the captain looked over the second page of the brief report. "We're well outside normal sensor range. And with the convoy gone, there probably won't be much friendly traffic out here for a while."

"If ever," Hernandez said.

The captain's downbeat manner troubled Fletcher. "Being a bit pessimistic, aren't you?"

Worry lines deepened on Hernandez's brow. "If yesterday's events are any guide, this entire sector is likely to be under enemy control soon." Her countenance darkened. "This was only the beginning—the first salvo in a war with the Romulans."

"You don't know that," Fletcher said. "It might have been an isolated skirmish, or—"

"They ambushed us," Hernandez interrupted. "They came in numbers, and they turned our own weapons on the convoy. This was planned. They've been preparing for a long time, and now they're making their move—and we're stuck out here, with no way home and no way to send a warning." She launched herself from her chair and then halted, a coiled spring with nowhere to go. Turning away to look out the compartment's single, small viewport, she added with simmering frustration, "The goddam war's actually starting, and we're stuck on the sidelines."

Fletcher sighed. "So, what are we supposed to do?"

Several seconds passed while Fletcher waited for the captain's answer. The exposed overhead conduits, normally alive with a low buzzing, were silent, exacerbating Fletcher's sense of the ship's predicament. Finally, Hernandez turned away from the window and back toward her first officer. "We survive," she said. "If the war has begun, Earth won't have any ships to spare on a search-and-rescue mission this far from home. Whatever else happens, we have to assume we're on our own now."

Fletcher wasn't ready yet to embrace the worst-case scenario. She asked, "What if Earth *does* send a rescue ship? Our best bet of being found would be to return to our original course, at any speed."

"That's also our best chance of being found by the enemy," Hernandez said. "They knew our route well enough to hit us with almost no warning. Using the same route to limp home strikes me as a bad idea." She covered her eyes and massaged her temples with one hand. "Besides, without the transceiver array, we're mute. Even if someone came looking for us, we can't respond to their hails. At anything less than close range, we might be mistaken for an alien ship that doesn't want to make contact."

The captain stepped past Fletcher and crossed the cramped room to another short desktop wedged into the opposite corner. She poked through a jumble of papers and bound volumes on the shelf above it, then pulled down and opened a large book. "Have a look at this," she said to Fletcher, who got up and joined the captain at the other desk. Hernandez continued, "This is from our last mapping run before we met the convoy."

Studying the dense cluster of symbols and coordinates on the map, Fletcher was unable to anticipate the captain's plan. "What are we looking for?"

"The basics," Hernandez said. "A nice Minshara-class planet where we can stock up on food and water. Preferably, one with enough expertise to help us make some repair parts for the warp drive." She planted her finger on an unnamed star system that so far had merited no more than a brief footnote in the galactic catalog. "That's what I'm talking about. Nitrogen-oxygen atmosphere, liquid water, and subspace signal emissions."

Fletcher shook her head. "Shaky readings, sir. And at that range? They could have been caused by a sensor malfunction."

"All right," Hernandez countered. "How do you explain the high-energy particles flooding out of that system?"

"It could be anything," Fletcher said. "That star's pretty dense. For all we know, we might be picking up signals from a system behind it, due to gravitational lensing."

The captain looked unconvinced. "I don't think so," she said. "If we were seeing a lensed signal, there'd be other distortions. These readings may be scarce, but they're clear. There's a planet there with the resources we need, and it's the closest safe harbor in the sector."

"We don't know that it's safe, and 'close' is a relative term," Fletcher said. "It's eleven-point-four lightyears away. How are we supposed to get there without the warp drive?"

Hernandez shut the book with a heavy slap. "We still have impulse engines, and I mean to use them."

As the captain put the book back on the shelf, Fletcher was compelled to ask, "Are you serious? Even at full impulse—"

"Forget full impulse," Hernandez cut in. "I want the main impulse system in overdrive. We need to get as close to lightspeed as we can without hitting it."

Fletcher was aghast. "You're talking about time-dilation effects," she said.

"Yes, I am," Hernandez said. She returned to her desk in the other corner. "Don't give me that look. Think about it for a second, and you'll see why we have to do this."

The captain's urgent tone made her point clear to Fletcher. "To ration our provisions," she said, and the captain nodded in confirmation. The *Columbia* had been fueled and supplied for a two-year deployment before leaving Earth. Without warp drive, interstellar travel to a world capable of restocking the ship's stores and repairing its damaged systems might take years or even decades. "What fraction of c are we talking about?"

"Within one-ten-thousandth," Hernandez said.

After a quick round of mental calculations, Fletcher said, "So, a time-dilation ratio of about seventy-to-one?"

"Give or take," Hernandez replied.

"So why not just make a run for home?"

Hernandez raised her eyebrows in a gentle expression of mock surprise. "Because 'home' is over eighty light-years away. I'd rather not waste the better part of a century getting there. If I'm right, we can find what we need to fix the warp drive in that star system and get home while at least a few people we know are still alive."

The prospect of twelve years being transformed by the laws of relativity into a short-lived purgatory disturbed Fletcher, but the notions of starving to death in deep space or returning home as a centenarian troubled her even more. "I'll get Graylock to work on the impulse drive," Fletcher said. "It'll take a few hours to remove the safeties before we can overdrive the coils past one-quarter c."

The captain nodded. "Tell him to beef up the main deflector, too. At the speeds we're talking about, the mass and kinetic energy of oncoming particles'll be pretty intense."

"And once we hit relativistic speeds, our sensors'll be blind to just about everything," Fletcher said. "We'll also become a serious X-ray source."

Hernandez smirked. "I prefer to think of it as becoming our own interstellar emergency flare."

Fletcher chortled. "We'd just better hope we don't get noticed by the Romulans or the Klingons."

"They'd probably mistake us for some kind of primitive colony ship," Hernandez said. "Maybe we'll get lucky and be taken prisoner aboard a ship that actually has a working warp drive. Now, if you want something to worry about, try the hard radiation from blueshifting."

Fletcher nodded. "We'd better have Dr. Metzger start us all on radiation-treatment protocols. And I'll have Thayer restrict access to the outer compartments."

"Good thinking," said Hernandez.

With a tired grin, Fletcher added, "Then the only things we still need are a deck of cards and some good books. If you like, I can loan you the first six *Captain Proton* novels."

"Thank you, Number One," said Hernandez, who no longer seemed to be paying attention. She sounded unusually somber.

"Are you sure you're all right, Captain?"

A rueful grimace twisted the captain's mouth. "I'm fine," she said. "It just bugs me that the time when Earth needs us most is the one time we can't be there." She turned her gaze out the viewport. "All we can do is hope that when we finally bring our ship home, there's still a home worth bringing it to."

———◆———

Stephen Foyle pivoted from one foot to the other while he dribbled the basketball from hand to hand, turning his body to keep his opponent at bay. Sweat dripped from above his hairline, tracing winding paths out of his gray brush cut and down his face. A thick sheen of perspiration on his arms and legs caught the glare of the overhead lights in the ship's gymnasium.

Gage Pembleton taunted him in a tone of crisp superiority. "What are you waiting for, Major? An invitation?"

"Patience, First Sergeant," Foyle said. He lurched forward, and Pembleton matched his stride. Then Foyle passed the ball backward between his own legs, spun, and slipped behind Pembleton's back for a drive at the basket. By the time the younger, brown-skinned man had caught up to Foyle, the major had made a graceful layup, banking the ball off the back-board.

The orange ball hushed through the net, and Pembleton caught it off the bounce. "Not bad," he said. He tossed the ball with a single bounce at Foyle. "But it's still eleven-eight."

Foyle checked the ball and passed it back. "For now."

A musky scent of deodorant overpowered by exertion trailed Pembleton as he dribbled the ball back to the top of the key to start his possession. "What time is it?"

The major smirked. "Getting tired?"

"No, I want you to sing me 'Happy Birthday' at 1340 hours."

"That's not funny," Foyle said, irked to be reminded of Captain Hernandez's decision to send them all on a slow-time cruise into oblivion. He imagined that he could feel an hour slipping away with every minute, days vanishing into every hour.

At the center-court circle, Pembleton turned and waited for Foyle to strike a defensive pose. The lanky Canadian started dribbling and pivoted to show Foyle his back. "I'll spot you three points if you can take the ball before I score," he said in his drawl of a baritone. "Give you a chance to tie it up."

Foyle grinned. "Don't go getting—"

Pembleton was off the deck, spinning in midair, hefting the ball high over his head with his long, wiry arms and massive hands. Foyle sprang to block the shot, hands flailing, but the ball was gone, sailing on a long and poetic arc into the basket. It slapped through the net, bounced twice off the deck, and rolled behind the end line as Foyle watched with a tired frown.

"Thirteen-eight," Pembleton said. As the major opened his mouth to protest, the sergeant pointed at their feet and added, "Behind the line, two points."

"Now you're just showing off," Foyle said. They walked downcourt together to retrieve the ball. The major's nostrils filled with the funky stench of his sweat-soaked tank top and sodden socks, and his thighs and calves felt as if they were tying themselves in knots and turning to wood. He palmed the excess perspiration from his face and dried his hands on his cotton athletic trunks. Then he squatted to pick up the ball and was unable to stop himself from exhaling a pained grunt. "I think I need a time-out," he said.

"No time-outs in one-on-one," Pembleton taunted. Unfazed by Foyle's bitter glare, he added, "Your rules."

Foyle tucked the ball under his left arm and walked toward the benches at the sideline. "Don't make me pull rank."

"It's your game, Major. I just play in it."

Pembleton followed him to the bench and sat down on the other side of a stack of soft, white towels. He kept his back straight and his head up, and his breaths were long and slow.

Foyle slumped as soon as he was seated, and he reached under the bench for his squeeze bottle of water. The major lifted the nozzle to his lips and clamped his hand tight, filling his mouth with a stream of cool liquid. He downed a third of the bottle in half a minute. "I can't believe she's doing this," he said after catching his breath.

The sergeant maintained an attentive silence. He picked up a towel and dried his shaved head as Foyle continued.

"There has to be some way to get a signal back to Earth. We could've cannibalized something to fix the transceiver array and sent a Mayday to Starfleet—or even to Vulcan, if we had to." He took another swig of water. "Instead, she's got us sitting out the war. Didn't even ask me before she put us all on the slow boat to nowhere."

Pembleton chided him, "She didn't *ask* you? Tell me, Major, when did the ship become a democracy? Do I get a vote, too?"

"You know what I mean, Pembleton," Foyle said, weary and frustrated. "It's the same old story. She thinks just because we're MACOs, we don't need to know. Hell, even the illusion of being consulted would be nice once in a while."

"So, if she had let you speak your mind, and then did the same thing anyway, you'd be fine with that?"

The question forced Foyle to stop and think for a moment. "No," he admitted, "I wouldn't. I mean, what if this planet we're going to can't help us? What then? Should we just keep making these near-light trips while the galaxy changes around us at warp speed? It's just so damned stupid. There has to be a better answer than wasting twelve years of our lives."

"It's not our lives she's wasting," Pembleton said. "It's everyone else's. I was supposed to be home in time to see my oldest start school. He'll be in college by the time we drop back to normal spaceflight. I feel like I've missed his *whole life*." He dried his arms and then tossed away the towel. "For us," he continued, "this'll just be a couple of boring months. But for my wife and my boys . . . I might as well be dead."

That same thought haunted Foyle, as well. They were five days into their journey, and he knew that home on Earth, his wife Valerie was likely marking the anniversary of the last time she had seen him or heard his voice. The *Columbia* and its crew had been missing in action for more than a year in Earth time.

She won't have given up on me yet, he assured himself. *But she won't wait forever. Sooner or later, she'll go on with her life, without me. I might get home while she's still alive, but it won't matter, because* my *life will be gone. Our* life.

"There's still time for a change of plan," Foyle said. He watched Pembleton to measure his reaction. "If we drop the ship back to quarter impulse, we can focus on repairing the transceiver, maybe get a message home before everybody we know gives up on us."

Pembleton smirked. "Nice idea," he said. "But if that was a possibility, I have to think we'd be doing it already."

"Maybe," Foyle said. "But what if it's just that Graylock needs to take orders from someone who knows how to motivate him?" He glanced at Pembleton.

The sergeant kept his expression a cipher. For as long as Foyle had served with him, Pembleton had been a master at encrypting his feelings. "It might take a pretty big shakeup in the command structure to cause a change like that," the sergeant said. His eyes betrayed nothing as he returned Foyle's stare. "Permission to speak freely, sir?"

"Granted."

"Considering the amount of damage to the ship, and the skill we've seen Graylock use to keep it running, I'm inclined to believe him when he says the transceiver can't be fixed. And if the captain thinks this is our best shot, I'd say trust her."

Foyle responded with a slow nod. "So, you don't think a change in strategy or leadership would be in our best interest?"

"Under these circumstances? No."

Something about the tenor of that answer prompted Foyle to press on. "And if, at some future juncture, our circumstances were to change . . . ?"

Pembleton shrugged and replied with an ominous nonchalance, "Well . . . that's a different question."

2381

7

———•———

Melora Pazlar felt as if she were the stillness at the center of everything. Floating in the womblike zero *g* of *Titan*'s stellar cartography lab, she was surrounded by a holographic sphere of stars, a virtual front-row seat to the universe.

Aloft and held in place by tractor beams so gentle that even her fragile senses couldn't feel them, she turned in slow degrees. She manipulated images of science-department reports and sensor analyses that were superimposed over the holographic backdrop, rearranging them with fluid arcs of her arms and subtle turns of her wrist. It was like a silent ballet.

She marveled at Ra-Havreii's handiwork. *He really is a genius,* she thought with admiration and delight. Then she remembered their almost-kiss and her reflexive retreat. She had pondered it for the past several hours while she worked, and she still didn't know why she had rebuffed him. The Efrosian was handsome and charming, and had a whispered reputation among the ship's female humanoids as a considerate companion. He had everything going for him, and he clearly was more than a little interested in her, and she knew that a few years earlier she might have welcomed him eagerly.

Now, however, she couldn't imagine letting his lips touch hers without a shiver traveling down her spine. The idea of his hands on her flesh made her pull her arms to her sides, and her entire body tensed and began to fold in on itself.

Bending forward, she propelled herself into a slow tumble around her center of gravity. She forced her arms wide, as if to take the stars and nebulae into her delicate embrace, and she cleared her mind while drawing deep breaths. Tuvok had taught her well how to master her emotions and calm her mind. He had even imparted some wisdom in the area of self-defense, by emphasizing styles and techniques based on evasion. She had become expert at slipping away from people.

A soft but insistent synthetic tone beeped in quick triple pulses, breaking her moment of reflection. The sound made bright echoes against the unseen surfaces of the holotank. Pazlar used bend-and-stretch gestures to arrest her forward rolling. It took a few seconds for her to become still once again. All the while, the computer's alert continued chirping at her. When at last she was steady, she stretched out her arm and waved her hand in a semicircle to halt the shrill signal. "Computer, report."

"Anomalous energy signature detected," replied the feminine voice of the ship's computer.

Pazlar tried not to get her hopes up. *Titan's* crew had charted many unusual energy signatures in this region, and few had proved worthy of even a cursory follow-up. "Elaborate."

"Concentrated pulses of triquantum waves with a subspatial distortion factor of four-point-six tera-cochranes."

This was something new. "Have we identified the source?"

"Affirmative. Bearing 335.46, mark 291.14, distance eighteen-point-two light-years."

"Show me what we have about the pulses' point of origin," Pazlar said. "Provide a false-spectrum display of the pulses' trajectories and superimpose over my starmap interface. Prepare secondary data displays." More focused now, Pazlar began her fluid choreography of data screens as she called them into existence. "Particle analysis of the wave pulses." Down and to the left. "Cross-reference with past energy emissions from this sector." Right and up diagonally.

The luminosity of her holographic environment became blinding as several beams of laser-intense white light radiated in all directions from what looked like an empty point in deep space. Pazlar squinted against the glare. "Computer, tone it down a bit, please." The beams faded to a dim blue, and she was grateful that Ra-Havreii's user interface had been programmed with a sophisticated grasp of idioms in several languages.

There was nowhere in the holotank that Pazlar could position herself without being intersected by multiple beams. "Computer, estimate the power level of these bursts."

"Unable to comply. Power levels have exceeded the limits of our sensor capacity. Severe subspatial distortion is interfering with scans of the origin point."

Now Pazlar was worried. *Subspatial distortion? At that power level? Not good.* She pulled the empty sector-grid chart to the front of her array of screens. "Pazlar to Lieutenant Rager."

Titan's senior operations officer answered over the comm, *"Go ahead."*

"Sariel," Pazlar said, "I need a priority reassignment of the main sensor array." She felt a low-power force field give her tactile feedback as she entered commands on her holographic interface. "I'm sending over a grid reference, and I need to see every last bit of it in maximum detail as soon as possible."

Rager was apologetic. *"Melora, I can't do that. Some of the scans we're running were ordered by Commander Tuvok. If you want to cancel his assignments, you'll need approval from the XO."* A computer feedback tone was audible over the channel. *"Hang on, I just got your file."* A few moments later, Rager muttered, *"You sent me a* blank *grid reference? You want me to drop everything to point the main array at* nothing?"

"I don't think it's nothing," Pazlar said. "Something at those coordinates is sending out high-energy bursts in every direction. More to the point, it's something *we can't see.*" She sent over her readings of the wave pulses and waited until she heard the chime of its arrival through the open channel.

"All right," Rager said. *"That is interesting. I can bump a couple of the research projects and let you have the gravi—"*

"Sariel," Pazlar snapped, "look at the energy profile for the pulses! Now look at the ambient readings in the center of that grid reference. Are you looking?"

Anger put an edge on Rager's voice. *"Yes, but I don't . . ."* She paused for a few seconds. Then she answered with understanding and alarm, *"Triquantum waves."*

"Also known as a telltale sign of transwarp conduits."

"The array's all yours."

"Spell it out for me," Riker said to Pazlar, whose holographic avatar sat at the conference table with the rest of *Titan*'s senior bridge officers. "How close are these pulses to Borg transwarp signatures?"

"Similar, but not identical," Pazlar said. "Their energy levels are greater than anything we've ever seen the Borg use, but their subspatial distortions share a number of properties with transwarp conduits. They might be related."

Keru leaned forward to look at Riker. "I agree, Captain. It's possible the Borg have developed a new form of transwarp to replace the network they lost."

Riker was troubled by Keru's speculation, but at the same time he was grateful to have something to work on. It was just after 2300 hours, nearly the end of beta shift, his normal time for retiring to bed with Deanna. This situation would give him a reason to stay awake a few more hours and let her go to sleep first, before he returned to their quarters. He looked at Lieutenant Rager. "Do we know what's generating these pulses?"

The brown-skinned woman shook her head. "No, sir. We've made the most detailed scans we can from this distance, and so far we haven't seen anything at the pulses' origin point. But we have come up with a few anomalies."

"Naturally," Keru quipped. "Never a shortage of those."

After shooting a glare at the chief of security, Rager continued, "Most of our scans showed the sector as empty, except for a pretty harsh radiation field. But when we mapped the currents of cosmic particles passing through the sector, we found this." She entered a command on her padd, and a computer-generated animation appeared on the conference room's wall-mounted viewscreen. It showed countless overlapping streams bending around a central point. "Even though we can't read any sign of space-time curvature in that area, particles moving through it have their directions and velocities altered as if they'd run into something big."

Intrigued and worried in equal measure, Riker asked, "Big like a Borg transwarp hub?"

"No," Pazlar said. "Big like a star system."

"All right," Riker said. "I remember seeing a planetary cloaking device during my first year on the *Enterprise*. It's not hard to imagine someone taking it to the next step."

"The question, then," Keru said, "is who that someone is."

Rager keyed in more commands on her padd and changed the animation on the viewscreen to show the trajectories of several of the energy pulses. "It's worth noting," she said, "that a few of these bursts appear to be targeted at Federation space. The energy signatures taper off after about twenty light-years from their point of origin, so if they are the leading ends of transwarp conduits, there's no telling where they let out."

Riker looked at his first officer, who had been unusually quiet so far during the meeting. "Chris? What do you think?"

Vale addressed her reply to Pazlar. "Sounds like you might have stumbled onto a Borg installation," she said. "This might be how they've been bypassing our perimeter defenses."

"Hang on," Rager said. "Don't you think we might be jumping to conclusions here? She only said there are *similarities* to Borg transwarp frequencies."

Tuvok added, "I concur with Lieutenant Rager. There is no evidence that the Borg have ever ventured into this region of the Beta Quadrant. Furthermore, if we are dealing with a cloaked star system, such an undertaking would, presumably, take a great deal of time to accomplish. Because we are within eighteen light-years of the pulses' source, the cloaking would have to have occurred at least eighteen years ago, or else light from the star would still be visible to us."

Pazlar's avatar perked up. "That's right," she said. "I need to check something." She picked up her padd—which was part of her projected holopresence—and worked quickly while the conversation continued around her.

"You both make good points," Vale said to Rager and Tuvok. "However, the fact that energy bursts are being directed from here toward the Federation, at the same time that the Borg are slipping through our defenses, is highly suspect. Even if the Borg didn't *create* the thing sending the pulses, they might have discovered it and found a way to exploit it."

Keru added, "Or maybe *it* is using *them* against *us*."

"Also a possibility," Vale said. Turning to Tuvok, she added, "Either way, if there is a link between this phenomenon and the Borg, it'll be our job to stop it."

"To borrow a human expression," Tuvok said, "'easier said than done.' If the Borg have established a stronghold in a cloaked star system, there will be no way to estimate their numbers until it is too late to turn back. We might well find ourselves severely outnumbered."

Keru nodded and looked at Vale. "He's right. It's not like we can call for reinforcements out here."

"I've got something interesting," Pazlar interrupted. She relayed her padd's information to the wall viewscreen. "I cross-referenced the star charts we got from the Pa'haquel and the Vomnin to see if they'd ever noted a star at these coordinates. They have." She got up and walked to the monitor to point out details as she talked. "In fact, we noted it ourselves, in a wide-area mapping survey several months ago, before we entered its 'dark zone.' It was a main-sequence star, high metallicity. Its gravitational signature indicated several planets in orbit. About eight hundred years ago, it started fading, and its gravitational signature changed in a way that suggests it lost its planets. Approximately seven hundred years ago, it went dark. So, today, to anyone within seven hundred light-years, it's as good as invisible."

Riker asked with real curiosity, "What happened to it? Did it go supernova? Collapse into a black hole?"

"No, sir," Pazlar said. "It just . . . went dark."

Keru deadpanned, "Gee, that's not ominous." He turned to Riker. "If they don't want to be seen, maybe we don't, either."

"Agreed," Riker said. "Tuvok, do what you can to reduce our sensor profile. Rager, deploy subspace radio boosters at shorter intervals, in case we need to get a signal back to Starfleet in a hurry. Keru, get your security teams ready to make an assault on the Borg, and be ready to repel boarders. Pazlar, keep analyzing the energy pulses, and report any new findings." As he pushed his chair back from the table, he said to Vale, "Commander, put us on an intercept course for the source of those pulses, maximum warp." Riker stood and made a quick exit, followed by the other officers.

They moved as a unit down a short passage to the bridge. There, Riker settled wearily into his chair as Vale ordered the course change. The pitch of the engines' whine climbed rapidly as *Titan* accelerated to its maximum rated warp speed. On the main viewscreen, the stars were no longer just streaks or even blurs so much as snap-flashes of light racing past, forming a tunnel of light around the *Luna*-class starship.

Vale finished making her circuit of the bridge and placed herself just behind Riker's left shoulder. "I just had a worrying thought," she said in a confidential tone. "It seems to me that someone who'd turn their star system invisible probably won't be thrilled to receive visitors."

"Good point," Riker said. "Take the ship to Yellow Alert."

Ranul Keru took two steps inside the auxiliary engineering lab and realized he was surrounded.

Machines of alien grace were grouped together in what seemed to Keru like a haphazard fashion, leaning against one another, clumped in tight clusters, or set front to back in ragged lines along the lab's bulkheads. The odors of chemical solvents and superheated metal assaulted Keru's nostrils, and he stepped carefully through the maze of incomplete inventions.

He followed his ears. Despite the blanketing hum of whirring generators, hissing ventilators, and purring servos, he still discerned the irregular tapping and scraping of a tinkerer at work. On the other side of an incomplete frame snaked with wires and patched with isolinear arrays, he caught the flash of a phased-pulse welding iron. When the red-ringed indigo afterimage faded from his retina and he could see again, he spied his friend Torvig eyeing a misshapen gadget on the bench.

"Hi, Vig," Keru said, making a small wave of greeting. "I buzzed a couple of times but got no answer, so I let myself in."

The Choblik engineer rolled his head to one side, an oddly endearing affectation that Keru had learned was used by Torvig's people as a gesture of trust—an unspoken show of faith that the new arrival would not go for one's jugular. "It's good to see you, Ranul," Torvig said. He trotted in bouncing steps toward Keru, his prehensile tail undulating behind him to help preserve his balance. When the squat, cervine young officer was closer to the burly Trill security chief, he craned his head back to make eye contact. "Is there something I can make for you?"

Keru grinned, being careful not to bare his teeth. "Maybe," he said. "You seem busy enough, though. What're you working on?"

"Prototypes and scale models," Torvig said. He gestured with one of his silvery bionic arms toward his workbench. "Let me show you." He flounced like an excited child back to his U-shaped work area, and Keru followed him.

Long, mechanical arms studded with tools and utilities reached down from the ceiling, where they swiveled from ball joints. A few curious devices hovered or tumbled in place, like tools abandoned in zero gravity. One side of the dark gray work surface was littered with dust, metal shavings, stray isolinear rods, optronic cables, and hundreds of sparkling bits of debris. Heat lingered in the air, a testament to interrupted efforts.

Standing upright at the end of Torvig's work area was a narrow, rectangular slab more than two meters tall, half a meter wide, and barely four millimeters thick; it was black and cast a mirror-quality reflection. "I've been working on this for many weeks," Torvig said, aglow with pride. "What do you think?"

Keru was at a loss for words. He wasn't certain if the slab was meant to represent an engineering achievement or an artistic one. Not wanting to offend Torvig, he finally settled on a neutral and factually incontrovertible declaration. "Shiny."

"Yes, it resists biological and synthetic residues even better than I had hoped," Torvig boasted. He directed an expectant stare at Keru. "Go ahead. Try it."

Again, Keru had no idea how to respond. He looked at Torvig, whose stare did not waver. *All right,*

Keru told himself, *he asked you to try it out. That implies it does something. It's functional. Just look for an "on" switch or something.*

He leaned close to the black slab, eyed it with unblinking intensity, and traced its edges with his vision, desperate to suss out some clue to its purpose. Then he caught his reflection on its flat surface, and he paused to wince at the new gray hairs that had crept into his dark beard. Torvig's voice was close behind him. "You don't know what it is, do you?"

"Sure I do," Keru lied—and then he remembered how proud Torvig was of the slab's resistance to biological residues. "I was just admiring your workmanship, was all." He reached out and lightly touched it with one calloused fingertip.

The slab came alive with color and motion. Information scrolled across its surface just below Keru's eye line, and images and schematics arranged themselves in convenient blocks beneath a command interface with links to every officer and noncom he supervised. He was so impressed at the streamlined efficiency of it that it took him a moment to notice that all of the written elements of the interface had been rendered in his native language—and not merely the dominant version of Trill, but his own local dialect. "That's amazing," Keru said. "It's like it was made just for me." Suspicious, he asked, "You didn't make this just for me, did you?"

"No, of course not," Torvig said. He nuzzled the slab with his snout, and the entire interface changed, muting its colors, reconfiguring its iconography and even the audible qualities of its feedback tones into something completely unfamiliar to Keru. "I made this for everybody," Torvig continued. "It can recognize the biometric signature of every *Titan* crew member and present the data and options they are most likely to need at any given moment. When one is on duty it displays work-related options. During one's off-hours, it becomes more personal, recreational." The Choblik snagged a small remote control from the workbench with the bionic hand at the end of his tail. "Best of all," he added, "it's even configured for our shipmates who prefer to see in other spectra than visible light, and it has ultrasonic as well as subsonic modes." Torvig entered a few commands on his control device, and Keru felt a few fleeting pulses of heat from the slab, which was otherwise blank and silent.

Keru recalled an incident from several months earlier, when Torvig—then a midshipman cadet—had decided to research the mysterious humanoid phenomenon of "gut feelings" by secretly infesting his crewmates' replicated meals with nanoprobes.

"Vig, if I ask you how you obtained the biometric profiles of everyone on the ship, do you have reason to suspect I'll be unhappy about your answer?"

"I believe it to be a distinct possibility," Torvig said.

The Trill sighed. "Then I won't ask." He nodded his approval at the slab. "Amazing work, by the way."

"Thank you. I have an appointment to show it to Commander Ra-Havreii tomorrow afternoon. I'm asking his permission to install them throughout the ship."

"Good luck," Keru said.

Torvig deactivated the black panel, put the control device back on his workbench, and puttered around a moment, imposing a bit of order on the chaos, before he turned back toward Keru. "You said there might be something I could build for you."

"Well, not exactly," Keru said. He felt awkward about his true motive for the visit. "I'm more interested in having you work with one of my security teams. We might have a dangerous away mission ahead of us, and I know you're good at finding ways to help people work together more effectively."

The young ensign's interest took on a keener edge. "What manner of challenge do you expect to face?"

That question brought Keru into territory he would have preferred never to discuss again. "The Borg," he said.

Torvig's enthusiasm dimmed in one surprised blink of his enormous, round eyes. "I see."

It was a delicate subject between them. When they had first started serving together on *Titan*, Keru had found himself more than a little unnerved by Torvig's cybernetic enhancements. They had reminded him of the biomechanical fusions of the Borg, who years earlier had claimed the life of his lover, Sean.

As a result, for his first few months of shared service with Torvig, Keru had treated the young Choblik unjustly, singling him out for harsher discipline and stricter oversight than he had deserved. Only after Counselor Haaj had forced Keru to start confronting his own prejudices had he been able to put his fears aside and start treating Torvig fairly.

After Torvig graduated from Starfleet Academy and received his field commission to ensign, he and Keru had—to Keru's surprise—started becoming friends.

This, however, was the first time Keru had ever come to ask Torvig for a favor.

"I think your expertise with cybernetics will be useful in helping us learn to defend ourselves against the Borg," Keru said, "but I want to make it clear that I'm *not* asking you to do this simply because you have bionic enhancements. I've learned over the years that brains are often a lot more valuable than brawn in a dangerous situation. I want you on my away team because you're a great engineer—a great *problem-solver*."

Torvig extended his neck as tall as it could go, and he tilted his head left and then right. Strong emotions made his voice tremble. "'A great problem-solver,'" he said. "That's one of the highest compliments my kind ever bestow upon one another."

"It's got some cachet among my people, too," Keru said.

The Choblik offered one bionic hand to Keru, who took it in a friendly clasp. "You honor me," Torvig said. "Thank you."

"Don't thank me, Vig," Keru said with regret as he released Torvig's hand. "Because if I'm right, we're going to war—and I just put you on the front line."

8

—•—

Though the *Enterprise* was alone in orbit above a dead planet, its bridge buzzed with activity.

Captain Picard sat in his chair, at the center of the elevated aft level. He was surrounded by the muted chatter of voices over the comms, hushed replies from his senior command officers, and the mechanical clatter of a damage-control team replacing a number of blown-out companels. Worf moved among the bridge's many stations and supervised the crew's intelligence-gathering efforts, while Commander Kadohata directed several simultaneous repair projects from the operations console.

In his hand, Picard held a padd that displayed the most recent dispatches from Starfleet Command. Most of the news from Earth consisted of updated fleet deployment profiles. During normal peacetime conditions, Starfleet might have several dozen ships temporarily out of service for maintenance or upgrades. In addition, up to ten percent of the fleet in service was expected to be assigned to deep-space exploration at any given time.

Over the past four weeks, every ship in Starfleet had been recalled to Federation space and deployed into defensive battle fleets. The only exceptions were a handful of vessels that were simply not fit for service, and a few dozen, including *Titan* and some of her *Luna*-class sister ships, that were too far away to return in less than two months. The situation had become so desperate that even large civilian vessels were being armed and pressed into service to defend some of the more remote worlds.

Picard shook his head and wondered, *How much more of this can Starfleet take?* The losses were mounting more quickly than reinforcements could be mustered. If the steady stream of Borg incursions wasn't halted soon, within a matter of weeks rapid attrition would leave the Federation defenseless.

He looked up as Worf and Lieutenant Choudhury approached his chair. "Yes, Commander?"

Worf looked at the security chief and then at the captain. "Lieutenant Choudhury has a theory," he said.

Hopeful, Picard asked Choudhury, "About the Borg ship's entry point into Federation space?"

Choudhury pursed her lips slightly. "No, sir," she said, straightening her posture. "We haven't been able to track its prior movements beyond half a light-year outside the system."

"I see," Picard said, masking his disappointment. "Then what does your theory concern?"

He noticed Worf casting a sidelong glance at her before she said, "I think I know where the next Borg attack will be, sir."

That commanded Picard's full attention. "Explain."

Worf spoke first. "We have detected new Borg signals and energy signatures in this sector."

"And I think there's a Borg ship closing in on Korvat," Choudhury said. "If we go now at maximum warp, there's a chance we could get there ahead of the Borg." Her eyes fell for a moment on the main viewer, which still showed the burned-black northern hemisphere of Ramatis.

Her use of the singular pronoun—"*I think*"—gave the captain pause. He looked to his first officer. "Do you concur with Lieutenant Choudhury, Mister Worf?"

The Klingon shifted uncomfortably for a few seconds, and then he said in his most diplomatic baritone, "I agree that it is possible Korvat is the next target."

"Possible?" Looking back and forth between Choudhury and Worf, Picard said, "Do I detect a lack of consensus?"

More cryptic looks passed between the two officers. Then Worf replied, "We agree that there is another Borg ship in the sector, and that we should destroy it."

"But you have reservations regarding the lieutenant's analysis," said Picard, who was trying to get to the heart of the matter with as much tact as possible.

Choudhury was soft-spoken in her response. "Commander Worf's doubts are reasonable, sir," she said. "My conclusion that the Borg are headed to Korvat is more a hunch than a deduction—but I still recommend that we break orbit, set course for Korvat, and proceed there at maximum warp."

"Based on what, Lieutenant?"

She spoke with quiet confidence. "Based on the facts that Korvat is just as likely to be the target as three other worlds in this sector, and, of the four possible targets, it's the only one we can reach ahead of the Borg. If I'm wrong, and one of the other worlds is the next target, we won't reach them in time anyway. And if I'm right, we might be able to give Korvat a fighting chance to survive."

The security chief returned Picard's gaze with steady surety. The captain looked at Worf, who in turn looked at Choudhury and deadpanned, "When you put it that way . . ."

Picard nodded. "Very well." He raised his voice to be heard across the bridge. "Helm, break orbit and set course for Korvat, maximum warp. Commander Kadohata, send a warning ahead to the *Gibraltar* and the *Leonov*. Let them know we'll join them at Korvat as soon as we're able."

"Aye, sir," Kadohata said from the ops console.

"Mister Worf," Picard said. "Step up our damage-control efforts. I need the ship ready for combat when we reach Korvat." The Klingon first officer nodded his acknowledgment of the order and moved away to carry it out.

On the main viewer, the curve of the planet sank below the screen's bottom edge, leaving nothing but the star-flecked vista of the Milky Way. "We've cleared orbit, Captain," reported the conn officer, Lieutenant Gary Weinrib.

Pointing forward with an outstretched hand, Picard set his ship in motion with a word. "Engage."

"Absolutely not, Captain," said Admiral Alynna Nechayev over the subspace comm, her angular fea-

tures and silver-blond hair framed by the edges of the desktop monitor in Picard's ready room. *"The risk is too great, and you know it."*

Picard found it difficult to remain calm when he knew the stakes were so dire. "I think the potential benefits outweigh those risks, Admiral. If my officers' analysis is correct, and a Borg cube is on course to attack Korvat, our best chance of defending the planet is to give the new torpedo designs to the ships that are already there."

Nechayev shook her head. *"We've reviewed your analysis, Jean-Luc. It's inconclusive, at best. The cube you've detected could be en route to any of a number of targets. The only reason your ship is en route to Korvat is because it's the only potential target you can reach in time to make a difference."*

"That's true, Admiral," Picard said. "But if you're wrong—if Korvat is the target, and the Borg attack it before we can arrive—you'll be committing two Federation starships to a futile battle, and condemning millions of people on that planet to death. And my instincts tell me that my chief of security is correct—Korvat *is* the target."

"I'm not dismissing your instincts, Jean-Luc, especially not when it comes to the Borg. But this isn't a matter of second-guessing your tactics in the field. Beyond the possibility that the Borg might adapt to transphasic weapons if we overuse them, transmitting that data over a subspace channel creates an unacceptable risk of its interception by the Borg. What if they break our encryption protocols, assimilate the transphasic torpedo, and turn it against us?"

She was right, and that only added to his frustration. "I acknowledge the risk," he said, "but an entire world and millions of lives hang in the balance."

"No, Jean-Luc," replied Nechayev. *"Hundreds of worlds are at stake, along with nearly a trillion lives. And I can't let you jeopardize all of them on a gamble to save one that might not even be under attack."*

"What if we can confirm that Korvat is the next target?"

He heard the regret in her voice as she said, *"The answer would still have to be no."*

Picard sank into a quiet despair. "Has it come to this? Are we prepared to sacrifice entire worlds because we're not willing to risk our own safety for theirs? Shall we let simple arithmetic dictate who should live and who should die?"

Remorse stole the certainty from Nechayev's eyes and left her with a grim and weary mien. *"You see the battlefield, Jean-Luc. I have to see the war."*

Lieutenant Rennan Konya felt the tension in the air.

Commanders Kadohata and La Forge flanked a wall-mounted companel in the chief engineer's office, adjacent to main engineering. Konya and Dr. Crusher stood opposite them. Coursing between them all was a palpable aura of anxiety that emanated from everyone in the office, including Konya himself.

He suspected that only he could detect the tangible quality of the group's shared concern, thanks to his carefully trained Betazoid empathic talent. By the standards of his own people, he was a weak telepath, one whose limited gift was unequal to the profound task of making reciprocal contact with the higher minds of others. Instead, he'd focused on teaching himself to read a more primitive region of people's minds—the motor cortex. Its signals were simpler to interpret and far more accessible.

In hand-to-hand combat it gave him an almost imperceptible advantage: He could feel what opponents intended to do a split second before they did it. It also had distinctly pleasant uses in more personal situations, but sometimes it worked a bit like empathy, to tell him when people were fearful or anxious. This was one of those times.

"We need something new," said Kadohata, who had summoned the others to this midnight brainstorming session. "Our best weapon against the Borg was neutralized when they captured our multivector pathogen at Barolia, and Starfleet's worried that the Borg will adapt to the transphasic torpedoes if we use them too often." She lifted her chin in a half nod at a star system diagram on the companel's screen. "If Choudhury's right, we'll be seeing the Borg again in less than an hour. So think fast."

Crusher shrugged. "Unless we can get a sample of the new 'royal jelly' the Borg are using to gestate their queens, I'm not sure I can update the androgen formula."

Kadohata asked, "What kind of changes could the Borg have made to block the formula from working?"

"Protein resequencing, or maybe new antigens," Crusher said. "Even a targeted biofilter would be enough to screen out the formula."

La Forge cut in, "Then there's still the 'Royal Protocol' to deal with." He turned his synthetic eyes from Kadohata to Konya as he explained. "The Borg don't have to grow new queens from scratch—they can just reprogram existing female drones with the operating system for one."

He looked back at Kadohata as she noted, "That's where your nanobot sabotage came into play."

"Right," La Forge said. The chief engineer's face showed no anger, but Konya could feel the man's ire coiling inside him. "It was designed not to give the Borg time to adapt once it was deployed. But it sounds like they acquired an unreleased specimen and reverse-engineered it."

The unrelenting negativity was raising Kadohata's pulse and blood pressure. She asked La Forge, "Isn't there any other way to disrupt their link?"

"Maybe," said the chief engineer. "But I have no idea how to go about looking for it. We have no access to the Collective, no living Borg drones to experiment on, and no time to do the research. Plus, last time—" Words seemed to catch in his throat, and Konya felt La Forge's profound discomfort as the man made himself finish his sentence. "Last time I had Data to help me."

Konya had never met Data, but like most people in Starfleet he had heard more than a few tall tales about the android. The last such story had not had a happy ending: Data had sacrificed himself to save Captain Picard's life and destroy a ship-based thalaron weapon that had boasted enough power to exterminate entire planets with a single shot. Judging from La Forge's pained expression, Konya surmised that Data and the chief engineer had been close friends as well as colleagues.

"Mister Konya," Kadohata said, commanding his attention. "For now, transphasic torpedoes still work against the Borg. Do you know what makes these warheads tick?"

"Sort of," Konya said. "They're based on creating dissonant feedback pulses in an asymmetrically phased subspace compression wave." As he had expected, his answer provoked nods from La Forge and Kadohata and a confused stare from Crusher. For the doctor's benefit, he added, "Essentially, the torpedo spreads out the energy of the wave among multiple subspace phase states. When the Borg modulate their defenses against one or more phases of the compression pulse, they make themselves vulnerable to the remaining pulses. And the phase shifts vary randomly, so the Borg can't anticipate the transphasic state of one torpedo based on the previous one." Crusher nodded.

For the first time since the meeting had started, Kadohata sounded hopeful. "How else can we apply that theory?"

"I've started working on creating a transphasic mode for our shield generators," Konya said. "If I'm right, they should make it very hard for the Borg to score direct hits on us. But we still have to be careful—it won't take them long to change over to wide-dispersal firing patterns. And the downside of these protocols is power drain. Running them'll cut our maximum warp speed down to nine-point-one, and there's a risk we could burn out the shield emitters in a prolonged battle."

Crusher asked, "How about the phasers? Could we rig them to fire a transphasic pulse?"

"Sure," Konya said, "if you feel like blowing up all our emitter crystals." Putting aside his sarcasm, he continued, "An iron-60 crystal matrix might be able to handle it, but not at power levels high enough to be effective. The essential problem is that phasers are designed to synchronize energy streams, and transphasic weapons rely on unsynching them."

"Apples and oranges, then," Crusher said.

"More like apples and trout," La Forge replied.

Kadohata keyed in some notes on her padd. "Konya, can you have the transphasic shields working before we reach Korvat?"

"Yes," he said. He looked at La Forge and added, "I'll need some help from you and your team in engineering, though."

"You've got it," La Forge said. "Send down the specs and we'll make it happen."

The second officer finished tapping on her padd. "Keep me posted on your progress. I'd like to have at least one bit of good news for the captain before we go into combat." She looked around at the other officers and nodded. "Thanks, everyone."

Crusher was the first person out of La Forge's office, followed by Konya and Kadohata, who walked together to the same turbolift. His psionic sense of the second officer's physical state made him aware of her myriad minor aches and pains.

As the two of them stepped into the turbolift, he tried to sound sympathetic as he said, "Stressed out, huh?"

"A little," Kadohata said, her London-like accent enhancing her gift for understatement. "I never look forward to giving the captain bad news, but that's all we seem to have lately."

He nodded. "You carry most of your stress in your lower back," he said. "It must get uncomfortable."

"Yes," she said with a suspicious glance. "It does."

"If you'd like to relieve some of that tension, I could—"

"I'm married, Lieutenant. Happily. With three children."

Konya blinked, amused by her reaction. "That's nice. I was going to say that I could recommend some excellent massage-spa programs in the holodeck that would help. . . . Sir."

"Oh," Kadohata said. Keeping her eyes on the turbolift doors, she added, "Thanks." After a moment, she added, "Sorry."

Konya felt Kadohata's pulse quicken and her temperature rise. But even without his empathic senses, he would have been hard-pressed not to notice her intense blush response. *Red is a good color on her,* he decided with a mischievous smirk.

Worf carried his *bat'leth* and walked at a quick step through the corridor, eager to reach the holodeck. The *Enterprise* was still at least two hours from Korvat and ready for action; now it was time for him to clear his thoughts and sharpen his focus, and for him that meant sixty minutes of exertion in his most intense "calisthenics" holoprogram, which La Forge had facetiously nicknamed "Nausicaans with Knives."

A female Bajoran ensign cast a wary look at the weapon in Worf's hand as he passed by her. The Klingon honor blade, which had become a familiar sight to many of Worf's shipmates on the *Enterprise*-D, continued to draw bemused stares from his new comrades. It had only added to his already fearsome reputation.

He arrived at the holodeck portal and reached over to activate his calisthenics routine. To his surprise, there was already a program running, one that he didn't recognize. It wasn't marked as private, and the portal wasn't locked, so he tapped a control on the companel to open the doors.

Magnetic seals released with a soft, rising hum. Then a quasi-hydraulic hiss of escaping air accompanied a muted rumbling of servomotors as the doors parted, revealing a majestic vista of jagged stone, ethereal mist, and azure sky.

Jasminder Choudhury stood on the mountaintop ledge with her back to Worf. She raised her arms in a fluid motion from her sides until her palms met high above her head. Her rib cage retracted as she exhaled and lowered her arms. Then she finished the traditional yoga breathing exercise by bringing her hands back together, palm to palm, in front of her chest.

Worf stepped into the serene-looking holographic simulation and caught the scent of alpine sage in the cool, thin air. Behind him, the holodeck doors closed with an obtrusive whine and an echoing thud, and then they vanished into the panorama of mountain peaks jutting up through a slow-rolling sea of clouds.

Choudhury inhaled and lifted her arms again, and she seemed to take no notice of Worf's arrival. As her palms met above her head, he cleared his throat with a resonant grunt of annoyance.

She continued her exercise until she had completed another slow exhalation, and her hands were once again pressed together in front of her. Then she let her arms drop to her sides as she turned and cast an untroubled smile in Worf's direction. "Yes, Commander?"

"What are you doing here?"

The trim, tall woman smirked. "Yoga."

He furrowed his brow at her flippant answer. "I reserved this hour for my private use."

"I thought you'd reserved Holodeck Two," she said.

"No, I reserved *this* holodeck." As he studied her face, he became convinced that she was not surprised by this apparent and unusual scheduling mistake. "This was not an error, was it?"

Choudhury shook her head. "I don't know what you—"

"I have served with you long enough to know that you are methodical, organized, and precise. You would not use another person's reserved holodeck time by mistake." He stepped closer to her, his demeanor one of overt challenge. "Why are you here?"

Even as he loomed over her, she maintained her enigmatic, close-lipped smile. "All right," she said. "You've caught me. I was hoping to catch you alone, and your exercise hour seemed like the best time."

"The best time for what?"

"To learn about your training regimen," she said, as a gust of wind fluttered her loose, brightly colored silk exercise clothes. "I hope you won't think it's out of line for me to say so, but you're one of the most *stoic* Klingons I've ever met."

"Stoic?" He reflected on the boundless reservoir of angst with which his life had afflicted him. "Hardly."

She responded with a reproving tilt of her head. "Compared to most Klingons I've met, you're a man made of stone. I know it's rude to describe someone based on racial stereotypes, but there have been times, when we've been working together, that you've seemed almost . . . well, *Vulcan*."

Her comment reminded Worf of his mind-meld with the famed Ambassador Spock, many years earlier, during a mission to stop the ancient telepathic tyrant known as Malkus. The meld had been a profound experience, one that had imparted lasting effects of which he had been unaware at the time. Lingering traces of Vulcan stoicism now infused some of his mannerisms, and snippets of Vulcan sayings sometimes infiltrated his discourse. He had, until this moment, thought that he and Captain Picard—who also had melded with Spock, on a separate occasion— were the only ones who would ever notice his echoes of those affectations.

Choudhury interrupted his moment of reflection. "I'm sorry if I offended you just now," she said.

"Not at all, Lieutenant," Worf said. "It is an *interesting* observation." He smirked. "Is this what you hope to learn more about by emulating my training regimen?"

With a coquettish shrug of one shoulder, she replied, "It's *one* thing I'd like to learn about you."

Intrigued by her forthright manner, he asked, "What *other* aspects of my life do you find of interest?"

"Permission to speak freely, sir?"

"Granted."

She stepped forward into his personal space. "You're one of the most intriguing people I've ever met, Worf, and I'd like to learn whatever you're willing to teach me."

"Are you certain that you are ready?"

"I'm a quick learner."

He liked her attitude.

"Computer," he said. "New program: Worf Calisthenics Number Four." The mountaintop yoga retreat dissolved and was replaced by the interior of a Klingon martial-arts school. A cold stone-tile floor appeared under their feet, and walls of thick, dark wooden beams surrounded them. The ceiling rose high overhead, but, compared to the open dome of sky in the previous simulation, it felt oddly close. Red and black banners emblazoned with the Klingon trefoil were draped high on the walls, above racks loaded with a variety of bladed Klingon weapons. Above Worf and Choudhury was a balcony level, from which a master could observe training drills for new students.

"Let me teach you *Mok'bara*," Worf said.

9

———•———

Dr. Simon Tarses had seen some gruesome spectacles during his nearly fifteen years in Starfleet, but the pair of crispy-molten corpses that had been beamed into his sickbay from the *Columbia* qualified as one of the most unique and horrifying.

After completing the preliminary autopsies, he had decided to beam down from the *Aventine* with a mixed team of medical investigators and security specialists, all of whom, including himself, had some measure of training in forensics.

He and the rest of the group emerged from the coruscating haze of the transporter beam inside an oppressively dark section of a passageway on D Deck of the *Columbia*. Before he or the members of his team could activate their palm beacons, a blue light snapped on in front of them. Its beam was aimed into his eyes, half blinding him.

As he raised his arm for shade, he pierced the darkness and saw the dour, squamous frown of Lieutenant Kedair. "I told the captain no one should come down here," Kedair said.

"She didn't agree," Tarses replied, as the other members of his team activated their own lights, filling their section of the passage with pale blue light and overlapping shadows. "I have orders to collect evidence. Lead the way, please."

Kedair scowled as she turned and led the group through the curved passageway. The *Columbia* was a small ship compared to some on which Tarses had served, and it was a short walk to the scene of the mysterious homicides. They were still a few sections away when the odors of putrefaction started to become overwhelming. Tarses suppressed his gag reflex—a skill he had learned while dissecting cadavers in medical school.

Then they arrived at the scene of the two deaths, and it was every bit as horrible as Tarses had imagined it would be when he'd seen the corpses. With the bodies removed from the passageway, all that remained were isolated pools of congealed fatty liquids and stains of scorched blood, all surrounding humanoid-shaped patches of clean metal deck plating.

"Have at it," Kedair said, and she stepped away and tapped her combadge. "Kedair to Darrow. Regroup at location alpha, we have visitors."

"Acknowledged," said a female voice via Kedair's combadge.

Tarses squatted beside the pockmarked puddle of boiled flesh and half-disintegrated synthetic fabrics. He lifted his tricorder and activated a series of preprogrammed scans. "All right, folks," he said. "Let's work quickly, before the good lieutenant here has an apoplexy worrying about us."

"I don't worry, Doctor," Kedair said. "I anticipate

undesirable events and outcomes, and try to prevent them."

"Well, you should take it easy," Tarses said. "At this rate, you'll *anticipate* yourself to death."

The security chief rolled her eyes and walked away. Tarses turned his attention to the results of his tricorder's molecular scan. Around him, the forensic specialists worked at a brisk pace, keeping their conversations to a minimum. Some were removing core samples from the deck or bulkheads; one was gathering scrapings of charred tissue or swabs of still-tacky liquefied biomass. One of the security specialists was creating a holographic documentation of the passageway section.

A crunching squish of a footstep near Tarses turned his head, and he saw one of Kedair's security officers, a human woman, making an awkward passage of the narrow gap between him and a Benzite ballistics expert. Tarses berated her, "Do you mind?" When she looked down with a confused expression at the crouching chief medical officer, he added with a frantic wave at her feet, "You're standing in my blood!"

She backpedaled until she was clear of the forensic team, and then she took up a sentry position a few meters away.

Tarses continued working and fighting the urge to retch. Ignoring the rotten-perfume odor of burned skin and fat did not make it go away, but Tarses clung to the fading hope that his nose might soon acclimate to the sickly stench so he could concentrate solely on his work.

Outside the cocoon of light in which Tarses and his team worked, a dim sparkle formed in the impenetrable darkness. That faint glimmer multiplied with a sonorous rush. Sound and light blossomed a few sections down the passageway, and a humanoid figure took shape inside the transporter beam's prismatic halo.

Captain Dax emerged from the fading glow and found herself illuminated by a half-dozen palm beacons. Lifting her hands in front of her face, she said, "As you were. Please." The beams were redirected, leaving her in a penumbra of reflected light.

Kedair slipped past the forensic team and moved to meet the captain as she approached. Tarses flipped his tricorder closed and followed Kedair. Together they intercepted Dax, who raised her chin toward the forensic team. "What've we got?"

"Still no definite cause of death," Tarses said.

Before Tarses could elaborate, Kedair said, "We've ruled out friendly fire, and my team has kept this deck secured since the bodies were found. Except for the doctor and his forensic team, no one's been down here."

Tarses was quick to add, "My preliminary autopsies found evidence of neuroelectric damage in both subjects' brain tissues, and their bodies exhibit molecular dissociation on all levels, from the epidermis to the marrow."

Dax looked to Kedair and asked, "What can kill like that?"

"The caustic effects are similar to damage inflicted by the Horta," the Takaran woman said.

"Except that the caustic injuries were highly localized," Tarses pointed out, "and instead of fusing synthetic and organic matter on the corpses, it dissolved them without mixing them."

Kedair narrowed her eyes and clenched her jaw.

"Which is what made me think of a Denebian preda-tor called a *teblor*," she said with ill-masked irritation.

"Interesting," Tarses said, deriving more than a touch of schadenfreude from poking holes in Kedair's guesses. "But the *teblor* doesn't possess anything like a neuroelectric attack. And if memory serves, it lives and hunts in environments with a peak temperature of no more than two degrees Celsius."

Crossing her arms, Kedair said, "Yes, I admit, it's a bit warm for a *teblor* on this rock with no name. Of course, an Altairan cave-fisher—"

"Would leave a trail of easily followed slime back to its watery lair, neither of which seems to exist within a thousand kilometers of here," Tarses said.

"Doctor," said Dax, "instead of telling me what the killer isn't, can you offer any insight about what it might be?"

It was Kedair's turn to smirk as Tarses admitted, "Not at the moment, Captain."

"We're running out of time down here," Dax said. "Starfleet Command wants us out of orbit in just over fifteen hours. I've asked for an extension because of what happened to Yott and Komer, but I wouldn't count on it." To Kedair she continued, "Send nonse-curity personnel back to the *Aventine* and run a hard-target search of every compartment, locker, crawl space, nook, and cranny on this ship. If whatever killed our people is still here, I want it found."

"We could use some extra sensor capability," Kedair said.

Dax nodded. "I'll have Leishman free up whatever you need." She looked at Tarses. "Has your team col-lected enough evidence for analysis?"

"Enough for a start," Tarses said. "But I'd really like to widen the search to see if—"

"Denied," Dax said. "I need you on the ship, analyzing the data we have in hand."

Disappointed, Tarses replied, "Aye, sir. I just hope we haven't missed anything."

"Time is short, Doctor," said Dax. "And the perfect is the enemy of the good. Make do with what we've got—and do it fast."

Its hunger was all.

Radiant shells of organic matter glowed in the empty spaces that surrounded it. They appeared and vanished in bright curtains of energy, in columns of fire shot down from someplace far above this crude prison of thwarted desire. They skated the surface of the gravity well, clutching blinding sparks.

Temptations, one and all.

Streams of data moved faster than light, traveling between the shells and the sky and their own glowing stones. There were fewer of the shells now, and they continued to diminish in numbers.

Panic pushed the hunger in pursuit of a cluster of shells. So little of its strength remained that even gravity, nature's most feeble instrument, threatened to overcome it and drag it down to its final dissipation in the silicon sea.

It risked everything to pierce the new stone: every iota of will, every drop of fear. Annihilation or escape—either would be better than limbo.

All that mattered now was the sky.

2168

10

—◆—

The flight of the *Columbia* had lasted sixty-three days, and it had lasted just over twelve years.

The high-frequency overdrive whine of the impulse engines fell rapidly as a pinpoint of light on the bridge's main viewer brightened and grew larger. Captain Hernandez gripped the armrests of her chair as her ship shimmied around her, its inertial dampers struggling to compensate for the extreme stresses of rapid deceleration from relativistic velocity.

Lieutenant Brynn Mealia, the gamma-shift helmsman, declared in a soft Irish lilt, "Thirty seconds to orbit."

"Katrin," Hernandez said to Ensign Gunnarsdóttir, the bridge engineering officer, "can we shore up the dampers?"

Gunnarsdóttir started flipping switches and adjusting dials on her console. "Patching in emergency battery power, Captain."

Seconds later the ship's passage became smoother, and Hernandez used the moments to lament the years that she had let pass by her ship, her crew, and herself. For weeks she had been imagining Earth spinning in a blur, its billions of people playing out the dramas of their lives while the crew of the *Columbia* pushed themselves beyond the normal boundaries of space-time—cheating it, evading it, living in the past while the rest of the galaxy moved on without them. She had heard the grumblings of her crew grow increasingly bitter as the weeks had dragged past, and just a few days—months?—earlier she had heard one of the ship's MACO troopers jokingly refer to the *Columbia* as "the *Flying Dutchman.*"

"Slowing to full impulse," Mealia said. "Three-quarters impulse . . . half . . . one-quarter impulse, Captain."

A lush blue-green sphere dominated the viewscreen. It looked like a pristine, uncolonized world, with no traces of habitation. Hernandez looked over her shoulder at Lieutenant el-Rashad, who was monitoring a sensor control station. "You're sure the energy readings from the planet are artificial?"

The thin, serious-looking second officer lifted his eyes from his console and said, "Positive, Captain." Thumbing a few switches, he added, "I can't lock in on the sources, but I can narrow it down and switch to a visual scan. Magnification to five hundred." On the viewscreen, at the edge of a greenish swath of richly forested planetary surface, she beheld what looked like a scintillating jewel.

Hernandez stood from her chair and studied the image on the screen. "Is that a city?"

"If not, it's the strangest rock formation I've ever seen," said Commander Fletcher, who was watching from beside the weapons console with Lieutenant Thayer. The first officer had a quizzical look on her face as she stared at the viewscreen. "Kalil, are we reading any life-forms at those coordinates?"

El-Rashad looked surprised by the question. "We're not reading anything at those coordinates, Commander. There's some kind of scattering field blocking our scans of the city."

Hernandez looked back at her bridge officers. "Thayer, can you compensate for that?"

Thayer poked at her console. "Negative, Captain." She patched in a new image on the main viewer: another brilliant speck on the surface. "We're seeing dozens of cities, spread around the planet. They're all extremely similar in mass and configuration . . . but we can't get precise readings, because they're all protected by scattering fields with an average radius of two hundred kilometers."

Every new report deepened Hernandez's curiosity, and for a moment the heartbreak of a dozen lost years was forgotten. "What about the other planets in the system?"

"Uninhabited, Captain," said el-Rashad. "No evidence of colonization or exploration."

Thinking ahead, Hernandez asked, "How's the air down there?"

"Breathable," said el-Rashad. "Maybe a bit on the thick side for most of us."

Hernandez pondered the top-down image of the city on the viewscreen for a moment longer, captivated by its symmetry and its mystery. Then she returned to her chair and sat down. "Kiona, can you detect any sign of patrol ships in this system, or defensive batteries on the planet?"

"Nothing of the kind, Captain," Thayer replied.

The captain was intrigued. She wondered aloud in Fletcher's direction, "Odd, don't you think? This close to both Romulan and Klingon space, and the planet has no obvious defenses."

"Just because they aren't obvious doesn't mean they don't exist," Fletcher said.

"True," Hernandez said. She looked to the communications officer. "Sidra, can we hail them on a regular radio frequency?"

Ensign Valerian shook her head. "I've been trying for a couple of minutes now. No response so far." She looked up from her console and added with a note of seemingly misplaced optimism, "It's possible there's no one down there."

Thayer replied, "Then why are all the scattering fields still active?"

"Good question, Lieutenant," Hernandez said. "And it begs another one: Can we find a way through them?"

El-Rashad checked his readings, tossed a few switches, and said, "If we were on the surface, we could walk through. They block signals, but they aren't harmful."

"Captain," Thayer cut in. "One of the scattering fields is contracting." She used an override switch to change the image on the main viewer. "A city near the equator seems to be reducing its field radius in response to our scans."

The captain was on her feet. "Current radius?"

"Still shrinking," Thayer said. "Thirty kilometers. Twenty." She adjusted some settings and added, "Holding at fifteen kilometers, sir."

Fletcher flashed a crooked grin at Hernandez. "Walking distance. If you ask me, that looks like an invitation."

"Agreed," Hernandez said. "Assemble a landing party and fire up the transporter, Commander. We're going down there."

Less than an hour after he had beamed down into the heart of a tropical rainforest along the planet's sun-baked equator, Major Foyle's camouflage fatigues were soaked with sweat.

His second-in-command, Lieutenant Yacavino, and his senior noncom, Sergeant Pembleton, who had beamed down with him, also had become drenched in their own perspiration. Like the major, they were victims of the hot, soupy air in the densely overgrown tropical forest. Privates Crichlow, Mazzetti, and Steinhauer had beamed down ten minutes behind them, after chief engineer Graylock had reset the *Columbia*'s temperamental transporter, and their uniforms were beginning to cling to them, as well.

The six MACOs had deployed in pairs, with each of the decimated company's leaders escorted by a private. Pembleton was on point, along with Mazzetti. Foyle and Crichlow stayed several meters behind them, on their left flank, moving parallel with Yacavino and Steinhauer, who were on Pembleton's right flank. For this mission they had traded in their standard gray-ice camouflage for dark-green forest patterns.

Foyle stepped over tangled vines and thick fallen branches while gazing down the barrel of his phase rifle, which he braced against his shoulder. A bright, sawing tinnitus of insect noise enveloped him, and shafts of intense light slashed through the sultry after-noon mists drifting down from the jungle's canopy. Thorned plants tugged at his fatigues, and underfoot the ground gave way to mud.

Something snapped in the underbrush ahead of Pembleton, who raised his fist to halt the team. Then he opened his hand and lowered it, palm down. Foyle and the others kneeled slowly, all but disappearing into the thick, waist-high fronds and ferns. Crichlow kept his rifle steady with one hand; with the other, the gawky Englishman pulled his hand scanner from his equipment belt and thumbed it open to its "on" posi-tion. A few quick inputs by Crichlow set the device for silent operation, and he began a slow sweep of the area around the landing party.

A flash of fur and motion. The creature was tiny, smaller than a squirrel, and it was very fast as it skit-tered up the trunk of a tree that put Earth's most mag-nificent redwoods to shame. Foyle watched the little beast skitter away into the leaves, and then he looked at Crichlow, who nodded in confirmation. Satisfied, the major looked ahead to Pembleton and twirled his raised index finger twice, then pointed forward. The sergeant acknowledged the order, stood, lifted his weapon, and advanced through a narrow pass into a shadowy thicket, followed closely by Mazzetti. Foyle and the rest of his team moved forward as well, con-tinuing on their patrol of the beam-in site's outer perimeter.

It was easy to get disoriented in a forest such as this; Foyle had seen it happen even to experienced soldiers. He had recommended to Pembleton that he use a hand scanner to verify that he was maintaining a consistent five-hundred-meter radius from the beam-in site, a clearing that at this distance was not the least bit visible through the claustrophobic press of trees, lichen, and hanging vines. Pembleton had refused the suggestion, preferring to trust his own instincts.

As much as Foyle had faith in his sergeant, he believed even more strongly in taking precautions. Consequently, he had Steinhauer monitoring their position with a hand scanner; if Pembleton wandered more than twenty meters outside of the radius, it was Steinhauer's job to alert Foyle. They had been walking for nearly an hour, covering almost three and a half kilometers of linear distance, and Steinhauer had not yet found any cause to speak up. *So far, so good,* mused Foyle.

He squinted as he passed through a shaft of bright light that had speared its way through the ceiling of boughs to the lush vegetation at his feet. Much of the forest remained shrouded in viridian twilight. He and his men waded the shallow green underbrush, scouting for natural hazards and predators that might lie between the rest of the landing party and the massive urban center the flight crew had detected, approximately fifteen-point-two kilometers to the west.

Ahead of the major, Pembleton and Mazzetti stood at the base of a colossal tree and waved the other two pairs toward them. As soon as the six men had regrouped, Pembleton pointed at a pair of crossed sticks stuck in the ground beside a gnarled, meter-tall root. Foyle recognized the twigs instantly; the sergeant had planted them there to mark the starting

point of their perimeter patrol. "Full circle," Pembleton said. "Perimeter's clear, Major. Site secure for
beam-in."

"Very good," Foyle said. "Take us back to the clearing. We'll set up a tight perimeter there and signal the
ship."

"Yes, Major," replied Pembleton, who made a
quick survey of the area to get his bearings and led the
landing party through a sea of green leaves with nothing resembling a trail.

The hike back to the clearing was slow going, and
not only because of the heat, the humidity, the uphill
terrain, and the need to circumnavigate massive arboreal obstacles. More than two months of combating
radiation effects caused by the *Columbia*'s near-light
journey had taken a heavy toll on the crew, in the
form of chronic mild radiation sickness and severe
fatigue.

*A climb like this never would've bothered me
before,* Foyle ruminated. *I guess it's true what my
grandfather used to say: "It's not the years, it's the
mileage."*

Minutes later, as the MACOs emerged from the tree
line and entered the forest glade, Foyle pulled his
communicator from his equipment belt and flipped it
open. "Foyle to *Columbia*."

Hernandez answered, *"This is* Columbia. *Go ahead,
Major."*

"Site secure," he said. "You can beam down when
ready."

"Glad to hear it. Any last-minute advice?"

"Yes," he said. "Make sure everyone packs a full
canteen."

———◆———

The twelve-person landing party moved single file through the humbling grandeur of the primeval forest, which was composed of trees wider in circumference and taller than any that Hernandez had ever seen before. The forest canopy was an unbroken ceiling of green nearly two hundred meters overhead, thick enough to block all but hints of the planet's searing daylight.

Hernandez was the second person in the formation. Pembleton walked ahead of her, serving as the point man on the long march to the alien city. Behind her was her first officer, Fletcher. Then followed Major Foyle, Private Crichlow, chief engineer Graylock, Lieutenant Thayer, Private Mazzetti, Lieutenant Valerian, Dr. Johanna Metzger, Private Steinhauer, and the MACOs' second-in-command, Lieutenant Yacavino.

Rivulets of sweat trickled between Hernandez's shoulder blades and down her spine under her uniform as she looked back at Fletcher. "How old do you think these trees are?"

Fletcher retrieved a hand scanner from her belt and made a quick sweep of the forest. The soft whirring sound of the device made Pembleton look back and scowl at them, though he apparently respected the privileges of rank too much to say anything. Then Fletcher closed the scanner and said, "Some of them might be as old as fourteen thousand years. There are carbon deposits from old forest fires that probably cleared away a lot of smaller, competing trees several millennia ago."

"It's a botanist's dream," Hernandez said. "But I can't figure out why the forest floor is so overgrown when it gets barely any light. What's feeding all this greenery?"

"Maybe they don't rely on photosynthesis," Fletcher said. "Or maybe they have a symbiotic relationship with the trees."

From the back of the line, Ensign Valerian asked with rhetorical sarcasm, "Are we there yet?"

"People," Foyle interjected, "it'd be safer for all of us if we didn't talk."

Dr. Metzger replied, "Safe from what? There's no sign anyone even knows we're here."

The stern-faced MACO commander directed his answer to the group. "When in doubt, *always* assume you're being watched."

"Just do as he says, folks," Hernandez said. "Keeping us alive till we make contact is the major's job. Let him do it."

She ignored the unintelligible grumbles from Valerian and Metzger and resumed her focus on Pembleton's back. He had stressed to her the importance not only of following his path, but of making the effort to step exactly where he'd stepped, both for her safety and to help conceal the landing party's numbers in case they were tracked. The same instructions had been passed to all her personnel, and so everyone concentrated on the monotony of walking in someone else's footprints.

After a sweltering and—in Hernandez's opinion—interminable stretch of hiking, Sergeant Pembleton stopped and raised his fist, halting the group. It was their first break since the march had begun. He waved everyone to a relaxed crouch. While the group settled and sank into the concealing fronds, Pembleton leaned his phase rifle against a tree trunk. Then he removed his hard-shell backpack, opened it, and took out a canteen. He took a drink and passed it to Hernandez. "One swallow," he said, "then pass it to the next person."

She looked at the wet ring around the mouth of the canteen. "Why can't I just drink from my own?"

"Only two kinds of canteen are quiet on a march," he said. "Full ones and empty ones. If you take just a few swigs from one, it'll swish while you walk, or give you away when you're trying to hide. But if we all drink from one canteen until it's empty, that won't happen."

Unable to fault his reasoning, she took a mouthful of water from the canteen and passed it to Fletcher, who helped herself to a drink. Person by person, it was handed back along the line.

Fletcher wiped a sheen of perspiration from her brow and said in a low voice to Hernandez, "Y'know what I'm gonna do when we get home? Buy a vineyard in Napa Valley."

That was certainly news to Hernandez. "A vineyard? Really?"

"Yeah," said the vivacious New Zealander. "I bet I can drink enough wine to make myself rich."

Still suspicious, Hernandez asked, "How can you afford to buy a winery? Last time we were on leave, you couldn't afford to pick up a round of drinks."

"Well," Fletcher said with a shrug, "I figure I've got twelve years of back pay coming to me when we get home. And since a Romulan ambush put us in this mess, I figure I'm entitled to twelve years of combat bonuses, too."

Hernandez chuckled. "I knew if anyone could find the silver lining to this mess, it'd be you."

Foyle tapped Fletcher's shoulder. When she turned her head toward him, he handed her the now-empty canteen. She passed it forward to Hernandez, who returned it to Pembleton.

He tucked the canteen inside his pack. Then he closed the pack and put it back on. As he stood and grabbed his rifle, he said, "Everybody up. We're moving out."

"Sergeant," Hernandez said, "what's our ETA to the city?"

"About six hours, if we can keep this pace. It'll be hard in this heat."

Fletcher said over the captain's shoulder, "Maybe we should wait for nightfall. Might be cooler then."

"It'll also be pitch-dark in this forest," Pembleton said. "That won't hurt our ability to navigate, but it will make us more vulnerable to predators. The best thing we can do is keep going until we at least get clear of the trees."

"And how long will that take?" asked Hernandez.

"Four hours and forty minutes," Pembleton said. "That'll put us at the edge of the grasslands that lead to the city."

"All right, then," Hernandez said. "Let's get going."

Pembleton adjusted his grip on his rifle and advanced through the waist-high waving greenery that dominated the relatively narrow gaps between the giant trees. Hernandez fell in behind him, watching the ground for signs of where he had placed his feet with each step. The muted shuffle of people walking seemed to be swallowed up by the steady drone of insect noise and the soft scratching of wind-rustled foliage.

Every few minutes, Hernandez stole a look backward to make certain the entire landing party was still accounted for, even though it was Lieutenant Yacavino's job, as the rear guard, to make certain no one went missing. After a while, she stopped looking back and kept herself focused on their destination.

The hours dragged on, seemingly multiplied by the heat and Hernandez's exhaustion. At her request, Pembleton increased the frequency of their stops, to once per hour. Each break consumed another canteen of water, and on the fourth stop they rested a bit longer and picked at their cold rations. After lunch ended, the landing party segregated by gender, and each person sought out some small measure of privacy in the thick undergrowth.

As the landing party regrouped, Hernandez looked around and realized that the trees in this part of the forest, while still larger than anything on Earth, were smaller than those they had left behind, and they were spaced a bit more generously. Looking ahead in the direction they had been traveling, she could almost see some faint glow of white daylight in the distance.

The sharp, crisp sound of finger snaps turned her head and silenced the murmuring of the group. Private Steinhauer had his hand scanner out and open, and as the other MACOs looked at him, he made short chopping movements with his hand in several directions around the landing party. Hernandez followed his gestures and was barely able to notice unusual flutters in the thick greenery, like ripples in water.

In slow, steady motions, Major Foyle and the other MACOs raised and braced their rifles. Sergeant Pembleton motioned the rest of the landing party to get down. Then he selected a target and put himself between it and Hernandez. Around the rest of the landing party, the MACOs formed a tight circle.

"Set for stun," Hernandez reminded everyone in a whisper. "Remember this is a first-contact mission."

The MACOs checked their rifles' settings and nodded to Foyle, who said in a low monotone, "Weapons free."

The forest erupted with bright flashes of phased energy and echoed with the screeching of rifles discharging in three-shot bursts. Piercing shrieks added to the cacophony as the soldiers' shots found their marks. Enormous, semi-transparent creatures that reminded Hernandez of millipedes reared up out of the fronds, their antennae twitching and their multi-segmented bodies wriggling from multiple hits by the phase rifles. Within seconds, all the creatures were in retreat.

Foyle shouted, "Cease fire!" The staccato roar of rifle fire stopped, leaving only its distant echoes reverberating in the cavernous spaces of the forest.

Hernandez noticed only then that she had drawn her own phase pistol without realizing it. She tucked the weapon back in its holster on her belt. Then she looked around and saw the other flight-crew officers doing the same thing.

Foyle and his men lowered their rifles and grinned at one another as they watched the *Columbia* personnel holster their sidearms. "Thank you for the backup," the major said, "but we have it under control."

"*Gracias,* Major," Hernandez said.

"*De nada,* Captain," Foyle said. He waved to Pembleton, who gave him his attention. "Sergeant, I want a defensive formation until we clear the forest."

"Yes, sir," Pembleton said. "Mazzetti, Crichlow—each of you take a flank. Steinhauer, join Yacavino on rear guard. Major, will you join me on point?"

"Absolutely," Foyle said, stepping past Fletcher and Hernandez. When he reached the front, he turned back and said to the landing party, "We're less than an hour from clearing the forest. I'd like to pick up the pace and get this over with. Anyone who doesn't think they can handle it, speak up now." No one said anything. "All right. Double-time. Let's move out!"

The jogging pace was twice as difficult to sustain as Hernandez had expected, but she was determined not to set an example of frailty. Inhaling the muggy air was a labor, and within ten minutes her chest hurt with each heaving breath. Her black bangs were matted to her forehead by sweat, and knifing pains between her ribs felt as if they penetrated into her lungs. Exertion left the muscles in her calves and thighs coiled and burning, and each running step sent jolts of impact trauma through her knees. Only the widening slivers of light through the trees kept her stride from faltering.

She noticed Fletcher striding alongside her, her longer legs making it easy for her to overtake the captain. Fletcher asked with a smirk, "Hangin' in there, Captain?"

Lacking the air to respond, Hernandez shot a venomous glare at her XO and kept loping along behind Foyle and Pembleton.

After almost twenty minutes of jogging, the tree line was within sight. A dark wall of Brobdingnagian trunks rose like columns in front of a curtain of pale illumination. Hernandez found it hard to let her eyes adjust; she stared at the light until she could make out the details. A narrow, vertical slice of landscape emerged from behind a veil of shimmering haze: green land below, a crimson shine on the horizon, and a cloud-streaked sky above. But then the forest became a black mass around her, and she was unable to see where she was going.

She blinked and cast her eyes toward her feet, so that her eyes could readjust to the shadowy realm beneath the arboreal giants. The landscape beyond the tree line was washed away once more in a radiant, white flood. As the landing party neared the forest's edge, the ferns and fronds that choked the ground became taller, and the spaces between them narrower and harder to traverse. Within moments, the lush green foliage towered over their heads, aglow with the intense light that slanted almost horizontally into the forest near its perimeter.

Pembleton slowed to a walking pace and called back to the others, "Regroup and stay close till we get clear of this stuff."

The heat from above grew stronger, and the light became much brighter. Filtered through the tall plants, it bathed the landing party in an emerald glow.

Then they broke through the wall of green into daylight.

Slack-jawed and silent, the landing party fanned out in a long line and stared at the vista before them.

Rolling knolls covered in knee-high flaxen grasses and brightly hued wildflowers punctuated the otherwise gradual downward slope of the landscape. The crescent border of the forest stretched north and south for hundreds of kilometers, disappearing into the misty distance. Flatlands stretched west toward the horizon, in front of which rose a jagged mountain range backed by a seemingly endless bank of storm clouds.

Rising from the center of the golden plain was a massive city unlike any that Hernandez had ever seen. Metallic white and shaped like a broad bowl filled with fragile towers, it looked as if it were perfectly symmetrical, but her eyes couldn't discern all the minuscule details of its architecture from this distance. Its surfaces gleamed with reflected light.

"No air traffic," Fletcher said. She took her hand scanner from her belt and activated it. After making a few adjustments, she added, "And we're inside the scattering field, so scanners are drawing a blank."

Hernandez eyed the landscape around the metropolis. "No roads," she said. "It's like this place has no history."

Major Foyle asked, "What are you talking about?"

"A city this big doesn't just spring up from nowhere," Hernandez explained. "Urban centers are hubs for commerce, industry, and travel. Even in a society long past the age of ground travel, you'd expect to find evidence of old roads leading to a city this size."

"Not to mention infrastructure," Fletcher said. "I'm not seeing any signs of civil engineering outside the city. No water or sewage-removal systems, no power grids, no comm lines."

"I'm sure this is all fascinating, Captain," said Major Foyle, "but I just need to know one thing right now: Are we going forward, or going back?"

Hernandez nodded at the city. "Forward, Major. We have to see if anybody's home."

"Then we'd better get going," Foyle said, pointing at the kilometers-long shadow of the city that was angled in their direction. "We're losing the light."

Hernandez looked up at the blinding orange orb of the sun, which was making slow progress toward the horizon. "Move out," she said, and she started walking to lead the way.

Her officers fell in as a group behind her, while Foyle silently directed his MACOs with hand signals to spread out in a triangle-shaped formation around the *Columbia* team.

Though the alien city was still nearly three kilometers away, it loomed large above the wild spaces of the plains, an intricate jewel standing like a citadel of order and authority amid the undefiled chaos of nature. Hernandez's admiration of the city's austere beauty was enhanced by its contrast with the storm-bruised dome of sky in the distance.

Fletcher seemed wary of the majestic white metropolis as she asked Hernandez, "What'll we do if it's deserted?"

"Plant a flag," Hernandez said, only half joking.

Still leery, Fletcher said, "And if it's *not* deserted?"

"We'll start with 'hello' and see how it goes from there."

"Some plan," Fletcher quipped. "Showing up on their front porch empty-handed. Maybe we should've brought a gift."

Hernandez grinned and played along. "Like what?"

"I dunno," Fletcher said. "A nice casserole, maybe. Or a basket of muffins. Everybody likes a basket of muffins."

"I'll put that on the first-contact checklist from now on," Hernandez said. "Phase pistol, universal translator, first-aid kit, and a basket of muffins."

Fletcher shrugged. "Couldn't hurt."

The slight downhill grade made the hike to the city an easy one, and the group picked up speed as they continued.

Hernandez sighed and muttered, "Damn you, Fletcher." When she saw her first officer's aghast reaction, she added, "Now I can't stop thinking about blueberry muffins. Thanks a lot."

"My work here is done," Fletcher said.

It was half an hour before anyone spoke again.

As the landing party crested the last knoll between them and the city, they saw that the metropolis didn't rest at ground level. The center of its convex underside hovered several dozen meters above the planet, and its outer edges were hundreds of meters off the ground. It was like standing beneath a giant, levitating bowl of dark metal. Hernandez saw no obvious means of reaching its surface.

Pembleton craned his neck and stared up at the city's edge. "Well, that's just great."

Fletcher said to Hernandez, "We could walk under it. There might be an entrance somewhere along its bottom."

Karl Graylock, who hadn't said a word since beaming down several hours earlier, peered through a pair of magnifying binoculars and shook his head. "*Nein*," he said. "The ventral surface has no apertures. Going under the city is a waste of time, Captain."

Hernandez saw Ensign Valerian fiddling with the settings of her communicator. "Sidra. Anything?"

Valerian shook her head. "Sorry, Captain. No signals on the standard channels. I'm scanning a wider range now, but all I'm getting is background radiation."

Lieutenant Thayer folded her arms and stared upward at the unreachable city. Hernandez stepped beside the tactical officer and asked, "Ideas, Kiona?"

Thayer look dismayed. "Short of throwing rocks at their windows, no."

Foyle interjected, "My men and I could fire a few shots, get their attention."

"I don't think that's a good idea," Hernandez said.

The major shrugged. "Then I have nothing."

Hernandez stared up at the majestic structure looming above them, and she watched it dim as the planet's massive, tangerine-hued star sank behind the mountain range in the west. She sighed heavily. "Well," she said, "that's just great."

Then she saw it.

Hernandez backed away from the city's edge, her gaze still directed upward as she said, "We've got company."

The rest of the landing party backpedaled alongside her as they turned their eyes to the rim of the megalopolis, hundreds of meters above. A vaguely humanoid shape, its limbs barely discernible in the twilight, stepped off the city's edge and descended as if borne aloft on the breeze. Its feet and head seemed large, ponderous, and not at all delicate, even from a distance. The landing party regrouped in a semicircle around Hernandez, who stepped forward to meet the being that floated with steady grace to the ground in front of them.

Only in the broadest possible sense would Hernandez have described the creature as humanoid. It had a torso, two arms, two legs, one head, and a face, but any resemblance to a human ended there.

Its skull was bulbous and quite large, and had two valvelike protuberances high up along the back. Two almond-shaped, upswept, lidless eyes of silver-flecked sea-green were set wide apart on the alien's face, which looked as if it had been stretched until the nose flattened and disappeared, leaving only a taut, lipless mouth curled into a permanent frown. It had no chin to speak of; its face continued to its chest in an unbroken slope of loose, leathery skin folds.

Segmented, tubular growths emerged beneath the base of the being's skull and hugged its shoulders as they curved down into its chest and blended into its mottled hide. Overlapping ridges concealed its shoulders, upper arms, and elbows, like interlocking plates in a suit of well-made armor.

As it took a cautious step in their direction, Hernandez froze, and the landing party tensed silently behind her.

Seeing the creature in motion had emphasized how different its physical proportions were to their own.

Its arms were freakishly long by human standards, and its legs seemed impossibly thin to support its weight, even though its chest was birdlike. Its wide, long feet had two enormous forward toes of equal length on either side of a deep curve, and a clawlike third toe near the heel, along the instep.

Loose strips of violet fabric hung over its ungainly body, wrapped around its bony thighs, and were draped between its legs to just above its ankles. Underneath the fabric was a fitted piece of armor that covered the being's torso. A circular plate attached to the back of the armor rose up behind its shoulders and framed its head in a manner that for Hernandez evoked the images of haloed saints on stained-glass windows.

It gestured at the landscape with three delicate-looking, undulating tendrils at the end of its arm. "Welcome to Erigol," it said, in a voice with a deep male timbre. "I am Inyx, the chief scientist of Axion."

"Hello, Inyx," Hernandez said. "I'm Captain Erika Hernandez of the Earth vessel *Columbia*." She pivoted and nodded at the landing party. "These are members of my crew."

Inyx turned his head slowly one way and then the other, gently twisting the rough, mottled waddles of green-and-purple skin between his face and chest. "You have come seeking aid."

"Yes," Hernandez said. "Our ship—"

"—was damaged in a conflict," Inyx said. "We observed the incident, and we noted your approach."

Hernandez traded confused glances with Fletcher and Foyle before she replied to Inyx, "You've been watching us travel here for over twelve years?"

"Yes," Inyx said. "Do you wish to enter Axion?"

His casual response to her question and the matter-of-fact manner in which he had proffered his invitation left Hernandez feeling conversationally off balance. "Yes, we would," she said finally. "It's why we're here."

"An ingress is being extended," Inyx said. He lifted one arm and waggled one of his ribbonlike digits upward. Hernandez and her team looked up and saw that a cylindrical shaft had sprung from the ostensibly unbroken shell of the city's underside and was quickly extending toward the surface near them. It touched the ground without a sound or vibration, despite its apparent mass. Inyx walked toward it. Hernandez hesitated for a moment before she followed him. Foyle and Fletcher flanked her as the landing party fell in behind them.

A pinpoint formed on the column's silvery-white metallic surface and opened like an iris, into an aperture wide enough for the landing party to pass through three across. The interior of the cylinder glowed with amber light. Inyx stepped inside first and then moved to the left of the entrance to facilitate the others' passage. As soon as everyone had stepped in and was clear of its threshold, the aperture spiraled shut.

Hernandez stood beside Inyx and stared at his unexpressive face. She felt an awkward need to make small talk. "Our species is known as human," she said.

"We know," Inyx replied. "You are one of many species in this part of the galaxy who have recently developed starflight capabilities—an occurrence of dubious virtue."

Masking her concern over the possible meanings of his remark, she asked, "What are your people called?"

"Caeliar. For simplicity's sake, you may use it in its noun form as a singular or as a plural, and also as an adjective."

Overhead, the top of the cylinder retracted, revealing the late evening sky. Then the walls of the cylinder fell away, and Hernandez saw that she, Inyx, and the landing party stood on the far perimeter of a magnificent city.

Below the ramparts, wide thoroughfares of moving walkways were flanked by lofty towers that looked like sketches of steel and glass. Great vertical columns rose side by side hundreds of meters above the city, their edifices decorated with intricate, repeated designs, and all of them linked by tenuous filaments, as if they had been wrought from platinum and gossamer.

"It's beautiful," Fletcher said over Hernandez's shoulder.

"This is Axion," Inyx said. "Our capital city."

Under their feet, the elevator disk that had lifted them from the surface detached from Axion's foundation and drifted upward. Then, without any sense of acceleration, it sped forward into the city, which filled its enormous, concave foundation. Canyons of gleaming metal and unearthly light blurred past. The disk transited a circular tunnel through the base of a skyscraper, then shot out beneath a network of airy, open walkways that bridged the yawning space between two clusters of buildings. Swaths of the metropolis were lush with vegetation, some of it wild, some of it artfully landscaped. Lights sparkled to life in the spires as the night at last took hold over the city.

As the hoverdisk carried the landing party deeper into Axion, Hernandez asked Inyx, "Where are we going?"

"To your accommodations," Inyx said.

"I guess I could use a rest, after the day we've had," Hernandez said. A look at her landing party garnered no objections. Looking back at Inyx, she continued, "When can we talk to someone about getting help fixing our ship?"

"Your ship will not be repaired," Inyx said.

The landing party's expressions of wonderment at the city's beauties were replaced by surprised and indignant glowers. Hernandez felt her own features harden with anger, then she forced herself to relax and remain diplomatic. "We wouldn't expect you to perform any labor, of course. You obviously have remarkable manufacturing capabilities. If your people could just help us fabricate some spare parts—"

"Perhaps I was not clear," Inyx interrupted. "We will not aid you in the restoration of your vessel."

Hernandez's temper began to get the best of her. "Could you at least send a subspace signal back to Earth so another ship can come out here and get us?"

"We have that capability," Inyx said. "But we will do no such thing. Multiple warnings were sent over subspace radio to your vessel during its approach and were not heeded."

Fletcher adopted a defensive tone. "Our subspace array is damaged," she said as the hoverdisk blurred through another tunnel. "We can't send or receive any signals via subspace."

"Yes," Inyx said. "We realized that when we conducted a more intensive scan of your vessel. It was the only reason we allowed you to proceed without interference."

The breeze that accompanied their flight felt good to Hernandez after the heat of the day, but she was too upset to appreciate it. "What are you saying? That if our comms had worked, you'd have destroyed us?"

"No," Inyx said. "Most likely we would have shifted you to another galaxy, one relatively devoid of sentient forms but still capable of sustaining your lives." As the disk glided around a long, shallow curve, he continued, "For many of your millennia, we have lived in seclusion. In recent centuries, as the local forms began traveling the stars, we masked our power signatures and obstructed scans of our world, to preserve our privacy. Clearly, however, our efforts have been ineffective."

Major Foyle snapped, "So you were going to fling us into another galaxy?" He tried to step toward Inyx and was restrained by Hernandez's hand on his chest as he continued, "Why not just send us back to Earth?"

"Preventing you from coming here would only have aroused your interest," Inyx said. "Your curiosity would have compelled your inevitable return, and others would have followed. We could not permit this. Allowing you to depart now that you have been here would pose the same threat. For this reason, we cannot allow you to transmit any signals back to your people."

Seething, Foyle asked, "Then why don't you just kill us?"

"We will not destroy sentient life," Inyx said. "But we will protect our privacy. Only the fact that you could not reveal your discovery of our world enabled me to petition the Quorum for leniency on your behalf."

The hoverdisk stopped in front of a tower and made a vertical ascent at a dizzying speed. A touch of vertigo left Hernandez unsteady on her feet, and Fletcher and Foyle each gripped one of her arms for a moment to steady her. Then the disk edged forward and docked at a rooftop garden that led to a sprawling interior space of open floors, skylights, and walls of windows offering panoramic views.

Inyx stepped off the disk and ushered the landing party into the penthouse suite with a wave of his disconcertingly long arm and rippling fingers. "I hope that you find your new accommodations satisfactory," he said. "We have interfaced with your ship's computer to acquaint ourselves with your nutritional requirements and other biological needs. This space has been configured accordingly."

"Nicest jail cell I've ever seen," Fletcher said.

"Do not think of yourselves as prisoners," counseled Inyx.

Hernandez fixed him with an icy stare. "What are we, then?"

"Honored guests," Inyx said. "With restrictions."

She had to know. "And my ship?"

"It will not be harmed," Inyx said. "But, like yourselves, it can never again leave Erigol."

2381

11

———

"The Borg cube is approaching Korvat," Lieutenant Choudhury announced to the rest of the *Enterprise*'s bridge crew.

Picard felt the tangible malevolence of the Collective in his gut, and he heard its soulless voice whispering at the gate of his thoughts as his ship hurtled at high warp toward another hostile encounter. "Time to intercept?"

From the tactical station, Choudhury said, "Six minutes."

Against the Borg, Picard brooded, *six minutes can be an eternity.* "Status of the planet's defenses?"

Kadohata answered as she reviewed data on the operations console. "Orbital platforms charging, surface batteries online. *Gibraltar* and *Leonov* are moving to engage."

Watching the relayed tactical data scroll across his left-side command screen, Picard feared for the two Federation starships defending Korvat. Even though the *Gibraltar* was a *Sovereign*-class vessel like the *Enterprise,* and the *Alexey Leonov* was a hardy *Defiant*-class escort, neither was armed with transphasic torpedoes. Without that advantage, their part in the coming battle might prove tragically short-lived.

To Picard's right, Worf shifted with visible discomfort in the first officer's chair. The Klingon had always preferred to be on his feet during times of battle. Now, however, his place was here, beside Picard, coordinating the command of the ship's vast resources and hundreds of personnel.

"Number One, what's our status?"

Worf didn't need to look at his console as he answered. "Shield modifications active, Captain. All weapons ready."

"Take us to battle stations," Picard said.

"Aye, sir," Worf said, and he acted without delay. He triggered the Red Alert klaxon, which wailed once shipwide. Then he opened a shipwide comm channel. "Attention all decks, this is the XO. All hands to battle stations. This is not an exercise. Bridge out." He closed the channel and continued issuing orders in rapid succession around the bridge—raising shields, arming weapons, and preemptively deploying damage-control teams.

In the midst of his crew's preparations for combat, Picard was paralyzed in his chair, his face slack, his thoughts erased like scratches on a beach washed smooth by a rising tide. Control, composure, and focus all vanished as the voice of the Collective spoke to him, its malice and contempt undiluted by the gulf of empty space it had bridged to touch his mind. All its hatred for him was expressed in a single word, one that always made him recoil in disgust, as if from an unspeakable obscenity.

Locutus.

The memory from which he could never hide. The atrocity he could never forget. It had been fifteen years since the Borg had first assimilated him and appointed him to speak on their behalf to humanity and the Federation. For a brief time he had been their unwilling intermediary, their instrument of conquest and intimidation. They had stolen his knowledge and experience and used them against his friends and fellow Starfleet officers; as a result, thirty-nine starships were destroyed and more than eleven thousand people were slaughtered at Wolf 359.

Picard's former first officer, Will Riker, along with the senior officers of the *Enterprise*-D, had liberated him less than a day after he had been taken. The physical wounds of his brief assimilation had healed soon thereafter, but the true scars of that horrible violation had lingered ever since, like a shadow on his psyche—a shadow with a name. *Locutus.*

It revolted him to hear the Collective in the privacy of his thoughts; he despised it as much for what it had done to him as for what it was. There was no shutting it out, no matter how hard he tried. Some part of that horrid, soul-devouring nightmare had left its imprint in his memory, its mark upon his essential nature, and now it could compel Picard's attention whenever it so desired.

One voice stood apart from the hive mind: the Queen. Once she had tried to seduce him. Now her voice was dark with spite.

The hour for humanity's assimilation is past, Locutus. The time has come for you and your kind to be exterminated.

He refused to respond to her in thought or deed. Instead, he took advantage of his momentary intimacy with the Collective to eavesdrop on its secrets, to use its intrusions to his own advantage against his old adversary. It seemed fitting to him that, in keeping with the Borg's culture of interdependency, his perpetual weak spot should be its Achilles' heel, as well. Eight years earlier, during the Battle of Sector 001, he had sussed out a vulnerability in the design of the Borg's ubiquitous cube-shaped vessels. To stop a gigantic Borg cube months earlier, he had risked letting himself become Locutus once again, to restore his link to the Collective and gain access to its secrets.

He hoped to uncover another such tactical advantage now, in the crucial moments before the battle.

A dark revelation unfolded in his mind's eye.

The Collective's agenda—in its alacrity, aggression, and scope—surpassed his worst fears. Aghast, he retreated from the vision, into the redoubt of his own thoughts. Denial was the natural response, but he knew better than to indulge it; there were no lies within the Collective, only certainties.

A gentle shaking dispelled the susurrating group voice of the Collective from his thoughts, and he blinked once to reorient himself. He was still seated in his chair on the bridge; Worf leaned down beside him, with one large hand on Picard's shoulder. He asked, "Are you all right, Captain?"

"No," Picard said, his emotions numbed from contact with the Collective. He stood, took a step forward, and said in a low voice, "We've underestimated them." Then he turned to face Worf and Lieutenant Choudhury. "We've made a terrible mistake."

Choudhury looked taken aback by the captain's words. "Well," she said with a glance at the image of

Korvat on the main viewer, "at least we were right about their next target."

Picard felt his countenance harden with anger and regret. "No," he said. "We weren't." He faced the main viewscreen and continued, "Korvat isn't *the* target, it's *a* target—one of five the Borg are about to attack in unison. Commander Kadohata: Send code-one alerts to Khitomer and Starbases 234, 157, and 343."

"Aye, sir," Kadohata replied, her hands already translating his order into action on her console.

"Captain," Worf said. "There might still be time to send the new torpedo designs to the starbases."

"We can't," Picard said, his frustration churning bile into his throat. "Admiral Nechayev's orders were quite specific." His hands curled into fists. "All we can do is fight the battle in front of us."

Dropping his voice, Worf protested, "Sir, if the starbases try to fight the Borg without transphasic torpe-does—"

"It's too late," Picard said, as another flash from the Collective assaulted him with images of carnage. "It's begun."

"They're locking weapons again, Commander! What do we do?"

Smoke and fumes filled the bridge of the *U.S.S. Ranger*. Voices crying out for orders or for help buffeted the ship's first officer, Commander Jennifer Nero, as she kneeled beside the fallen Captain Pachal and searched in vain for his pulse.

Another blast from the Borg cube rocked the *Nebula*-class starship hard to port, hurling Nero's crewmates toward the bulkhead and sprawling her atop the burned and bloodstained body of the captain. She pushed herself off him and struggled to her feet. "Schultheiss, th'Fairoh, get back to your posts!"

As the shaken human woman and timorous Andorian *thaan* scrambled back to their seats at the ops and conn consoles, Nero moved to take the center seat. She sat down and swept stray wisps of her red hair back behind her ears. "Ankiel," she said, looking over at the sinewy, crew-cut tactical officer, "where are the *Constant* and the *Arimathea*?"

"Coming up behind the Borg," replied Ankiel, whose eyes stayed on his console. "They're firing." He shook his head. "No effect. The Borg's shields are adapting too fast."

"Let's see if we can adapt faster," Nero said. "Bridge to main engineering."

"*Braden here,*" answered the chief engineer over the comm.

Nero crossed her fingers. "Is the captain's plan ready?"

"*Almost,*" Braden said. "*One minute till we arm the MPI.*"

Unable to remain seated, Nero got up and strode forward. "Th'Fairoh, overtake the Borg cube. Schultheiss, transfer weapons power to the warp drive. Ankiel, stand by to activate the MPI on my command."

The MPI—molecular phase inverter—wasn't a device that had seen much use on the *Ranger*. On the rare occasions when it had been put into service, it had been used to restore phase-shifted matter to the normal space-time continuum. Typically, objects were

knocked a few millicochranes out of phase by transporter mishaps or by exposure to severely miscali-
brated warp fields. It had taken the imagination and
rare technological expertise of the *Ranger's* now-slain
commanding officer, Peter Pachal, to conceive of a
new use for this obscure piece of technology: They
would employ it to turn their ship into an unstoppable
missile with catastrophic destructive potential.

In the end, it would be all about timing—intercepting the Borg cube before it got too close to Khitomer,
and activating the MPI late enough in the attack that
the Borg wouldn't have time to adapt to the tactic and
counteract it.

Ankiel called out, "The *Constant's* been hit!"

Nero watched the main viewer as lifeboats ejected
from the *Akira*-class vessel like spores from a dande-
lion. A fiery conflagration erupted from the ship's aft
section and broke the ship into wreckage before consuming it in a blinding flash. The explosion was vast,
and in seconds it swallowed the loose cloud of
lifeboats, none of which emerged from its burning
embrace. Then the firestorm passed below the bottom
edge of the viewer, left behind as the *Ranger* continued its desperate pursuit of the Borg ship speeding
toward Khitomer.

Between the *Ranger* and the Borg was the *Arimathea,* which continued to harry the Borg with woe-
fully ineffective phaser fire and steady photon-torpedo
barrages.

"Schultheiss," Nero said, "tell the *Arimathea* to
break off before they—" She was cut off by the sight of
emerald-hued beams from the Borg vessel crisscross-
ing the *Centaur*-class cruiser and obliterating it in a

flash that would spread its wreckage across millions of cubic kilometers as its warp field collapsed.

Grim silence fell over the *Ranger*'s bridge crew. *It's up to us, now,* Nero realized. "Bridge to engineering, report."

"Arming the MPI now," Braden said. *"Make sure we keep her steady—we'll be getting a pretty big boost in speed once we slip out of phase."*

"Noted," said Nero. "Schultheiss, stand by to trigger the MPI. Mister Ankiel, arm all quantum warheads and release the log buoy. Th'Fairoh, lay in a ramming trajectory for the Borg cube and prepare to increase speed to maximum warp."

"Trigger ready," Schultheiss replied. "At helm's command."

From the tactical console, Ankiel said simply, "Armed." Nero forced herself not to dwell on the fact that the *Ranger*'s sizable inventory of quantum torpedo warheads had been linked to the ship's antimatter fuel pods. If the captain's plan worked, and they slipped inside the Borg's defense screens long enough to detonate the warheads—and themselves— even the Borg's amazing regenerative abilities would be unable to withstand total, instantaneous subatomic annihilation.

She was about to give the order to proceed with the final attack when she eyed the conn and saw that the intercept course had not been locked in. "Th'Fairoh," she said, "lay in the course. It's time."

The wiry young Andorian sat with his blue hands side by side in his lap and stared at his console. He made slow, almost imperceptible swivels of his head, side to side, the movement so fluid that it didn't impart the slightest quiver to his antennae. "No," he muttered, his voice below a whisper.

Nero spoke in sharper tones this time. "Mister th'Fairoh, I gave you an order. Lock in the course and prepare to engage."

Her directive made his head tremble in nervous microturns, and his hands curled closed, with his fingernails biting into his palms. "No," he repeated. "I can't." He looked up at her, his countenance fearful and his eyes wide. "This is pointless! Don't you get it? It's a lost cause. We can't beat them! They'll just keep coming, over and over. Why throw our lives away? What good will stopping one Borg ship do?" Growing more hysterical, he continued, "We don't even know if this plan'll work! The captain's already dead, we've lost a third of the crew, and Khitomer's not even a Federation planet! What are we still doing here? We have to break off, we have to run—"

The Andorian *thaan* scrambled up from his seat. Nero yelled, "Stay at your post!" It didn't stop him. She stepped forward to restrain him, to force him back into his chair at the conn, but she underestimated the strength advantage that panic had given him. He tried to push past her, and it was a struggle to hold him back. "Dammit, th'Fairoh! Sit dow—" His fist caught her in the chin and knocked her backward onto the deck.

The angry screech of a phaser was loud enough to be painful in the confines of the bridge. Nero watched as the blazing orange beam slammed into th'Fairoh's torso and held him paralyzed, twitching in front of the energy stream like a puppet on a taut wire. Then the beam ceased, and the Andorian collapsed face-first to the deck.

A few meters away, Ankiel stood with his arm outstretched and his sidearm still aimed at the unconscious flight controller. Seconds later he seemed satisfied that th'Fairoh would not be getting up any time soon. He holstered his weapon. "Looks like you'll have to do the honors, Commander," he said.

Nero grabbed the seat of the conn officer's chair and pulled herself up into it. A deep, throbbing pain blossomed in her jaw, and she tasted the salty-metallic tang of blood between her loosened molars. Rather than spit it onto the deck of the bridge, she forced herself to swallow it. Then she coughed once to clear her throat and eyed the controls in front of her.

Entering the first few commands was easy. "Patching in all power," she said, talking herself through the steps to reduce it to the level of mere process and avoid thinking about what it meant. "Intercept trajectory plotted," she said. Making her fingers key in the next action was more difficult. She felt herself resisting the inevitable. Through will alone she entered the order and announced, "Course locked."

Then she froze, her hands hovering above the console.

She stared at the main viewscreen. On it was the image of the Borg cube, accelerating away from them, opening the gap on its way to the historic planet of Khitomer, where the Federation and the Klingon Empire had taken their first, uncertain steps toward détente and, ultimately, alliance. But Khitomer was not merely a political landmark; that lush world was home to a thriving Klingon colony of more than half a million people, all of whom would now live or die based on what the crew of the *Starship Ranger* did next.

Schultheiss leaned over from the ops console toward Nero. "Commander," she said without raising her voice, "we have to attack in the next twenty seconds, or we won't be able to stop the Borg without causing serious casualties on the planet."

Nero felt tears welling in her eyes as she faced the terrible finality of their situation. She looked around at the other bridge officers, all of whom were looking at her, waiting for the signal to proceed. Her voice faltered slightly as she asked, "Everyone ready?" Heads nodded in unison. She smiled sadly. "It's been an honor serving with you all." Turning back to face the main viewer, she poised her finger above the blinking control pad that would trigger the MPI and accelerate the ship to its rendezvous with the Borg. She paused just long enough to say to Schultheiss, "Thanks, Christine."

"My pleasure," Schultheiss said.

One deep breath in, one last breath out. *I only have to be brave for a moment,* Nero told herself. She triggered the MPI.

A moment later, it was over.

Governor Talgar stood on the balcony outside his office and watched the sky of Khitomer. Age and political duty had robbed him of the chance to take up arms and meet the Borg in honorable combat, but he refused to be shepherded like some weakling into the secure bunker beneath the administrative complex. When death came for him, he wanted to meet it with a smile.

The colony's regiment of soldiers were defending all the checkpoints that led inside the walled section of Khitomer City, and manning the surface-to-space artillery units, for whatever good it might do. Talgar had no illusions about the Borg's ability to eradicate his colony and the world on which it stood. Their preparations for war were little more than a formality.

His aide, a tall Defense Force lieutenant named Nazh, lurked just inside the doorway behind him. The younger Klingon's anxiety was palpable and irritating to Talgar, who had long resented being forced to employ the *petaQ* simply because Nazh was a kins-man of a member of the High Council. Talgar turned and growled at him, "Did you bring it?"

"Yes, sir," Nazh said.

"Then give it to me, *yIntagh*," Talgar said, reaching out his hand. Nazh pushed a carved-onyx goblet into his grasp, and Talgar lifted it to his lips and guzzled three bitter mouthfuls of *warnog,* until all that remained in the cup were dregs.

The sky was a blank slate, blue-gray like gunmetal, clear under the noonday sun, unblemished by clouds or air traffic. It seemed so serene, but Talgar knew that a deathblow was coming, a killing stroke that would fall without preamble. The Borg were not noble, and they neither had nor lacked honor; what they were was decisive and swift. The governor appreciated his enemy's ruthless efficiency for what it was: a weapon.

Inside his office, a shrill buzzing emanated from his desk. He grimaced at the disruption and said to Nazh, "Get that."

His lieutenant walked in quick strides to the desk, silenced the alert, and worked for a few moments at the desktop console. Then he looked up and declared, "Governor, it's from Colonel Nokar. He says you should see this."

Talgar grumbled incoherently out of frustration, turned, and walked back inside to his desk. He brusquely pushed Nazh aside and eyed the data and images on his wide desktop display. Despite having been informed hours earlier by the High Command that there were no Defense Force vessels close enough to reach his world before the Borg attacked, he clung to the hope that a *Vor'cha*-class attack cruiser or two might have defied the Council or the limitations of their own engines to join the fight at the last minute.

Instead, he saw a trio of Federation starships engaged in a futile, running battle with the Borg cube, which did not deviate from its course even as it pummeled their shields and blasted rents in their hulls. Over an audio channel, he heard Colonel Nokar remark with his typical snideness, *"Looks like Starfleet's in the mood to lose a few more ships today."*

Nazh let out a sardonic *harrumph* and said, "At least *they* think Khitomer's worth fighting for."

The governor punched the impudent lieutenant and sent him sprawling backward over a guest chair. "No one asked you." He turned his attention back to his desktop, in time to see the first of the three Starfleet vessels disintegrate under a steady barrage from the black cube. Several seconds later, the second of the three vessels was sliced into fiery debris by the Borg, and the third began to fall steadily behind.

"A valiant effort, friends," Talgar muttered to the diminishing image of the last Starfleet ship as he watched the image of the enemy vessel grow larger. He expected the Federation cruiser to abandon its hopeless pursuit in a few moments, since there appeared to be no way for it to overtake the cube, and no means for it to fight the cube if it did.

Then the Starfleet vessel, which the colony's sensors had just identified as the *U.S.S. Ranger*, accelerated instantly to a velocity that was almost off the scale. The sensors tried to keep up with it, but all that Talgar saw on his display was a jumble of conflicting data—and then the Borg cube vanished in a blaze of white light. His display went dark, but from outside his office came a blinding flare at least twice as bright as Khitomer's sun. It faded away within seconds, but a tingle of heat lingered in the air.

Talgar poked at the unresponsive desktop interface for a moment before he glared at Nazh and said, "Get Colonel Nokar on the comm, now."

Nazh, for once, didn't complain or procrastinate. He powered down the interface and triggered its restart sequence. It took nearly half a minute before the system was working again and a comm channel had been opened to the underground command bunker, from which Nokar had been directing his pointless, surface-based defense campaign.

"Colonel," Talgar said, "report!"

"We're still analyzing the Starfleet ship's attack," Nokar said. *"It looks like they shifted their vessel just far enough out of phase to breach the Borg's shields before sacrificing their ship in a suicide attack."*

Wary of being too optimistic, Talgar asked in a neutral manner, "Status of the Borg vessel?"

"Destroyed, Governor," Nokar said. *"Vaporized."*

Talgar marveled at the news. *"Qapla',"* he said, as a salute to the fallen heroes of the *Ranger*. Then, to Nokar, he added, "Where be your gibes now, eh,

Colonel? A thousand times I've heard you mock our allies, and now you get to keep drawing breath because of them." He wasn't surprised that Nokar had no riposte for that, and as he cut the channel he imagined a sullen expression darkening the colonel's weathered, angular face.

Turning to Nazh, Talgar said, "The Empire hasn't seen an act of courage like that since Narendra, and it's time the High Council heard about it. Open a channel to Chancellor Martok."

Decades of diplomatic service had taught Talgar to make the most of opportunities when they presented themselves. For years, the chancellor's foes on the High Council had been impeding his efforts to forge a tighter bond with the Federation. Their most recent obstructions had entailed diverting Defense Force ships and resources to avoid aiding the Federation in its renewed conflict with the Borg. Calling the escalating struggle "an internal Federation matter," a bloc of councillors, led by Kopek, had begun undermining Martok's influence and authority in matters of imperial defense. But that was about to change.

An image flickered and then settled on the governor's desktop display—it was the stern, one-eyed visage of Chancellor Martok himself. *"What do you want, Talgar?"*

"The Borg have come to Khitomer, old friend," Talgar said, "and our allies have defended us with their lives." Over the subspace channel, he sent Martok the colony's sensor data of the three Starfleet ships' battle and the *Ranger*'s decisive victory over the Borg cube. As he observed the chancellor's reaction to the news, he knew that his assumption had been correct: This was the ammunition Martok had been waiting for to sway the Council.

In his guttural rasp of a baritone, Martok asked rhetorically, *"You know what this means, don't you?"*

"Yes, my lord," Talgar said. "It means this is the hour when men of honor go to war."

The command center of Starbase 234 was collapsing in on itself, and all that Admiral Owen Paris could think about was finding a working comm terminal.

Fire-control teams scrambled past the admiral on both sides as he stumbled over the wreckage strewn across the floor. Flames danced in the shadows between buckled walls, and a cloud of oily smoke gathered overhead, obscuring the ceiling.

Paris grabbed a lieutenant whose black uniform was trimmed at the collar in mustard yellow. "Is your console working?"

Grime and blood coated the woman's face, which contorted in frustration as she replied, "No, sir." She freed herself from his grasp with a rough twist and continued on her way.

He tightened his left fist around the data chip he'd carried from his office and staggered forward, through the mayhem of firefighters shouting instructions over the tumult of tactical officers issuing battle orders. A thunderclap of detonation rocked the station with the force of an earthquake.

Someone called out above the din, "Shields failing!" Then another bone-jarring blast knocked Admiral Paris off his feet and reminded him that even a bunker of cast rodinium was no match for the weapons of the Borg. He landed hard atop a mound of twisted metal and shattered companel fragments that tore through his uniform and lacerated his forearms and knees.

With only his right hand free, he found it difficult to push himself back to his feet. Then a pair of delicate but strong hands locked around his bicep and pulled him upright.

He turned his head and saw the base's chief of security, Commander Sandra Rhodes, nod toward a short stairway to the command center's lower level. "This way, sir," said the lithe brunette. "I've got a channel ready for you." A resounding boom seemed to tremble the foundations of the planet, and more chunks of debris fell from above, crashing to the deck all around them. One close call coated them in dust. Rhodes stayed by Paris's side as she pressed one hand into his back to keep him moving forward.

Scrambling down the steps, Paris cursed himself for leaving something so vital until it was long past too late. He'd made his share of mistakes in life—not least among them the Tezwa debacle, in which he'd actually conspired with other Starfleet officers to unseat a sitting Federation president—and he'd borne his guilt and his regrets in silence. But there was one burden he could not bear to take with him to the grave.

The lights stuttered and went out, plunging the underground chamber into darkness. Only the pale, faltering glow of a few duty consoles remained lit, beacons in the night. From behind, Rhodes's insistent but gentle pressure guided him forward.

His ankle caught on something sharp and hard, and he tripped. By instinct he reached out to break his fall—

The data chip fell from his hand and plinked brightly across the rubble-covered floor, its tiny sound the only clue to where it had landed. Scuttling back and forth on all fours, he began to hyperventilate. Owen Paris, the model of stoicism, was on the verge of tears, his chest heaving with panicked breaths.

"I dropped it," he called out to Rhodes. "God help me, Sandy, I dropped it!"

He swirled his hands over the stinging shards of shattered polymer on the ground as he searched in blind desperation for the chip. His palms grew sticky with caked dust and his own blood. From close by he heard Rhodes shout to the firefighters, "We need some light over here! Now!"

Sharp cracks heralded the ignition of several bright violet emergency flares in various directions around him. Some were held by members of the base's command team, some by engineers struggling to contain the fires. A few of them worked their way toward Paris, who continued rooting through the debris until the scarlet glow cast everything into harsh monochrome shadows and highlights. Then a glint of light caught the data chip's edge, and he snatched it from the dust.

A deafening concussion was followed by the roar of an implosion that brought down half the command center's ceiling. More than a dozen Starfleet personnel vanished beneath the cascade of broken metal and pulverized rock.

No time to lose now, Paris admonished himself, and he left Rhodes behind as he lurched and barreled ahead toward the still-illuminated console. With his last steps he fell against it, and he fumbled the data chip in his bloody fingers for a few seconds until he inserted it into the proper port on the panel.

As he began entering the transmission sequence, another station nearby exploded. Shrapnel from the blast raked his face and body, and a dull thud of impact on the side of his neck was the last thing he felt before he landed, numb, on the deck.

Stupid old man, he chastised himself. *Slow and stupid.*

Rhodes was at his side a moment later, looking frightened for the first time that Paris had seen since his transfer to Starbase 234 four months earlier. "It's a neck injury, sir," she said. "Don't try to move." Over her shoulder, she cried out, "Medic! The admiral's down! I need a medic over here!"

Paris's voice was a dry whisper of pain. "Sandy," he rasped, fearful that she might not hear him over the crackling of flames and the settling of debris. He said again, "Sandy."

She leaned down and said, "Don't talk, sir. Moving your jaw might do more damage in your neck." She was trying to sound unemotional, but in his opinion she was doing a lousy job of it.

"Listen to me, Sandy," Paris said. "It's important."

"All right," she said, steeling herself.

He tried to swallow before he spoke, but his mouth was dry and tasted of dirt. "Message on the data chip," he said, his voice growing reedier with each word. "Send it. Hurry."

It was to her credit, he thought, that she chose not to argue with him. Instead, she clambered over to the console and wiped off the fresh blanket of soot and crystalline dust. After a glance at the settings he had already keyed in, she shook her head. "Encryption protocols are down without the main computer."

"Doesn't matter," Paris said. "Send it."

This time she resisted. "Sir, if we send a signal in the clear to Starfleet Command, the Borg—"

"No," Paris protested, marshaling the last of his strength to make sure she understood. "Not . . . to Starfleet. . . . To my boy."

Rhodes's teary eyes reflected Paris's sorrows as she replied, "Aye, sir." She worked at the failing console for several seconds, and then she returned to Paris's side, kneeled beside him, and took his hand. "It's done, sir."

"Thank you, Sandy," Paris said, the last vestiges of his ironclad composure deserting him as his strength faded. "I needed him to know," he confessed, " . . . that I'm sorry."

She cupped her hand under his cheek. "I'm sure he knows."

"Maybe. But I had to say it. . . . I had to *say* it."

As a final eruption of stone and fire engulfed the command center, Owen Paris was grateful that he'd been spared the indignity of tears,

Picard felt like the calm at the center of a hurricane. He had plunged his ship and crew into battle with a single order: *Destroy the Borg cube.* Telling his officers *what* to do was his role; telling them *how* to do it, he left to Worf.

"Helm, lay in attack pattern Sierra-Blue," Worf said over the steady comm chatter of tactical reports from *Gibraltar* and *Leonov*. The two vessels were already engaged in a losing battle against the Borg cube that had entered Korvat's orbit and begun bombarding the surface. Worf continued, "Lieutenant Choudhury, arm transphasic torpedoes."

"Armed," Choudhury replied, entering commands with fast, quick touches on her console. "Twenty seconds to firing range."

Picard stared at the magnified image of Korvat on the main viewscreen. The planet's orbital defense platforms had all been reduced to tumbling clouds of glowing-hot junk. Crimson blooms of fire erupted on the planet's surface. From ops, Kadohata reported, "The planet's surface defenses have been neutralized."

Picard flashed back for a moment to the scenes of devastation he'd witnessed on Tezwa less than two years earlier. Then the damage had been inflicted by Klingons using photon torpedoes; he shuddered to imagine what horrors the Borg had just wrought. *If only we'd been here a few minutes sooner,* he cursed silently as the situation unfolded around him.

"The Borg are locking weapons on the planet's capital," Choudhury said. Then she added with surprise, "The *Gibraltar*'s maneuvering into their firing solution!"

Everyone on the *Enterprise*'s bridge turned their eyes to the main viewscreen as the other *Sovereign*-class ship positioned itself between the Borg cube and its target, rolling to present as broad a barrier as possible. A searing beam of sickly green energy from the cube slammed into the *Gibraltar* just behind its deflector dish. The *Gibraltar*'s shields collapsed, and the green energy beam ripped into its underside. Fissures spiderwebbed across its exterior, spread through its elliptical saucer section, and buckled the pylons of its warp nacelles. Vermillion flames and jets of super-heated gas erupted from broad cracks in its hull. Picard winced as if he were watching his own ship fall beneath a mortal blow.

Then a flash of white light filled the screen, and when it faded seconds later, the *Gibraltar* was gone.

"We're in firing range," Choudhury said. "Locking weapons."

"Fire at will," Worf said.

On the screen, a quartet of brilliant blue projectiles raced toward the Borg cube as it fired again at Korvat's capital city. The *Alexey Leonov* tried to emulate the *Gibraltar*'s self-sacrifice, only to be picked off by a dense fusillade from the Borg cube. Another blinding flare whited-out the main viewer.

All four of the *Enterprise*'s transphasic torpedoes found their target. Even as they broke the Borg cube into pieces and consumed them in blue fire, the Borg got off one last shot—a massive pulse of emerald-hued energy that arrowed down through Korvat's atmosphere and laid waste to its capital.

Two fire clouds blossomed like obscene flowers on the screen in front of Picard, who for the second time in one day bore witness to a burning world and its dispersing black halo of collateral damage.

Worf left his chair and prowled from station to station. "Commander Kadohata, scan the planet's surface for survivors."

The svelte second officer tapped at her console and sighed. Her dry, Port Shangri-la accent leached the emotion from her voice as she reported, "Isolated life signs in a number of highland regions and on a few antarctic islands." She filtered the data on her screens. "I'm reading roughly twenty-nine thousand people left alive on the surface, sir." Picard appreciated her artful omission, her choice to emphasize the number of survivors rather than confirm the deaths of more than ten million people. Then she continued, "Toxins in the atmosphere and water are spreading rapidly. If the survivors aren't evacuated in the next seventy-two hours, they'll receive lethal doses of theta radiation."

"Lieutenant Choudhury," Worf said, "send Starfleet Command a priority request for evacuation transports."

Kadohata turned from her station to look at Worf. "Shouldn't we start rescuing them ourselves?"

"We do not have room for that many refugees," Worf said. "We also have nowhere to relocate them to."

The slim human woman looked back and forth in frustration between Worf and the captain. "So we're just going to leave those people there?"

Picard replied, "We have other mission priorities, Commander." He looked away from Kadohata's accusing stare and said to Choudhury, "Any reports from the other four targets?"

"Starbase 234 was destroyed," she said, "but it looks like they took the Borg down with them. Khitomer's safe—thanks to a kamikaze attack by the *Ranger*." Glancing at her console, she added, "The battles at Starbases 157 and 343 are still in progress." She frowned. "Starbase 157 is sending a Mayday, sir."

Against his better judgment, Picard said, "On speaker."

Crackles of static, wails of feedback noise . . . and then panicked shouts over the cries of the dying and the erratic percussion of explosions. "*. . . phasers overloaded . . .*" More static. "*. . . hit them with everything we've got . . . still coming . . .*" A scratch of deep-space background radiation noise. "*. . . all power . . . can't break our shields . . .*" A screech and a high-frequency tone pitched in and out on a long oscillation. "*. . . coming right at us! They're on a ramming trajectory!*"

A long, loud burst of noise was followed by silence.

"They're gone," Choudhury said, her eyes downcast as she closed the channel.

An incoming signal chirruped on Kadoháta's console. She reviewed it in a glance and reported, "Priority message from the *Excalibur,* sir. They're signaling all-clear at Starbase 343."

Choudhury looked perplexed at the news. "How'd they stop the Borg without using transphasic torpedoes?"

"With a miracle, Lieutenant," Picard said with dry humor. "That's Captain Calhoun's ship. I've learned to expect the impossible from him and his crew." He shook his head as he thought of the hotheaded young Xenexian man he'd coaxed into Starfleet all those years ago—and the unorthodox, nigh-infamous starship commander he'd become.

From an auxiliary console, the *Enterprise*'s half-Vulcan, half-human contact specialist and relief flight controller T'Ryssa Chen heaved a tired sigh. "I'm just glad it's over."

Her comment rankled Picard. "Glad *what's* over, Lieutenant?"

The young woman recoiled from Picard's curt response, as usual favoring the human half of her ancestry over the Vulcan. Her reply was hesitant and uncertain. "The invasion. The Borg cubes were destroyed."

Picard knew that he had to make the situation clear to Chen, and to anyone else who might have made the same, misguided assumption about the outcome of the battle they'd just fought.

"This isn't over," he said to her. "It's only begun." He got up from his chair and made a slow turn as he continued. "The Borg have been planning this invasion for years, and it won't end as easily as this. They're going to keep coming—hammering us every day, week after week, for as long as it takes . . . until we, or they, are gone."

His officers watched him with grim, resolute expressions as he revealed what he'd learned in his latest brush with the Collective. "This is a clash of civilizations," he explained, "and it will end when one of us falls."

12

———•———

Tuvok found the zero-gravity environment of *Titan*'s stellar cartography lab inconvenient but manageable, though he had to suppress a deep, subtle tinge of envy at Lieutenant Commander Pazlar's graceful ease of motion.

Envy. The presence of such a petty emotion shamed him, despite being known to no one but himself. Over the years his control of his emotions had been degraded by one incident after another. It had started years earlier, with a mind meld to his *Voyager* crewmate Lon Suder, a Betazoid man who also had been a violent sociopath. In his effort to stabilize the homicidal Suder, Tuvok had almost unhinged himself.

Other traumas—including a period of brutal incarceration on Romulus before he'd joined the crew of *Titan*—had exacerbated Tuvok's difficulties. Most recently, Tuvok's mind had been telepathically hijacked into the service of space-dwelling life-forms known to Starfleet by the nickname "star jellies." While in their control, he had assaulted Pazlar and compromised the ship's security. Under the care of

Counselor Troi, he had begun learning Betazoid techniques for channeling and controlling his emotions, but he remained wary of his feelings and the damage that they could do when he failed to master them.

"I have the next set of projections ready," Pazlar said. The delicate Elaysian reached out, her arms wide, and pulled the holographic image of the galaxy closer, compressing its scale with a balletic drawing together of her palms until they were centimeters apart. She and Tuvok towered like cosmic giants in the midst of the spiral majesty of the Milky Way, which girdled their torsos in a broad band. "That's the source of the signals," she said, pointing out a blinking red pinpoint half a meter in front of them. "And here's a model of the signals' trajectories." She waved dozens of pale-blue beams into existence, all of them emanating in a tight, fan-shaped cluster from the pinpoint and reaching toward Federation space.

"Highlight the segments of those trajectories that fall within Federation space," Tuvok said.

Pazlar sighed. "Sure, since you asked so nicely." She entered the command into the holographic interface, which left an odd pattern of blue lines cutting through a tiny, red-tinted region demarcating Federation territory. "There's no way to tell where any of them terminate," she said as Tuvok patched his padd into the computer and began noting major UFP star systems along the beams' paths. "For all we know, they're looking at another galaxy and we just happen to be in their way."

"That is a possibility," Tuvok said. "However, unless we investigate it, we cannot know for certain." A list of star systems appeared on the screen of his padd. He skimmed it and said to Pazlar, "Please enlarge the map of the Federation."

The simulation zoomed in on the red patch and expanded it until it surrounded them and all but filled the hololab. At that magnification, the angles between the various beams became far more subtle. "There must be dozens of populated systems within a light-year of each pulse," Pazlar said.

"Eighty-three, to be precise," Tuvok said, correcting her careless approximation. "However, I propose that we can limit our search to a specific region." He transmitted a set of data to the computer, and it appeared in the simulation as a dense cluster of yellow dots in a corner of the three-dimensional map. "Magnify, please." He waited until Pazlar had enlarged that isolated region, and then continued, "The recent Borg incursions into Federation space have all occurred along the border between the Klingon Empire and the Federation, from Acamar to Ramatis." Pointing at the lone bold, blue streak that cut through the image, he added, "If these energy pulses are being used by the Borg, then this would likely be their conduit."

"I don't see any populated star systems near it," she said. "But if its terminus opens in interstellar space, that might explain why Starfleet hasn't been able to locate it."

"Possibly," Tuvok said. He paused as he traced the beam's path through the cloudy stain of the Azure Nebula. A tiny detail snared his attention. Pointing at the nebula's center, he said, "Magnify again, please." Pazlar reached out and cupped the nebula in both hands, then she spread her hands and arms apart, instantly ballooning the gaseous cluster to dozens of times its previous size. The narrow beam of blue light cut straight through an astrocartographic marker. "Most curious," Tuvok said.

"That's one way of putting it," Pazlar said, eyeing the image with surprise and wonder. "It passes right through that supernova remnant." She chuckled. "If the Borg are using that beam as some kind of subspace passage, that remnant's the end of the line. Even in subspace, if they hit that, they'd be dead."

"Indeed," Tuvok said. "And if that is their entry point into Federation space, the radiation from the remnant and the nebula would provide them with excellent cover from the region's sensor network." He arched one eyebrow in satisfaction. "We should inform the captain immediately."

Pazlar mumbled, "Mm-hm," and she began entering a new series of commands into the hololab's interface.

Tuvok watched her for a moment, expecting her to explain her sudden burst of activity and inspiration. After several seconds, he concluded that the intensely focused and independent-minded science officer was not going to volunteer such information. He would have to ask her for it.

"What are you doing?"

"Setting up new parameters for the simulation," she said, still keying in commands. "Seeing that beam run smack into the supernova remnant got me thinking: We cast the net too wide."

"Explain," Tuvok said.

She made some minor adjustments via the interface as she answered him. "Well, instead of looking for all the systems that fall within a certain range of the beams, why not just look for the ones that actually intersect? In other words, ignore the near misses and just look for the direct hits. It's bound to yield fewer results, and if what we saw in the nebula's any indicator, they might be a lot more relevant."

"An interesting hypothesis. How long will it take to run the new simulation if you include all known galactic points?"

"Another hour," she said, "but I think it'll be worth it."

"Very well," he said. "Computer," Tuvok said, "platform." He felt the gentle tug of a tractor beam nudge him toward the circular platform below him and Pazlar. He could have navigated his way out of the zero-*g* environment with minimal difficulty, but because of his lack of recent experience with free fall, the effort might have taken him a few minutes, and he was eager to meet with the captain and continue his work. Allowing the computer to facilitate his exit from stellar cartography was both logical and expedient.

His feet touched down on the platform, and the tractor beam gradually released him into the low-gravity zone. He looked up at Pazlar, who hovered several meters above him. "Notify me when the results are ready for analysis," he said. "I will continue my research in science lab one after I've informed the captain of our discovery."

"Aye, sir," Pazlar said. Then she returned to her work, and Tuvok walked toward the exit. As the hatch to the corridor opened, he stole a look back at Pazlar, floating free in her faux heavens, manipulating millions of ersatz stars with waves of her hands, blissfully submerged in her labors.

As he departed into the corridor, Tuvok struggled once again to extinguish that same troubling spark of envy.

Dr. Shenti Yisec Eres Ree paced on taloned feet, awaiting his patient's arrival in sickbay. Delivering bad news had never been a pleasant experience for him, and he had found it was often best done as soon as possible and with little or no preamble. All the same, he despised the task. He had considered letting the matter lie until morning, rather than forcing himself to remain awake well into his regular sleep period. Then he had seen the report, realized its importance, and issued his urgent summons.

Caught up in his tests and his analysis, he had missed the scheduled hour for the crew's carnivores to dine in the mess hall. Hunger burned in his gut, so intensely that he could almost taste the raw meat and the fresh marrow he craved. Despite the lateness of the hour, he knew that he could still use the mess hall and eat as he liked, but he would miss the camaraderie of his fellow flesh-eaters. The omnivores and herbivores on *Titan* had grown accustomed to witnessing the bloody feeding spectacle of carnivores playing with their food, though the majority of them remained discomfited by the idea of sitting in proximity to it while consuming their own meals.

Too bad, Ree decided. *They'll just have to deal with it. A little bit of splatter never hurt anyone.*

The door sighed open and Counselor Troi walked in, attired in civilian clothes. She was bleary-eyed from being woken up, and she appeared anxious, clenching her right hand into a fist and cupping it in her left hand. "You said it was urgent?"

"Yes, Counselor," Ree said. He turned and led her toward his private office. "Please come in and sit down."

She shook her head. "I'd rather stand."

"As you prefer." He continued inside his office and waited until she was inside before he closed the door for privacy. As it closed, it shifted from transparent to translucent, along with the windows that looked out on sickbay. "I've finished my tests. I'm sorry to say the news isn't good."

Laying a hand on her belly, she asked, "You know why this is happening?"

He bobbed his long, therapodian head in a rough imitation of a nod. "I do." He reached over to his desk and scooped up a data padd with his long, clawed fingers. "According to your medical history, sixteen years ago, on Stardate 42073, you became pregnant after contact with an unidentified alien being composed of energy. Hours later, you gave birth to a son."

Tears rolled from Troi's eyes. "Ian," she said.

"Yes." Reviewing her file, he continued, "The boy matured at a remarkable rate—approximately eight years in a single day. At the same time, a sample of plasma plague supposedly in stasis started to grow, its development accelerated by a field of Eichner radiation—the source of which was your son, Ian."

Troi covered her mouth as if to hold back a cry of alarm. Her eyes were shining with tears, and her voice was a throaty gasp through her fingers. "No, please don't tell me . . ."

"I'm sorry, Counselor," Ree said. "But you should know all the facts." He handed her the padd. She took it in one shaking hand and stared at it while he continued. "Research conducted a few years ago at the Vulcan Science Academy showed that sustained exposure to Eichner radiation can cause erratic mutations in mitochondrial DNA. For the purpose of their study, 'sustained' exposure was defined as anything longer than four hours. You gestated Ian for more than thirty-six hours."

She covered her face with her hands. "No," she said through a keening cry. Struggling for control, she said, "Dr. Pulaski said there were no complications. She said all my readings were as if I'd never been pregnant."

Ree bowed his head a moment. "Her exam was as accurate as it could have been," he said, looking up. "But she relied on hormonal data and basic cellular analysis. The damage occurred on a much deeper and more subtle level."

The counselor's stance became unsteady, so Ree took her gently by the shoulders and eased her into a chair beside his desk. She was all but imploding in front of him.

"Forgive me," he said. "There's more." The data padd started to fall from her hand, and he plucked it gingerly from her grasp. "The Eichner radiation caused subtle, random genetic defects in all of your unreleased ova."

Troi peeked out from behind her hands. "But you can fix that, can't you? Reconstruct the genetic sequence . . . ?"

Where a human might have sighed, Ree stifled a low, rasping growl. "No, I can't," he said. "If it were a single, uniform mutation, I might have been able to extract an ovum, resequence its chromosomes, fertilize it in vitro, and reimplant it. But that's not what has happened here." He keyed up a screen of visual guides on the padd to illustrate his point. "The damage to your ovaries hasn't resulted merely in *corrupted* genetic information. It's also led to *lost* information. It would have been extremely difficult to resequence a mutated ova without a healthy specimen as a template. I wouldn't know where to begin filling in the blanks of an incomplete chromosome."

The half-Betazoid woman bowed her head into her hands and wept. All that Ree could do was sit in silence and let her cry. Though he found the parasitic nature of mammalian pregnancy to be unnerving, he understood the profound sense of connection that it created between female mammals and their young. *This would be so much easier if she were a Pahkwa-thanh,* he thought sadly. Among his kind, when an egg failed to hatch, its mother would break it open and devour both young and yolk, to conserve resources and provide for the next offspring. *So much simpler than stillbirth,* he reasoned. *Not to mention cathartic.*

After a few minutes, Troi ceased her lamentations and calmed herself. Wiping tears from her reddened eyes, she asked, "What's my prognosis, then, Doctor?"

"That depends on the actions you take. Are you asking for my recommendation?"

"Yes, I am."

He scrolled to the final page of information on the padd and handed it back to Troi. "As your physician, I advise you to terminate your pregnancy immediately. The fetus is not viable, and if it's not removed, I predict its growth will rupture your uterine wall and cause a potentially fatal hemorrhage."

"When?"

"I'm not certain. It could be tomorrow, or next month."

Troi's expression was grave and distant. "What are the odds of this happening with my next pregnancy?"

Medical ethics compelled him to tell her the truth. "Almost certain," he said. "My medical opinion is that the odds of you and Captain Riker having a healthy offspring are negligible, and I would recommend you cease trying. Since the damage to your ova cannot be repaired . . ." He hesitated, and was sorry that he'd let the first half of the sentence leave his tongue. He felt as if he had failed her, though he knew that he had done everything he could.

"What?" prompted Troi. "Since it can't be repaired . . . what?"

Ree turned away a moment, then decided to finish what he'd started. "I'd recommend a radical hysterectomy, Counselor. To prevent further failed pregnancies, and to protect you from the risk of future oncological complications."

She looked stunned, as if he had just hammered her with a whack of his long, muscular tail. He waited for her to say something. Instead she turned her face away from him and blinked slowly a couple of times. Then she got up and moved to leave.

"Counselor," he said. "We should schedule your procedure before you go."

Troi ignored him. She got up and made her exit; his office door and windows reverted to their normal, transparent state as the portal slid open. She crossed sickbay at a hurried pace and was out the door without a look back at the concerned surgeon.

Her refusal of his medical advice put him in a precarious position. Ree had no doubt that Troi would have the support of the captain, and that Riker would obstruct any effort he might make to exert his medical authority for Troi's own good. Worse, he was appalled at the idea of performing a surgical procedure on a patient against her will. In his opinion it would be little different from assault, his good intentions notwithstanding.

On the other hand, his responsibilities as *Titan*'s chief medical officer were unambiguous and defined in stark terms by Starfleet regulations and the Starfleet Code of Military Justice. He could not, either by action or omission of action, allow personnel under his medical charge to bring themselves to harm or to death—and by law he was empowered to protect them, if need be, from themselves. The counselor's disregard for her own safety had made this his responsibility.

The fact that his patient was the captain's wife made the situation rather more incendiary than he was accustomed to, however. If he was going to make a stand, he would need to make certain he wouldn't be standing alone.

He sealed the door of his office and reset the windows to their frosted privacy mode. Then he used the companel on his desk to open a secure, person-to-person channel to the one individual he most needed to be certain he could trust.

"Ree to Commander Vale."

The first officer answered moments later. *"Yes, Doctor?"*

"We need to talk. In private."

Tuvok didn't need to look up from his work to know who had just entered the science lab behind him. Heavy, rapid footfalls and a faint hint of an obscure Risan cologne had told him who it was. "Good evening, Mister Keru."

"Pazlar says you two found something," said the Trill chief of security.

"Her report may have been premature," Tuvok said. "I am still conducting my analysis."

Keru sidled up to Tuvok and eyed the starmaps on several adjacent monitors. "Tuvok, you've definitely got something here. Fill me in—I want to know whatever you can tell me about this."

It was clear to Tuvok that Keru would not be willing to wait for his official report at the start of the next shift. He suppressed a surge of negative emotions and pointed out details as he spoke. "Lieutenant Commander Pazlar suggested that we narrow our investigation to those energy pulses that directly intersect known star systems. As she suspected, very few systems satisfy that criterion." He began augmenting the images on the screens with illustrative overlays. "The first, which led us to this method, is a remnant of the supernova that created the Azure Nebula. So far, we've identified three others." Pointing from each monitor to the next, he continued, "An uncharted system in the Delta Quadrant. A periphery system in globular cluster Messier 80. And an unnamed system in the Gamma Quadrant."

"What about the other energy pulses?" Keru asked. "There had to be dozens of them."

"If we assume that each one is targeted at a specific star or planet, then the remaining pulses appear to be focused on subjects outside of our galaxy."

A dubious look creased Keru's brow. "What if *we* have assumed wrong? What if the pulses are passageways that open in deep space, away from prying eyes?"

"Then we would need to modify our research accordingly."

Keru narrowed his eyes and lowered his chin, signaling his apparent displeasure with Tuvok's answer. "All right, then," he said. "Let's examine the facts in hand. Have you uncovered any connections between these four locations?"

"I have found no direct connections," Tuvok replied.

Displaying the interrogatory style that had served him so well as a security officer, Keru asked, "What about *indirect* connections? Or suspicious coincidences?"

"I had hoped to conduct a more thorough investigation before sharing my initial discoveries," Tuvok said, "in part because I am not yet convinced that they are relevant, to either the phenomenon ahead of us, or to the crisis currently unfolding within the Federation."

His attention fully engaged, Keru pushed, "So you did find some kind of link?"

"Possibly," Tuvok said. He changed the images on one of the monitors. "The beam intersection in the

Gamma Quadrant falls inside a star system where, eight years ago, the *Starship Defiant* discovered the wreckage of the Earth ship *Columbia*."

"I read about that," Keru said. "It went missing right before the Earth-Romulan war."

"Correct," Tuvok said, and he pointed at the monitor showing the first intersection point. "They vanished in 2156, while traveling from the Onias Sector with a convoy near this supernova remnant, which at that time was a main-sequence star."

Visibly intrigued, Keru asked, "When did it supernova?"

"In 2168," Tuvok said. "Which is most unusual, because main-sequence stars typically expand and cool for billions of years before such an event."

Now the security chief looked puzzled. "And what's the connection between that and the beams hitting those points now?"

"I do not know," Tuvok replied.

Keru was animated with enthusiasm for the mystery. "Is it possible these beams had something to do with how the *Columbia* got to the Gamma Quadrant? Could *Columbia* have made it out here, only to get tossed all the way across the galaxy?"

"Anything is possible, Mister Keru," Tuvok said. "Sensor readings made by *Defiant* indicated that the *Columbia*'s hull had been subjected to extreme subspatial stresses before it crashed. Consequently, the Starfleet vessel *Aventine* was dispatched over a week ago to recover the wreck for analysis."

The burly, bearded Trill leaned over Tuvok's shoulder to skim the mission reports about the downed *Columbia*. "Those subatomic fractures in the hull are pretty intense," he said. "Any theories on what could've done that?"

"There are some hypotheses," Tuvok said. "Including a few that bear pronounced similarities to the phenomenon we are now moving to investigate."

Keru nodded. "I'll bet." He folded his arms and leaned back from the bank of computer screens. "So, what about that beam intersection in the Delta Quadrant? Is it inside Borg space?"

"Not as such," Tuvok said. "But it falls very close to the known limits of their conquered territory. It would take them only a matter of weeks to reach it without the benefit of their transwarp network."

"Then this is a whole lot of coincidences," Keru said. "A mysterious power source with an energy profile that resembles transwarp, shooting beams that point at Federation space, Borg space, and a planet in the Gamma Quadrant where an old Earth ship has been sitting for nearly two centuries."

Tuvok arched one eyebrow to convey his incredulity. "I understand your zeal to draw links between the phenomenon and the recent Borg incursions into Federation space. However, I fail to see the relevance, if any, of the disappearance and rediscovery of a twenty-second-century Earth starship."

A crooked grimace tugged at Keru's mouth, though it was hard to see his expression behind his beard. "Yeah," he said, "I'm drawing a blank on that, too. I feel like that ship has to fit into this somehow—that it's not just a random fluke that it's sitting on a planet with one of these beams pointed at it. But I'll be damned if I can see the connection."

Tuvok sighed softly. "Indeed."

———————◆———————

Riker's eyelids fluttered and drooped with fatigue. Catching himself sinking into sleep, he jolted awake at his desk with a shudder. It was late, almost 0400, and his body craved sleep.

He took another sip from his third mug of half-sweet *raktajino* and savored the tingle of its caffeine infusing his bloodstream. Then he realized that he'd started drifting off again—he'd been dreaming of himself enjoying the Klingon coffee. He shuddered awake and sipped his now-tepid beverage for real.

His ready room's door signal chimed. Wiping the itch of exhaustion from his eyes, he said, "Come in."

The door opened and Christine Vale entered. He recalled the awkwardness of their last private meeting, several hours earlier, and he straightened his posture as she approached.

"Sorry to bother you so late," she said, "but since we're both up, I decided not to put this off."

That didn't sound good. "Put what off?"

Vale sat down in one of the chairs on the other side of his desk. "I just met with Dr. Ree. He's worried about Deanna."

Suspicion edged into Riker's voice, despite his efforts to remain calm. "I know about his concerns. Why is he discussing my wife's medical condition with *you*?"

"Because you and Deanna have made this into a crew-safety issue," Vale said. "Regulations require him to intervene—and they give him the authority to do so."

"I still don't see what—"

"And if he makes it an order, I'm required to enforce it," Vale cut in. "Whether you like it or not."

He was out of his chair and pacing like a caged animal. "Dammit, Chris, we talked about this a few hours ago. I'm not letting him force her to terminate her pregnancy."

She remained calm and seated. "It'd be best for everyone if it didn't come to that. If she doesn't have the procedure now, she'll need to have it when she becomes incapacitated. Except then there's a chance she'll die." Vale got up and stepped into Riker's path, disrupting his frantic back-and-forth. "Why let it come to that? Can't you talk to her?"

"No," Riker admitted. "I can't." He sighed. "I don't know what to say, and she wouldn't want to hear it if I did." Faced with the hopelessness of the situation, he turned away to gaze out the ready room's window. "She's not stupid, Chris—and she's not crazy. She knows her life's in danger, but that's not enough to change her mind." He stared at his dim reflection and realized it made him look the same as he felt—like he was only half there, half the man he used to be. "Our first miscarriage hit her so hard," he continued. "I think she just can't stand the idea of losing another baby."

Vale nodded. "I understand, Will. I really do. But if she's in that much distress, should she still be on active duty? And if her grief, or her depression, or whatever she's struggling with . . . if it's so overwhelming that she can't take action to save her own life, is she really fit to be making medical decisions?"

"Maybe not," Riker said. He turned from the window to face Vale. "But I am."

The first officer steeled her gaze. "Are you, sir? Do you really think you can be completely objective about this?"

"I don't need to be objective," Riker said. "I'm in command, and I'm not letting Ree force this on her."

"I see," Vale said, her temper starting to show. "This is *exactly* the kind of conflict of interest I was worried about when you told me your wife would be part of your command team. You promised me that your personal feelings wouldn't get in the way when it came to ship's business. But the first time there's a tug-of-war between what she wants and what the regs demand, the book goes out the window, doesn't it?"

Riker shot back, "This isn't about ship's business! We're talking about my wife's health, and maybe her life!"

"What if she collapses in the middle of a crisis situation? Have you thought about that?" He tried to turn away, but she kept after him, putting herself in front of him, hectoring him with increasing fury. "What if we're in combat, or handling an emergency, and she starts bleeding out? You think you'll be at your best when that happens? Think you'll stay focused on the mission when your baby's dying and taking her with it?"

He bellowed, "That's *enough!*" The force of his voice silenced Vale's harangue and made her take a step back. "I know what's at stake here, Chris—I don't need you to lecture me. Do I know my unborn child's going to die? *Yes.* Do I know that Deanna's risking her life by not ending the pregnancy? *Yes.* Am I going to let Dr. Ree force a solution on her? *No.*" His face and ears felt feverishly warm. "If the doctor overrules me and makes the surgery compulsory, Deanna won't comply. If he declares me unfit for command, I'll refuse to step down. Then you can put me in the brig—and decide for yourself how *you* feel about terminating a woman's pregnancy against her will."

The captain and first officer regarded each other in a tense standoff for several seconds. Vale's eyes burned with resentment. She took a breath, calmed a bit, and seemed to be searching for the right words with which to reply.

Then a deep shudder of impact resonated through the deck and bulkheads, and a jolt of arrested motion hurled Riker to the deck as Vale slammed against the side of his desk. Darkness hiccuped in and out for a few seconds before settling on them. Outside the ready room's window, the slow pull of warp-distorted starlight had vanished, replaced by a static starfield. As the captain struggled back to his feet, dim emergency lights snapped on overhead and at regular intervals along the bottoms of the bulkheads. Vale clutched her ribs and had trouble straightening her posture. Riker asked, "You all right?"

"Just bruised," she said, and she glanced toward the door to the bridge. "I guess we ought to go see what happened."

"Might be a good idea," he said, patting her shoulder as he stepped past her.

She followed him and said, "You know we're not done talking about this, right?"

"I know," Riker said. "One thing at a time, though."

They stepped back onto the bridge, him first and her close behind, and found the gamma-shift team shaken and still out of sorts. Lieutenant Commander

Fo Hachesa, the gamma-shift officer of the watch, was about to sit down in the center seat when he saw Riker and Vale. "Captain," said the trim, muscular Kobliad, "we've lost warp drive and main power."

"I've gathered that," Riker said. "What caused it?"

"The source of those energy bursts we've been tracking," Hachesa said, worry lines creasing on either side of his broad naso-cranial ridge. He nodded to the young Cardassian officer at the ops console. "Ensign Dakal picked up a high-power sensor beam directed at us from the energy source. On the chance it might be a Borg early warning system, I had Lieutenant Rriarr raise shields." The golden-furred Caitian at the security console nodded in confirmation to the captain and first officer. Hachesa gestured to the other side of the bridge, where a Benzite engineering officer stood at an auxiliary companel. "Ensign Meldok is analyzing what hit us after we raised shields."

Riker nodded once to Meldok. "Ensign? Any damage?"

"Yes, sir," the Benzite replied, with seemingly misplaced enthusiasm. "A broad-spectrum, high-nutation sensor pulse caused degenerative feedback loops in our warp field and shield grid, collapsing both in point-zero-zero-four seconds. I am still running diagnostics on all systems, but preliminary results suggest serious damage to our subspace communications array and weapons grid, and main power is offline. There may also be coil failures in the warp nacelles."

Vale asked Rriarr, "Casualty report?"

"Minor injuries in engineering," Rriarr said.

The captain nodded. "Understood. Commander Hachesa, carry on with repairs and keep Commander

Vale informed of your progress. Let me know as soon as we have warp speed."

"Aye, sir," Hachesa said.

Riker looked at Vale and gestured with a subtle tilt of his head that she should follow him. He led her off the bridge, into the turbolift. The doors closed and he said, "Deck Five."

"Deck Six," Vale added. As the turbolift began its descent, she quipped, "Hachesa finally got the hang of verbs, I see."

Riker grinned as he recalled the well-meaning Kobliad's propensity for mangled conjugations. "Took him long enough." He folded his arms and looked at his shoes. "I'll try and talk to Deanna. Tonight, if she's awake, in the morning if she's not. I can't promise she'll change her mind, but maybe we can find a compromise."

Vale nodded. "I'll ask Dr. Ree for more options."

They rode together in silence until the turbolift stopped, and the doors parted to reveal the Deck Five main corridor. Riker stepped out. Before the doors closed, Vale stepped between them to hold the lift. "Am I the only one who finds it hard to believe we just got our ass kicked by a *sensor beam*?"

Riker cocked his head. "What are you saying?"

"That I don't think what that beam did to us was an accident. Think about it: Someone or something goes to a lot of trouble to black out a whole star system. We start flying toward it, pelting it with sensor sweeps, and what happens? It knocks us out of warp, frags our weapons, and fries our comms. If you ask me, I'd say whatever's out there doesn't want to meet us, and it doesn't want us talking about it to anyone else."

Riker couldn't help himself. He grinned. "Then it shouldn't have messed with my ship—because now I'm *really* curious."

"You and the cat, sir." She smirked back at him.

He chuckled softly. "Go get some sleep. I get the feeling tomorrow's gonna be a very busy day."

2168

13

Veronica Fletcher popped her head around the corner from the foyer and said to Erika Hernandez, "We're ready, Captain."

Hernandez lifted her feet from a reasonable facsimile of an ottoman and got up from the wraparound sofa that bordered three sides of the penthouse suite's sunken main room. She climbed the few stairs in quick steps and passed the open dining area. It was well stocked with fruits and a wide variety of faithfully re-created Earth foodstuffs. Before she left, she stole another look at the warm, natural light slanting through the suite's panoramic windows, which rose to great arches near the vaulted ceilings. As gilded prisons went, this one, intended for her and the rest of the landing party, was truly first-rate.

She joined Fletcher in the foyer and followed her out to the floor's central corridor, where a transparent pod waited for them in an alcove. They stepped inside. It began a swift descent, devoid of any sensation of movement, into a glowing shaft of pale, pulsing rings. In seconds they emerged into what seemed like thin air, dropping in a controlled manner toward a pool of water shimmering with rippled sunlight.

The towers of the city surrounded them, and through slivers between the platinum spires, Hernandez caught flashes of the jagged mountaintops in the west. Peach-colored clouds were pulled taut across the sky.

"It really is a beautiful city," Fletcher said.

Hernandez allowed herself a tired grin. "Nice place to visit. Wouldn't want to live here."

Their pod touched down on the surface of the water without so much as a ripple. The dancing sparkle of sunlight on wind-teased water transformed into a dull glow of reflected illumination on a solid, matte surface, and the pod itself sublimated and dissipated into the hot summer air.

Fletcher led the way across a sprawling plaza paved with white marble. Hulking granite sculptures and massive, flowering topiaries depicted alien creatures unlike any the captain had ever seen before.

At its far end, flanked by densely grown trees, was a rectangular reflecting pool. Its surface was serene and black, and it cast razor-sharp reflections of everything in sight. At its farthest end, a tall, thick-trunked, droop-boughed tree stood on a low, wide island of earth, whose mossy shores reached to within a meter of the low wall that bordered the pool.

The rest of the landing party was gathered in a cluster on the miniature island in the shade of the tree, crouched like ancient primates wary of abandoning their arboreal redoubts.

Fletcher and Hernandez hopped across the narrow channel of water to the tree's island and slipped into the middle of the huddle. Hernandez folded her arms across her bent knees. "What did we learn?"

Before anyone else could speak, Major Foyle asked, "Captain, are we sure it's safe to talk here?"

"Why wouldn't it be, Major?"

He looked at the other MACOs and then replied, "What if we're being monitored?"

Fletcher fielded the question. "If the Caeliar want to listen in, I don't think it matters where we go in this city. Or on this planet, to be honest. With technology like theirs, I don't think we could stop them."

"Then maybe we shouldn't make plans verbally," Foyle said. "Maybe we should do it all in writing and destroy the notes."

Hernandez exhaled sharply. "They know about Earth, they've accessed the *Columbia*'s computers, and they speak English without translation devices. I think they can probably read our writing. So let's just get on with it, shall we?"

"As you wish, Captain," said Foyle. "But I object to this unnecessary risk to our operational security."

"Noted," Hernandez said, hopeful that she'd heard the last of Foyle's paranoia. "You spoke up first, so why don't you make your report first? How's our access to the Caeliar's city?"

"Almost unlimited," Foyle said, and he nodded to Yacavino, his second-in-command, to continue.

"Our men had no trouble coming or going from our residence tower," Yacavino said. "The Caeliar admitted us without search or challenge to a variety of spaces, both indoors and outdoors."

Hernandez nodded. "Good. At least we have mobility."

"Until they decide to take it away," injected Sergeant Pembleton. "All they have to do is turn off our see-through elevators and we'll be stuck in that four-star penitentiary."

"One problem at a time," the captain said. She looked to her first officer. "Veronica, what did you and Dr. Metzger find out about our hosts?"

Fletcher arched her eyebrows and frowned, as if she found her own report hard to believe. "They can change shapes."

Metzger added, "And they can turn into vapor or liquid."

"Change shapes?" Hernandez threw a quizzical look at Metzger and Fletcher. "Can you be more specific about that?"

The *Columbia*'s middle-aged surgeon pushed her short, gray bangs from her forehead and replied, "I saw them get larger and smaller, change from bipeds to quadrupeds—one of them even seemed to think it was funny to mimic the two of us down to the last detail."

The first officer nodded. "It was impressive," she said. "And a bit troubling, to be honest."

"That's an understatement," Hernandez said. "They can impersonate us?"

Fletcher waved her hand. "Not our behavior, just our appearance and voices. They don't seem to have any sense of personalities."

"Thank heaven for small mercies," Foyle quipped. He added, "Though what worries me is their ability to levitate."

Around the huddle, several heads nodded, and Hernandez's was among them. "Do we know how they do it?"

"Yes, sir," Fletcher said. "Catoms."

"I'm sorry, could you repeat that?"

Graylock cut in, "Claytronic atoms—also called programmable matter. They're like nanomachines, but more complex, and a lot more powerful. Bonded together, they operate on a human scale instead of a microscopic one. They can change their density, energy levels, a whole range of properties. Teams in Japan and the United States made a few prototypes about ninety years ago. Proof-of-concept models. It was all very primitive, never made it out of the lab. It was supposed to change telepresence, but it was scrapped after the last world war."

Hernandez asked, "And this is the same thing?"

"*Nein*," Graylock said, stifling a laugh. "What we had was a spark. *This* is a supernova. They can change their mass, their state, anything—all on a whim."

That made the captain think. "What's their power source?"

Graylock shook his head. "They wouldn't say. I'd guess it's an energy field generated at a remote facility."

"Let's make identifying that energy source a priority," Hernandez said. She looked to Foyle. "Did you or your men find any access to the underground regions of the city?"

"No," Foyle said. "On the surface we moved freely. But there's no sign of any way into the guts of this thing. Of course, we've had only a few days to search. It's a big place."

"True." The captain turned to her communications specialist. "Sidra, what's your take on Caeliar culture?"

Valerian pondered the question a moment. "Complicated," she said. "They don't seem to mind answering questions, which helps. A lot of the public spaces I've seen have been dedicated to the arts—mostly music and singing, but also some dance and visual performance art. They used to have narrative arts like theater and literature, but they fell out of favor a long time ago."

Fletcher asked, "How long?"

"Maybe a few thousand years," Valerian said. "They also don't seem to have anything resembling economics, and there's no agricultural production or animal husbandry that I could find."

"What about politics?" asked Hernandez.

The Scottish woman shrugged. "They have a ruling body here in Axion called a Quorum, with members from each of their cities, but they're all picked by lottery. I'm not sure how often they hold lotteries, but no one campaigns for it."

A balmy breeze carried the scent of green things and flowers in bloom, but made no ripples on the reflecting pool. Hernandez wondered if she was the only one who noticed. She turned her attention back to Valerian. "What else? What are their habits? We know they're pacifists; what else do they believe?"

"They hold art and science in the same esteem," Valerian said. "All the ones I talked to are both artists *and* scientists. One who makes mosaics in the plaza is also an astronomer; one who composed a symphony I heard is also a physicist."

Crichlow, a MACO from Liverpool, said, "They're also really polite. And they all seem to know who we are—I mean, these blokes knew me *by name*. Caught me by surprise, it did."

"Me, too," Pembleton said.

"One of them asked me to try sculpting," Graylock added. "Said I should nurture my creativity. But when I asked to learn more about their sciences, he lost interest in my artsy side."

"Our loss, I'm sure," Hernandez said with a grin. "Kiona, did you see anything we could use to send a subspace message back to Earth, or even just a signal up to the ship?"

Thayer shook her head. "Nothing. I tried using my hand scanner in case the scattering field didn't extend inside the city itself, but I think the Caeliar drained its power cell. It's been dead since yesterday."

"Everybody check your gear," Hernandez said. "Weapons, hand scanners, all of it. Quickly."

Hernandez inspected her own equipment while the rest of the landing party did likewise. A minute later, everyone looked up and around with the same flustered, dumbfounded expression. Her inquiry was almost rhetorical: "All drained?" Everyone nodded.

Fletcher tucked her hand scanner back into its belt pouch. "Captain," she said, "it's been almost three days since we contacted the ship. If we don't signal them by 1600 today—"

"I know," Hernandez said. "They have orders to break orbit." She gazed in dismay at the gleaming city. "Except they can't, because the Caeliar are holding them here." She sighed. "I guess all we can do is hope El-Rashad follows orders and doesn't try to send down a rescue team." With one hand she started smoothing out a patch of dirt in the middle of the huddle. "So much for fact-finding. Let's start working on—"

"One more thing, Captain," Major Foyle said. "It might interest you to know that the Caeliar never sleep."

That news silenced the group.

The captain blinked once, slowly. "Never?"

"Assuming they told me the truth," Foyle replied. "I figured they were being so helpful that I might as well ask how much sleep they needed and how often. That's when they told me."

"Well, that's *wonderful* news," Hernandez said with soft sarcasm. "For a moment there, I was afraid our escape would be too easy. Thanks for setting me at ease on *that* point."

Foyle dipped his chin, a half nod. "You're quite welcome."

"Now, let's start talking about—"

Private Steinhauer interrupted in a whisper, "Captain." Everyone looked at the MACO, who flicked his eyes to his right, toward the reflecting pool. "Company."

The group turned to face the pool. In its center, Inyx rose from the black water without a ripple of disturbance on its surface or a drop of moisture on his person. He ascended with an eerie floating quality and a perfect economy of motion. Then, once his body was fully in view, he strode across the pool without seeming to make actual contact with it. Hernandez found the spectacle quite surreal.

As he neared the tree's island, he spread his long, gangly arms and gesticulating tendril-fingers in a pantomime of greeting. "Hello again," he said to the landing party. "Are all of you well? Do you require anything?"

Hernandez stepped out of the tree's dappled shadows to meet the Caeliar at the edge of the tiny island. "Aside from our freedom and a way to contact our ship and our home? No."

His inquiry and her rejoinder had already become a ritual. Since the landing party's arrival, Inyx had visited them twice per day, always asking the same bland question and receiving the same pointed answer in return. It didn't seem to bother him.

"I have important news," Inyx said. "The Quorum has agreed to grant you an audience, Captain. It's a most unprecedented turn of events."

Fletcher grumbled behind Hernandez's ear, "Took them long enough. You've been asking to see them for three days."

The captain ignored her XO's grousing and asked Inyx, "When do they want to talk?"

Inyx reached out toward her with one undulating hand.

"Now, Captain."

At the heart of Axion, concealed by a ring of delicately complex interlocked towers and slashed with stray beams of late-afternoon sunlight, stood an intimidating, colossal pyramid of dark crystal and pristine metal: the Quorum hall.

Inyx stood at the leading edge of the transportation disk that was ferrying him and Hernandez toward the pyramid. She didn't know whether he was guiding the disk or merely riding on it as she was. He did seem more confident in its safety than she was; he was perched on its rim, while she preferred to remain near its center. Like every other conveyance she had used since coming to the alien city, it imparted no sensation of movement—no lurch of acceleration or deceleration—and there was far less air resistance than she would have expected, given the speed at which it traveled.

The disk slowed and drifted at a shallow angle toward a broad opening in the middle of one side of the pyramid. From a distance it had looked to her like a narrow slash in the building's façade, but as she and Inyx were swallowed into the structure's interior, she appreciated how huge it and the pyramid really were.

Somewhere close to what Hernandez guessed was the core of the building, the disk eased into a curved port. As it made contact, Inyx stepped forward. Under his feet, the disk and platform fused into a solid structure with no visible seam.

Hernandez followed her Caeliar guide down a cavernous thoroughfare that cut all the way through the pyramid. In the distance, another narrow, rectangular opening framed a strip of cityscape aglow with daylight. Halfway between her and it, the massive passageway was intersected by another; the two paths formed a cross. Then she became aware of moving faster, as if in a dream, and she realized that she and Inyx were on an inertia-free moving walkway. Within seconds they slowed again and came to a stop at the very center of the intersection.

She looked at Inyx. "Let me guess: Now another disk takes us up to the top of the pyramid."

No sooner had she spoken than the disk started to ascend, through a vertical shaft that hadn't been there a moment before.

Inyx crossed his arms in front of his waist and bowed his head slightly. "I apologize if our civil engineering aesthetic has already grown monotonous for you. If you like, I can task an architect to prepare some surprises for your next visit."

"That won't be necessary," Hernandez said.

They reached the top of the shaft in a blur, slowed just as quickly, and rose the last few meters with languid grace. The sunlight was blinding in the pyramidal Quorum chamber, whose four walls were composed of towering sheets of smoky crystal suspended in delicate frames of white metal.

Four tiers of seating surrounded her, one sloping down from each wall, each suspended more than a dozen meters above the main level, which was open and empty except for her and Inyx. The floor was decorated with a fractal starburst pattern, each grand element echoed in millions of miniature designs. Hernandez strained to see how intricately the pattern had been reduced and surmised that it might well continue to the microscopic level.

A masculine voice resonated in the cathedral-like space. "Welcome, Captain Erika Hernandez." She turned until she saw the speaker, a Caeliar in scarlet raiment, standing in the middle of the lowest row of seats on the eastern tier. He continued, "I am Ordemo Nordal, the *tanwa-seynorral* of the Caeliar."

Hernandez tried to conceal her confusion. "*Tanwa* . . . ?"

Inyx whispered to her, "An idiomatic expression. You might translate it as 'first among equals'. Call him Ordemo."

She nodded her understanding and then addressed Ordemo. "Thank you for meeting with me."

Ordemo's reply was cool and businesslike. "Are your accommodations and provisions acceptable?"

"They are," Hernandez said. "But our captivity is not."

"We regret that such measures are necessary," said Ordemo.

Keeping her anger in check was difficult for Hernandez. "Why are they necessary? We pose no threat to you."

"Your arrival on the surface of Erigol left us little alternative, Captain. As Inyx already told you, we greatly value our privacy. Once it became clear that you were aware of our world, we were forced to choose between banishing you to a distant galaxy and making you our guests. The latter option seemed the more merciful of the two."

Hernandez rolled her eyes and let slip a derisive huff. "Don't take it personally, but we don't see it that way."

"That's not surprising," Ordemo said.

Reining in her temper, Hernandez said, "If it's isolation you want, we can arrange that. I could have your system quarantined. None of our people would ever return."

"Not officially," Ordemo said. "However, in our experience with other species and civilizations, we have often found that telling people not to come here inevitably attracts visitation by those who disregard authority—hardly the sort of guests we'd want to encourage. I'm certain you can understand that."

"Yes, of course," Hernandez said. "But if it's anonymity you want, we could wipe our records of your world from our computers—"

Inyx interrupted, "Forgive me, Captain, but we have already done that. And we have rendered them blind to any new data about our world and star system." When she glowered at the lanky alien, he added, "It seemed to be a sensible precaution."

"Do not be angry with Inyx," Ordemo said. "The decision to tamper with your ship's computers was made by consensus. He only carried out the will of the Quorum."

Diplomacy had never been Hernandez's strong suit, and the Caeliar were making this overture more difficult for her than she had expected. Through gritted teeth she said, "All right." After a deep breath, she continued, "So, if my ship's databanks are clean, and I swear my crew to secrecy, there's no reason you can't let us go on our way."

The *tanwa-seynorral* seemed unconvinced. "Except that when you reached your people, they would expect an explanation for your absence. And you and your crew would still know the truth, Captain. Coaxed by threat or temptation, one of you would talk."

"Then erase our memories!" She knew she was getting desperate, but she had to press on. "We can't reveal what we don't know. With all this crazy technology of yours, I bet you've got something that could whitewash our minds, make us forget we ever saw you. You could erase everything since the ambush of our ship, send us back, make us think we blacked out—"

"And that twelve of your years passed in the interval?" Now the first-among-equals sounded as if he was mocking her. "How would you and your crew react to *that,* Captain? Would you accept a circumstance so bizarre without seeking an explanation? And if you did, who's to say that once taken back to that moment, you wouldn't make the same choice you did before, and set course once again to our world?"

Hernandez felt tired—of arguing, of plotting, of all the little battles that had marked every hour of her command since the ambush. Softening her approach, she said, "You make good points, Ordemo. I really can't refute them, so I won't try. But I just don't understand your motives. You cite this need for privacy as the reason my crew and I are being held prisoner. Why are you so afraid of contact with other races?"

"Our impetus is not fear, Captain," Ordemo said. "It is pragmatism." He looked at Inyx, and Hernandez did likewise.

Inyx turned to her and explained, "When less-advanced species become aware of us and what we can do, they tend to respond with either intense curiosity or savage aggression—and sometimes both. In the past, alien civilizations have inundated us with pleas for succor, expecting us to deliver them from the consequences of their own shortsightedness. Others have tried to steal the secrets of our technologies or force them from us. Because we will not take sentient life, even in self-defense, it became increasingly difficult to discourage these abuses. Some sixty-five thousand of your years ago, we concluded that isolation and secrecy would best serve our great work, so we relocated our cities and people here, to what was, at that time, a relatively untraveled sector of the galaxy. However, the recent development of starflight by several local cultures and your arrival on Erigol have reminded us that while changes are never permanent, change is."

"Yeah, life is hard," Hernandez said to Inyx. "Cry me a river." While the scientist struggled to parse her sarcastic idiom, she aimed her ire at Ordemo. "So let me get this straight: My ship, my crew, and myself are doomed to spend the rest of our days here because you don't like getting hassled?"

The angrier she became, the calmer Ordemo seemed. "It is not quite so simple a matter, Captain. These conflicts tend to escalate, despite our best efforts to contain them. Often, as we take bolder steps to defend ourselves and our sovereignty, several less-developed civilizations will band together out of fear or avarice. When that happens, we often must take . . . extreme measures, up to and including their displacement."

She held up a hand to interrupt him. "Displacement?"

"A shifting, en masse, of an entire civilization and its people, often to another galaxy. To use an analogy from your own world, it's like catching a spider in your home and expelling it to the outdoors rather than killing it." He paused and grew more somber. "It's a tactic we find distasteful and distressing. Having been forced to it in the past, we now choose to conceal ourselves rather than risk provoking another such travesty."

Begging and pleading both had proved ineffective. All that Hernandez could do now was try to lay groundwork for a future opportunity. "If my people and I have to stay here, we'd at least like to get to know more about your culture," she said. "In particular, I'd like to learn more about this thing you keep referring to as 'the great work.'"

Inyx looked up at Ordemo. "With the Quorum's permission?"

"Granted."

"The great work," Inyx said, "is a project that has spanned several millennia and is only now reaching its fruition. Reduced to its core objective, it is our effort to detect, and make contact with, a civilization more advanced than our own."

Hernandez smirked. "Finally . . . something we have in common."

Inyx left the humans' penthouse suite after escorting Captain Erika Hernandez back to her fellow guests. He guided his disk along the outer edge of Axion, to a narrow promontory that extended beyond the city's edge and faced the setting sun.

Sedín, his companion of many aeons, waited for him at the end of the walkway. They met frequently at this place to watch the sky's ephemeral changes. Often they eschewed conversation, having long since run out of anything new to say. Silent presence now passed for friendship between them.

The disk under Inyx's feet melded back into the memory metal of the city, and he stepped onto the walkway and willed it into motion beneath him. It whisked him with speed and precision to within an arm's reach of Sedín, and then it halted. With an ease born of many thousands of years of practice, he strode off the walkway and took his place at Sedín's side.

Beyond the mountains, the ruddy orb of the heavens made its descent, its colors bleeding into the darkness above it.

"You brought the human ship commander to the Quorum," Sedín said, her enunciation neutral but still intimating disapproval.

"She asked to see them," Inyx replied. "They consented."

The sky grew darker and swallowed the jagged silhouette of distant mountaintops. Stars peppered the sky before Sedín spoke again, her affectless manner betraying her disdain.

"They could have been displaced."

Inyx countered that statement of fact with another. "That was not the Quorum's decree."

"I audited the debate through the gestalt," Sedín said. "You shaped that decree. If not for you, they would have been displaced, like all the others. You advocated custody."

"Displacement was not warranted," Inyx argued. "They had no means of communication—"

"I've already heard your justifications," Sedín said. "And I know they swayed the Quorum. The matter is decided."

Darkness swallowed the last glimmers of twilight, and overhead the cold majesty of the galaxy stretched across the dome of the sky. Soon it would be time for Inyx to return to his research for the night, before paying another visit to the humans at daybreak. Tired of the hostility in his discourse with Sedín, he turned to leave.

He paused as she asked, "Why did you bring them here?"

"They came of their own accord," Inyx said, turning back.

"But you secured them permission to make orbit and come to the surface. *You* welcomed them to Erigol. Our *home.*"

In time, Inyx knew, it might be possible to persuade Sedín to let go of her anxiety toward the unknown. That time, however, would not be this night. For now, he could only tell his comrade the truth and hope that it would suffice to postpone the rest of their discussion until the next sunset.

"I argued my conscience," Inyx said. "Nothing more."

Sedín was not appeased. If anything, she sounded more suspicious. "Your conscience? Or your curiosity?"

A new transportation disk appeared beside the end of the platform. Inyx stepped onto it and faced toward the city. He chose to ignore his friend's question—not out of guilt or anger, but because he did not, in fact, know the answer.

He willed the disk forward. "Good night, Sedín."

In the shade of the tree by the pool, violent ideas were taking root.

Most of the landing party was still asleep back at the penthouse suite. The MACOs, however, had risen at dawn, stolen away in silence, and gathered here.

They circled around Major Foyle, who used a green twig snapped from a low branch to draw designs in the rich, black earth of the tree's island.

"Our biggest challenge right now is the scattering field around the city," Foyle said, etching a circle in the dirt. "We can't transport through it, and we can't get signals out."

Lieutenant Yacavino tumbled three small stones in his hand while he stared at the circle Foyle had drawn. "Depending on our objective, we need to either get outside the field or collapse it. It's fifteen klicks to get clear, and we don't even know how to get back to the planet's surface from up here, so I'd suggest we focus on knocking out the field."

"That's a good plan," said Sergeant Pembleton. "Except for the fact that we don't have any power left in our gear."

Foyle waved away the complaint with his twig. "There are ways to fix that," he said. "Worst-case scenario, we can use solar power to recharge the rifles."

"That would take weeks," Crichlow protested.

Pembleton deadpanned, "Are you going somewhere, Private?"

"The city has to have some kind of power-generation," said Yacavino. "Maybe we can find a way to tap into it."

"Talk to Graylock," Foyle said. "But let's remember that we have options. The rifles and hand scanners might be out cold, but we still have chemical grenades, flares, and our hands."

Private Steinhauer said, "I don't want to sound negative, Major, but CQC with the Caeliar sounds like a bad idea."

"He's right," Pembleton said. "Going hand-to-hand with a shape-changer that can levitate is a good way to get killed."

"Except that the Caeliar are pacifists, Sergeant," said Private Mazzetti. "They won't kill."

"Not on purpose," Foyle said, feeling the urge to clarify the situation for the younger men. "But accidents happen. Just because they aren't trying to kill us doesn't mean they have to save us when we make mistakes." The three enlisted men nodded.

Yacavino massaged his stubbled chin with his thumb and forefinger. "We need an objective." The Italian-born MACO looked at Foyle. "I assume we're trying to get back to the ship?"

"Yes," Foyle said. "And from there, out of orbit."

"And home," Pembleton added.

"Then we have to take down the scattering field," Yacavino said. "That's job one. Then we need to neutralize the Caeliar's ability to hurt the *Columbia*. Once that's done, we contact the ship, beam up, and get the hell out of here."

Foyle nodded. "It sounds like there's a good chance we could achieve the first two goals by causing a major disruption of the city's power supply. Do it right, and we might gain a useful distraction while we're at it."

"A useful distraction?" parroted Yacavino. "An explosion?"

"Correct," said Foyle. "Is there a problem?"

The second-in-command looked troubled. "We don't know what kind of damage we might do with demolitions. We might be talking about a lot of collateral damage." His jaw clenched and he swallowed. "I don't think the captain will go for that, sir."

"No," Foyle said. "I don't imagine she will. Which is why we're treating that part of the plan as need-to-know information until further notice—and the captain doesn't need to know."

That seemed to mollify the privates, but Yacavino looked away to hide his agitation, and Pembleton had a cautious air about him as he asked, "What if she finds out anyway?"

"Funny thing about collateral damage," Foyle replied. "It can happen to anyone. Even captains."

2381

14

His cup of Earl Grey was long since cold, and Jean-Luc Picard stared at the padd in his hand and found no answers, only the gnawing emptiness of unanswered questions.

Why had the Borg changed their tactics against the Federation? What was the reason for their mad frenzy of murder, the wholesale slaughter of worlds?

Picard had thought he knew the Borg, understood them even as he'd loathed them. He'd been perplexed by their desperate pursuit of the mysterious and elusive Omega Molecule as an emblem of "perfection," but at least their obsession with it had been consistent with their cultural imperative toward the assimilation of technology and biological diversity. Genocide, on the other hand . . . It *didn't fit*.

The pragmatist in him didn't want to look beyond the surface. From a practical standpoint, all that mattered now was fighting the Borg, halting their advance, and ending the war.

But the part of him that was still an explorer needed to know *why*. Something had changed, and he needed to understand.

He paced in front of his desk, padd in hand, trying to reassemble the pieces of the puzzle into something that made sense. The timing, the targets—he saw no patterns in them.

His door chime sounded, and he was grateful for the interruption. "Come."

The portal hushed open, and Worf entered, followed by La Forge. "Captain," Worf said, "we have something." He nodded to the chief engineer, who continued the report.

"Sensor analysis of the Borg cube we just destroyed picked up something odd," La Forge said. "Traces of sirillium."

Picard lifted an eyebrow. "Sirillium? Out here?"

"That's what I said." La Forge stepped beside a wall companel and activated it. He accessed the ship's computer with touch commands as he continued. "I figured there were two likely explanations. One, the Borg might've started using it in their ships or weapons."

That struck a chord in Picard's memory. "The Tellarites used to arm torpedo warheads with sirillium, back in the twenty-second century."

"Right," La Forge said. "So did the Andorians. But that'd be a fairly primitive solution for the Borg, so I took a closer look at the samples we detected." He called up a series of images on the companel screen. "All the traces we found were on external hull fragments from the Borg ship, or floating free with other atomized matter. We recovered debris from their weapons system, and it had no traces of sirillium. Neither did interior bulkhead plates, or sections of their life-support system. And that led me to my second possible explanation: They picked it up in transit."

With a flick of his finger, La Forge changed the display to a starmap of the surrounding sectors. "There are only two sites near Federation space with high enough concentrations of sirillium gas to leave deposits that rich on a Borg cube. One is the Rolor Nebula, on the Cardassian border, past the Badlands."

A glance at the starmap revealed the Rolor Nebula to be, quite literally, on the far side of the Federation from the *Enterprise* and the recent spate of Borg attacks. Picard asked, "And the other?"

La Forge enlarged a grid of the map—the sector adjacent to the *Enterprise*'s position. "The Azure Nebula, precisely twenty-point-one-three light-years from here. I ran an icospectrogram on the Borg cube's most likely route from there to here, and I found sirillium traces at regular intervals."

Picard looked to Worf. "ETA to the nebula at maximum warp?"

"Twenty-two hours," Worf said. "Course plotted and laid in, ready on your command."

Picard gave his XO a curt nod. "Make it so." To both Worf and La Forge he added, "Excellent work, gentlemen."

"Thank you, Captain," La Forge said. "I'm heading back to engineering—see if I can push a few more points over the line and get us there in twenty-*one* hours." He nodded to Worf and the captain, and then he made his exit from the ready room. Worf, however, remained behind.

"Something else, Worf?"

The XO frowned. "If Commander La Forge is correct, we can expect to face significant resistance when we reach the nebula." He looked Picard in the eye. "Permission to speak freely, sir?"

"Granted."

In a quiet but still forceful baritone, Worf said, "You need to rest, sir."

Picard turned to walk back to his desk. "Your concern is appreciated, Commander, but I—"

"Captain," Worf said, blocking Picard's path. "You have been on duty for more than twenty hours. I suspect you have been awake for at least twenty-two."

The captain stiffened in the face of his first officer's confrontational behavior. Even though Worf generally respected human customs and courtesies, moments like this served to remind Picard that having a Klingon for an XO would take some getting used to. Taking care not to blink or demur, he looked into Worf's eyes and replied gravely, "Do you mind, Mister Worf?"

Worf made a low growl of protest and stepped aside. As Picard walked by him, the brawny first officer grumbled, "You know I am right. Sir."

Picard stood behind his desk and rested his hands on the back of his chair. "What I *know*, Mister Worf, is that you've been awake even longer than I have."

Worf grunted. "True. It would be best if you and I were *both* well rested before taking the ship into battle."

The dead weight of his own feet and the dull aching in his muscles persuaded Picard to admit that his first officer was right. "I trust you've assigned new watch commanders for the next two shifts?"

"Yes, sir," Worf said. "Commander Lynley is on the bridge now, and Lieutenant Commander Havers will relieve him at 0800."

Picard sighed. He found Worf's new ability to anticipate his decisions both reassuring and irritating. "Very good. I'll be in my quarters—and I'll see you back on the bridge at 1600."

"Aye, Captain." He walked toward the door and paused before stepping in range of its motion sensor, so that he could turn back and add, with his unique brand of irony, "Sweet dreams."

Picard's valediction was a good-natured warning: "Good night, Number One." Worf answered with a wry smirk and left the ready room. Picard sighed and returned to his desk. He picked up his half-consumed cup of tea, carried it back to the replicator, and keyed the matter reclamator. The cup and its cold contents vanished in an amber swirl of dissociated particles.

Around him, the *Enterprise* resonated with the swiftly rising hum of the warp engines rapidly pushing the ship to its maximum rated velocity, and perhaps even a fraction beyond. The stretch of starlight outside the ready room window, normally a soothing backdrop, now raced by in frantic pulses. Even the stars knew that the *Enterprise* was headed into danger.

Picard had promised Worf he would rest, but he doubted he would sleep tonight, with the Collective looming on the horizon.

The voice from the overhead comm roused Miranda Kadohata from her troubled, fitful slumber a few minutes shy of 0500.

"Bridge to Commander Kadohata," said Lieutenant Milner, the gamma-shift operations manager.

Kadohata's eyes snapped open. Her heart was palpitating furiously, and the muscles in her chest and arms twitched with nervous energy. Rescued from one of a night-long series of anxiety dreams, she was grateful to be woken. "Kadohata here."

"You asked for notice when we had a comm window," Milner replied. *"I have one coming up in twenty seconds. It'll be short—a couple minutes, tops. You still want it?"*

She was already out of bed and scrambling into her robe. "Yes, Sean. Patch me through as soon as the channel's up."

"Will do. Stand by."

Leaning left, she caught her reflection in the mirror beside her bedroom desk and finger-combed her straight, sable hair into a smooth ponytail and twisted it into a knot on the back of her head. Her eyes were a bit red, and the circles under them were too dark to hide. *It doesn't matter,* she told herself. *There's no time. It'll be fine.*

She had left standing orders with the junior operations managers to let her know whenever there was an opportunity for her to get a real-time signal out to her family on Cestus III. When she'd first come aboard the *Enterprise,* she'd made a point of speaking to her husband and children via subspace every day. Their infant twins, Colin and Sylvana, couldn't understand her words, of course, but she wanted them to hear her voice as much as possible while she was away. She had recorded herself reading them bedtime stories while she had been pregnant, and Vicenzo, her husband, made a point of including those recordings in the twins' nightly routine.

Aoki, their first born, was another matter. It was chiefly for the five-year-old's benefit that Kadohata was so diligent about these comms home, however brief they might be. The girl was old enough to miss her mother, to feel the ache of absence, and for Kadohata it was worth any amount of lost sleep and expended favors to keep herself in Aoki's daily life.

Her comm screen snapped to life, the bright blue-and-white Federation emblem almost blinding in the night-cycle shadows of her quarters. Milner's voice filtered down from overhead as a string of numbers and symbols flashed past along the bottom edge of her screen. *"Hang on,"* he said. *"I'm routing the signal through about four different boosters in the Klingon Empire."*

The second officer grinned. "How'd you swing that?"

"I know a bloke who knows a bloke who has friends on the High Council." She understood his meaning: Worf had used some of his old diplomatic connections with the Klingon chancellor's office to secure this extraordinary favor.

She made a mental note to thank Worf the next time she saw him privately. Then the screen in front of her blinked to an image of her husband, Vicenzo Farrenga. She smiled at the sight of his round, jovial face and immaculate coif of dark hair. "What time is it there, love?"

"We're just sitting down to dinner," he said. With a quick tap of a key, he switched the comm's feed to a wider angle that revealed him, Aoki, and the twins around the dining room table. *"How 'bout there?"*

"Middle of the night, as always." She hadn't

worried about the differences in local times. As her calls home had become less frequent, Vicenzo had made it clear that he didn't mind being woken at any hour. Ringing in at dinner had been a lucky break, though; it meant she got to see the children.

Sylvana grabbed up fistfuls of strained-something and flung it in globs on the floor. Colin seemed content to smear his dinner on his bib. Aoki waved frantically from the far end of the table. *"Hi, Mummy,"* she said, her bright voice echoing.

"Hello, sweetheart." Kadohata wished she could teleport to her daughter's side and just hold her. "Have you been helping Daddy with the twins?"

Aoki nodded, and Vicenzo replied, *"I couldn't do it without her."* He winked at the girl, then continued, *"She's a natural."*

"I'm happy to hear that, love. What's for dinner tonight?"

Vicenzo pointed out each dish. *"Colin's turning mashed peas into a fashion statement, Sylvie's doing some redecorating with her strained carrots, and Aoki and I are enjoying some vegetable moussaka, fresh corn, and spinach salad."*

"Impressive," Kadohata said, nodding her approval. With a teasing lilt, she asked, "Real or replicated?"

He gave a small shrug. *"Mostly real. I think the dairy products are replicated, but all the vegetables were grown here in Lakeside, and the pasta's made fresh at a market in town."*

"Glad to see my lectures about eating healthy have stuck with you," she said.

Nodding, he replied, *"We're being good, I promise. Looks like you have, too. You look great."*

She shook her head. "I look horrid."

"*No,*" Vicenzo insisted. "*You really don't.*"

It was true that she had lost weight in recent weeks, restoring the fine angles of her mixed European-Asian ancestry. What she didn't want to tell him was that most of her weight loss had been stress-induced, as the *Enterprise* had become the Federation's principal instrument of defense against the Borg.

"Thank you, love," she said, lowering her eyes. On the other end of the channel, Vicenzo sensed her fatigue and her fear, and like her he masked it with a sad smile of quiet desperation, for the sake of the children.

Oblivious of the unspoken tension, Aoki asked in a loud and shrill voice, "*When are you coming home, Mummy?*"

"*Inside voice, honey,*" Vicenzo murmured, hushing the girl.

Kadohata shook her head. "Don't know, love. Soon, I hope."

Aoki pressed on, "*Where are you?*"

"*She can't tell us that, sweetie,*" Vicenzo said, circling the table to pluck Aoki from her chair and into his arms. "*It's not safe for her to say things like that over the comm. Bad people might be listening.*" Watching him comfort her made Kadohata miss the embrace of her little ones that much more.

The little girl locked her arms around her father's neck and rested her head on his large, rounded shoulder. "*I'm sorry, Mummy,*" she mumbled.

"No need to be sorry, love," Kadohata told her. Forcing a smile, she said to Vicenzo, "Happier thoughts, right? Big day coming up next month."

"I remember," he said. "Eight years."

"What's the gift for that anniversary?"

He chuckled. "Bronze. Had a devil of a time thinking up a gift for that one."

"You've already bought my gift?" He nodded, and she grinned. Vicenzo had never been one to leave things until the last minute. "I should've known." Feigning seriousness, she added, "I suppose you'll expect me to get you something, now."

"I wouldn't want you to go to any trouble."

She almost laughed. "Liar."

A double-beep over the channel heralded an interruption. From the overhead speaker in her quarters, Lieutenant Milner warned, "Twenty seconds, sir."

Kadohata looked away from the image of her family on the screen and said, "Thank you, Sean." Then she looked back. "Time's up, loves. I have to go."

Vicenzo looked as if he'd had his heart cut out. "Stay safe, Miranda. We miss you." Aoki lifted her head from his shoulder and crowed, "We miss you, Mummy!"

"I miss you all, too," Kadohata said. "Very much. I'll comm again as soon as I can, but I don't know when that'll be."

"We'll be waiting. . . . Love you."

"Love you, too."

She and Vicenzo reached out and each pressed a fingertip to their comm screen, an illusion of contact transmitted across light-years, for the last few seconds before the signal was lost and the channel cut to black and silence.

A sinking feeling became an emptiness inside of her as she plodded back to her bed and slipped under the covers. It had been barely two hours since she'd watched the Borg lay waste to Korvat. If they weren't stopped, sooner or later they would reach Cestus III. It would only be a matter of time.

Visions of her beautiful children being turned to fire haunted her when she closed her eyes. There was nothing she wouldn't do to prevent that, she was certain of it. She would kill, die, or sacrifice the ship and whoever or whatever was necessary, if doing so saved her children.

But tonight, alone in her quarters, her face buried in the soft clutch of a pillow, all she could do was sob with rage for the lives she had already failed to defend.

From dead asleep to wide awake—Beverly Crusher blinked her eyes open wider and inhaled. There had been no sound, no sudden change in her surroundings. She had been on the edge of slumber's gray frontier, inching her way over the border, when a jolt and a shiver had pulled her back.

Rolling over, she looked for her husband. Jean-Luc's side of the bed was empty, his pillows untouched. He hadn't come to bed yet. It was just after 0500. She had gone to bed at 0315, after the ship had secured from general quarters. *I guess I did doze off,* she realized. *For a little while, at least.*

A small, soft bump of a sound carried into the bedroom, through the doorway that led to the suite's main room. Crusher pushed off the lightweight but pleasantly warmed sheets and blanket and eased herself out of bed, into the relatively chill air. She suspected that Jean-Luc had been at the climate controls again; he preferred a crisp coolness in their living quarters, a temperature a few degrees below where she was comfortable. And so they wrangled. It had been the same way with her first husband, Jack, decades earlier.

The skin on her arms and legs turned to gooseflesh until she shivered into her bathrobe and tied it shut. She was grateful that at least the deck in their living area was carpeted. The plush, synthetic fabric was warm under her feet as she padded to the doorway and peeked into the main room.

Jean-Luc sat on the floor with his back to her. He was still wearing his uniform. On the floor beside him, a tarnished, engraved copper box with a foampad interior lay open and empty. In his hands he held his Ressikan flute, a keepsake recovered from an alien probe that years earlier had gifted the captain, in the span of a few minutes, with the memories of another lifetime, the last message of a dying world and people.

In that other life, he'd lived as a man named Kamin, raised a family, and learned to play the flute. Its music, he'd told Crusher, often soothed his nerves and dispelled his sorrows. She knew how much he treasured that instrument. He turned the narrow, bronze-hued flute in his hands and gently straightened a twist in the silken cord of its white tassel.

Taking sudden note of her presence, he looked over

his shoulder. "Beverly," he said in a hushed voice. "I'm sorry. I didn't mean to wake you."

"You didn't," she said. "I just woke up. Don't know why."

Jean-Luc nodded once and looked back at the flute. He pulled the tassel cord taut with one hand and placed the instrument back into its custom-cut indentation on the foam pad, taking care to lay the silken thread parallel to the metal body of the flute. Then he closed the lid gently, picked up the box, stood, and carried it to a nearby shelf. He bore it as if it was a holy relic. Setting the box beside some leather-bound volumes of classic works, Jean-Luc was somber, like a man moving with great care because he might be doing everything for the last time. Crusher found the deliberateness of his manner worrying.

"You look exhausted," she said. "Are you coming to bed?"

He sighed. "To what end? I can't let myself sleep. Not with the Collective waiting for my guard to fall."

"I could prescribe a sleep aid that would—"

"No," Jean-Luc said. "No drugs. I have to be ready."

She stepped beside him and put her hands on his shoulder. "How ready will you be if you don't sleep?"

"Worf said the same thing." His eyes became distant, disengaged from the moment. "Neither of you can hear them, not the way I do." He frowned. "I can't sleep. Not now."

Crusher let him shrug off her hands. She didn't take it personally. Instead, she walked toward the replicator. "All right," she said. "If you're not sleeping, neither am I. Computer, lights one-half."

"Beverly," he said in protest as the room brightened.

"Shush." She stopped in front of the replicator. "Two peppermint herbal teas, hot." A singsong whine filled the room; two delicate porcelain cups took shape in a spiral of glowing matter inside the replicator nook. When the sequence ended, Crusher lifted the cups and carried them back to Jean-Luc. She offered him one.

"I'm not thirsty," he said.

"It'll soothe your nerves," she countered, but still he made no move to accept the tea. She set the cup down on an end table beside the sofa. "When was the last time you ate?"

He took a few steps into the middle of the room and gazed out the window at the passing streaks of starlight. "I don't recall," he said. Then he added, "Breakfast, I think."

"Jean-Luc, you have to make time to take care of—"

"Beverly," he said. There was a deadness in his voice. Crusher had heard it before, in combat veterans suffering from shock. "In the past twenty-four hours, I've seen two worlds destroyed. Billions of lives, each one unique and irreplaceable, all extinguished." He turned to face her. "And it's only just started. Something terrible is coming, I can feel it. Watching Korvat burn was like seeing an omen."

She inched closer to him. "An omen? Of what? A disaster?"

His jaw trembled. "An apocalypse."

Closer now, she took his hands, tried to anchor him, keep him from being swept away by the undertow of his fears. "You don't know that," she said. "The worst of it might be over."

"No, Beverly. It's not." His voice fell to a whisper, as if he feared eavesdroppers. "The worst is still out there, waiting to fall, like a hammer in the dark." She watched his eyes glisten with tears as he freed his right hand and placed it softly against her cheek. "We're out of our depth, now."

"I can't believe that," she said. "I won't. Starfleet's destroyed six Borg cubes in the last few weeks, and five more today. We can stop them."

"And what have we lost in the bargain?" He lowered his hand from her face, and his tone became harder. "More than a dozen ships of the line. Three major starbases. Four worlds. *Worlds,* Beverly! *Billions* of lives." Pacing away from her, he continued, "I've read Kathryn Janeway's reports from her years in the Delta Quadrant. Her encounters with the Borg. They have *thousands* of ships." He stopped near the replicator and turned back to face Crusher. "They control vast regions of space, have almost unlimited resources at their command. Beverly, the Collective *dwarfs* the Federation. They're gearing up to fight a war of attrition. That's a war we can't win. We just don't have the numbers. Not enough ships, not enough people. Not enough *worlds.*" His voice deadened again. "We can't win."

Crusher crossed the room and stood in front of him. He looked up at her with a vacant, fearful expression.

She slapped his face.

The smack was sharp and loud against the quiet hum of the engines and made contact with enough force to knock Jean-Luc back half a step and leave her palm stinging. She fixed her husband with a feral glare. "Snap out of it, Jean-Luc! The man I married is a *starship captain*. He doesn't declare defeat when he's still fighting the war."

To her surprise, he smiled. Almost laughed. "You don't think I'm the man you married?"

"The Jean-Luc Picard I know would never talk this way."

His smile soured. "'Do I contradict myself? Very well, then, I contradict myself. I am large, I contain multitudes.'"

"Don't quote Whitman at me. You don't even *like* Whitman." She sighed. "Do you want to know what I've always liked about you, right from the very first time we met?"

"Tell me," he said sincerely.

"Your faith that there was more good than bad to be found in the universe. I heard you once tell Jack on the *Stargazer,* 'That's why we do this—it's what makes going to the stars worthwhile.'"

Jean-Luc massaged his reddened cheek. "Perhaps I was wrong," he said. "Those are the beliefs of a young man. A man who hasn't felt the harsh embrace of cruel machines." He collapsed on the sofa. Crusher sat down beside him. "Words will never capture the horror of losing myself that way, Beverly. I can't describe what it's like to be erased. Absorbed. To have everything I am become lost inside a force untouched by love or joy or sorrow. To know that it's *stronger* than I am."

"That's where you're wrong, Jean-Luc," she said. "It's not stronger than you. It's not stronger than us." She grasped his hand and lifted it, moved it onto her belly, above her womb. "We'll survive as long as we have hope," she said, trying to project her shaken optimism onto him, hoping he would reinforce it with some small gesture, however minor. "As long as we don't let them take that from us, we can still fight. And they can't take it if we don't let them." She touched his face as tears rolled from her eyes. "Don't let them."

His free hand closed tenderly around hers. "I won't," he said, but some part of her knew that he was lying. He was clinging to hope for her sake, but she felt it slipping from him, as the Borg drove it from him by degrees.

"Don't let them," she said.

15

———◆———

Federation President Nanietta Bacco led a procession out of her chief of staff's office on the fourteenth floor of the Palais de la Concorde. "Don't tell me there aren't any ships available, Iliop," Bacco snapped at her secretary of transportation. "Your job is *making* ships available."

As soon as she stepped through the door, a phalanx of four civilian security guards fell into step around her. Iliop—a tall Berellian man whose spectacles, mussed hair, and ill-fitting toga made Bacco think of him as a cross between an absentminded professor and a Roman senator—lingered half a step farther behind her as he followed her out of the office. "Madam President, my mandate was to restore the avenues of commerce and normal—"

"We're way past 'normal,' Ili," said Esperanza Piñiero, the president's chief of staff, who was the next person to exit the office. "Here's your new mandate: Get those twenty-nine thousand survivors off Korvat in the next three days." The Berellian opened his mouth to argue, and Piñiero cut him off. "Get it *done*, Ili." He nodded and slipped away down a side corridor as Safranski, the Rigellian secretary of the exterior, and Raisa Shostakova, the secretary of defense, followed Bacco and Piñiero from the office and down a central hallway to the turbolifts.

"Korvat's the least of our worries, Madam President," said Shostakova. "FNS is whipping up a panic with images of the attack on Barolia."

"The Borg are making the panic, Raisa," Bacco said. "The media just report it. Besides, corralling the media is Jorel's problem." To Safranski she said, "Any word on the summit?"

The Rigellian replied, "No."

As ever, his brevity bordered on the passive-aggressive and added frown lines to Bacco's brow. "Why not?"

"No one's taking our calls."

"Not good enough," Bacco said. "Keep trying."

Shostakova shouldered her way past Safranski—not an easy feat for the squat, solidly built human woman from the high-gravity colony planet known as Pangea. "We've got an antimatter problem," she announced as Bacco turned a sharp corner.

Piñiero replied for Bacco, "What kind of problem?"

"A shortage," Shostakova said. "We need fuel for the Third Fleet and the reserves are tapped out."

The chief of staff pulled a personal comm from her jacket pocket, flipped it open, and pressed it to her ear. "Ashanté," she said, addressing one of her four deputy chiefs of staff. "We need an executive order authorizing Starfleet to commandeer civilian fuel resources, on the double. Work up a draft with Dogayn and have it in the Monet Room in thirty minutes." She slapped the device closed and tucked it back into her pocket in a fast, well-practiced motion.

The group passed through a set of frosted double doors into a comfortably furnished reception area. Its honey-hued wood paneling and warm lighting cast a pleasant glow over the off-white carpet, which was adorned by a pale blue outline of the Federation emblem. Long sofas and a few armchairs surrounded a C-shaped formation of coffee tables.

Standing between them and the bank of turbolifts was a presence as austere as the surroundings were relaxed. Shoulder-length gray hair framed his proud countenance, and the pristine blacks and grays of his Starfleet uniform flattered his tall, heavily muscled frame. He nodded to Bacco, who strode ahead of her security detail, hand outstretched to greet him.

"Admiral," she said, shaking the hand of Leonard James Akaar, the official liaison between Starfleet and the Office of the Federation President. "Any good news to report?"

He pressed his lips together, making his chiseled features appear even more stern. "I am afraid not, Madam President."

She frowned. "Why should you be any different?"

The doors of a large turbolift gasped open a few meters away. A burly Zibalian man from Bacco's security detail stepped inside, made a quick scan with a handheld device, and motioned everyone inside. Bacco entered and moved to the back of the turbolift. Akaar, Piñiero, Shostakova, Safranski, and the other three security men followed close behind. The doors hissed shut. The senior agent on the detail, an ex–Starfleet officer named Steven Wexler, issued the turbolift command with a whisper via his subaural implant. The lift began a swift descent.

Bacco said to Akaar, "Give me the bad news, Admiral."

"We've lost three critical starbases near the triborder," Akaar said in his rich rumble of a voice, referring to the region of space where the territories of the Federation, the Romulan Star Empire, and the Klingon Empire collided. "In the past hour, Epsilon Outposts 10 and 11 have gone dark. We're proceeding on the assumption that they've been destroyed."

"What about Khitomer?" asked Shostakova. "What went right at Khitomer?"

Akaar directed his reply to the diminutive defense secretary. "The *Starship Ranger* used phase-inversion technology to penetrate the Borg's shields and sacrificed itself as a single, massive warhead to vaporize the cube."

Shostakova recoiled, shut her eyes, and inhaled sharply, almost as if by reflex. Safranski, unfazed by the report, replied curtly, "Can we do it again?"

"Too late," Akaar said. "Captain Calhoun tried to sacrifice the *Excalibur* using the same strategy, but the Borg had already adapted. His chief engineer rigged a salvo of torpedoes with phase-inverters, each set to a different variance. Enough made it through to destroy the cube, but it's safe to assume the Borg will be ready for that tactic next time."

The doors sighed open, revealing a windowless corridor with soft, indirect lighting. Agent Wexler was the first person out of the turbolift, followed by another agent, an Andorian *thaan*. They sidestepped clear of the others who were exiting the lift, and remained just ahead of Bacco on her left and right as she led the rest of the group toward the Monet Room.

Bacco said to the admiral, "What's Starfleet doing before there *is* a next time?"

"The *Enterprise* is following a lead that may reveal how the Borg are reaching our space," Akaar said. "We've deployed every available ship to reinforce the *Enterprise,* but it will take a couple of days before they arrive. Until then, she'll be on her own, out by the Azure Nebula."

From behind Bacco and Akaar, Safranski inquired, "That's near the tri-border, isn't it?"

"It *is* the tri-border," Akaar replied.

Anticipating the president's next order, Safranski said, "I'll have K'mtok and Kalavak summoned to the Palais." Bacco nodded her approval; she expected that she would soon have an urgent need to talk to the Klingon and Romulan ambassadors.

She turned left at an intersection and neared the door to the Monet Room. "Admiral," Shostakova said, "we need an update from Starfleet on its evacuation plan for the core systems in the event of a full-scale Borg invasion."

"We don't have one," Akaar said, and his matter-of-fact tone made Bacco bristle. "If the Borg get past us at Regulus, there will be nothing between them and the core systems. In essence, Madam President, if the Federation had what was once called, in Earth history, a 'doomsday clock,' its hands would now be set at one minute to midnight."

A grim pall settled over the group, which became very quiet as they strode the final few paces to the Monet Room. Agent Wexler stopped just shy of reaching its door, letting President Bacco move past him.

Bacco resolved not to surrender to the paralysis of despair. "All right, Admiral," she said. "If we can't evacuate the core systems, we damned well better find a way to defend them. Which is why I've brought you all down here to meet my new deputy security adviser." She stepped to the door, which slid aside with a soft swish, and she led the group into the Palais's unofficial war room.

On one wall hung an impressionist painting from earth's preunification period, *Bridge over a Pool of Water Lilies,* by Claude Monet. Panoramic viewscreens dominated the other walls. Most of the middle of the dimly lit room was taken up by the long, dark wood conference table, which comfortably seated up to twenty people. The group filed in and spread out to Bacco's left and right on one side of the table.

Standing on the other side were two people. The middle-aged Trill man was her senior security adviser, Jas Abrik. An irascible former Starfleet admiral, he actually had managed the presidential campaign of Bacco's opponent, Fel Pagro, during the special election the previous year. In exchange for his silence on a potentially explosive matter of national security that had emerged during the election, she had appointed him to this key position in her cabinet. He had treated it like a coup.

He didn't seem quite so enthused about his new deputy.

Bacco introduced the statuesque, fair-haired human woman, who had jarring patches of silver machinery grafted to her left hand and temple.

"Everyone," said the president, "this is Seven of Nine. She's here to help us stop the Borg."

Struggling bodies and flaring tempers added to the musky heat of the Klingon High Council Chamber. Shouts of "Federation lackey!" were met with angry retorts of "Traitorous *petaQ*!"

Instead of calving into partisan ranks on either side of the dim, sultry meeting space, as the councillors normally did, they were a shoving, bustling mass in the brightly lit center of the room, atop the enormous red-and-white trefoil emblem that adorned the polished, black granite floor.

Elevated above the mob, on a dais at the end of the chamber, Chancellor Martok struck the metal-jacketed end of his ceremonial staff on the stone steps before him. Explosive cracks of noise resounded off the angled walls and high ceiling, to no avail. With his one eye he glared at the disgraceful thrashing and longed for days of honor that had long passed into history.

Martok stepped forward and hammered the end of his staff down on one of the marble tiles, harder than before. This time the percussive banging was loud enough to halt the melee and shatter one of the square tiles into dusty, broken chunks. The councillors all set their feral gazes on him.

"This is war!" he boomed. Then his voice turned to gravel. "The hour for debate is over. You stand for the Great Houses of the Empire. It's time you showed our enemies what *greatness* is!"

The chancellor descended the stairs and prowled forward through the muddled ranks, which parted, disturbing the humid air and creating a current that was rich with the odors of sweat and *warnog*-tainted breath, and the traditional scents of *targ*-tallow candles and braziers of sulfur and coal. "Some of you"—he aimed a lacerating stare at Kopek, his longtime bitter political rival—"say this is not our war. That it's an internal matter for the Federation. *Use our strength for conquest,* you say, *and let the Federation defend itself.*" He spat on the floor and scowled at Qolka and Tovoj, who in recent months had become vocal backers of Kopek's verbal sabotages. "I never want to hear that excuse again." He continued stalking through the knot of councillors, making eye contact with each one as he passed—with Mortran and Grevaq, Krozek and Merik. "Don't pretend you haven't heard the news from Khitomer," Martok growled. "The Borg came gunning for *us*. It was no *accident*. No *coincidence*."

On his way back to the dais steps, he passed Kryan, the youngest member of the Council. Behind him, and closest to the dais, were Martok's three staunchest allies in the chamber: K'mpar, Hegron, and Korvog. He nodded to them, ascended the steps, and turned to face the assembled councillors en masse.

"When the Borg came to destroy one of our worlds, our allies *bled* for us. They died *defending* us. Three Federation starships sacrificed themselves for Khitomer, a colony world of less than half a million Klingons. Do you remember the last time that happened? I do." He let the implication sink in before he pointed at his nemesis, Kopek. "And so do you." Over his opponents' shamed silence, Martok said simply, "Narendra III."

Grunts of acknowledgment came back to Martok in reply.

He pressed on, "Blood shed for a friend is sacred, a debt of honor. And if you won't stand and fight beside a friend in blood, then you are not a Klingon. You are not a warrior. Run home to your beds and hide, I have no use for you! I won't die in the company of such *petaQ'pu*. The sons of our sons will sing of these battles. Time will erase our sins and fade our scars, but our names will live on in songs of honor.

"The Borg are coming, my brothers. Stand and fight beside me now, and let us make warriors born in ages to come curse *Fek'lhr* that they were not here to *share our glory*!"

His partisans in the chamber roared the loudest, but even Kopek's allies joined the chanting war cries, their bloodlust inflamed with rhetoric. Martok would never admit it aloud, but he suspected that a full-scale conflict with the Borg might be enough to push the Empire past its breaking point. It did not matter; better to die in the struggle than to surrender. As long as he and his people perished with honor and not as *jeghpu'wI'*, he would not consider it a defeat.

Unity in the Council would be critical to the war effort, Martok knew. He saw Kopek step forward, away from the others. Martok took one step down to meet him, maintaining his one-up power position for its symbolic and psychological advantages. Making eye contact with his adversary, he said, "Choose, Kopek."

He saw that the choice was galling for Kopek, and that pleased him. Despite years of political maneuvering, Martok had never been able to halt Kopek's dirty tricks. It had taken a Borg invasion to outflank the ruthless *yIntagh*. Where scheming and coercion had failed, circumstance had prevailed.

With a clenched jaw and bitter grimace, Kopek extended his open right hand to Martok, who took it. "*Qapla'*, Chancellor." A feral gleam shone in his eyes as he released Martok's hand, turned, and declared with a raised fist, "To war!"

The councillors roared their approval, and Martok flashed a broad, jagged grin. "It is a good day to die . . . for the Borg."

Lieutenant Commander Tom Paris sat alone in his quarters aboard the *U.S.S. Voyager* and picked lethargically at his dinner. He had ordered a platter of deep-fried clams with a side salad of spinach and sliced tomatoes. The clams were rubbery and tough, but he knew that was because he had let them sit too long and get cold. *Can't blame the replicator for that,* he brooded.

More troubling to his palate was that the clams seemed to have no flavor. They were just a texture without a taste. He felt the same way about the salad. The leaves were the perfect color and crispness, but they were an empty crunch. The grape tomatoes felt right as his teeth cut through them, but they delivered none of the sweetness that he'd expected.

Can't blame that on the replicator, either.

He didn't figure there was anything wrong with the food itself. The problem was him. Nothing had been right since B'Elanna had left and taken Miral with her.

Food no longer tasted good. Synthehol had no effect. Sleep brought no rest, only dreams of loss and regret.

It had been several months since he'd last seen his wife and daughter. He had wondered if B'Elanna would return for Kathryn Janeway's memorial service. Captain Chakotay had been there, of course, along with Seven, and just about everyone else who had served with Janeway on *Voyager*—with the exception, of course, of Tuvok, who by that point was already hurtling away into sectors unknown as the new second officer of the *U.S.S. Titan* under Captain Riker.

During the outdoor services, Paris had stood with his friend and shipmate Harry Kim. Tom's father, Owen Paris, though he'd come to the memorial, had remained distant and avoided him. Despite the cool, breezy weather that had graced the event, the skies over San Francisco had been unusually clear that day, and the sunlight had beaten down on their dress-white uniforms with great ferocity.

The crowd had been packed with familiar faces, including people Paris hadn't seen since graduating from the Academy. He'd even stolen a glimpse of captains Picard and Calhoun, standing together in front of the gleaming pillar that had been erected in Janeway's honor.

But there had been no sign of B'Elanna.

He'd understood her reasons for leaving. The fact that their child had been hailed as the messiah—aka the *Kuvah'magh*—by an obscure Klingon religious cult was a better reason for separating than most couples could claim. But it didn't make her absence or her silence any easier to bear.

If the separation had plunged Paris into new depths of melancholy, it had rocketed his father to new heights of recrimination and wrath. The admiral had excoriated his son without mercy when Paris had first broken the news, and only the strict decorum of Janeway's military funeral had likely prevented Owen from an encore performance at their last meeting.

They hadn't spoken since. Paris had received a few messages from his mother, each carefully crafted to make no mention of his father, except one noting his transfer to take command of Starbase 234. A few times, he had considered writing to the old man, but he'd never been able to find anything to say. The situation with B'Elanna was what it was, and nothing he could tell his father was going to change it.

So he sat alone in a compartment of gray bulkheads, darker-gray carpeting, and institutionally drab taupe furniture replete with rounded corners for his safety. His food tasted like cardboard, and going to sleep meant waking up to find each day a little bit darker than the one before.

And I'm supposed to be in charge of morale on this ship, he thought with grim amusement. *How's that for irony?*

He stood, picked up his plate, and carried it back to the replicator to dispose of it. As he placed it back in the nook from which it had come, a soft double tone from the overhead comm preceded the voice of Ensign Lasren, the ops officer.

"Bridge to Paris."

"Go ahead," Paris said, activating the matter-reclamation sequence. The plate dissolved and vanished in a whorl.

"You've received a priority signal from your—" Lasren changed course in midsentence. *"—from Admiral Paris, sir."*

Paris wondered what would be important enough to make his father break his silence after all these months. He assumed the worst. "Patch it through." He crossed the room quickly to his desk and activated the comm screen.

A prerecorded image snapped to life in crisp colors and sharp shadows. His father sat at a desk in an office; Paris presumed it was his father's office at Starbase 234. An unsteady percussion of explosions was like a subliminal track underneath Owen's halting words.

"Tom," he began. He paused and looked around in confusion before he continued. *"I had meant to do this the right way, son. Not like this. But we don't always get to choose, do we?"*

Objects trembled on the shelves in the background of the shot as Owen continued. *"I said terrible things when you told me about B'Elanna, Tom. Stupid things. It wasn't my place."* Lights stuttered for a few seconds, distracting the admiral. *"I was so upset about my granddaughter being taken from me that I forgot it was your* daughter *being taken from you. It's just that—dammit—we were all so happy not so long ago. How'd it go so wrong?"*

The question, though probably rhetorical, stung Paris. It was something he'd asked himself daily since B'Elanna and Miral had left him behind on Earth, a family man with no family.

"Can you forgive a dumb old man for words spoken in anger? Can you believe me when I tell you that it kills me to know how much you must miss your wife and little girl?" In the space of a breath, Owen was on the verge of tears. *"I don't know how I'd live if I lost your mother. I don't think I'd want to."*

Owen rubbed his eyes and forced himself back into a state of composure. *"I was wrong to blame you for what happened. It's your marriage, not mine, and I shouldn't have said anything, except that I'm sorry . . . and that I still love you, no matter what. But most of all, just that I'm sorry."* He flashed a bittersweet smile at the screen. *"For everything."*

His composure began to slip again as louder, closer explosions rocked the image. *"No matter what happens, Tommy, you'll always be my boy. Take care of yourself."* A dark expression descended on him. He reached forward, said, *"Good-bye, son,"* and terminated the recording.

The screen cut to black, and Tom Paris had the icy feeling of gazing into the void or the depths of a grave. Unable to contain his alarm, he called out, "Paris to bridge!"

Harry Kim replied immediately, *"Bridge. Go ahead."*

"Harry, get me a channel to Starbase 234, *now*!"

The delay before Kim's response was long enough for Paris to anticipate what his old friend would say, and dread swelled in his heart even as he prayed that he was wrong. But he wasn't, and he was already sinking into shock, tears streaming down his face as Kim broke the news, his voice freighted with remorse.

"Tom . . . Starbase 234 is gone."

16

———

The desert swelled around Lieutenant Lonnoc Kedair and seemed poised to reclaim the husk of the *Columbia* in its shifting embrace. She stood near the top of the downed ship's saucer section, watching the evacuation grind forward by degrees.

She tapped her combadge. "Kedair to Hockney. How much longer till you're ready to beam up?"

Through the beige veil of the growing sandstorm, she looked aft and saw the harried engineer turn and look her way as he answered over the comm, *"A few more minutes."* The wind howled and whistled, and he had to shout to be heard over the wail. *"We're rounding up the last of the small stuff."*

"Quickly, Ensign," Kedair said. "We're scheduled to break orbit in an hour. It'd be a shame to have to leave you here."

Hockney replied, *"Just a few minutes, I promise."*

"Notify me the moment you're ready. Kedair out."

Below, the engineer turned away and resumed work, helping researchers and their enlisted assistants carry equipment out of the *Columbia* through an aft hatch on one of the lower decks. The crates were gathered in a neat, stacked cluster several meters from the ship, between its broken and off-kilter warp nacelles. Through it all, the wind whipped sand at Kedair's face.

Raging winds, shifting sands . . . the desert was ever-changing, but the desert never changed, as if it were a cousin of the sea. Kedair had remained on the surface during the overnight shift and through the dawn. The deep watches of the night had settled, starry and frigid, on the broken bones of the *Columbia* until it coaxed out the away team's breaths in huffs of thin mist. The gray majesty of predawn twilight had been short-lived, blasted away by the swift ascent of one sun and then another.

Another blistering afternoon had seemed to be in store until minutes earlier, when the leading edge of a kilometers-wide sandstorm hove into view, turning the sky the color of burnt umber. It was hurling the desert at Kedair and the away team, and the force of it felt like millions of flying insects slamming against her uniform from every direction. She felt the sand working its way into everything—her boots, her uniform, her hair, her ears, her mouth, her nostrils—and it was still better than spending even another minute inside the *Columbia.*

She preferred the blinding stings of the storm to the rank odor of decaying flesh and blood, the grotesque perfume of scorched tissue, and the sharp stink of burned hair. After spending the night belowdecks with the forensic investigators, Kedair was relieved to be free of the bowels of the *Columbia,* and she had no intention of going back inside, not even if this damned storm buried her alive.

The section of D Deck where Chief Komer and Crewman Yott were killed had been sealed less than an hour earlier. The investigators had collected so many samples and scrapings that they'd nearly scoured the deck plates clean. All that evidence was now secured aboard the *Aventine,* where it was being subjected to an endless, ad nauseam battery of tests—none of which had so far yielded a single clue to the identity or even the nature of the killer.

Kedair blamed herself. As far as she was concerned, her shipmates were all under her protection, and it was her job to prevent tragedies like this. And she'd failed.

If only they weren't all so fragile, she lamented. Of all the moments of culture shock she had endured when she made the decision, upon reaching adulthood sixteen years earlier, to emigrate to the Federation and apply to Starfleet Academy, none compared with her discovery that most of her classmates—indeed, most of the species she would meet from then on—were absurdly delicate organisms when compared to Takarans. Specialized internal organs, limited disease and toxin resistance, no cellular stasis abilities—their myriad shortcomings astounded her. She had assumed that all species were like hers, with distributed internal anatomy, resilient hides, and tissue-regeneration genes. Instead, she had found herself living in a galaxy of hopelessly vulnerable people. Even relatively sturdy species, such as the Klingons, the Vulcans, and the Andorians, could be slain easily enough if only one knew where to strike.

Defending them, she'd realized during her first year at the Academy, was her charge to keep, her purpose for being. The deaths of Komer and Yott had been a painful reminder of that duty. In the hours since the attack, she had tripled the security presence in and around the *Columbia*. Armed guards had shepherded every research team, open channels had been maintained, and everyone had been made to stick together.

The last warm bodies on the planet's surface now were herself, the two rifle-toting guards down below, and the four engineers and two scientists they were protecting.

"Hockney to Kedair." The engineer's voice, filtered through her combadge, was all but lost in the roar of the wind and the white noise of sand scouring the hull of the *Columbia*.

She shielded her eyes and squinted aft through a crack in her fingers. If Hockney was still down there, she couldn't see him. "Go ahead," she said.

"Stand by to beam up in sixty seconds," Hockney shouted over the storm. *"Cupelli and ch'Narrath are upgrading the cargo transporters to quantum resolution to preserve our biosamples. As soon as they're done, we're outta here."*

Lifting her own voice, she replied, "Thank you, Ensign. Kedair out."

She hated to leave while the deaths of her shipmates remained unsolved. Abandoning the ship, letting it be swallowed up by the sands, felt to Kedair like a dereliction of duty. If the answer was still in there, it might be lost by the time the wind next deigned to liberate the *Columbia* from its shallow desert grave. But orders were orders. It was time to go.

Another voice squawked, weak and hollow, from her combadge. *"Aventine to away team: Stand by for transport."*

Her muscles tensed and she closed her eyes while she waited for the hazy white embrace of the transporter beam. Buffeted by the dry, hot gale and stinging granules, she held her breath and focused on continuing the investigation, by whatever means were available, when she returned to the ship.

Did we find anything here that was worth two people's lives? Kedair wondered. *Or was this all for nothing?*

She suspected that, at that very moment, on the *Aventine,* Captain Dax was learning the answer to that question.

"That doesn't answer my question, Lieutenant," said Dax, who was starting to think the briefing was going in circles.

Helkara stood in front of a diagram of the subspace tunnel phenomenon on the conference room's wall monitor, his mouth slightly agape. "I'm sorry, Captain," said the Zakdorn science officer. "Which question didn't it answer?"

"Any of them," Dax said. "We've suspected since day one that a subspace phenomenon carried the *Columbia* here from the Beta Quadrant. I want to know how it entered the phenomenon, as well as where and when."

Another stymied pause. Helkara cast bemused looks at the other officers seated around the table behind Dax: Mikaela Leishman, Sam Bowers, and

Nevin Riordan, a young computer specialist with a slight build and a disheveled bramble of short, spiky white hair. Then the Zakdorn said, "I don't have the data to answer that question right now, Captain."

And we're back at square one, Dax grumped to herself. "Why not?" She directed her next statement to Riordan. "I thought we recovered all of *Columbia*'s logs and databases."

"We did, Captain," Riordan said. "But as I was saying before you—" He stopped as he noticed Bowers's warning glare, but he'd already crossed the conversational Rubicon and had to continue. "—before you cut me off—we detected a gap in their log chronology. Eight months separate their last data on the ambush from the start of their sensor logs about the phenomenon."

As much as Dax wanted to be upset with the ensign for his impolitic reproach of her, she knew, in hindsight, that he was right. She had run roughshod over him in her impatience to reach some answers. To make some progress before the clock ran out and it came time to break orbit.

She asked Riordan, "Is it possible that it was a malfunction, or the result of damage?"

Riordan shook his head. "No, sir. No sign of damage or erasure. It's as if the ship's sensors just got turned off for eight months, then snapped back on inside the phenomenon."

Turning back to Helkara, Dax said, "What are the last regular entries in the *Columbia*'s log?"

"A Romulan ambush," Helkara said. "Based on the dates, it looks like the Romulans were testing some new tactics right before the start of their war with Earth. The ship's chief engineer tricked the Romulans into thinking the *Columbia* was destroyed, but it was left without communications or warp drive, a few light-years from Klingon space."

Dax drummed her fingertips on the tabletop. "Any indication what their next plan of action was?"

"None," Helkara said. "The last entry in Captain Hernandez's log is that their engines and subspace antenna were irreparable."

Leishman leaned forward and added, "The damage in their warp reactor and the internal components of their comm system still hadn't been fixed by the time they crashed here."

Helkara continued, "For what it's worth, Captain, the data from their passage through the phenomenon was completely intact, and as detailed as sensors of that era could be."

"All right," Dax said, surrendering to the realization that her other questions would have to wait for another time. "What, exactly, do we know about their journey through subspace?"

Bowers took over the briefing from Helkara, who returned to his seat as the first officer got up and stepped over to the wide companel monitor. "The *Columbia* was inside the phenomenon for just over forty-five seconds," he said. "There were thirty-one human life signs on board at the start of its journey, and one Denobulan. That leaves ten of its crew unaccounted for."

Dax interrupted to ask, "Could they have been killed during the Romulan ambush?"

Bowers looked to Helkara, who said, "The logs identified fifty-three ambush casualties and forty-two survivors."

Satisfied, Dax nodded to Bowers, who continued. "Once the ship passed inside the phenomenon, it got kicked around pretty good. The subspatial stresses were more volatile than those inside a wormhole or a controlled warp bubble."

"I can see the difference between this and a warp bubble," Dax said. "But what makes this different from a wormhole?"

Again, Bowers nodded to Helkara. The Zakdorn used a touch-screen interface in front of him on the tabletop to display animations on the large wall monitor. "Topologically, not much. Both, in essence, serve as passages for rapid travel between distant points in the same universe, or possibly different universes. Both are tubes with a topology of genus one, with a mouth, or terminus, at either end, and the throat, or tunnel, between them. The chief difference is where and how they exist."

He enlarged one of the schematics. "This is the Bajoran wormhole, a relatively stable shortcut through normal space-time. Its structure is made possible by a twelve-dimensional, helical verteron membrane and a series of verteron nodes, which tune its as-yet-unknown energy source to maintain its tunneling effect through space-time."

Switching to the second schematic, Helkara continued, "This is the subspace tunneling effect the *Columbia* encountered. Its shape is basically identical, but there are two major differences between this and the Bajoran wormhole. First, it doesn't exist in normal space-time, it only exists in subspace. Second—and I just want to say that this next point is pure conjecture, because no one has ever seen this work before—all of the *Columbia*'s data suggest this phenomenon is powered by dark energy drawn from normal space-time." He highlighted part of the display. "We think that's what led to the deaths of the crew."

Dax asked, "They were killed by the dark energy?"

"Not directly," Helkara said. "It was the by-product that did them in: hyperphasic radiation."

Bowers made a clicking noise with his tongue against the roof of his mouth. "That would do it. How fast did it hit?"

"I'd estimate every organic particle on the ship was disintegrated within twenty seconds of entering the subspace tunnel," Helkara said.

"But the ship spent forty-five seconds inside the phenomenon," Dax said. "Yesterday, Mirren said the ship's autopilot had been engaged. When did that happen?"

Bowers answered, "About fifteen seconds after the ship exited the subspace tunnel and returned to normal space-time."

"In other words," Dax said, doing the math in her head as she spoke, "about forty seconds after every living thing on that ship was dead."

Her first officer cocked one eyebrow and responded with a crooked grin. "Give or take."

"And there's no record of who or what triggered the autopilot," Dax said, and Helkara and Riordan nodded in confirmation. "Maybe it's some kind of creature that lives out of phase most of the time. Could it be the same thing that attacked Komer and Yott last night?"

With a shrug, Bowers said, "We don't know yet."

"Captain," Helkara said, "there's one more important note I'd like to share about the subspace tunnel."

She nodded. "Go ahead."

He got up and walked to the companel and pointed out some details as he spoke. "The energy field inside the tunnel was remarkably stable, much more than a conventional wormhole would be. If my analysis of its graviton emissions is correct, I think there's a very good chance the subspace tunnel is *still there*."

Dax looked at Bowers, who seemed as surprised by this news as she was. Intrigued, she asked Helkara, "Are you sure?"

"I'm almost positive," he said. "If we can locate the terminus and make a successful passage of the tunnel, we might be able to figure out how it was created. It could open up new areas of the galaxy for exploration—maybe the whole universe."

As if Dax needed more convincing, Bowers added, "If it leads back to a point in the Beta Quadrant, it might also be a major strategic discovery for Starfleet."

"Okay," Dax said. "How do we find the terminus?"

"I have a few ideas," Helkara said. "It's too soon to say which approach will work. But if I'm right and it's still there, with Lieutenant Leishman's help, I'm fairly certain I could track it down in a few hours."

She frowned. "We're supposed to be heading back now. I can hold us here for an hour, maybe two at the most. You have that long to find the subspace tunnel and figure out how to open it."

"You know," Bowers said with a mischievous gleam in his eyes, "if we find it and it still works, we could be back on the line in Federation space today instead of next week."

"Let's not get ahead of ourselves," Dax said. "The tunnel's still flooded with hyperphasic radiation."

Leishman waved away the problem. "I can work around that. A properly harmonized multiphasic frequency channeled into the shields should be able to cancel out their effects." She flashed an expectant look at Dax. "So what's the word, Captain?"

Dax grinned. "The word is go. Mikaela, get to work on those shields. Gruhn, start looking for the subspace tunnel. Sam, think up some excuse I can give the admiralty for why we're not out of orbit yet." She got up from her chair. "If there's—"

An alert Klaxon whooped once over the shipwide comm.

"Kedair to Captain Dax."

"Go ahead," Dax said.

"Captain, I need to see you and Commander Bowers in shuttlebay one, right away."

Bowers followed Captain Dax out of the turbolift on Deck 12 and followed her at a quick step toward the shuttlebay. At the first curve in the corridor, they were met by four security officers armed with phaser rifles. The quartet of guards fell into step around the two command officers and walked with them until they approached the open door to shuttlebay one, which was blocked by another duo of armed security officers. The pair stepped aside and let Dax and Bowers pass.

The first clue that something was amiss was the odor. Bowers wrinkled his nose at the sickly stench, which only became stronger as he and Dax neared the cluster of armed security personnel that surrounded the runabout *U.S.S. Seine.*

GODS OF NIGHT

Security chief Kedair noticed their arrival. She stepped away from the group to meet them. Her complexion was an even richer shade of blue-green than Bowers was accustomed to, and he took it as a sign of agitation. "Captain," she said, "I think we have an intruder."

Before Dax could ask Kedair to elaborate, the guards between them and the *Seine* parted, revealing a troubling sight through the runabout's open side hatch.

It was the slagged remains of a humanoid body, mixed with the burned tatters of a Starfleet uniform. Much of the victim's skin was gone, exposing jumbled viscera, half-dissolved muscles, and bones wet with liquefied fats and spilled blood. The half of its face that Bowers could see looked normal from the scalp to the nose, but everything from the upper lip to the chin looked as if it had been blasted away, down to the morbid grin of the skull. Its tongue was draped across its throat.

Forcing himself to remain detached and businesslike, he asked Kedair, "Have you identified the victim?"

"Crewman Ylacam," Kedair said. "Flight technician, first class. He was logged in for routine maintenance on the *Seine*."

Dax stepped forward, studying the scene with the eyes of a scientist. "How much do we know about what happened?"

"Not much more than we know about what happened to Komer and Yott on the *Columbia*," Kedair said. "Mirren's pulling the internal sensor logs and starting a forensic review."

DAVID MACK

Bowers averted his eyes from the stomach-churning carnage inside the runabout. "Are we sure it's the same cause of death that we saw on the *Columbia*?"

"All but certain," Kedair said. "I'm just waiting on final confirmation." Looking over Bowers's shoulder, she added, "And here it comes now."

Dr. Tarses entered the shuttlebay, followed by a female medical technician with a stretcher. The CMO paused as he saw the state of the body inside the runabout. He looked back at the medtech and said, "We don't need the stretcher. Go back and get some sample jars and a stasis pouch." The technician nodded and reversed course, quick-timing her way out of the shuttlebay and looking relieved for the opportunity.

Tarses approached the runabout with a wary frown. "Not again," he mumbled as he passed Kedair. He opened his satchel, removed a medical tricorder, activated it, and started a scan of the half-burned, half-melted corpse. "Molecular disruption," he said, reading from the tricorder's screen. "Acute thermal effects. Major breakdown in all organic material."

On a hunch, Bowers asked, "Is the damage consistent with hyperphasic radiation exposure?"

"No, it's not," Tarses said, putting away his tricorder. "Hyperphasic radiation desiccates organic matter and disperses it into subspace. Basically, it turns people into gas and dust. Whatever did this turns people into soup."

Dax asked the doctor, "Was this done by the same thing that killed our people on the *Columbia*?"

As he considered his answer, Tarses crossed his left arm over his torso and tugged gently with his right hand at the lobe of one of his pointed ears. "The effects are all but identical," he concluded. "So I'd have to say yes, it was."

"Lonnoc," Dax said to the security chief, "sound a shipwide intruder alert. All nonessential personnel are restricted to quarters. Have your people sweep the ship, bow to stern. Use sensors, hard-target searches, whatever it takes. Something followed us up from the planet, and I want it found, now."

Turning to Bowers, the captain added, "Sam, tell Starfleet Command we're not going anywhere—not until I find out what we're dealing with."

2168

17

An electric charge in the air raised the fine hairs on Commander Veronica Fletcher's forearm. She gazed into the chasm beyond the catwalk and felt humbled.

"This is as close to the apparatus as I can permit you," said Inyx, who led Fletcher, Karl Graylock, and Kiona Thayer on a guided tour of the enormous machine at the center of the Caeliar's "great work." They had come here by way of a disk ride and a swift descent through a nondescript tube set into a promenade beside a vast, darkly translucent dome. It wasn't until they'd reached the catwalk that Fletcher realized their destination lay beneath the hemispherical shield, which from this side appeared to be transparent.

A massive, clear cylinder with dozens of meter-wide vertical gaps placed asymmetrically along its entire length was connected at its top to the dome's center, two hundred meters overhead. Suspended from it was a huge, circular platform whose surface was divided into a silver ring around the cylinder and a black outer ring of equal thickness. Both surfaces were polished to mirror brilliance and reflected the steady, pulsing display of prismatic energy inside the central column.

"It's magnificent," Thayer said, awestruck.

Fletcher continued to study the platform's other large details. From her vantage point, she could see five of what she presumed was a total of eight narrow arms with chisel-shaped ends reaching down and away from a second layer of the platform; the arms were mounted on broad, ring-shaped joint mechanisms and spaced forty-five degrees apart. Between them were bevel-edged, blocky structures that resembled docking ports. From the center of each squarish mass bulged a black hemisphere set inside a bright metallic ring.

Underneath the thick lower ring of the platform was a shimmering globe of incandescent coils. The top of the sphere was connected by a weblike conglomeration of machinery and cabling, all of it silhouetted by the blinding ball. Its glow illuminated the distant sides of the silo-shaped abyss, but it was not powerful enough to reach the bottom, from which came an echo of the low, throbbing pulse of the machine.

"The apparatus serves two major functions," Inyx said. He walked forward, and the *Columbia* officers followed him along the curved, railing-free catwalk that ran the perimeter of the silo. "It is a means of observation, and a tool for communication. With it, we can listen for signals from the farthest extremities of the universe, and we can establish real-time contact with anyone or anything we discover."

As Fletcher's eyes adjusted, she discerned the shapes of Caeliar moving about in pairs on the surface of the sprawling platform. Watching them move in and out of portals in the blockhouse structures, she asked Inyx, "So, this is how you plan to talk with something more advanced than yourselves?"

"Yes," Inyx said. "We realized several thousand years ago that many of the galaxies we were investigating were either long dead or had never been capable of supporting life. In order to find a civilization that meets our criteria, we limited our search to those billions of galaxies that were not inherently hostile to life, and that had remained stable for the estimated billions of years that might be necessary for it to develop."

"I'm sorry," interrupted Thayer. "Did you say you searched *billions* of galaxies?"

Inyx faced the dark-haired young woman. "Yes. We were extremely selective. I confess that limiting our candidates in this manner might have led us to overlook viable systems, but I felt the risk of oversight was statistically insignificant."

Fletcher watched a trio of Caeliar levitate and float from the platform, across the hundred-meter-wide void, to a catwalk below the one on which she walked. "So now you're looking for contacts at the end of the universe," she said to Inyx, to keep him from making note of her silent observations. "At what range? Fourteen billion light-years?"

"Slightly less," Inyx said. "Approximately thirteen-point-eight-seven billion light-years, using your metrics."

Graylock took his turn drawing their host's attention. "Hmmph. Must take a lot of power to send a signal that far."

"More power than your species has harnessed so far in its entire history," Inyx said.

Graylock pointed at the distant platform and asked in amazement, "All through *that* machine?"

Inyx bowed his head in a stiff imitation of a nod, a habit he'd picked up from interacting with the *Columbia*'s landing party. "Yes," he said.

Goading the Caeliar, Graylock inquired, "What if that generator on the bottom overloads?"

"As that is not the generator, there is little possibility of that," Inyx said.

Thayer cut in, "See, Karl? I told you. They generate the power remotely, just like for everything else around here."

"Quite correct, Kiona," Inyx said in a patronizing tone.

She replied, "You must use up a lot of that power punching through the scattering field, though."

"*Nein*," Graylock said before Inyx could answer. "They use a subharmonic to collimate the signal after it leaves the field."

"Hardly, Karl." The visage of the Caeliar always seemed to convey hauteur, but Inyx's tone was rife with it. Graylock visibly tensed whenever one of the Caeliar addressed him by his given name. Inyx continued, "At the power levels involved here, a phase-shifted soliton pulse is the only choice."

"Really?" Graylock's feigned ignorance was painfully obvious to Fletcher, but the Caeliar seemed so oblivious of human behavior that they took the landing party's statements at face value. In this case, Graylock had made good use of the Caeliar scientist's almost reflexive habit of correcting erroneous hypotheses. Had the question been left for Inyx to answer, his reply would have been vague. To correct Graylock's blatant "errors," however, Inyx seemed frequently compelled to elaborate and underscore his superior expertise.

Part of Fletcher's task was to keep changing the subject, in the hope of distracting Inyx from the purpose of their many inquiries and ruses. "Assuming you locate a culture more advanced than yours," she said, "what do you hope to learn?"

"We don't know, exactly," Inyx said. "One might say we are in search of our next step as a culture."

Thayer said, "Are you certain there's nobody worth talking to anywhere closer than the edge of the universe?"

"It has been hundreds of your millennia since we eliminated all the habitable galaxies within one billion light-years as viable candidates," Inyx said. "Every failed search has spurred us to press on and look deeper into space and time. We believe that we are only days from opening contact with the civilization we have sought. If my analysis is correct, I have located a harnessed galaxy, an achievement unlike any I have ever seen."

Fletcher looked at the giant machine, brilliant and held aloft over a pit of midnight blue shadows. She grinned at Inyx. "That thing really must be one of a kind."

"Not at all," Inyx said. "There is an identical apparatus in each of our cities." Conspiratorial glances passed between Fletcher and the other two officers, unnoticed by Inyx. He continued, "If your curiosity is now sated, may I suggest we—"

"Can we go to the platform for a closer look?" asked Fletcher. It had taken her months of pleading and assurances to secure permission from the Caeliar for this tour, and she wasn't going to let it end without trying to make the most of it.

Inyx stiffened at the request, and his normally cordial demeanor chilled. "I'm afraid that would be quite out of the question," he said. "It's time to go back. Please follow me."

The lanky alien led the three humans off the catwalk and down a narrow passage, one of several that radiated away from the vast empty chamber of the apparatus. Their visit to the Caeliar's signature achievement had been brief but educational. Fletcher hoped that she and her officers had learned enough to find a way off this planet—and a way home.

Sheltered under the gnarled boughs of the tree at the end of the black reflecting pool, the stranded members of the *Columbia*'s flight crew sat in a circle around their captain.

"The clock is definitely ticking, folks," Fletcher said. "Inyx says they're only days away from powering up this super gadget of theirs, so if there's any way it can help us get back to the ship, we need to figure it out fast."

Graylock and Thayer reached into the pockets on the legs of their jumpsuits and removed three hand scanners each. It had taken Graylock months to juryrig a solar cell and then recharge the drained devices. From then until that day's tour of the "apparatus," the landing party had kept the scanners powered down and hidden to avoid detection by the Caeliar. As Thayer had hoped, the scattering field was configured as a shell around the city; the hand scanners functioned normally inside the protected zone but were blind to anything beyond it.

"We had these set for passive scans," Graylock said as he handed two of them to Hernandez and Fletcher. "Each scanner was set to look for something different."

Metzger and Valerian each accepted a scanner from Thayer, who noted, "Security on the 'apparatus' is tighter than other spots we've been to. It's completely sealed in and underground."

A warm breeze tossed locks of Hernandez's black hair into her eyes, and she swept it away with a pass of her hand. "Karl, what is this thing?"

"The final word in subspace radio," said the Austrian. "Inyx says it can make real-time contact between here and the end of the universe."

Lifting her eyebrows in mild surprise, the captain asked, "Any idea how it works?"

Graylock tapped at the screen of his hand scanner. "The platform creates an intense subspace phase-distortion field. And the pulses inside the column—" He looked around, made a hasty swap of scanners with Thayer, and continued. "—are soliton waves, just like Inyx said. I think this thing sends the waves through subspace, uses them like a drill to make a hole. Then the phase distorter . . ." He leaned forward and traded scanners with Valerian. "The phase distorter acts like a nut and bolt, pulling the two ends of the hole together, until they meet."

"Now my brain hurts," mumbled Dr. Metzger.

Hernandez turned off her hand scanner and looked at Thayer. "Thoughts, Kiona?"

"With all the power that thing uses, it might make a hell of a feedback pulse if it got disrupted during their big event, maybe enough to knock out their power source and drop the scattering field so *Columbia* can beam us up and break orbit."

Graylock let out a derisive snort of laughter. "Or it might blow up the city—or maybe the planet."

"That's not the only flaw," Fletcher said. "It would have to take the Caeliar out of commission for at least six minutes: one minute for *Columbia* to find us after the scattering field falls, four minutes to beam us up three at a time, one minute to break orbit at full impulse. And that's assuming the crew on the ship is standing by and ready to act on a moment's notice."

"Actually," Hernandez said, "we don't even know if the rest of the crew is still up there. They might have abandoned ship and beamed down to the planet by now."

Thayer added darkly, "Or the Caeliar might have displaced them." Grim stares around the circle confirmed that she wasn't the only one who had considered that scenario.

Valerian said, "Even if we do get back to the ship, what then? We're still at least twenty light-years from the nearest friendly system, and there's no tellin' what's moved into the space between while we've been tootlin' around for the last twelve years. Are we just gonna limp home, show up thirty-four years late, and ask if we have any messages?"

Speaking like a man who knew a secret, Graylock asked, "Who says we have to get home late?"

Hernandez was not in a mood for a mystery. "Explain."

"The tunnels the Caeliar are making through subspace are a lot like Lorentzian wormholes," Graylock said. "Even though they're in subspace, most of the rules still apply. If it makes a shortcut through space, it can make a shortcut through time—forward *or* backward."

"Whoa," said Hernandez, dragging out the word like she was reining a wild horse to a halt. "Time travel, Karl? Are you out of your mind? We've barely got the hang of warp speed, and you think you're ready to break the time barrier?"

The chief engineer got red in the face. "Why not? If this thing's as powerful as Inyx says, we can get back to Earth—not today, but twelve years ago, when it might make a difference!"

"He's right," Thayer said. "If we go back, we could warn Earth about the Romulans, tell them about the ambush. It might save who knows how many lives."

Captain Hernandez frowned. "And it might destroy the time line. The Vulcans *warned* us about this kind of thing."

"Oh, screw the Vulcans," Thayer said. "Us getting back might be the thing that decides who wins the war. We have a duty to try and get home."

Graylock nodded. "*Ja,* and for all we know, Captain, it's what *supposed* to happen. Maybe we've already done it. And if we prevent our earlier selves from coming here, the Caeliar would never *know* that we did it."

On some level, Hernandez found the idea tempting. It would be a chance to erase the biggest mistake of her career, maybe even save the convoy, hundreds of lives, and change the course of the war. . . . Then she reminded herself that tampering with history and with temporal mechanics might be a task with zero margin for error; the slightest mistake could destroy everything and everyone that she cared about. And then there was the reaction of the Caeliar to consider, whether they succeeded or not.

"No," she said. "Messing with time is too damn dangerous. We might end up making things worse. For all we know, we were meant to be lost in action twelve years ago, and we're meant to be here now. I want to go home just as much as the rest of you, but I'm not willing to risk undoing twelve years of history—twelve years of *other* people's successes and sacrifices—just so I can feel like I didn't miss anything." She scanned the reactions of the group as she added, "Even more important, if we actually escape and get home, think about what the Caeliar will do—not just to us, but to Earth. We might end up condemning our entire world to oblivion. And I can't allow that." She let go of a heavy, dispirited sigh. "I'm sorry, but our first duty is to protect Earth, and in this case that means making a sacrifice and accepting our fate. Is that clear?" Thayer and Graylock gave reluctant nods, in contrast to the easy assent from Valerian, Fletcher, and Metzger. "All right," Hernandez said.

"So, what now?" asked Fletcher. "If we're really giving up on escape, what's left for us?"

Hernandez shrugged. "I'm not sure. Maybe I'll ask for permission to bring down the rest of the crew. Let the Caeliar decide what to do with the *Columbia*." She looked around at the city. "It's not exactly where

I'd planned on spending my retirement, but I can think of worse places."

"If we're staying here," Fletcher said, "there'll have to be some changes."

Hernandez arched one eyebrow. "Such as?"

Fletcher smirked. "For starters, I want my own apartment."

Major Foyle stood on the penthouse suite's terrace and stared beyond the sharp edges of the Caeliar city, to the distant peaks of mountains hidden under blankets of autumn fog. "So . . . she's lost the will to fight?" He turned and regarded his visitors.

The *Columbia*'s chief engineer and senior weapons officer both looked and sounded nervous—appropriate enough reactions for officers going behind their captain's back.

"They've broken her," Thayer said. "Not only is she telling us not to try and escape, she wants to bring down the rest of the crew. She's talking about *abandoning the ship*."

Foyle's brow creased with intense concentration as he pondered the situation. He asked Graylock, "Do you concur with Lieutenant Thayer's assessment?"

"*Ja, Herr* Major," said the broad-shouldered Austrian.

Behind the two flight officers, the rest of the MACOs perched like gargoyles along the lip of the penthouse's roof, which was a jumble of odd shapes and angles. It was lunchtime, and the men were all snacking on small pieces of fruit, as well as on sticks of dried, synthetic meat that they had conserved and rationed from their provisions for the past few months.

The switch to a predominantly vegetarian diet had given all the members of the landing party a distinctly lean and hungry look.

"I wish there was some satisfaction in being able to say I told you so, Lieutenant, but there isn't." Foyle sighed and turned back toward the faraway range. "If Captain Hernandez isn't willing to use force to secure our freedom, then I have to question her fitness to command." At the edges of his vision, he saw Graylock and Thayer stake out positions on either side of him, leaning on the terrace's railing. "If I place this mission under military authority, will I have your support?"

"Absolutely," Thayer said.

"*Jawohl,*" said Graylock. "It's why we came to you."

The major nodded. "And the others?"

"*Nein.* They won't go against the captain."

"I'd suspected as much," Foyle said. Turning his head toward Thayer, he said, "Tell me about your diversion."

There was excitement in her eyes as she detailed the plan. "It entails coordinated strikes on the 'apparatus' in two of the other cities, preferably ones as far as possible from Axion."

"I don't have that much manpower," Foyle argued.

She pulled a hand scanner from her jumpsuit's leg pocket and handed it to him. "We only need to seize one node of the apparatus in person. In the second city, we'll use a timer-detonated munition to blow up a different node while it's all juiced up for their big experiment. The tachyon pulse alone should be enough to collapse the scattering fields worldwide."

"For how long?"

Thayer glanced at Graylock, who said, "No idea. We hope it'll last for at least six minutes so we can beam back to the ship and break orbit."

Foyle considered the power that their captors had already displayed on the planet's surface. "Once we're on the ship, what then? Do we really think we can outrun the Caeliar at impulse?"

"We may not have to," Graylock said. "The technology they're using for their 'great work' could be modified to send us back home in a snap."

The major gritted his teeth and twisted his mouth into a rueful grimace. "Let's remember what the good captain said about our hosts' bad habit of 'displacing' entire civilizations. Do we want to risk bringing that kind of attention to Earth?"

Graylock smirked. "If we do this properly, *Herr* Major, the Caeliar might never know we were here."

"That's the other proposal the captain rejected," Thayer said. "The Caeliar's machines can move us through time *and* space. We'd have to run afoul of the predestination paradox, and deal with meeting ourselves, and about a dozen other temporal no-nos . . . but we could go back, warn Earth about the Romulans, and save ourselves from getting stuck here in the first place."

From behind the trio came the scuffle of men climbing down from the rooftop. Foyle and the *Columbia* officers turned to see Pembleton and Yacavino stride toward them, while Crichlow, Mazzetti, and Steinhauer scrambled over the edge and sought purchase with their hands and feet.

"Did I just hear that?" asked Pembleton. "We can go back? I can see my wife again and watch my boys grow up?"

"In theory," said Graylock.

The MACOs gathered around, a wall of intense focus and dark forest camouflage, as Foyle asked the engineer, "What will it take to make your theory a reality?"

"Phase two of the plan," answered Thayer. All eyes turned to her, the only woman on the terrace, as she continued. "Karl has a good idea what the Caeliar's machines are capable of, but he doesn't know how to make them do what he wants. I think the Caeliar do know how, and if they're properly motivated, they might be . . . *persuaded* to assist us."

Pembleton threw a sidelong stare at Foyle. "That does sound like our specialty, Major."

Foyle was torn. Mucking about with time was dangerous business, no matter how cavalierly his men embraced it. He hadn't been trained for decisions such as this. Small-unit tactics, SERE protocols, psyops, boarding procedures—those were his areas of expertise. Altering the flow of history had not been covered at the war college in Credenhill. But the human cost of his decision was staring him in the eye. This was a chance to reunite his sergeant with his family, bring his men and the crew of the *Columbia* home to their friends and loved ones, and spare all those people back on Earth the grief of believing the ship and its crew lost in action.

A chance to go home to Valerie. To his life. Their life.

For all I know, the Romulans conquered Earth because we couldn't get a warning out, he brooded. *What if everyone we care about is gone because of that mistake? What if our going back in time is Earth's only hope?*

He climbed up from the deep well of his thoughts to find everyone staring at him and waiting for his answer. "Graylock, if my people get you into one of those machines and compel the Caeliar to cooperate, are you sure you can pull this off?"

"I'm certain it's our only chance, *Herr* Major."

Foyle studied Thayer's eyes, looking for the resolve of a soldier. He asked her, "When this turns ugly—and I promise you, it will—can I count on you to go the distance?"

"Whatever it takes, sir," Thayer said. "I refuse to die as a prisoner, here or anywhere else."

That was an answer Foyle could accept and respect. "All right, then," he said. "Forget what Captain Hernandez wants. If we're going to make a go of this, we have to hit the Caeliar where it'll hurt them most." He worked his way around the circle with speed and certainty. "Yacavino, you and Crichlow get munitions in place before they start their big experiment. Have Lieutenant Thayer tell you which site to mine. Pembleton, go over the scans of the Caeliar with Lieutenant Graylock and see if we can bring them down to our level and hurt them once we get them there. Mazzetti, Steinhauer—you're both with me."

Yacavino looked worried. "What will you be doing, sir?"

"I expect Captain Hernandez will object to our plan," Foyle said. "She and the other flight officers will have to be kept in sight and out of the loop. When it's time to attack, they'll have to be contained until we're ready to beam up." He saw Yacavino's expression of concern mirrored on the faces of Thayer and Graylock. "Trust me," he added. "She'll thank us after we all get home." That seemed to mollify the three lieutenants. Foyle snapped everyone into action with a clap of his hands. "We have a lot to do. Let's get to work."

The group moved off and segregated into duos according to the assignments that Foyle had made. The lone straggler was Sergeant Pembleton, who waited until the others were out of earshot before he confided to the major, "You know containment won't be enough, don't you? She won't stand for it."

"I know," Foyle said. "And we can't take a chance on her alerting the Caeliar before we break orbit." He patted the taller man's shoulder. "I'll handle it."

"One more thing bothers me, sir," Pembleton said. Foyle nodded for him to continue. "What if the Caeliar have taken the rest of the ship's crew prisoner? What if there's no one up there to beam us aboard?"

Foyle looked to the horizon. "Then we're already dead."

2381

18

———•———

Commander Geordi La Forge walked through the mechanical jungle of assembly lines that occupied three converted cargo bays on Deck 23 of the *Enterprise*. A tang of overheated metal filled the ozone-rich air, and the long, open space buzzed with the hum of motors, plasma welders, and industrial replicators.

The death factory. That was La Forge's secret nickname for this hastily erected manufacturing complex. Here was where the crew struggled to produce a steady supply of the one weapon that so far had proved consistently effective against the Borg: transphasic torpedoes.

Flashes of light from the welding teams pierced the blue haze that lingered between checkpoints on the line. Lighting in the munitions plant was kept glare-free and diffuse, to avoid hard shadows and reduce eyestrain. Most of the line was powered by antigravs, which kept the noise to a low rumble.

For those who toiled here, the only relief from the monotony was to be rotated between different stations each day. Watching the dull routine, the grind of repetition, La Forge found it hard to believe that it made much difference. One set of rote tasks was as mind-numbing as another.

He stopped to check the phase variance circuit on a finished warhead that was awaiting delivery to the forward torpedo room. He used the warhead's built-in touch-screen interface to perform a quality-control inspection of its internal systems. The data was still crawling up the screen as he noted someone approaching from his left.

"Geordi," said Beverly Crusher, who had a medical satchel slung at her hip. She stopped beside him and noted the inspection in progress. "Am I catching you at a bad time?"

It was a terrible time, but the chief engineer shook his head and replied, "Not at all. What can I do for you?"

"Actually, I'm here to do something for you," she said, opening her satchel. She removed a small gadget that La Forge recognized as a recalibration tool for his ocular implants. "I'm sorry I didn't have time to tend to your injuries personally when you came to sickbay." Lifting the device to his temple, she continued, "Dr. Tropp said you left sickbay before he could fix the damage to your implants."

La Forge tried to dismiss her concern with a half-hearted smile. "It's no big deal, Doc. Just some false-spectrum artifacts in the ultraviolet range. I just tune it out."

"Mm-hmm," she mumbled, adjusting the calibrator's settings. "I'll have it fixed in a few seconds, so just hold still." With a mischievous gleam she added, "And don't say I never make house calls."

As promised, the distortion cleared instantly. Crusher switched off the device, and he nodded to her.

"Much better. Thanks." He turned to resume his diagnostic of the warhead he'd been inspecting when she came in. A moment later he noticed that Crusher didn't seem to be making any move to depart. Over his shoulder, he asked, "Want to tell me why you're *really* here?"

"Because I don't know who else to talk to," she confessed.

He turned and folded his arms. "This sounds interesting."

Now that she had his full attention, Crusher looked very self-conscious. "It's about the captain," she said, copying La Forge's guarded stance, arms crossed in front of her chest. "I'm worried about him. About what this mission is doing to him."

"Are you sure I'm the right one to talk to?" he asked. "If it's a command issue—"

"It's not," she interrupted. "And it's not something for the counselors, or for Starfleet Command. I don't even want to take any action, I just want to talk to someone about it. Someone who won't have to file a report."

Crusher didn't mention Worf by name; she didn't have to. All at once, Geordi understood her dilemma. Worf, by nature, would always err on the side of supporting his captain, and if Crusher raised an official concern, Worf would be required to note it in his log. The same would likely be true of the ship's staff of counselors. With the recent departures of so many of Crusher's longtime friends on the senior staff—including Will Riker and Deanna Troi—La Forge was probably the last of the "old guard" whom she felt she could trust to lend a discreet and sympathetic ear to her concerns.

He conveyed his understanding with a single, slow nod. "If anyone asks, this conversation never happened."

"Thank you," she said.

He gave a final glance at the warhead's data readout and was satisfied that all its ratings were nominal. He shut it down and moved on, walking between two long lines of automated machines cranking out a steady parade of warhead casings. Crusher followed along. As she fell into step beside him, he asked, "So what is it we aren't talking about?"

"Obsession," she said. "Specifically, Jean-Luc's fixation on eradicating the Borg. I guess I'm worried because I'm hearing him advocate strategies that I never thought he'd endorse."

La Forge rolled his eyes at the understatement. "I know what you mean. Every line I think he won't cross, he goes over in a broad jump. Truth is, it's starting to scare me."

She reached out and touched his arm in silent affirmation. "Me, too," she said. Gentle pressure from her hand brought him to a halt with her as she continued. "One minute he seems ready to surrender, just throw himself on his sword, and the next he's channeling Henry the Fifth, 'once more unto the breach,' and all that. And neither seems like him."

"Except when he deals with the Borg," La Forge corrected her. "Then everything he's ever done and said goes right out the window. Logic, discipline, principles . . . he burns 'em all when he's up against the Collective."

"I know," she said. "When he fights them, he becomes like them—an extremist. A conformist one moment, a radical the next. And I feel like he's pushing us and Starfleet into a full-scale confrontation, no matter what the cost. He keeps talking about a 'clash of civilizations' as if it's inevitable, but then he says we can't win that kind of war with the Borg. So what is he trying to do? Is he just looking to end it, even if it means dying and taking the Federation down with him?"

La Forge resumed walking, and Crusher stayed by his side. "I wouldn't say the captain has a death wish," he said. "Not yet, anyway. But I look at this place"—he gestured around them at the munitions plant—"and I feel like he's already decided there's only one way the war can end, and it's in fire."

"It's not like the Borg are giving us much choice, Geordi, especially now that they're bent on extermination instead of assimilation. Shutting down the Collective might be our only chance of survival."

A gust of heated air washed over them as they kept walking. Shielding his face, he replied, "It's not as simple as shutting them down, and you know it. The Borg aren't just machines. Most of the drones in the Collective used to be individuals, just like us." La Forge raised his voice as they passed a noisy bank of plasma cutters. "We've seen drones come back from that—Hugh, Seven of Nine, Rebekah Grabowski, even the captain himself. No matter what the Borg look like on the outside, there are still people in there, Beverly—people who've been enslaved. I know the Collective's the enemy, but I can't help but feel like killing the drones is just punishing the victims without getting to the source of the problem."

They turned left at the end of the aisle and circled around to walk past a row of specialists who were performing precision calibrations on magnetic containment cores for variable-phase antideuterium. One mistake here could spark a blast that would destroy the *Enterprise* in a microsecond. Ion fusers in constant operation cast dull, ruddy glows beneath thick, rodinium glare shields while technicians monitored their work via nanocams.

Crusher walked with one hand pressed protectively over her abdomen. The sight of Beverly, as the bearer of a new life, surrounded by instruments of death and destruction made La Forge want to hurry her out of the munitions plant and as far away from these infernal machines as possible.

She sounded worn out as she asked, "What are we going to do if Jean-Luc loses control, Geordi? Where do we draw the line?"

"I don't know. I'm not even sure I'm qualified to say if or when he's crossed it. He's always been hard to gauge when it comes to the Borg. One minute he's ready to kill them all, the next he says wiping them out is wrong . . . and then, when you least expect it, he turns himself back into Locutus." He stopped next to one of the photon chargers and stared into the rhythmic workings of the assembly line until his sense of depth flattened and its details fused together. "I'm just afraid we won't know which Captain Picard we've got *this* time until it's too late."

"Whatever we're flying toward, it's big," said Miranda Kadohata, "and eight minutes ago it started jamming all known subspace frequencies within thirty light-years of the Azure Nebula."

The announcement by the ship's second officer added to the already grave mood of the emergency staff briefing. Dismayed glances were volleyed across the conference table, from Choudhury to Worf, and then from Kadohata to the captain. Absent from the meeting was Commander La Forge, whom Worf had excused so the chief engineer could give his full attention to making the ship itself ready for combat.

Worf decided to try and preserve a sense of momentum in the meeting. He asked Kadohata, "What is our ETA to the nebula?"

"Nine hours. We're following the sirillium traces from the Borg ship we destroyed at Korvat, but the jamming field is blocking our sensors. We could be heading into a trap."

Captain Picard sat at the head of the table and regarded the senior officers with his careworn frown. "I think it's safe to say that we'll be facing stiff resistance when we reach the nebula," he said. "We need to be prepared."

Lieutenant Choudhury replied, "The security division is good to go, sir. With your permission, I'd like to post extra guards on all decks, in case we get boarded."

"Granted," Picard said, "but you might find their effectiveness limited against the Borg."

"I'm aware of that, sir, but in combat, sometimes a few extra seconds make the difference. My people are ready to give you those seconds if you need them."

Worf noted the captain's dour nod of approval but no change in his mirthless visage. "Well done," was all Picard said to the security chief. Then he turned to Lieutenant Dina Elfiki. "Can you break through the interference at short range?"

"I think so," Elfiki said. The soft-spoken science officer—whose brown hair framed her tanned, elegant cheekbones and dark, beguiling eyes—looked younger than her years. "The subspace interference shouldn't stop us from finding transwarp signatures or anything similar. Once we close to within a few billion kilometers of the nebula, I can start my sweep."

"Good," Picard said as he got up from his chair. He seemed pensive as he paced behind it and laid his hands on top of its headrest. After a few moments, he said, "Before we lost communications, I received a message from Starfleet Command. It was a reply to my request for reinforcements to rendezvous with us at the nebula." He stepped to the wall panel and activated it with a touch of his hand. A starmap of the surrounding sectors appeared. "Starfleet's losses have been heavier than expected," he continued. "Less than an hour ago, a previously undetected Borg cube destroyed Starbase 24, along with the starships *Merrimack, Ulysses,* and *Sparta.* The only ship besides us in this sector is the *Excalibur,* and she's all but crippled after stopping the attack on Starbase 343. Which means we'll be facing this threat alone."

Tense anticipation filled the room. Worf could almost smell the anxiety—he was too polite to call it *fear*—of his human shipmates. "The *Enterprise* is ready, Captain. As are we."

"Of that I have no doubt, Commander. But I need to make clear that combat is not our principal mission. Our assignment is to find out how the Borg are reaching our space undetected, and then deny them that ability. Furthermore, we, and this ship, are to be considered expendable in the pursuit of that goal." The captain looked at the faces around the table. "Clear?"

Everyone nodded in confirmation.

Picard's already serious manner turned grim. "I've made no secret in the past of my . . . *unusual* connection with the Borg Collective, or that it's as much a liability as an asset." He strolled behind the officers seated on Worf's side of the table as he continued, talking as if to himself. "I can sense them now. The voice of the Collective is getting stronger as we get closer. There are at least three Borg cubes waiting for us. Maybe more." The captain avoided eye contact with everyone else as he paced around the far end of the conference table. "And they know we're coming. We won't enjoy the element of surprise." Returning along the other side of the table, Picard stared into some deep distance only he could perceive. "If we had the luxury of time, I'd wait for the fleet. But I can feel the fury that's driving the Borg. It's like a whip of fire on their backs."

The captain returned to the head of the table, eased his chair aside, and stood tall before the group. "We don't have long—hours, perhaps days—to stop this invasion before it goes any further. The Federation has suffered more casualties from hostile action in the past five weeks than in all the previous wars of its history combined. And it's only going to get worse, unless we put an end to it. This ship is the Federation's last line of defense, and nine hours from now we will have to hold that line, outnumbered by an enemy that doesn't negotiate, won't surrender, and never shows mercy. It's an impossible mission."

Picard's frown became a smirk as he added, "Fortunately, we have some experience with those here on the *Enterprise*."

19

———◆———

"Of course you don't like it," Vale said to Riker, Troi, and Ree. "I don't like it, either. That's how I know it's a good compromise: We're all equally unhappy."

Troi shifted uncomfortably on the end of the biobed where she was sitting. Riker stood beside her. They were both sullen, and their eyes searched *Titan*'s sickbay for everything except each other. Vale watched them, worried they might reject the agreement she had negotiated with Dr. Ree on their behalf.

Ree carried himself with an even greater aura of menace than usual. The dinosaur-like physician's tail waved behind him in slow, steady swishes, a Pahkwa-thanh affectation that Vale intuited was indicative of suppressed irritation.

Standing between the vexed doctor and the unhappy couple, Vale was determined not to say anything more until one side or the other broke the stand-off. As she'd hoped, the captain took the initiative. "How long will the stasis last?" Riker asked.

"Strictly speaking, it's not stasis," Ree explained. "The treatment will slow your child's growth almost

– 332 –

to the point of halting it, but she will still draw nourishment from—"

Troi interrupted, "Did you say 'she'?"

The doctor's tail halted in mid-swing, and he seemed frozen, as if he were trapped by invisible amber.

Vale knew from some of her earlier conversations with Ree that he had been avoiding using gender pronouns when referring to Troi's terminally mutated fetus, because he felt that calling the child "it" would somehow depersonalize her and make her loss easier for Riker and Troi to cope with. Although Vale had no medical or psychiatric training to speak of, she was convinced that Ree was crazy if he believed that his choice of pronoun would ease Troi's and Riker's pain one damn bit.

A low rasp rattled deep inside Ree's long, toothy mouth, and his head dipped in a gesture that Vale thought might suggest shame, disappointment, or perhaps both at once. "Yes," he continued, with an air of resignation. "She will continue drawing sustenance from your body, even as her growth is impeded by the targeted synthetase inhibitor."

Riker nodded. "Is this a onetime treatment?"

"Unfortunately, no," Ree replied. His tongue darted from between his front fangs, two quick flicks. "To avoid harming the fetus—and your wife—I have to keep the dosages very small. She will need daily injections to maintain a safe equilibrium. I also wish to make clear that this is not a solution, merely a delaying tactic. It will postpone the imminent risk of the fetus growing and puncturing the uterine wall, but it doesn't change the fact that the pregnancy itself is unviable."

Troi asked, "How long can we use this treatment?"

"I don't know. It's experimental, and there are many variables. We might be able to stall your pregnancy for months, or your body could reject the TSI, and we'd be back where we started. I can't guarantee it will work for long, or at all."

"Until it does," Vale said to Ree, "I need to insist you remove Commander Troi from active duty."

The captain cut off Ree's reply. "Absolutely not. If this works, there won't be any imminent threat to her health, so what would be the point?"

Vale modulated her voice into a diplomat's tones. "The point is that until Dr. Ree can observe her reaction to the treatment, we won't know how safe she really is."

"Commander Vale is correct," Ree said to Riker. Then, to Troi, he added, "A period of observation would be in your best interests, my dear counselor."

"Fine," Troi said. "Monitor my bio-signs with a transponder and let me go about my business. I don't need to be confined to a bed—here *or* in my quarters."

Riker added, "Would that be acceptable to you, Doctor?"

"It won't be ideal," Ree said. "But it will be sufficient." He reached over to a nearby surgical cart and picked up a hypospray and a biometric transponder implantation device. "Are we agreed, then, on this futile and utterly—"

"*Doctor*," Vale snapped, terminating another potentially inflammatory elocution of the doctor's sarcastic rant about patients ignoring his advice.

Ree's tongue flitted twice in the cool, antiseptic-scented air of sickbay. Ostensibly accepting defeat, he sagged at the shoulders and said to Troi, "May I proceed?"

The counselor nodded her assent, and Ree went to work. A gentle press of the hypospray against Troi's left bicep injected her with her first dose of TSI. He switched to the transponder implantation device, manipulating it and the hypospray with one clawed hand, whose digits, Vale saw, were capable of surprising dexterity. Ree placed the tip of the squat, cylindrical device against Troi's left forearm, a few centimeters above her wrist. "This might sting a bit," he warned.

A soft popping sound from the device was overlapped by Troi's stifled yelp of discomfort. Then it was done. Ree put away his tools while Troi massaged her forearm. The doctor turned back with a medical tricorder in hand. He activated it, made a few adjustments, and mused aloud, "Yes, it's working. Signal is strong and clear. Very good."

Riker sounded edgy as he asked, "Are we through here?"

"You may leave any time you wish, Captain," said Ree. "I need your wife to remain a few moments longer while I gather baseline data from the transponder."

"Just go," Troi said to her husband, in a tired, resentful monotone. "I'll be fine." Riker seemed both angered and relieved by her dismissal, and he marched out of sickbay without so much as a glance backward.

The door sighed closed after his departure, and Ree turned off his tricorder. "I'm finished," he said to Troi. "Please come back for a more detailed checkup tomorrow at 0900."

"Thank you," Troi said, without sounding the least bit grateful. She got up from the biobed, glared at Vale, and walked out of sickbay in a hurry.

Vale waited until she was gone and the door once again closed before she berated the doctor. "A biometric transponder? Thanks a lot, Doc. I wanted her relieved of duty, not tagged for research."

"And I wanted her pregnancy terminated, not stuck in slow motion." Ree plodded away from her in heavy steps. "As it is, we are only postponing the inevitable."

The first officer sighed. "Story of my life, Doc."

As the phaser blasts started flying, Ranul Keru almost forgot that it was only a holodeck simulation.

The passageways of the Borg transwarp hub complex were so close that he could touch both sides at once by extending his elbows. Through the open-grid framework that surrounded him, Lieutenant Gian Sortollo, and Chief Petty Officer Dennisar, he saw the fast-moving silhouettes of Borg drones. The enemy was converging on them from every direction, swarming on levels above and below them, harrying them with a steady barrage of energy pulses that screeched through the thin air and stung the back of his neck with hot sparks as they flashed off the dark bulkheads around him.

Keru filled the corridor ahead of him with covering fire as he yelled to Dennisar, "Block the side passage!"

The Orion security guard pulled a finger-sized metallic cylinder from his equipment belt, thumbed open its top cap, and pressed its arming button. Then he pitched the capsule underhand down an intersecting corridor that led to a ramp from the upper level. He leaped past the corner and yelled, "Fire in the hole!"

Sortollo and Keru ducked against a solid block of infrastructure and turned away.

A thunderclap and a brilliant flash. The plasma blast rocked the structure, and a rolling cloud of fire spilled out into the main passage, between Dennisar and Keru. Through gaps in the walls, Keru watched several levels of the Borg facility collapse inward, glowing hot and dripping with slag.

Then a deep groaning resonated around the three men, and a powerful tremor robbed them of solid footing. A grinding of metal was underscored by a deep, steady rumble. The walls around them began moving, reshaping themselves, sealing off the damaged area and making new paths inside the complex.

"Sortollo," Keru shouted over the din, "send in the scouts."

The human security officer detached a hexagonal block from his equipment belt and pressed a button in its center. Then he hurled it with a sideways toss and sent it skidding along the deck ahead of them. In the span of seconds it seemed to break apart into thousands of pieces—and then all the pieces skittered away in different directions, vanishing into the tiny spaces between the machines, the slots in the deck grilles, and the open ports of various machines.

Moments later, the lights began to flicker, plunging entire levels of the complex into darkness. Some of the deep hum of machinery faded, making the clanging footsteps of approaching drones all the more ominous.

Sortollo pulled his phaser rifle from its sheath on his back and checked the tactical tricorder mounted on the top of the weapon. "Nanites are working," he said. "I've got a signal. Ahead and right to the central plexus."

Keru motioned the two men forward. As he followed them, he plucked a cylinder from his own equipment belt, twisted its two halves each a half turn in opposite directions, and lobbed it behind them. He heard its soft pop of detonation and knew that Ensign Torvig's cocktail of virulent neurolytic pathogens was spreading in a thick, syrupy puddle across the deck, a lethal greeting for any Borg drone that came into contact with it. Then he drew his own rifle and quickened his step.

Ahead of him, Dennisar stopped short of passing a T-shaped intersection, poked his rifle around the corner, and fired off a fusillade of shots to cover Sortollo, who jumped forward and tumble-rolled to safety on the other side.

It was Sortollo's turn to lay down cover fire as Dennisar waved Keru to continue past him. "Go ahead, sir," the Orion said. "We'll cover your—" His eyes went wide and his body started to twitch. Then snaking tubules erupted from the wall behind him and mummified him in a blur of black movement. The wall split open, transformed into a biomechanoid maw, and the hideous tendrils pulled Dennisar inside.

Sortollo lurched away from his corner as more assimilation tubules sprang from it, writhing like ravenous bloodworms. He fired frantically at the wall, vaporizing chunks of it.

Keru sprinted forward, trying to find a position from which he could cover Sortollo, but then the floor was no longer beneath his feet. He fell forward into a pit of churning cables, tubing, and wiring that coiled like serpents around his legs and pulled him down-ward. Struggling to steady his aim and avoid shooting off his own foot, Keru pumped a dozen full-power shots into the tangled mass that held him. The blasts had no effect.

"Go forward!" he shouted to Sortollo. "Get to the plexus!"

Sortollo hesitated, clearly torn between a desire to try and save Keru and his training to obey orders. As the synthetic tentacles of the Borg complex yanked Keru's rifle from his hands and pulled him down until only his head was left exposed, Sortollo turned to continue down the pitch-dark corridor—and was felled by a single, massive pulse of green energy.

Only after the shot had struck home did the telltale red targeting beam of a Borg's ocular implant slice the darkness.

Then everything halted, frozen in time and space.

From behind Keru came the deep thunks of mag-netic locks being released, followed by the hiss and whine of the holodeck doors opening. A broad shaft of warm light from *Titan*'s corridor spilled into the chill-ing, hostile darkness of the simulated Borg facility. Then a long shadow bobbed into view, and Ensign Torvig said, "Computer, end program."

The industrial architecture and biomechanical trappings of the Borg complex vanished, along with the security trio's simulated weapons and equipment. It took a moment for Keru's perception to adjust, because the simulation had fooled his senses into believing he had been pulled to a lower elevation than Sortollo and Dennisar, but now all three of them sat on the deck and massaged their aches and pains.

"Maybe it's just me, Vig," Keru said, "but I think you went a little overboard with this program."

Torvig responded with a bemused tilt of his head. "Odd that you would say so, sir. If the mission reports from *Enterprise* and *Voyager* are accurate, then this simulation might not be aggressive enough."

The other two security officers cast alarmed looks at each other. Sortollo said to Torvig, "You've gotta be kidding me."

"I'm not, Lieutenant," Torvig said. "Borg drones are now capable of very fast individual action in combat, and there is reason to believe that Borg ships and structures have become active combatants during battles to repel invaders."

Dennisar looked stricken. "Even the walls are going to attack us? How are we supposed to fight that?"

"That's what we're here to figure out," Keru said, forcing himself to stand. "Torvig's right. The Borg are getting faster and smarter all the time. If we underestimate them, we won't have a chance. So we train until we're ready for anything." He turned and said to Torvig, "Good work on those new gadgets, by the way. Can you protect us from getting eaten by the walls?"

The young Choblik engineer waggled his bionic fingers. "Avoiding or preventing physical attack may not be possible," he said. "However, my research indicates that neural-suppressant injections once rendered persons temporarily immune to the psychological effects of assimilation. Implanted neutralizer chips performed a similar function, as did nanites developed by Lieutenant Commander Data and Dr. Kaz. Though all these methods are known individually to the Borg, I have synthesized a hybrid that they will not yet have adapted to. Even if the Borg inject you with nanoprobes, you will not submit to the Collective."

"Won't stop them from just killing us," Keru said, "but I'll have Dr. Ree inoculate the away team, just in case."

That seemed to trouble Torvig, who replied, "Sir, a neural suppressant will prevent my body from interacting with my cybernetic implants. I would, in effect, be incapacitated by the injection. If you still wish me to be a part of your away team, I will have to forgo that protective measure."

Keru frowned. "Is that a risk you're willing to take?"

"If necessary, yes."

"In that case," Keru said, "stay close to me and Dennisar, and load us up with as many of your gadgets as we can carry."

Torvig's tail flipped anxiously behind him. "Sir . . . I should warn you that my devices are made to exploit weaknesses of the Borg that might already be known to the Collective—and which they might already have remedied. There is no guarantee that any of the devices I've created for your team will be effective."

Sortollo muttered to Dennisar, "Now he tells us."

Ignoring his comrades' pessimism, Keru said, "Don't worry about that. Now that you've given us some tools for offense, we need to focus on defense. Any ideas on that front?"

"Yes, sir," Torvig said. "I've sent you a new deployment plan for your people here on the ship. It should enable your team to defend the same areas with fewer personnel, freeing up additional strength for such key locations as the bridge, sickbay, and main engineering."

Keru nodded. "Sounds good. Anything else?"

"Defending *Titan* from external attack by the Borg will be very difficult," Torvig said. "The difference in power between a Borg cube and our vessel is too great to overcome. Assuming we evade destruction by overwhelming force, the Borg will likely resort to infiltration and sabotage." The Choblik shifted his weight from side to side, like an anxious child. "I have a response strategy," he continued, "but I don't think Commander Ra-Havreii will like it."

"Don't worry about him," Keru said. "What's your idea?"

"We need to isolate system functions throughout the ship," Torvig said. "Not with firewalls, but by shutting down the data network. Each console must be dedicated to one task, so that Borg drones can't seize low-priority stations and use them to access the ship's main computer and command systems."

Imagining the potential consequences of Torvig's strategy, Keru winced. "That could be a real handicap in combat, Vig. If a dedicated station goes down and we can't reroute its functions to a working console, we could end up in big trouble."

"As I said, Commander Ra-Havreii will not like it."

Dennisar grumbled to Sortollo, "He'll like being killed by the Borg even less."

"We all will," Keru said, shooting a silencing glare at the human and the Orion. Turning back to Torvig, he said, "Write up a contingency plan for combat situations. We'll bring it to the XO and let her decide."

"Yes, sir."

The Choblik looked at the deck, then away from Keru, which gave the Trill security chief the impression that there was something else on the engineer's mind. "What's wrong, Vig?"

"I am concerned that I might be a liability to the away team," Torvig said. "While I'm honored to help you and your team prepare, I'm not sure how much help I'll be inside a Borg facility. My talents are better suited to working in a lab than fighting in a battle."

Keru patted Torvig's back. "Relax, Vig. You'll be fine." He grinned at his friend. "Most of my people can only hold two phasers at a time. You can hold three. You'll be a natural."

Torvig seemed unconvinced, but he replied, "I will do my best, sir." He glanced at the doorway. "With your permission, I will draft my contingency plan for Commander Vale."

With a nod, Keru said, "Dismissed."

The young engineer bounded out of the holodeck. Keru looked at Dennisar and Sortollo, who were still sprawled behind him. "Go get some chow, and be back here at 1800," he said. "We're running this sim again until we can get past the first level."

The two security officers pushed themselves to their feet and limped out of the holodeck. Watching them go, Keru had to wonder if maybe Torvig was right. He was starting to feel as if he was asking too much of him. After all, Torvig had been an ensign for less than six months.

Doubts plagued Keru's thoughts. *How can I expect someone so young to face something like this? What if he's not ready? Do I really want to risk getting him killed just so he won't think I've lost faith in him?* He shook off that notion. *I haven't lost faith in him. He can do this, I'm sure of it. He'll be fine.*

Then he imagined his friend falling into the hands of the Borg, just as his beloved Sean had fallen years ago.

No, Keru promised himself. *Not this time. Not to Vig. I talked him into joining this mission, and I'm making sure he comes back from it . . . even if that means I won't.*

He had an hour before Dennisar and Sortollo returned.

"Computer," he said. "Restart program. From the top."

Riker stepped out of the turbolift onto the bridge and was met with anxious stares. Vale, who was manning the center seat, rose to surrender the chair to him. He nodded and said, "Report."

"Warp drive and main power are back online, but long-range communications are down for the count, along with most of the sensor array." Vale handed him a padd with a summary of the ship's status. He skimmed it as she continued. "Ra-Havreii networked the subspace transmitters on the shuttles, only to find out that the subspace booster relays we've been leaving behind us are all offline."

He almost had to laugh. "Of course they are." Settling into his chair, he ruminated aloud, "Whatever we're moving toward just muzzled us, but it left our tactical systems alone. Why?"

Lieutenant T'Kel looked up from the security console and offered, "Perhaps because it doesn't see us as a threat."

"Then why did it disable us?" asked Riker.

The Vulcan woman shrugged. "A warning shot?"

From the other side of the bridge, Tuvok added, "It might also have been an accident. An entity with such power could easily have destroyed us while we were incapacitated. The fact that it did not suggests that its intention was not to kill."

"Or that it thought it *had* killed us," Vale offered.

Sariel Rager swiveled her chair away from the operations console and joined the conversation. "Sir, I think it's worth noting that the pulse that hit us did so only after we'd run some fairly high-energy scans of our own. It's possible we provoked the target's curiosity, and it may not have realized we'd be so vulnerable to its sensors."

"All good points," Riker said. "Cease active scanning of the target. Passive sensors only from this point forward."

Rager nodded. "Aye, sir."

"Ensign Lavena," Riker said to the Pacifican flight controller, "resume our last course, maximum warp."

The thrumming of the engines grew louder and pitched quickly upward as the stars on the viewscreen shot past.

"Course laid in and engaged, sir," replied Lavena, her voice filtered through her aquatic breathing mask. "ETA to target is approximately seven hours, nine minutes."

To Vale, Riker added, "Get ready for a hostile reception."

Vale turned to T'Kel. "All security personnel to stations." Then she pivoted toward Tuvok. "Shields to ready standby, weapons hot." As the two officers carried out her orders with cool, quiet efficiency, Vale turned back to Riker and lowered her voice to a sub rosa level. "Without comms, we won't be able to report our findings to Starfleet. If we get into trouble, we won't even be able to send a Mayday. We'll be completely alone out here."

"We're already alone out here," Riker replied in the same hushed tone. "But I'm not breaking off or going back. Whatever's hiding out there in the dark, it's got my full attention."

2168

20

———◆———

Erika Hernandez awoke struggling and flailing as a gloved hand clamped over her mouth and nose.

A German-accented voice snapped, "Quick, tie her!"

She lashed out and cuffed Private Steinhauer on the ear before someone else snared her wrist and yanked it backward.

Steinhauer and Mazzetti pulled Hernandez from her bunk. The German's hand slipped from her mouth, and she inhaled, a prelude to a shout—then Mazzetti wedged a rolled-up sock between her teeth, muffling her panicked cry for help.

There were sounds of struggle in the rooms adjoining hers, more sharp-but-hushed orders, heavy thuds of bodies striking the floor, the meaty smack of fists against flesh.

Her attackers flipped her facedown on the floor. One of them, she couldn't see which, kneeled on her back and held her wrists behind her while the other bound them. The odor of their exertion was heavy in the air. She kept trying to pull free, and they tightened their hold. Beads of sweat rolled from beneath her hair, soaking her forehead and neck.

Mazzetti and Steinhauer each grabbed one of her arms, under the shoulder, and dragged her backward out of her quarters, into one of the corridors of their penthouse suite. At the same time, Commander Fletcher was dragged, bound and gagged, from her room by Sergeant Pembleton and Private Crichlow. Lieutenants Yacavino and Thayer pulled the similarly restrained Lieutenant Valerian into the hallway, while Major Foyle and Lieutenant Graylock towed Dr. Metzger from her chambers.

"Bring them to the main room," ordered Foyle. The group did as the MACO leader said and pushed, pulled, and prodded their four prisoners into the suite's sunken living area, near the terrace entrance. Foyle released his hold on Metzger and said, "Seat them back-to-back and tie them together."

Hernandez eyed Foyle as he stepped away and watched Pembleton and the three privates lash the four *Columbia* officers together, each of them facing out, like points on a compass.

The major conferred in whispers with his second-in-command for a moment before he acknowledged Captain Hernandez's baleful glare. "I won't insult you by apologizing," he said. "And I can't say as I mind our conversation being a bit one-sided in my favor, for a change." He stepped down and kneeled beside her. "You understand why I had to do this, don't you?"

She wanted to spit at him, but the sock was in the way.

"Yacavino," said the major. "I'll brief our guests on what happens next. Deploy the others and wait for my signal." As the group began to leave, he added, "Pembleton, hang back."

The MACO sergeant turned and halted while the rest of the mutineers departed. Hernandez caught a backward, regretful glance from Lieutenant Thayer, but only a stern mask of resolve on Graylock. She was profoundly disappointed in both of them, but especially in her chief engineer.

I never should've let Tucker transfer back to Enterprise, she jokingly berated herself. *It's so hard to find good help these days.*

After the Caeliar elevator pod had departed, carrying the others back to street level, Foyle waved Pembleton over. "Take their communicators," he said. "And anything else you find."

Hernandez had suspected that Foyle would remember she had ordered everyone to carry communicators at all times, in case the scattering field ever lifted. All the same, as Pembleton plucked hers from her pocket, she felt a twinge of irritation at the MACOs' efficiency and thoroughness. The sergeant concluded his pat-down search of the four female officers and held up four communicators. "This is all they had."

"Stack them over there, against the wall." Pembleton did as Foyle instructed. Then the major added, "Frag them."

Pembleton tugged the strap of his phase rifle and swung it off his back and into his hands. He squeezed off a burst of charged plasma and reduced the four communicators to smoking, sparking sludge.

Then he aimed his rifle at Hernandez.

"Give the order, sir," said Pembleton, his index finger poised over the trigger, steady and certain.

Foyle absorbed Hernandez's murderous, defiant stare. His face was an icy cipher. After several seconds, he said to Pembleton, "Lower your weapon." He strode toward the elevator pod. "We'll leave them here."

Pembleton let his weapon's muzzle dip toward the floor as he watched Foyle walk away. "Sir, that wasn't the plan."

The major stopped, turned, and snapped, "I know that, Sergeant. Sling your rifle and get in the lift." He watched Pembleton engage the safety on his weapon and quick-step toward the returned elevator pod. Then he looked at Hernandez. "I've chosen not to kill you, Captain," he said. "Please don't make me regret my decision."

He followed Pembleton to the pod and stepped inside. Its transparent shell sealed itself around them, and then it vanished through the floor on its way to the plaza below.

Hernandez assessed her situation with dour cynicism. *I'm bound hand and foot, unarmed, with no communicator. And I've got a sock in my mouth.* She felt her nostrils flare as she sighed through her nose. *I wish he had shot me.*

Time was dragging for Kiona Thayer even as the wind whipped her long, dark hair above her head like Medusa's serpents.

She still had a sick feeling in her gut from helping Major Foyle and his men assault and restrain her four fellow officers. Everything had unfolded so quickly once the MACOs had set themselves in motion. Within minutes she and Graylock had been roused and pressed into service to restrain the captain and the others.

In the hour that had elapsed since they'd left the penthouse and persuaded the Caeliar to provide them with an automated transportation disk to the nearby city of Mantilis for "cultural research," Thayer had felt her pulse throbbing in her temples. At any moment her four betrayed shipmates would be discovered trussed like animals in the penthouse, she was certain of it. And then all of this would be for nothing.

Towers and spires blurred past in the darkness. Then the lines of the metropolis sharpened as the disk settled to a soft landing in the midst of a great plaza across from the opaque dome that shielded this city's majestic Caeliar apparatus.

The disk melted into the marbled stone of the plaza, and the eight-person team moved quickly toward the dome. A violet radiance shot up from the top of the dome and soared skyward.

"Nice thing about a species that never sleeps," Crichlow said softly, with a grin. "They don't ask why you'd want to take a trip in the middle of the night."

Pembleton smacked the back of Crichlow's crew-cut head, and said in a whisper laced with menace, "Shut up."

At the base of the dark hemisphere that loomed large before them, the group halted. The MACOs unzipped side pouches on one another's packs and removed rolls of wide medical tape from their first-aid kits. They worked strips of tape between their fingers and wrapped a few loops, adhesive side out, around their palms and the toes of their boots.

Pembleton handed a roll of tape to Thayer. "Just enough to give yourself some traction," he whispered. "Once we're past the first half, we should be okay without it."

Thayer tried to wrap her hands and boots with the tape; it was clumsy work, holding one end in place while manipulating the rest of the roll. After it slipped from her grasp for the third time, Pembleton and Steinhauer did the work for her. When they finished, Pembleton asked her, "Ready?" She nodded. "All right," he said. "Let's climb."

The sergeant and Major Foyle led the way, scrambling and fighting for purchase on the smooth surface. The rest of the group hurried behind them. In moments they were scratching and kicking their way up the dome like drunken bugs. Just as Pembleton had predicted, after they reached the halfway point they were able to move more quickly, jogging in a knuckle-dragging slouch, occasionally padding their palms against the dome for traction or balance. Recalling that the domes appeared transparent from inside, Thayer hoped that none of the Caeliar working on Mantilis's apparatus were looking up at that moment.

At the top of the dome, the eight-person team perched at the edge of the fifty-meter-wide aperture to the crystalline shaft that linked the dome to the enormous circular platform two hundred meters below. "Moment of truth," Foyle said as he stared down into the glittering empty space and the constantly moving mass of dark machines at its nadir.

All six MACOs doffed their packs, opened them,

and began extracting coils of high-tensile microfiber rope and carabiners that they snapped into reinforced loops on their standard-issue tactical vests. Their hands worked faster than Thayer could follow, threading ropes through the steel loops, tying knots, and securing pockets and packs.

Graylock carried a tube of cyanoacrylate from his emergency repair kit and moved down the line, stopping behind each person to affix a carabiner on the surface of the dome with a thick wad of the polymer superadhesive. Thayer eyed the fat dollop of glue with suspicion. "Will that hold?"

"*Ja,* but not long. Six, maybe seven decades." As Graylock moved on, Thayer reflected on the truism that there had never been any great German comedians.

Yacavino tapped her on the shoulder. "Lift your arms, *signorina,*" he said. "I need to tie you a harness." She did as he asked and watched as he worked careful loops in a cross over her torso and then secured them with a strong simple knot through the carabiner at her feet. Then he threaded her descent rope through a carabiner on her makeshift harness. "You know how to use this, *sì*?"

"I think I remember, yes," she lied.

A few meters away, Steinhauer finished strapping Graylock into his own jury-rigged harness. The MACOs secured their rifles and gear, slung their packs back into place, and looked to Foyle for orders. "Let's go," he said. "We're running out of time."

Yacavino whispered to Thayer, "Do as we do."

He turned his back to the aperture and took hold of the rope between himself and his glued-on anchor.

Thayer mimicked his actions but lacked the Italian man's ease or confidence as they began backing up in small steps toward the edge behind them. Watching and copying his every movement, she set her heels precisely over the edge, pulled her rope taut, and leaned back until she was almost horizontal, with only her grip keeping her from free fall. On either side of her, the others hovered over the shining abyss. Then Foyle said, "Now."

Reflex kept her in motion with the MACOs. She bent her knees just enough to coil up some energy, then she pushed away from the wall and let the slack rope fly through the carabiner. Then her old combat training came back to her, and she was right beside Yacavino and the others, plummeting and bouncing and feeling the exhilaration of acceleration, the rush of falling without losing control, all her focus on the present moment, the angle of her body, the placement of her hands, the tension in the rope, the rebound in her feet.

In less than a minute, they were standing on the narrow perimeter rim at the bottom of the shaft and unhooking their carabiners from their rappelling lines. Speed was paramount now. They had to act before the Caeliar had time to respond.

They slipped through a close grouping of meter-wide slits in the columns and sprinted across the giant, deserted circular platform, toward one of the entrances to the facility hidden within. Beyond the luminous halo of the platform, Thayer saw nothing but shadows and heard only the vital pulsing of great machines and the endless echoes of the yawning silo.

A portal irised open on the blockhouse as Foyle and Pembleton approached it, weapons held steady and level. Thayer was stunned by the lack of security. *Guess the Caeliar figured we'd never get this far, so why lock the door?*

Beyond the portal was a long, spiral-shaped ramp that led down and doubled back beneath Thayer's position. Foyle motioned Pembleton to take point, and the sergeant stalked forward in a low crouch until he was almost out of the team's sight. With a low wave, he ushered the rest of the team forward.

Mazzetti and Crichlow were the next to proceed. Then Foyle gestured for Thayer and Graylock to advance, placing them in the protected middle of the formation. Next, the major and Private Steinhauer followed the two flight officers, while Yacavino lingered a few meters back as the squad's rear guard.

Near the bottom of the ramp, the team halted while Foyle and Pembleton surveyed the situation. Thayer peeked over the low half wall that bordered the ramp and stared agape at the Caeliar laboratory. Beside her, Graylock was stealing a peek of his own.

Machines of crystal, light, and fluid ringed the nearly hundred-meter-wide open space, and a dancing sphere of light several meters in diameter hovered in the chamber's center. The ceiling was dozens of meters overhead, lending a cavernous aspect to the facility's total enclosure. But its real wonder were the Caeliar themselves.

There were only thirteen of them overseeing the entire works. Some stood and interfaced with the apparatus by contact, while others hovered in midair and manipulated two-dimensional screens that seemed to be made of silver liquid that rippled at their touch. A slow, oscillating song emanated from the machines, eerie and almost hypnotic in quality.

Pembleton looked back at Foyle, who nodded. It was time.

The team charged into the open, the MACOs brandishing their rifles, as Pembleton shouted, "Stop what you're doing!" His voice echoed back to him twice as the rest of the MACOs spread out around him. The Caeliar, if they were surprised or alarmed, gave no appearance of it. They regarded the invaders with the same curious annoyance that a human might have at discovering a troublesome pet in a forbidden room of the house.

Foyle stepped out in front of the group and addressed the Caeliar in a calm, even manner. "We are here because we desire your cooperation. And before you start vanishing in puffs of smoke or floating away, I should warn you that if you don't cooperate, there will be grave consequences."

The nearest Caeliar scientist said, with almost pitying boredom, "Your weapons pose little threat to us, Stephen Foyle."

"Yes, I'm aware of that." Foyle looked at Pembleton. "Sergeant, if you would."

Pembleton turned, fired, and shot Thayer's left foot.

She collapsed to the floor, screaming and bleeding.

Her ragged cries of horror and agony resounded in the vast enclosure, bringing her pain and shock back to her threefold. The initial needlelike blast of pain in her now-crisped foot became an unbearable burning that spread from her ankle into her entire leg. "*Putain de merde!*" she raged at Pembleton. To Foyle she added, "*Con de crisse!*" Blood flowed from the stump of her leg, forming an irregularly shaped puddle on the floor.

No one had told her this would be part of the plan.

Graylock tried to come to her, but Yacavino held him back.

The Caeliar crowded forward as if attracted to her pain. Foyle waited until they had circled around the squad and said, "Any closer and my sergeant will kill her."

"And if we drain the power from your weapons?" inquired another Caeliar.

Steinhauer pressed a combat knife against Thayer's throat.

"Then he cuts her from ear to ear," said Foyle.

Thayer fought to blink through her kaleidoscope of tears. She saw Graylock struggle against the MACO lieutenant's hold. "You're all *verrückt!*" shouted the furious Austrian.

"Be quiet, Mister Graylock," Foyle said. "We've come here to do a job, and I will see it done, by any means necessary." Returning his focus to the Caeliar, Foyle continued, "My chief engineer is going to ask you to make some adjustments to your apparatus. First, however, I want you to weaken the scattering field in a narrow radius around this facility, with a clear line of transmission to our ship in orbit. Do you understand?"

The Caeliar watched Thayer as she squirmed in agony on the floor and flailed desperately in a pool of her own blood. A few seconds passed before the first

Caeliar who had spoken to Foyle replied, "We understand."

That was when Thayer understood Foyle's logic. Unable to overpower the Caeliar, he had exploited their only weaknesses: their compassion and pacifism. Several times over the past six months they had reminded the *Columbia* team of their aversion to violence and their cultural prohibition against taking sentient life, through "action or omission of action."

It was a noble philosophy, in Thayer's opinion, and it was therefore completely unsuitable for dealing with such a ruthless political actor as Foyle, who had just put it to the test and found it wanting. He snapped at Graylock, "Stop staring at her and get to work on the time tunnel home." While Graylock stepped away and conferred with three of the Caeliar scientists about the modifications he wanted to make in their apparatus, Foyle looked to his MACOs. "Yacavino, hail the *Columbia*. Pembleton, if he can't break through the scattering field and raise the ship in the next fifteen seconds, shoot Thayer's other foot."

His order brought back all her pain, and the fear of an encore made it worse. She wanted to crawl away and hide, but the cold edge of Steinhauer's knife was firm against her throat. Her leg felt as if it was on fire, and her mouth was parched. A sick feeling swelled in her stomach, and adrenaline overload was shaking her with the force of a seizure while she watched her lifeblood seep away.

Yacavino held up his communicator and called to Foyle, "I have the *Columbia*, sir."

"Tell them to fire up the transporter," Foyle said. "Fast."

One of the Caeliar made cautious gestures to Foyle and then drew near. "Your engineer's time-travel formulae are crude," the scientist said. "We've made such adjustments as are necessary for your safe passage. However, I should warn you that the linked nature of the apparatus will make it obvious to the other loci in the network when we shift our focus to Earth. Also, the various stations all operate from a central command system, so your time-travel formulae will infect the system as a whole. These details will not go unnoticed. The Quorum will block your escape from orbit once your actions are noted by the gestalt."

"They'll try," Foyle replied with a sinister grin. He pulled back one sleeve of his camouflage uniform and checked his watch. He tapped its face and smiled. "Which is why, when we set our timers, I chose this as the perfect time for a distraction."

On the sunlit side of Erigol, in the city of Kintana, Auceo, poet-laureate and chief archivist of the Caeliar, worked with his colleagues in the core of the city's apparatus, awaiting the response to the hail they had projected across the universe, toward a civilization from the dawn of time.

"The aperture is steady," said Eilo, his research partner. She dragged the tip of one tendril across the liquid display that shimmered before her.

Attuning his will to the gestalt, Auceo rearranged the monads that infused the air around him. The same nigh-invisible cloud of raw matter surrounded all the Caeliar's cities and was free for the taking by all who could perceive its existence.

Subatomic particles coalesced at his behest and formed a curving liquid-silver sheet that he molded until its vista of images, all as sharp as reality, filled his peripheral vision. Streams of data flooded his senses, some of it numeric, some of it visual. "Subspatial harmonics are stable," he said. "Data stream integrity is—"

Errors and failures cascaded from every system, and Auceo and the others in the Kintana locus abandoned their previous tasks to attend the emergent crisis.

"The Mantilis node is misaligned," reported Noreth, the interlink engineer.

Auceo observed the feed from Mantilis. It fell farther out of synchronization with the other loci the longer he watched.

Then a hue of alarm resonated in the gestalt, and Auceo caught only the most fleeting sense of its warning—the humans had interfered in the Great Work somehow. Before he could learn more, a discordant wail of pain and terror engulfed the gestalt and drowned out all the other voices. At the same time, a surge of chaotic signals and unchecked power spikes blasted through the apparatus network, disrupting its global frequency.

For the first time that Auceo had ever known, the gestalt was silenced by its shared pain and horror.

Far beyond the horizon from Kintana, halfway between it and Axion, the city of Feiran had just vanished in a flash of fire.

"Massive detonation on the planet's surface," reported Ensign Claudia Siguenza, the *Columbia*'s gamma-shift weapons officer. "One of the alien cities just exploded."

"Hexter, report," said Lieutenant Commander el-Rashad.

Lieutenant Russell Hexter, the alpha-shift officer of the watch who had been serving for the past few months as el-Rashad's XO, punched up a new screen of data on the science station's monitor. "The scattering fields on the surface just collapsed."

"Do we have a transporter lock yet?"

"Almost," replied the lanky, rudder-nosed, red-haired American. "The explosion kicked up a lot of interference."

From the communications station, Ensign Remy Oliveira called out, "I have a lock on Major Foyle's communicator. Relaying coordinates to the transporter room now."

El-Rashad thumbed a switch on the arm of the command chair and opened an intraship comm to the engineering deck. "Pierce! Power up the transporter, and stand by for full impulse!"

"Aye, sir," said the acting chief engineer. *"We're patching in the coordinates now. Energizing in sixty seconds."*

"Acknowledged, bridge out." El-Rashad closed the comm channel and said to the entire bridge crew, "Look sharp, everyone. I get the feeling this one's going to be close."

At first, Erika Hernandez thought she and the other captive officers were being visited by a swarm of fireflies. Then the gently buzzing cloud of glowing motes fused together and formed an incandescent sphere, which swiftly reshaped itself into Inyx.

The looming Caeliar scientist took a moment to assess Hernandez's predicament. Then he extended his hand, conjured a small cluster of radiant particles that descended on her and the others, and sent the glowing specks into a dizzying spin. Seconds later the tiny lights faded away to nothing, and the ropes that had held her were gone. She plucked the sock from her mouth and looked for any trace of the ropes behind her, but there wasn't so much as a loose thread or a stray fiber.

Hernandez turned to Inyx and massaged her rope-burned wrists. "Foyle and his men are planning an attack."

"Their scheme is already set in motion," Inyx said. "They have destroyed one of our cities by sabotaging a node of the apparatus, and they have seized another."

Fletcher, Valerian, and Metzger gathered at Hernandez's sides. "Can't you stop them?" Fletcher asked Inyx.

"They are threatening one of their own to keep us at bay," Inyx said. "For her sake, we are exercising caution."

Hernandez fumed to think of Foyle and his men using Thayer as a pawn. Although Thayer had betrayed her by siding with the MACOs, she was still one of Hernandez's officers. "Is she okay?"

"No," Inyx said. "She's badly wounded. She may die."

Dr. Metzger said, "Take me to her, please, I can—"

"Unacceptable," Inyx said. "Allowing you to regroup with the others is forbidden by order of the

Quorum. I am here only because the gestalt saw that you four were not with the others, and we feared for your well-being."

The doctor looked ready to argue with him, but Hernandez silenced her CMO with a raised hand. "Inyx, take us to the Quorum, as fast as you can. We'll help you stop Foyle and his men before this gets any worse." She saw him bristle at the notion. "Please, Inyx. I'm begging you. Let us try to help. Bring us to the Quorum."

Inyx pondered her request for a few seconds. He turned away and bowed his head ever so slightly, then he extended his arm toward the terrace outside the penthouse and summoned a pool of quicksilver from the dark marble tiles.

Valerian stared at the shifting metallic liquid and muttered, "Talk about taking blood from a stone."

Thousands of drops of shining fluid floated upward and conglomerated a few centimeters above the terrace into a mirror-perfect, razor-thin transportation disk. Inyx walked forward, stepped onto the disk, and looked back at Hernandez.

"Events are accelerating," he said. "We should go."

Major Foyle's vision pierced the white haze of the transporter effect as he rematerialized on D Deck inside the *Columbia*.

To his left was Lieutenant Yacavino, and in front of them, with their rifles in its back, was a Caeliar scientist. As soon as the rematerialization sequence finished, Foyle prodded the lanky, bulbous-headed alien forward. "Move."

The two MACO officers and the Caeliar stepped off the small transporter pad and were met by Corporal Hossad Mottaki and Private Ndufe Otumbo. Mottaki nodded at the Caeliar and asked Foyle, "Who's your friend, sir?"

"He's not a friend, he's a prisoner," Foyle said. "Put him in the brig and keep an eye on him at *all* times. Understood?"

"Yes, sir," Mottaki said, and he aimed his rifle at the Caeliar. "Follow Private Otumbo." The corporal nodded to the private, who led them out of the transporter bay.

Standing behind the transporter control console was Ensign Katrin Gunnarsdóttir, from the ship's engineering division. The wide-eyed Icelander asked, "Are you all right, sirs? I've never had to run a transport sequence that fast before."

"We're fine," Foyle said. "Thank you, Ensign. I'm just glad you were ready when we needed you. Start scanning for the next round of transports, we don't have much time." He signaled Yacavino with a nod toward the door. "Let's get to the bridge."

As the two men headed for the exit, Gunnarsdóttir called after them, "Sirs? I'm only reading six communicator signals at the transport site. I can't get a lock on the captain, the XO, the doctor, or Ensign Valerian. Where are they?"

Foyle ignored his lieutenant's accusing stare and replied calmly, "They didn't make it. Let's get the rest of our people home as soon as we can, Ensign."

She averted her eyes and focused on her console. "Aye, sir," she said, with a vibrato of grief in her voice.

As he and Yacavino left the transporter bay, Foyle noted his lieutenant's tensed jaw and brooding glower. They didn't speak of his lie to the ensign as they moved down the corridor and entered the turbolift, and with every step they took, Foyle became more certain that they never would—because Yacavino was a good soldier, and he knew that war made its own demands.

Karl Graylock had only the vaguest idea what the machines in the Caeliar apparatus were, and he had no idea how the aliens made the system work. The Caeliar seemed to direct it by thought alone; so far as he could tell, it had no physical interface. The symbols that streamed past on the enormous liquid sheets that the Caeliar had produced in midair were gibberish to him.

He cast a wary look at the alien closest to him. "How do I know you're programming the variables I asked for?"

The scientist had to twist his upper body to look at Graylock. With their ever-frowning, impenetrable visages, the Caeliar always looked disdainful, and their hauteur always conveyed a degree of condescension. As this one answered him, however, he couldn't mistake its obvious contempt. "Shall I have the formulae translated into your primitive alphanumeric code?"

"If you wouldn't mind," Graylock said, answering sarcasm with more of the same.

On the silver sheet above and in front of him, a ripple transformed the alien script and symbols into Arabic numerals and Earth-standard mathematical expressions. It was the most beautiful thing Graylock had ever seen. It was elegant and economical, it was mathematics and physics and temporal mechanics fused into one and reimagined as poetry.

He looked around, hoping to share his wonder with one of the other members of the *Columbia* landing party—and then he saw Thayer, lying on the floor, her jumpsuit soaked with her own blood, which still seeped from the ragged and meaty mess that used to be her left foot.

A Caeliar scientist said, "It is ready."

Graylock turned back to the formula and its creators. "Then let's proceed. Open the passage."

The apparatus resonated with a deep droning, and Graylock felt it vibrating the fillings in his molars. Several liquid displays indicated sharp increases in power output, and another set its puzzle of Caeliar symbols racing. As they began to melt into a blur, he imagined he could almost see in it numbers and notations he understood. Then the image dissolved into a view of a dazzling rift in space-time, in orbit of Erigol. Looking like a speck poised on its event horizon was the *Columbia*.

"*Mein Gott*," Graylock said under his breath. "We did it." For a moment he could only stare in fascination at the temporally shifted subspace tunnel. He was unable to fathom how much raw energy was being expended to keep it open and stable. Recovering his wits, he grinned as he called over his shoulder to Pembleton, "Hail the ship! The road is open."

The last time Hernandez had visited the Quorum, the Caeliar had seemed aloof and reserved. Now, as she and her loyal officers ascended with Inyx into the center of the hall's main level, the clamor in the soaring space was deafening. Scores of sliver-thin, levitating liquid screens raged with riots of color and sound. The hall was lit by thirty-six sunlike orbs, arranged in a circle high overhead, near the pyramidal chamber's peak.

None of the Caeliar spoke. Instead, they filled the air with an atonal humming punctuated by deep, vibrato drones, like the low groan of a didgeridoo she had once heard on Earth, in the silence of the deep Outback.

Fletcher stood on her right, Metzger on her left, and Valerian was close at her back. Inyx stepped a few paces ahead of Hernandez and spread his arms in a submissive gesture before the eastern tier, where the scarlet-robed *tanwa-seynorral* looked down at them. Ordemo Nordal appeared to be the only member of the Quorum who wasn't lost in the throes of a droning swoon.

"Captain Hernandez," said the first-among-equals, "you told us a short time ago that you and your kind posed no threat to us." A wave of his hand united the many liquid screens around the hall into one enormous floating wall of quicksilver. An image rippled into focus—it was a Caeliar city being consumed in a fiery flash. When the blinding glare faded, it revealed an image of the MACO-led hostage crisis taking place in another city's apparatus control center. Her cheeks burned with shame as she watched her mutinous crew coerce the Caeliar by threatening the already wounded Lieutenant Thayer. "It seems you underestimated your people's capacity for brutality."

The Caeliar leader continued, "Inyx, these savage beings were welcomed into our home at your urging. Now they have extinguished countless lives, minds that were integral to the gestalt, and they have interfered at a critical moment during the great work. Our link to the far galaxy has been corrupted."

Inyx bowed low from the waist. "Forgive me, *tanwa-seynorral.* I sought only knowledge and understanding."

"I trust that you will remember this the next time you are tempted to indulge your curiosity at the expense of our safety."

"I will," said Inyx, the top half of his body still parallel with the floor.

Hernandez stepped forward. "Can we play the blame game later, please?" Inyx straightened and looked back at her in surprise, and Ordemo seemed taken aback by her tone. "We need to act quickly if you want to stop this from getting worse."

Ordemo's contempt was bilious. "What do you propose?"

"Let me talk to them," Hernandez said. "Now."

"That seems ill-advised."

She gritted her teeth and sighed to dispel the swell of anger in her voice. "They're manipulating you," she said. "You're not used to dealing with strangers, so your people told us anything we wanted to know. My men are using that knowledge to make you help them. You don't understand us well enough to put an end to this. But I do. Stop cooperating with them and open a channel, and I'll try to end this."

Ordemo replied, "I find it difficult to believe you are so concerned with our well-being."

"You're right," Hernandez admitted. "I'm not. But I know how seriously you take your privacy, and I have a good idea what you'll have to do to my homeworld if I don't put a stop to this. I like Earth where it is. I'd rather not see it displaced."

Inyx interjected, "She sounds sincere, Ordemo."

Hernandez got the impression that Inyx's support did little to bolster her position with the *tanwa-seynorral*. Regardless, a few seconds later Ordemo turned toward the image of the ongoing hostage situation and declared, "Your people in Mantilis can hear you now, Captain."

She surveyed the scene, noted that Foyle and Yacavino were both absent, and surmised that the two MACO officers had likely already beamed up to the *Columbia*. Technically, Graylock was the ranking officer on the scene, but the one in charge was obviously Sergeant Pembleton. He was in command of the MACOs, and the one who she would have to negotiate with. "Sergeant," she snapped, "this is Captain Hernandez. Stand down."

Pembleton looked up and around until he obviously found a screen near him that was displaying the captain's face. *"I'm sorry, Captain. I can't do that."*

"Yes you can, Pembleton. Ask your men if you're still in contact with the *Columbia*." She waited while he looked to Private Mazzetti, who fiddled for several seconds with a communicator, then shook his head and frowned at his sergeant. Hernandez continued, "The scattering field's back up, isn't it? Take my word for it, Sergeant: The *Columbia*'s not breaking orbit today. You've failed. Tell Private Steinhauer to let Thayer go."

He seemed ready to falter, just for a moment, and then he lifted his weapon to his shoulder and pointed it at Thayer. *"No, Captain. Major Foyle's orders were clear."*

"What did the major order you to do?" she asked.

"Whatever I had to," Pembleton said. *"As long as I secured the Caeliar's cooperation."*

Hernandez found it telling that Pembleton was reluctant to elaborate on Foyle's orders. She suspected that part of him regretted what he was doing. His hesitation and general unease told her he was rationalizing his way through this mess. "So," she said, "you were prepared to wound Thayer. But are you ready to kill her? Because she's bleeding out, you know. A wound like that's fatal if it's not treated."

"We'll treat her as soon as we reach the ship," he said.

"But you're not going to reach the ship, Sergeant. And neither is she. So you might as well kill her now, and let her death be quick instead of drawing it out like this."

Ordemo interrupted, indignant, "Captain, we cannot permit your sergeant to—" A vicious glare from Hernandez quelled his protest, and the *tanwa-seynorral* cast a long, silent look at Inyx, who responded with his own icy stare of reproof.

Pembleton intensified his focus on Thayer as he said to Hernandez, *"Don't bother trying to bluff me, Captain. I'll do what I have to. I'm going home. I'm gonna see my boys again."*

"No, you're not, Gage. I've asked the Caeliar not to cooperate with your demands. But I can't stand here and watch Kiona's life drain away like this. Let me

GODS OF NIGHT

make it easier for you. This is an order, Sergeant: Kill Lieutenant Thayer."

He looked perplexed. *"Sir?"*

"You heard me, Sergeant. Kill her. When she's dead, you've got nothing left. You can't kill Graylock, you need him to help the ship make the trip through the subspace tunnel. I don't think you and your men are ready to start killing one another. That makes Kiona your only pawn. So let's just end the game here, shall we? Kill her." Hernandez waited a few seconds. When, by the end of that interval, Pembleton had done nothing, she feigned disgust. "Fine, pass the buck, Sergeant. Private Steinhauer: Cut the lieutenant's throat. That's an order."

Only now did Hernandez notice that the din of the Caeliar had faded to silence and that a tense silence hung over the Quorum as everyone waited for the reaction to her stratagem.

Steinhauer removed the blade from Thayer's throat, dropped it on the ground, and sank to a sitting position on the floor. Without him to hold her torso upright, Thayer collapsed onto her back. Pembleton, sensing the surrender of his men, lowered his weapon and pulled his hand over his face, wiping away sweat, grime, and fatigue. In the background, Graylock leaned against one of the machines and covered his eyes with one hand.

"Private Mazzetti," Hernandez said, "get a first-aid kit and start treating Lieutenant Thayer's wound. We'll get the doctor to you as soon as we can."

"Aye, Captain," said Mazzetti, who took off his backpack, opened it, and removed the first-aid kit. He jogged over to Thayer and started taking steps to stanch her bleeding.

One of the Caeliar scientists in the Mantilis facility neared the comm interlink and addressed the Quorum. *"It will take time to dissolve the temporally shifted subspace aperture,"* she said. *"The Earth ship should be restrained until the phenomenon has been disincorporated."*

"Understood," said Ordemo. "Proceed with haste, Sedín." The massive silver screen vanished, leaving a faint mist that lingered in the air like a rain shadow. Ordemo looked down at the visitors and said, "Inyx, see the humans' physician to their wounded comrade in Mantilis."

Hernandez cut in, "One thing first: Let me talk to my ship. I need to have a few words with Major Foyle."

Foyle didn't seem to care that he was making a scene on the bridge. "I'm not interested in excuses, I want answers!"

Lieutenant Commander el-Rashad, the nominal commanding officer of the ship, shoved past Foyle on his way to the science console, which had once been his regular station. Punching buttons to skim several screens of data, he said, "If I had answers for you, Major, I'd give them to you. But all we know right now is that the scattering field is back, and we can't get a transporter lock."

"What about the subspace tunnel?" Foyle asked, pointing at the image of the dazzling passage on the main viewer.

"Stable," said el-Rashad, who lurched away from the science console to join Ensign Oliveira at the communications panel. "For now." To the ensign he added, "Patch in the boosters. Maybe there's a lingering frequency gap we can exploit."

The major stayed close behind el-Rashad, who was quickly tiring of his irate shadow. "We should go now," Foyle said, "while we still can."

"That wasn't the plan," el-Rashad said. "We've already lost the captain and the XO, I'm not leaving any more of our—" He was interrupted by the beeping alert of an incoming comm signal. "Oliveira, report," he said, moving back to the command chair.

Oliveira made some quick adjustments on her panel. "Signal from the planet's surface, sir."

"On-screen."

The image of the subspace tunnel was replaced by the faces of Captain Hernandez and Commander Fletcher, who stood with Ensign Valerian and Dr. Metzger inside a huge, ornate chamber. *"Mister el-Rashad,"* said Hernandez. *"Nice to see you again."*

"Likewise, Captain," el-Rashad said, confused at seeing his commanding officer and XO alive after receiving Foyle's report of their demise. "What are your orders?"

"Don't take the ship into the subspace tunnel, Kalil. If you do, the Caeliar will have to retaliate against Earth, and I can't allow that. Understood?"

El-Rashad nodded. "Aye, Captain." He felt the two MACO officers on the bridge staring at him, their malice a tangible presence. "Captain," he began, uncertain how to phrase the next part of his report, "Major Foyle . . ."

"Ah, yes," said Hernandez with a sinister grin. *"Major Foyle. He and Lieutenant Yacavino are charged with mutiny, conspiracy, assault on a supe-*

rior officer, assault on flight officers, and the attempted murder of Lieutenant Kiona Thayer. And tack on disobeying the orders of a superior officer."

"Aye, sir," said el-Rashad, his resolve galvanized by the captain's surety. He turned to his acting XO. "Mister Hexter, place Major Foyle and Lieutenant Yacavino under arrest. Ensign Siguenza, help the XO take our prisoners to the brig." Siguenza drew her sidearm and faced Foyle and Yacavino. It was a testament to the two MACOs' respect for military tradition that they showed no sign of resistance. Both men surrendered their sidearms with care to the XO, who directed them with a nod into a waiting turbolift.

After they had departed, el-Rashad felt a moment's regret that the plan to go home and erase the *Columbia*'s lost years would have to be abandoned. Then he cast aside those selfish desires and reminded himself that this was the captain's call to make, not his. The *Columbia* was her ship; he was just watching over it until she came back. "Sir?" he said, easing into his question. "We're running low on provisions up here. Is there any chance the Caeliar might let us settle on the planet's surface if we stay out of their cities?"

Hernandez sighed. *"I don't know, Kalil. That's a ver—"*

The signal went dead.

Then something hammered the *Columbia,* and el-Rashad realized that the ship's near-empty galley had just become the least of his problems.

Hernandez had sensed the reduction in tension among the Caeliar in the Quorum hall as soon as Pembleton had lowered his weapon. She hoped that her role in ending the crisis might persuade the Caeliar not to take punitive measures against her ship or against Earth for the crimes that Foyle and the others had committed.

Her thoughts drifted while she watched el-Rashad direct the officers on the *Columbia* to arrest Foyle and Yacavino. *How am I supposed to make amends for this? How do I apologize for the deaths of millions?*

She was pulled back into the present moment by el-Rashad asking, *"Sir?"* She blinked once and looked up at his larger-than-life image on the liquid wall high above her. *"We're running low on provisions up here,"* he said. *"Is there any chance the Caeliar might let us settle on the planet's surface if we stay out of their cities?"*

After what we just did? She sighed. "I don't know Kalil. That's a very good—"

A thunderclap rent the air, the glowing orbs at the top of the chamber were extinguished, and a flash reddened the night sky beyond the crystal-walled pyramid. Tremors shook the floor under Hernandez's feet and knocked her down. The other *Columbia* officers fell beside her. The liquid screens evaporated and rained down like stardust. Inyx and the other Caeliar levitated upward, and then Hernandez saw why—the tiers on which they had been seated were collapsing, shearing away from the crystal walls of the pyramid with sharp splintering sounds.

An earsplitting crack made Hernandez wince, and when she opened her eyes again, a ragged fissure had bifurcated the magnificent, fractal starburst pattern that adorned the floor.

Over the steady rumble of an earthquake, she called out, "Inyx! What's happening?"

Despite the tumult erupting around them, Inyx's voice resonated clearly, as if it were amplified. "It's a feedback pulse from the galaxy we contacted," he said. "A million times more powerful than we expected."

The reddish glow that suffused the chamber brightened. Outside the pyramid, the night sky had become almost bloodred.

Valerian shouted to Inyx, "A feedback pulse did this?"

"It disrupted all of our technology, including our deep-solar energy taps," Inyx said. "The gestalt is trying to contain the damage, but the signal appears to have been crafted with malicious intent. Please excuse me while I commune with the gestalt." Inyx turned away and stared into space with the other Caeliar. Outside, lightning blazed across the sky. Then Inyx looked back at Hernandez and her officers. "We are unable to contain the reaction. We have very little time left."

Fletcher traded a terrified look with the captain and asked their Caeliar liaison, "Until what?"

"Until this star system is destroyed."

Karl Graylock stared in anger and disbelief at the Caeliar scientist and asked, "Are you serious?"

"The feedback pulse from the extragalactic signal has caused a chain reaction in our solar and geothermal taps," the alien replied. "The core of our star has been pushed past its supercritical point. Its detonation is imminent, and the solar mass ejection will be propelled at faster-than-light velocity by a subspatial shock wave. At the same time, explosive conditions are being generated inside Erigol's core. The annihilation of this planet will be all but instantaneous."

Waving his hands at the darkened and sparking equipment in the sprawling laboratory, Graylock protested, "Can't you stop it?" A violent shuddering motion was followed by a low, metallic groan from the structures around them.

"It is too late to save Erigol," the alien said. "But if you will permit us to work without interruptions, maybe we can save this city—and you, as well."

Graylock stepped away from the machines and said, "Do whatever you have to do." As the Caeliar started moving atoms around by the power of thought, and another temblor rattled the apparatus control room, Graylock flipped open his communicator, in the hope that the impending calamity had once again disabled the scattering field. "Graylock to *Columbia*. Come in, *Columbia*."

Static and squalls of noise half-buried el-Rashad's reply. *"Go ahead, Karl,"* said the second officer.

The chief engineer spoke loudly and slowly to improve the likelihood of his message being understood through the interference. "Kalil, the star and the planet are going to explode. Break orbit now! Get the hell out of here!"

"What about the landing party?"

"Forget us," Graylock said. "Save the ship, Kalil!"

The channel was quiet for a few seconds before el-Rashad said, *"Good luck, Karl. To all of you."*

"*Danke*," Graylock said. Then he lowered his voice, pressed the communicator close to his mouth, and covered it with his free hand. "Kalil, the solar shock wave will be FTL. You can't escape on impulse. You know what you have to do. Graylock out."

He flipped the communicator closed and prayed that his warning to the *Columbia* had been delivered in time.

Hernandez was just starting to regain her footing when the violent shaking of Axion became a steady vibration, and then her sense of balance abandoned her and she tumbled backward. She expected to strike the floor and stop there, but she kept on rolling, tumbling sideways, realizing only after several disorienting seconds that the floor inside the Quorum hall was sitting at a steep angle and that she and her officers were being dragged across it by gravity.

All of this went unnoticed by the levitating Caeliar, who maintained their positions relative to the pyramid's walls.

Fletcher was the first of the group to slam into the pile of wreckage from one of the collapsed seating tiers. Hernandez plowed into the broken stone and metal behind her first officer, with Valerian and Dr. Metzger making impact seconds later. It was Fletcher who asked, "What the hell? Did the city fall over?"

"I don't think so," Hernandez said, as she watched forks of lightning dance across the dark crystal walls of the pyramid, which was engulfed in glowing red mist. "I'd say we took off."

The four women clung to the apparently stationary wreckage as the ruddy clouds outside the pyramid cleared and revealed the broad sweep of the planet, from low orbit. Along the horizon, other Caeliar cities were rising from the surface, which was aglow with volcanic eruptions and wreathed in ashen smoke.

Above the cerulean halo of the thinning atmosphere, Erigol's once-golden star had turned bloodred and expanded to frightening proportions. In higher orbit of the dying world, numerous tunnels of light were forming, and when Hernandez looked to the apex of the Quorum hall's pyramid, she saw another such passage directly ahead of Axion. They closed the distance to it in moments—then they stopped, hovering at its aperture.

Valerian was trembling and wide-eyed as she muttered, "What are they waiting for?"

Inyx was far away, but his voice was close. "We are trying to purge the equations that your engineer forced us to put into the system. The damage caused by the feedback pulse is slowing our efforts, but it is not safe to enter the passage until we have stabilized the phenomena."

Fletcher pointed at the distant cities hanging in space. "Why aren't they leaving?"

"All our cities are linked nodes in the apparatus," Inyx said. "An error in one is an error for all. Harmony must be restored before we can proceed."

The star was enlarging at a rate swift enough to be seen by the naked eye. "I don't think we have that much time," she said.

Shaking her head in denial, Valerian sounded hysterical. "It's not real, it can't be real. How can it be real?"

Dr. Metzger snapped, "What're you talking about?"

"The sun," Valerian said. "The sun. We shouldn't be able to see the effects yet. The inflation just started, it's nine light-minutes away, we can't really see it, it's not real. . . ."

"Subspatial lensing," Inyx's voice explained. "The same phenomenon that will carry the supernova's eruption to us is telegraphing its effects."

His answer didn't seem to placate Valerian, who buried her face in her hands. Hernandez watched the red star dimming and swelling, and she felt her own anxiety swelling in equal measure. "Inyx, how much longer?" When he didn't answer right away, she hollered at his distant form, "How long?"

"Not long," he said, "but too long, all the same."

"Fifteen seconds to the subspace tunnel," said helmsman Brynn Mealia.

El-Rashad watched the coruscating phenomenon grow larger on the main viewer as the *Columbia* broke free of the Caeliar's tractor beam and accelerated toward freedom. The captain had told him not to do this, but she had been motivated by a fear of retaliation by the Caeliar against Earth. Based on the cataclysm that was unfolding in front of him, however, he doubted the aliens would be in a position to take their revenge, or that they would even notice the *Columbia*'s departure.

"Commander," said Ensign Diane Atlagic, who had taken over for Siguenza at tactical, "none of the Caeliar city-ships are entering the subspace tunnels. They're all holding station at the apertures." He looked back at the dark-haired Croatian woman, who added, "Maybe they know something we don't, sir."

He had only seconds to decide—proceed or hold? *If the Caeliar don't trust the passages enough to use them, do I really want to take us in there?* "Helm, all stop!"

"Answering all stop," Mealia said.

"Oliveira," el-Rashad said, "hail the Caeliar capital-ship, find out why they—" The main viewer whited out for a fraction of a second, and when it reset, Erigol was breaking apart like a marble struck by a hammer. A subspatial shock wave blasted scores of city-ships into vapors, and the subspace passages dissolved in its wake. "Helm! Go!"

Mealia punched in full impulse power, and the *Columbia* hurtled forward into the breach.

The ship pitched and rolled the moment it was inside the subspace tunnel. Darkness blinked in and out on the bridge as consoles erupted into flames and sparks showered down from overloaded relays in the overhead. A brutal jolt hurled el-Rashad from the command chair and pinned Mealia to the helm.

El-Rashad clawed his way across the deck, back to the chair, and jabbed the comlink to engineering. "Bridge to . . ."

The next word refused to leave his throat. A dry rasp rattled in his chest. His mouth felt as if it were carved from sand, and a burning sensation filled his eyes, his sinuses, and then every cell in his body.

Everyone on the bridge was in agony, just as he was. He saw their faces contort in horror, watched them fall to the deck beside him. They were all going through the

DAVID MACK

motions of fighting for air, even though their bodies no longer had the ability to inhale. He felt his thoughts breaking down as his brain boiled and burned.

Mealia was the first to vanish in a cloud of ash, and Atlagic disintegrated into gray powder. Oliveira reached out to el-Rashad for one last moment of human contact before oblivion. He bridged the distance with his outstretched hand, but as she took it in hers, he couldn't feel it.

Then both their hands crumbled to dust, and a few seconds later he felt absolutely nothing at all.

Planetary debris slammed into the spires of the Caeliar city-ship Mantilis and pulverized swaths of its platinum-white majesty. Behind it, Erigol was an expanding jumble of rocks and fire and gases, and a subspatial shock wave shattered dozens of city-ships in seconds.

Karl Graylock watched the mayhem on one of the Caeliar's liquid screens as the alien scientists tinkered with numbers and symbols and generally acted as if nothing was wrong. The chief engineer grabbed one of them, spun the looming freak around to face him, and shouted, "Go! Go now! Or we're all dead!"

"Temporal balance has not—"

Graylock shook him silent. "If you don't go, you're *killing* us! Go, *scheisskopf*! *Schnell*!"

The scientist became as insubstantial as a ghost and slipped from Graylock's grasp. A moment later he resolidified in front of a large console of glowing liquid surfaces, waved his tendril-like fingers over it, and declared, "It is done."

- 384 -

On the liquid screen, the images of the cataclysm were replaced by the swirling, blue-white chaos of the subspace tunnel. A slight tremble in the floor made Graylock wonder if they would face turbulence inside the passage.

Then a savage quaking gripped the lab, and the liquid screen showed him mighty towers being shorn from the city-ship and cast away into the uncharted realms of subspace, flotsam in the ether beyond space and time.

"*Mein Gott*," Graylock said as the buildings were swallowed in the subspace vortex. "Don't you have shields?"

The Caeliar scientist didn't look at him as he replied. "They failed when we entered the passage, as I feared."

The chief engineer was aghast. "Are you saying we're exposed?"

"No," the Caeliar answered. "This lab is a protected environment. It will protect you from the passage's effects."

"But what about the rest of the city?"

All the Caeliar in the vast facility turned and faced him with their permanent frowns and cold, metallic-hued eyes. In an ominous tone, the one closest to him said, "The rest of the city is dead, Karl Graylock."

The city-ship Axion hurtled through the subspace passage, buffeted by forces more powerful than Erika Hernandez could imagine. She hung on to a bent piece of wreckage from the tier. Veronica Fletcher hung on to Hernandez's legs, and Valerian and Metzger were both clinging to Fletcher.

Hernandez and her officers all had watched in terrified silence as Erigol's sun had exploded and the shock wave, propelled toward the planet at faster-than-light speed, had atomized scores of Caeliar cities hovering in orbit of the broken world. She had seen only two of the other cities escape destruction, by entering their swirling subspace passages scant moments before the shock wave dispersed their apertures. Then Axion had raced into its own subspatial rift and left its shattered legacy behind.

Outside the dark-tinted pyramid of the Quorum hall, lashes of blue-white energy tore away chunks of the city's periphery. Hernandez winced as massive slabs of metal and landscaping were ripped from its edges and impacts flared against its protective energy shield, which appeared to be contracting. As the field's outer edge shrank below the tips of Axion's loftiest spires, the towers were rapidly shorn away and scattered into the blinding swirl of chaos that surrounded them.

Then the whirling brightness fell away and darkness returned. Hernandez felt the strain of gravitational forces release its hold on her, and Fletcher let go of her leg. Looking back, the captain saw her people all safe on the floor, looking scuffed and mussed but generally unhurt. The crystal walls of the pyramidal chamber lightened and became transparent. Once her eyes adjusted, Hernandez saw the vista of stars. Axion had returned to normal space-time.

Fletcher was the first to get up, and she offered a hand to Hernandez. The XO asked, "Where are we?"

"No idea."

Valerian and Metzger were slow getting to their

feet. The doctor rolled out a crick in her neck while the young Scotswoman brushed the dust off her blue jumpsuit uniform.

"I'm just glad we're still alive," Metzger said.

Valerian added, "Aye, I'll second that."

Above them, the hundreds of Caeliar, who had hovered undisturbed by the rougher moments of their subspace transit, floated down to the main level. They looked exhausted. As they descended closer, she realized that they actually appeared to be smaller than they had been before. Their bodies were emaciated and shorter, and the colors of their skin were blanched and dull. Once they touched down on the main level of the hall, the group quietly dispersed, wandering dazed like refugees from a war zone, singly and in small clusters. A few of them clung to one another for mutual support.

A lone figure emerged from the erratic, spreading crowd. Inyx limped in heavy steps toward the four humans, looking humbled and enervated. "Are any of you hurt?"

"No, Inyx," said Hernandez. "Thank you." Observing the slow, weary sway of his torso with every breath he drew and released, she asked, "How about you? Are you all right?"

"We are weakened. Much power was lost with our fallen cities. And the loss of minds has been a blow to the gestalt."

Fletcher said, "Looks like the city took a lot of damage."

"Nothing that can't be repaired," Inyx said, but the sorrow in his voice betrayed his optimistic words as a lie.

Valerian cast a nervous glance at the stars. "Inyx, how far did we travel?"

"In space, not far," Inyx said. "A few thousand light-years, by your species' reckoning."

His choice of words alarmed Hernandez. "*In space*?"

"Because your engineer's equations had polluted the neural network of the apparatus, the subspace tunnels we created were unstable. The induced detonation of our star introduced a cascade of high-energy tachyons that—"

Hernandez held up her hand. "No details, Inyx, just the summary. Where are we?"

"We are approximately half the distance from the galaxy's core to its rim . . . and, using your chronological units, we have been displaced six hundred fifty years, seven months, eight days, eleven hours, and forty-three minutes into what was the past . . . and is now our present."

Shocked reactions were volleyed between the four *Columbia* officers. It took Hernandez a moment to process the news. "Well, we can't stay here," she said to Inyx. "We have to go back."

"That will not be possible," Inyx said. "Not yet."

Commander Fletcher snapped, "Why the hell not? The subspace tunnel brought us here, it can take us back the way we came."

"It cannot," Inyx said. "Because it traversed time as well as space, it was extremely unstable. Only a focused effort by the gestalt was able to prevent its collapse before we reached its far terminus. As soon as we returned to normal space, it collapsed behind us. It no longer exists."

Ensign Valerian's temper flared, as well. "So? Moving forward in time can't be that hard! We skipped twelve years in two months on the *Columbia*. You lot must have somethin' better, what with all your fancy tricks and gadgets."

"It is not a matter of ability," Inyx said. "It is a matter of law. For as long as we have known the methods of time travel, it has been strictly controlled by the Quorum. Careless jaunts either forward or backward in time carry the potential for great harm. It was permitted in this instance only to save *your* lives. Had you not been among us, we would have let ourselves perish rather than risk the integrity of the time line."

Dr. Metzger inquired, "So, what happens now?"

"First, we heal," Inyx said. "Then we mask our presence, to avoid anachronistic encounters. When that is done, we will analyze the causes of our world's destruction, and we will attempt to determine if our presence in this earlier phase of the time line is an error that needs to be corrected."

"And what about us?" asked Hernandez. "We're just supposed to sit quietly while you do all this?"

"Yes," Inyx said. "We will not skip forward in time unless we are certain that doing so is necessary, nor can we permit you to leave or return to your time with knowledge of us. All we can do now is seek the truth and go forward."

As usual, Hernandez realized, there was little point in arguing with the Caeliar. Then another worrisome thought occurred to her. She asked Inyx, "Is the Quorum going to blame us for what happened at Erigol?"

The delay in his answer was both telling and troubling.

"That remains to be seen," he said.

Sergeant Gage Pembleton's only clue that the city-ship of Mantilis had exited the subspace tunnel was that the blinding flurry pictured on the lab's liquid screens had changed from blue and white to red and black. The turbulence was the same.

Pembleton and the other humans were huddled under the ramp they had descended during their ultimately futile assault on the laboratory. Mazzetti and Steinhauer were devoting their full attention to treating Thayer's wounded foot and keeping her sedated. Crichlow hid in the shadows, wrapped in a fetal curl around his rifle while he prayed. Graylock stayed near the edge of the ramp and observed the silent Caeliar scientists at work.

Tapping the engineer's shoulder, Pembleton asked, "What's going on?"

"My professional opinion? We're crashing."

The energy sphere in the center of the control facility had dimmed greatly during the brief journey through the subspace passage, and the current crisis wasn't making it any better. Pembleton tried to edge past Graylock. "I'm asking them."

The engineer grabbed his arm. "Let them work."

He dislodged Graylock's hand with a brusque shake of his arm and walked away, toward the nearest Caeliar. "Hey," he called out. "What's your name?"

"Lerxst," the alien replied.

"Hi, Lerxst. We'd like to know what's happening."

The scientist didn't look at Pembleton as he replied, "Your friend Karl Graylock is correct. We're crashing."

"Where, exactly?"

A rectangle of metallic liquid assembled itself in front of Pembleton and rippled to life. It showed a world that, despite being half-obscured by the curtain of fire around the Caeliar's city, appeared Earth-like—but which, based on the shapes of its continents, definitely was not Earth. "There," said Lerxst.

Pembleton began to understand why Graylock had tired so quickly of talking with the aliens. "Does 'there' have a name?"

"None that is known to us. If it's inhabited by sentient forms, they might have one they prefer."

Now he was annoyed. "I don't suppose you could give me a sense of where we are relative to, for instance, *Earth*?"

"We are fifty-eight thousand, nine hundred sixty-one light-years from your world."

Pembleton heaved a disgruntled sigh. *So much for a shortcut home.*

On the screen, plumes of superheated gas from Mantilis's atmospheric entry blasted vast areas of the city-ship's surface bare. Gone were the spires, the plazas of art and trees, the reflecting pools and foot-bridges and elegant architectural flourishes. The city resembled little more than a metallic disk with molten edges and a million ragged scars.

"Graylock says you told him the rest of the city was dead."

"You six and we twelve are all that remain," Lerxst said, apparently without either regret or bitterness.

Pembleton was surprised by the scientist's sangfroid in the face of tragedy. "Aren't you upset about this?"

"Do not mistake stoicism for an absence of emotion," Lerxst said. "Our anger and sorrow are greater than you can imagine, but the sacrifice of our people outside the apparatus was a choice, not an accident."

"What does that mean?" Pembleton asked.

Lerxst said, "It means that we will not destroy sentient life, or allow sentient life to be destroyed, by action or omission. Not for revenge, not in self-defense. We do not kill."

"Are you telling me that millions of Caeliar agreed to let themselves die to save the six of us?"

"Correct," Lerxst said. "Though making the passage would cost them their lives and violate our people's laws against time travel, the gestalt concurred that—"

"Time travel?" Pembleton interrupted. "Forward or back?"

"Backward," Lerxst said.

"How far?"

Lerxst told him the numbers, in years, months, and days.

Pembleton staggered back to the others in a daze. Liquid screens throughout the vast circular facility showed the flattened disk of the city-ship. It was aglow within a nimbus of fire and slicing through the atmosphere, toward a rocky, icy expanse of arctic tundra whose details were coming into focus all too quickly for comfort. The sergeant slumped to the floor next to the chief engineer, who asked, "What'd they say?"

"They said we're gonna crash."

The rippling images of the horizon flattened and fell away, and then the liquid screens went dark and scattered. Pembleton felt the ground rising to meet them. It would be a disastrous crash landing, and their chances of survival were slim. But even if they did live through planet fall, it no longer mattered.

He closed his eyes but didn't bother to pray— because it was much too late for that now.

2381

21

Ezri Dax emerged, bleary-eyed and aching-limbed, from her ready room shortly after 0200 and was surprised to see many of her senior personnel still at work on the bridge.

Sam Bowers was settled in the command chair as if he had been melted into it. The steaming beverage he held in one hand while perusing a report on a padd seemed to have done little to reinvigorate him. He looked up at Dax as she entered and was half a second slower than usual snapping to attention.

"Captain on the deck!" he announced as he bolted to his feet—and spilled his hot drink across the back of his wrist. Swearing under his breath, he dropped the padd on the chair and swapped the mug into his unburned hand. He waved his scorched appendage in the air to cool it as Dax approached and smiled.

"As you were," she said to the bridge crew. Joining Sam at her chair, she added sotto voce, "Guess how much I want to make a joke at your expense right now."

"I can only imagine, Captain." He wiped the liquid from the back of his hand onto the pant leg of his uniform. "I'm required by regulations to remind you that we're now ten hours overdue for departure, as per our last orders from Starfleet Command."

Dax fought the urge to roll her eyes and said simply, "I'll note your reminder in my log, Sam, thank you." She stepped past him toward the security chief's station, where Lieutenant Kedair was busy reviewing a steady stream of incoming data and reports. Catching the Takaran woman's eye, Dax said, "Give me an update on the manhunt, Lieutenant."

Kedair's hands continued to manipulate data on her console as she replied, "We've finished two full sweeps of the ship, Captain. So far, no intruder." She called up Dr. Tarses's forensic reports on one side of her station. "No new leads on the cause of death, and no progress devising a defense against it—whatever it turns out to be."

"That's not very encouraging, Lonnoc."

"No, Captain, it's not. But I'd still like your permission to keep the ship in lockdown until we complete a third sweep of all compartments. We've switched to some fairly exotic detection methods this time around. It's a long shot, but I want to be as thorough as possible."

She admired Kedair's refusal to admit defeat. "All right. Let's hope the third time's the charm." Kedair nodded her understanding and resumed her work as Dax moved on to the aft station, where Gruhn Helkara and Mikaela Leishman were immersed in conversation about their wall of schematics and sensor data. "How's *your* search going?" she asked the duo.

"We haven't found the subspace tunnel yet," Helkara said. "But not for lack of trying. We've been through the full range of likely triggers, and now we're trying the unlikely ones."

"Sounds like a familiar refrain around here tonight," Dax said. She nodded at a screen showing a diagram of the *Aventine*'s shield emitter network. "What about the hyperphasic radiation inside the anomaly?"

"*That* we solved," Leishman said. "If we ever find this thing, we'll be ready to try it out."

Dax smiled at the pair. "Finally, some good news. Keep at it, and let me know when we get a fix on the phenomenon."

"Will do, Captain," Leishman said. She and the Zakdorn science officer returned to their hushed conference about exotic particles and technological arcana.

The captain continued her circuit of the bridge, past the relief conn and ops officers, who were occupying their time at the starboard duty stations compiling data for Kedair's manhunt and tagging sensor reports for Helkara and Leishman. Ensign Erin Constantino, a human woman from Deneva, manned the conn, while Lieutenant Mirren was on her second shift of the day at ops.

Stopping beside the ops console, Dax peeked at the display panel. Mirren looked up. She sounded anxious. "Yes, Captain?"

"Just curious," Dax said. "Have we learned anything new from the *Columbia*'s databanks?"

"Maybe," Mirren said. "Most of it is log fragments and snippets of internal comm chatter, but there was one interesting bit." She called up a recovered data file on her console. "The *Columbia*'s transporter had a redundant activity log from the main computer. It shows four outgoing transports, for twelve people. The first six beamed down at 1100, and the rest followed at 1300. The time stamp on those transports is roughly sixty-three days after the Romulan ambush." Mirren called up the last line in the log. "There's only one beam-up sequence, for three subjects, about six months later—less than twelve minutes before the ship's flight logs put it inside the subspace tunnel."

Intrigued, Dax asked, "What's the connection?"

"No idea," Mirren said. "But I have to believe it's more than a coincidence—and it accounts for nine of the ten missing personnel. Or maybe for all ten, if we assume that one of the three who beamed up wasn't a *Columbia* crew member."

Dax nodded. "Okay. What if something beamed up with two of *Columbia*'s people? Could that something have killed Komer and Yott inside the wreck and the crewman in the shuttlebay?"

"Two hundred years later?" Mirren said, incredulous. "It would have to be something *really* long-lived if it—"

An explosion thundered belowdecks and resonated through the bulkheads. The *Aventine* pitched wildly and knocked Dax off balance. Then the ship's inertial dampers reset themselves, and the heaving and rolling of the deck ceased. "Report!" Dax said.

Kedair replied from tactical, "Explosion in shuttlebay one! Hull breach and explosive decompression in the bay."

"That bay was sealed after Ylacam's body was found," Bowers said. He joined Dax at ops. "Mirren, what the hell happened?"

Mirren reconfigured her console to assess the damage and review internal sensor logs of the explosion. "It was the runabout," she said, surprised. "The *Seine* destroyed the bay doors with a pair of microtorpedoes." She looked back at the captain and XO. "It's leaving the bay, Captain."

Looking back at Kedair, Dax said, "I want to know who's in that ship—*now*."

"No life signs inside the runabout," Kedair said. "But I'm picking up some wild energy readings."

Mirren added, "It's accelerating to full impulse and breaking orbit, bearing three eight mark seven."

"Pursuit course," Bowers said. "Full impulse."

"Aye, sir," Constantino replied. The *Aventine* veered away from the planet and fell in behind the fleeing runabout.

Helkara bounded away from the aft station. His face was bright with excitement. "Captain! There's a massive energy buildup in the runabout's sensor array. I think it's been reconfigured to emit a soliton pulse!"

"Locking phasers," Kedair said, as if by reflex.

"Hold fire," Dax said, and then she turned to watch the runabout on the main viewer. A moment later a shimmering beam lanced out in front of the tiny ship and seemed to cut through space-time like a scalpel. The slash through reality parted and revealed a tornado-like passage of coruscating blue light.

The runabout accelerated toward the subspace tunnel.

"Captain," Bowers said, "we can catch it with a tractor beam before it crosses the aperture."

Dax shook her head. "No, Sam. Whatever's on the runabout, I think it could've killed us all if it meant to. But that's not what it wanted. I think it came here from the other side of that passage. Now it's on a journey, and I want to see where it leads. Lieutenant Kedair, raise shields. Helm, take us into the subspace tunnel, full impulse."

Seconds later, the *Aventine* plunged into the blinding maelstrom, close behind the fugitive runabout. Erratic fluctuations in the inertial damping system had Dax hanging on to the edge of the ops console for balance, while Bowers clung to the flight controller's chair to keep himself upright. Twenty seconds into the passage, Dax directed a questioning look back at Kedair, who reported in a calm voice, "Shields holding."

Less than a minute later, a pulsing circle of midnight blue appeared ahead of the *Aventine,* the darkness at the end of the tunnel of light. The runabout shot out of the subspace passage, and the *Vesta*-class explorer followed it back into normal space-time moments later. The two ships were completely engulfed in a deep-indigo stain, a rich cloud of violet supernova debris that was, depending on where one looked, steeped in shadow or lit from within.

Dax stared at the cerulean majesty on the main viewer as she said, "Position report."

"Beta Quadrant," Constantino replied. She checked her readings while stealing glances at the vista on the screen. "Near supernova remnant FGC-SR37–758, in the center of the Azure Nebula."

Kedair looked up from the tactical console. "Captain, the runabout is reducing speed." She punched in a command on her console and added, "Its power levels are dropping fast."

"Helm, hold station at ten thousand kilometers," Dax said. "Mirren, put a tractor beam on it."

On the main viewer, a golden beam from the *Aventine* snared the runabout, which made no effort to evade it or break free. "Tractor beam locked, Captain," Mirren said. "Radiation levels inside the runabout are dissipating rapidly."

"It didn't even put up a fight," Bowers said. He lifted one eyebrow to express his suspicion as he said to Dax, "After all that, it's just giving up?"

"I don't know, Sam," Dax said. "That's what I'm beaming over there to find out."

The XO raised both eyebrows, bringing out the worry lines on his forehead. "With all respect, Captain, you should let a boarding team secure the runabout before you beam over."

She headed for the turbolift. "What? And miss all the fun? Not a chance." To Kedair she added, "Lieutenant, have two security officers meet me in transporter room one." The security chief nodded to Dax as she passed by. The turbolift door sighed open ahead of Dax, who stepped in and turned back to face the bridge. She leaned forward, just enough to poke her head out, and smirked at Bowers. "Well? Are you coming or not?"

"Do I have a choice?"

"Not really, no."

Bowers walked to the turbolift, issuing orders along the way. "Mirren, watch the runabout and make sure the transporter room keeps a lock on the away team. Kedair, lower the shields *only* for transport. Mister Helkara, you have the bridge."

Helkara crossed to the command chair as Bowers stepped into the turbolift with Dax, who directed the computer, "Deck Four."

As soon as the doors closed and the lift began its descent, he said, "I'm required by regulations to remind you, Captain, that this is a really stupid thing to do."

"Sam, what's the point of being a captain if I don't get to do something stupid once in a while?"

His mien shifted from annoyed to bemused to stymied in just a few seconds. Then he frowned, sighed, and replied, "Touché."

Shapes emerged beyond the white haze of the transporter beam, and Dax recognized the familiar close quarters of a runabout's empty aft compartment.

The transporter effect faded. She looked around to confirm that the rest of the away team was with her. Bowers was at her right side, and behind them were Ensign Altoss and Lieutenant Loskywitz from the ship's security detail.

Loskywitz and Altoss charged their phaser rifles. Bowers checked his tricorder and pointed the pair forward, toward the cockpit. The human lieutenant took point, with his rifle braced against his shoulder, moving in smooth, easy strides that kept his aim steady. His female Efrosian partner stepped to the control panel for the aft portal and, on Bowers's signal, opened the door to the middle compartment of the small ship. Then she aimed her rifle around the corner and covered Loskywitz as he stole forward, his body pressed close to the port bulkhead in the short connecting passageway.

Dax started to follow them, but she stopped when she felt Bowers's hand on her arm. He held out his tricorder so she could see the information on its screen. Although it wasn't reading any life signs in the forward compartment, its motion and air-density sensors had revealed a vaguely humanoid shape slumped against the cockpit's aft tactical console.

"Let them secure the ship first," Bowers said to Dax, with a nod toward the security officers. Loskywitz was keeping his weapon aimed at the hatch to the cockpit as Altoss advanced through the narrow passageway to the middle compartment.

As soon as both security officers reached the portal, they looked back to Bowers for the order to proceed. He motioned Dax to take cover near the corner, and she moved to a safe position from which she could still observe what was happening. Then the XO signaled Altoss and Loskywitz to advance.

Altoss reached up and tapped a button on a control panel. The hatch hissed open, revealing the darkened cockpit, whose only illumination came from the glow of the nebula outside.

Just as the tricorder's scans had indicated, a large, long-limbed alien figure was collapsed on the deck, its narrow torso resting against the support for the aft tactical console. The upper and rear portion of its head was enormous and round, but it had a fleshy quality, like that of a cephalopod. On either side of its head were tubules, whose ends dilated and contracted in a slow cadence. Pulsing in the same rhythm were ribbed, organic tubes that emerged from its neck and curved over its shoulders before tapering and vanishing into its chest.

DAVID MACK

At the ends of its gangly arms were limp tendrils, and its feet had two forward toes joined by a U-shaped curve and a prominently clawed third toe near the rear of its instep.

Its head swiveled slowly in Dax's direction. Lidless, almond-shaped black eyes stared at her from a narrow face with a mouth that seemed capable of no expression but a grimace.

Loskywitz and Altoss kept their rifles aimed at the weak and apparently defenseless being, even as they looked back to Bowers for new orders. Bowers, in turn, looked to Dax.

She emerged from behind the corner and walked forward before Bowers could tell her not to. "Lower your weapons," she told the security officers.

At the cockpit's threshold she stopped and examined the creature more closely. Its leathery hide was mostly gray and mottled with faint hues of violet and viridian.

"I'm Captain Ezri Dax, commanding the *Starship Aventine.*"

The alien's mouth barely moved as it replied in a fragile whisper, "I am Arithon of the Caeliar."

Dax stepped inside the cockpit and squatted next to Arithon. "You were on the Earth ship *Columbia*?"

"Yes. Taken as a prisoner. Before entering the passage."

Following her flashes of intuition, she asked, "Was it you who set the ship's autopilot after the crew died?"

"Yes. . . . Hoped to control the vessel, use it to return home. Too much damage. Couldn't stop the crash." The arm that Arithon was using to hold himself in place slipped, and he slumped lower to the deck. Dax reached out to steady him. His skin was cold.

"And that's why you stole the runabout," Dax realized, thinking aloud. "You were trying to get home. But what happened to my people? Did you do that?"

"Forgive me," Arithon said. "Did not mean to kill. Weak without the gestalt. Centuries alone. Drained energy from the ship's batteries until none was left. Hibernated in the machines, waiting for power." The Caeliar finished his slow collapse to the deck. His voice became hollow and distant as he stared at the overhead. "So hungry, so cold. Saw heat and fuel. Had to feed. Was nothing but the hunger. Did not remember myself until this vessel's power restored me. Made me tangible again."

"I don't understand," Dax said. "Made you *tangible*?"

Arithon's head lolled in her direction and came to a heavy stop. "Needed power to rebuild myself for the return. But all for naught. Voices silenced. Gestalt is lost."

Dax leaned closer. "What does that mean?" The alien didn't respond. She reached out and cradled its head in one arm and laid a hand on its bony, thin chest. "What is the gestalt?"

No answer came. Before she could ask her question again, she realized that Arithon's head was becoming less heavy in her arm—and then it weighed nothing at all. It disintegrated on her sleeve, along with the rest of his body. It all became a cloud of sparkling particles of dust that shimmered for a moment and then transformed into a dull, superfine powder.

Dax lingered in the shadows and dust and looked at the gray residue on her hands. She was torn between remorse at Arithon's demise and relief at being rid of the entity that had killed three members of her crew.

Bowers stepped into the cockpit and stood beside her. "You live to make my job difficult, don't you?"

"Yes, Sam, it's all about inconveniencing you." She stood and clapped the dust from her hands. "I just don't get it. What did Arithon hope to find here?"

The XO shrugged. "Whatever it was, it probably got fried in the supernova."

"We don't know that. Maybe it left without him."

"Maybe," Bowers said. "What I want to know is, if this is where the *Columbia* entered the subspace tunnel, why don't its logs have a record of its journey here?"

"No idea." Dax nudged the powder on the deck with the tip of her boot. "But I bet *he* knew." She looked out the cockpit windshield at the chaotic beauty of the supernova remnant. "I feel like we're on the verge of a major breakthrough, Sam. I wish we could see where all this leads."

Bowers replied, "I get the feeling Starfleet Command has other plans for us. Speaking of which, we should probably check in, since we're back in Federation space ahead of schedule."

"We'll check in with Starfleet as soon as we get back to the *Aventine,*" Dax said. "But I think we're on to something here, Sam—something *big*. One more ship defending Trill won't make any difference against the Borg. But this might."

"I have a new theory about you," Bowers said, his serious tone telegraphing his deadpan humor.

She mirrored his grave demeanor. "Let's hear it."

"You don't really like being a starship captain, and you're trying to get fired."

She smirked. "You'd have made a good counselor. If you want, I can arrange a transf—"

A comm warble was followed by Lieutenant Commander Helkara's excited hail: "*Aventine to Captain Dax!*"

"Go ahead, *Aventine.*"

"*Captain, we've just received a priority-one distress call. We're reeling in the runabout and beaming up you and your team in ten seconds. Stand by for transport.*"

"Hang on," Dax said. "A distress call from whom?"

"*From the* Enterprise, *Captain. They've engaged the Borg.*"

22

In the heart of night, *Titan* had found an iron sun.

Riker marveled at the dark orb taking shape on the main viewer. "It reminds me of a Dyson shell the *Enterprise* found twelve years ago," he said to Vale, who was standing next to his chair and watching the black globe grow steadily larger. "Except smaller, of course."

"Naturally," Vale said. "Heck, this one's only two million kilometers across. You can barely fit a star in there."

He looked up and caught the hint of a smirk at the corner of her mouth. "Exactly," he said with a subtle grin.

Melora Pazlar—or, as Riker had to keep reminding himself, her holographic avatar—turned from the aft science station and said, "Captain, we've picked up another sphere." She relayed her data to the main viewer, where it appeared as a small inset in the top right corner. "Equatorial diameter is eighteen thousand six hundred kilometers. Based on the gravitational field and subspatial displacement, it appears to be constructed of the same unknown alloy as the star-sphere."

Vale asked, "Distance from the star-sphere?"

"One hundred sixty-nine million kilometers," Pazlar said. "Orbital period estimated at four hundred nineteen days."

Riker asked Tuvok, "Any sign we've been detected?"

"None. I have detected no artificial signal activity in this system, Captain. No sensors, no communications."

"So far, so good," Vale said. "What about defenses?"

"Unknown," Tuvok said. "We remain limited to passive sensing protocols, and the spheres absorb a wide spectra of energy. Consequently, I have been unable to make detailed scans."

The captain felt his brow crease as he concentrated on finding the simplest and most direct solution to the issue. "What if we moved in closer? To within standard orbital range?"

Tuvok arched an eyebrow as he considered that. "That would enable me to make a more detailed visual analysis."

Riker nodded to Vale, who turned toward the conn and said, "Lavena, take us into orbit of the planet-sphere. Half-impulse approach, and have evasive patterns on standby."

"Aye, sir," replied the Pacifican through her liquid-filled respirator mask. "Sixteen minutes to orbit." The steady thrumming of the impulse engines lent an invigorating vibration to the deck, a tangible sense of impending action.

Riker swiveled his chair toward the other side of the bridge, where Lieutenant Commander Keru manned the security console, Ensign Torvig monitored the bridge engineering station, and Deanna Troi hovered at Keru's side. "Mister Keru, does any of this look like Borg technology to you?"

The brawny Trill security chief traded a glance with the deceptively meek-looking Choblik engineer before he answered, "No, sir. It doesn't look like anything I've ever seen."

"Ensign? Anything to add?"

"Yes, Captain," Torvig said. His tail undulated gracefully behind him. "I've confirmed that the planet-sphere is the source of the energy pulses we detected. Another such pulse has just been emitted, toward Federation space in the Alpha Quadrant."

Vale folded her arms across her chest. "That seals it. We have to go down there. Ranul, is your security team ready?"

"As much as they'll ever be," Keru said.

Tuvok interjected, "Whether there is a planet inside the smaller sphere or its interior surface serves as a habitat, I suspect its shell will prove impervious to transporter beams."

"Then we'll find a gap in the shell and jaunt down by shuttle," Keru said. "Failing that, we'll *make* a gap."

Troi stepped from behind Keru, toward the middle of the bridge. "Have we considered hailing them? Opening diplomatic negotiations *before* we send armed personnel to their planet?"

"For all we know, it's the Borg inside there," Keru said. "If the shell makes it as hard for them to see out as it makes it for us to see in, then we might have the element of surprise on our side. We'll lose that if we hail them."

"They sent a pulse that knocked us out of warp and destroyed our communications systems," Troi said to Keru. "I'd say we lost the 'element of sur-prise' quite some time ago." She turned toward Riker. "Captain, I respectfully suggest we not aban-don diplomacy before we've had a chance to try it. If it's not the Borg inside that shell, we should be pre-pared to greet its people in peace and make a proper first contact."

Riker was tempted to agree with everything Deanna said, but he didn't want to be too quick to side with his wife during a debate on the bridge. He also was unsure whether he might want to concur with her simply to avoid clashing with her again, to preserve some piece of common ground between them. Instead, he shifted his gaze to Vale and said, "Your opinion?"

"She's right," the first officer said. "There's no sign the Borg have been here, and our primary mission remains peaceful exploration and first contact. We may have come ready for a fight, but we don't have to force one."

Rising from his chair, Riker said, "I agree. Lieu-tenant Rager, open hailing frequencies to the planet-shell."

The operations officer keyed in the command on her console and replied, "Channel open, Captain."

He took a breath, then lifted his voice. "Attention, residents of the shelled planet. This is Captain William T. Riker of the *Starship Titan,* representing the United Federation of Planets. My crew and I have come in peace and wish to meet with your leaders or representatives. We intend to send a small, unarmed shuttlecraft to your world. If this is acceptable to you, please respond."

Several seconds passed in silence. Rager tapped at her console and cycled through all the known frequencies, searching for a reply. Then she looked over her shoulder at Riker and shook her head. "Nothing, sir."

"I might have something, though," Pazlar said. She replaced the inset system chart on the main viewer with a close-up detail from the surface of the planet's shell. Blocks of its exterior seemed to slide or melt away, revealing hollow spaces underneath. "It looks like a passage through the shell is being created, sir. More than wide enough for a shuttlecraft."

Vale asked, "What about a transporter beam?"

"Sorry," Pazlar said. "No line of sight to the planet. I'd guess they're willing to let us fly down but not beam down."

"Or up," Keru muttered, his suspicion evident.

"It still looks like an invitation to me," Riker said. "Chris, have a shuttlecraft ready to fly as soon as we make orbit. We're going down there."

His first officer glared good-naturedly at him. "What do you mean 'we'? You're not going anywhere, sir."

"Captain's privilege," Riker shot back.

"Starfleet regulations," Vale countered. "And yes, I'm invoking them for real. We don't know who's down there, and I agree with Keru—I worry about why they've made sure we can't use the transporters. Until we know more, you should stay on the ship and leave the away mission to me."

He was about to argue when Troi stepped closer and lowered her voice to tell him, "Listen to her, Will. Your place is here, in command of the ship. We'll handle the first-contact mission."

"With all respect, Counselor," Vale cut in, "you're not going down there, either."

"Yes, I am, Commander. I'm the diplomatic officer on this ship, and first-contact assignments fall under my authority."

"Counselor, this isn't the time or the place—"

"Enough," Riker said. He suspected their disagreement was about to ignite into something much worse unless he intervened. "My ready room, both of you."

He ushered them off the bridge into his private office. Vale entered the ready room first, followed by Troi and then Riker. After the door closed behind him, he asked, "Chris, did Dr. Ree clear Deanna for duty?"

"Yes, as long as she stays close enough for him to monitor her condition. In other words, on the ship."

Riker felt Deanna's ire intensify even as her voice became very calm. "The requirement was proximity to Dr. Ree, not confinement to the ship. The doctor can join the away team and monitor my condition at all times. If anything happens, he can stabilize me long enough to get me back to the ship."

"Seems reasonable," Riker said.

Vale frowned. "I doubt the doctor will agree."

"I'll leave it to you to persuade him, then," Riker said. "Assemble your away team and be ready to fly in ten minutes."

As Tuvok piloted the shuttlecraft *Mance* into the newly opened path through the planet's dull, black shell, he maintained a wary vigil on the environment outside the craft. A passage so easily provided could be just as easily revoked.

Commander Vale sat on his left, in the mission commander's seat of the shuttlecraft's cockpit. She, too, seemed to be keeping her attention focused outward, looking for any sign of a trap being sprung. Then her stare connected with his, and she rolled her eyes. He imagined it was her way of expressing frustration at their vulnerability.

Behind them, their six passengers faced one another, grouped in rows along the port and starboard bulkheads. Commander Troi, Ensign Torvig, and Dr. Ree were behind Vale. On the other side of the cabin were Lieutenant Commander Keru, Lieutenant Sortollo, and Chief Dennisar. The bench seating was awkward for Ree and Torvig, who both perched uncomfortably on its edge.

Outside the cockpit window was nothing but a dark tunnel that curved and dipped and doubled back on itself several times, creating a winding course through the shell. None of the *Mance*'s sensors were functioning inside the passage. Not even proximity detectors registered any contact with the shell's mysterious, black alloy. That left Tuvok no choice but to navigate by eye and instinct, trusting in his perceptions of parallax motion to guide his hand as he steered through hairpin turns with only navigational thrusters to control the ship.

Vale peeked upward through the windshield. "How thick do you think the shell is?"

"Without sensors, I could offer only a vague estimate," Tuvok said. "I would speculate that, so far, we have made seven-point-three kilometers of vertical descent while navigating inside the shell."

The XO half smirked at his report. "That's a 'vague estimate,' Tuvok?"

"Indeed. I suspect it might be inaccurate by up to three-tenths of a kilometer. Its value as a computational variable for assessing the shell's mass and other properties is negligible."

"Noted," Vale said. She resumed her anxious visual survey of the environment outside the ship as Tuvok guided the *Mance* through another banking turn, into a much brighter area.

The cockpit windshield dimmed automatically to reduce the glare, enabling Tuvok to see that the passage came to an abrupt end roughly sixty meters ahead of the shuttlecraft, at the source of the light flooding into the tunnel. He slowed the shuttle's forward motion to less than two meters per second as it drew within twenty meters of the light. The windshield dimmed again, revealing a gap along the bottom of the passage, an opening just more than wide enough to let the *Mance* through.

He guided the shuttlecraft to a stop with its nose less than a decimeter from the terminal wall of the passage. Then he nudged its vertical thrusters into a descent profile and eased the *Mance* straight down, past what he guessed was more than twenty meters of the same black metal . . . and into open space.

Tuvok had too much control over his emotions to be amazed by the spectacle that stretched out ahead of him, but as a disciple of reason and as an explorer, he was impressed.

Before them lay a lush, bluish-green world swaddled in clouds and bathed in ersatz sunlight projected from the interior surface of the shell. From their vantage point on the edge of the planet's uppermost atmosphere, the shell looked like nothing more than a starless night, as if this was the only world orbiting the only star in the universe.

Checking his systems panel, Tuvok reported, "Sensor functions restored, Commander. Scanning the planet's surface."

"Any sign of habitation?" asked Vale.

"Life signs are extensive," Tuvok said as he reviewed the data. "The planet appears to be rich with plant and animal life in all regions and climates." He adjusted the sensors. "Scanning for artificial power sources and signal emissions." It took only seconds for the *Mance*'s sensors to lock on to something large. "Intense power readings, Commander. From inside a large mass of refined metals and synthetic compounds. Range, nine hundred eighty-one kilometers, bearing two two one."

"Take us in, Tuvok."

"Should I raise shields?"

Vale shook her head. "Negative. Not unless they give us a reason. Let's try to make this a friendly visit."

"As you wish." He adjusted the shuttlecraft's heading and keyed its thrusters, hurtling the small ship forward through the atmosphere. They punched through massive cloud banks and made a slight detour around a black-bruised stormhead that was bursting with rain and flashing with electric-blue lightning. Far below, the surface blurred past, a verdant landscape marked by dramatic rock formations and pristine, azure lakes.

Then the *Mance* passed over a range of jagged peaks capped with snow and cruised over a twilit arctic sea, toward a shimmer on the horizon. Tuvok reduced the shuttle's speed and altitude as a glittering metropolis took shape above a sea of pack ice. The city covered the entirety of a vast, bowl-like platform, which hovered hundreds of meters above the water. Most of its highest towers were clustered in its center, and the airspace above and between them teemed with thousands of small objects in motion.

"Wow," Vale said under her breath. "I'm guessing that's our energy source?"

"Affirmative," Tuvok said. He responded to a soft beeping on his console and saw that a signal was being transmitted to the shuttlecraft. "Commander, we appear to be receiving a repeating signal from the city. I believe it might be a beacon intended to guide us to a landing site."

Vale nodded once. "Follow it." She adjusted the sensor protocols. "The energy levels are making it hard to detect any life signs inside the city . . . except one. It's carbon-based, but it doesn't match anything in the computer."

"I've locked on to our landing coordinates," Tuvok said, guiding the *Mance* through a wide turn past twisting, organically shaped towers of dark crystal and delicate metalwork. He pointed at a circular platform situated at the end of a narrow causeway, a hundred meters past the edge of the city's outermost rampart.

The XO seemed amused. "All this high technology, but the visitor parking lot's still out in the boondocks. I guess some things really are universal." She looked at Tuvok as if she expected him to return her volley of inane banter with one of his own. Noting his pointed lack of a response, she faced forward and muttered, "Tough room."

Tuvok centered the shuttlecraft above the landing pad and eased it downward. It made only the slightest bump of contact as it touched down and settled on the platform. As he switched off the thrusters and activated routine command lockouts to secure the craft during the away team's absence, Vale moved through the aft cabin and marshaled the passengers into motion.

"Everybody ready?" she asked. The others nodded. She opened the port hatch, letting in a blast of frigid air. "Let's go."

Troi and Torvig were the first to follow Vale out of the shuttlecraft, and then Keru, Dennisar, and Sortollo exited with their rifles slung diagonally across their backs. Tuvok paused at the threshold when he noticed Dr. Ree lingering in the middle of the passenger cabin. "Doctor? Are you all right?"

"Let's just say that extreme cold is not a friend of the Pahkwa-thanh," Ree replied.

"Your exposure will be brief," Tuvok said. "Scans of the city I made during our approach indicate that the average temperature inside its environmental maintenance field is thirty degrees Celsius. I suspect that our landing area has been placed outside the protected zone as an incentive for us to leave the ship and proceed inward."

Ree's tongue flicked twice from between his front fangs, and he rasped, "Doesn't mean I have to like it." Then he lumbered through the hatch and out of the ship. Tuvok followed him into the dry, arctic chill.

"What the hell took you two?" snapped Vale in between huffing warm breath onto her cupped hands. "We're freezing our asses off out here." She tucked her hands under her armpits. "Come on. Double-time, people."

She led the away team at a brisk jog across the causeway, toward the humbling majesty of the city, whose structures gleamed with reflections of the peach-and-indigo arctic sky and the silhouetted landscape of peaks flanking a virgin sea. Their breath billowed around their heads in short-lived gray plumes as they ran, dispersed by gusts of wind that roared in their ears.

It was not a long run, but the extreme cold made it seem like one. Ahead of Tuvok, a wave of exhaustion and relief seemed to wash over the away team members. Then he caught up to them and felt the balmy warmth of the city's protected climate. It was more humid than he would have preferred, but still mild by human standards.

Dr. Ree arched his head back until his long snout was pointed straight up, and he made several deep snorting sounds, followed by rich, trumpeting blares that sounded as if they had originated deep inside his torso. He relaxed then and noticed the surprised looks from the other away team members. "Warming breaths," he said. "Just something Pahkwa-thanh have to do after we're exposed to the cold."

Vale gave a tight-lipped grin and said, "Okay, then. If show-and-tell's over, let's get . . ." Her voice tapered off as she stared past the away team, back toward the shuttlecraft. Tuvok and the others turned to follow her gaze.

The causeway had vanished. A hundred meters

away, past a gulf of open air hundreds of meters above an ice-packed arctic sea, the circular landing platform hovered without support. The *Mance* did not appear to have been damaged; apparently, whoever had removed the causeway had been satisfied merely to render the vessel inaccessible.

"Well . . . that's just great," Keru said. He looked at Sortollo and Dennisar. "I don't suppose either of you can do a hundred-meter long jump?"

Holding up her palms, Vale said, "All right, we came here to work some diplomacy. Getting our ship back will just have to be one of our negotiating terms—right, Counselor?"

"I think you'll have to ask them," Troi said, pointing.

Tuvok pivoted back toward the city and looked up, along the line of Troi's outstretched arm. Hundreds of meters above them, from a breezeway connecting two massive but delicate-looking towers, three figures floated downward with swift grace.

The away team watched in silence as the descending trio neared. Vale, Tuvok, and Troi stepped forward to meet them.

When the beings came within ten meters of the ground, they slowed and positioned themselves in a line. The two mottled gray-and-blue aliens at either end had their tendril-like fingers folded together in front of them. Their heads were bowed slightly forward, revealing the enormous globes of their skulls. Their generally humanoid shape made the ribbed tubing that ran from their chests to what Tuvok assumed were respiratory tubules near the backs of their heads all the more curious.

Most curious of all was the figure standing between them.

According to his tricorder, it was a carbon-based life-form of a kind not previously encountered by the Federation. What he saw was an athletic, healthy, and attractive young human woman with a long and unruly mane of black hair. Judging from her appearance, he estimated her age to be somewhere between her late teens and her early twenties.

The woman stepped forward and looked at Vale and Troi. Her voice sounded guarded and cautious— and perhaps secretly excited. "Humans," she said, apparently not discerning that Troi was half-Betazoid. Then she looked at Tuvok. "Vulcan." She glanced past them at the rest of the away team. "Orion," she said when she saw Dennisar. Looking at Keru, she said, "Trill."

After eyeing Torvig, she said nothing at all.

Tuvok studied the woman's face. Something about her seemed familiar to him. He searched his memory and found the reason.

Troi asked her, "You recognize our species?"

Before the woman could answer, Tuvok said, "I'm sure she does, Counselor. She is *from* Earth." Everyone looked at Tuvok for the explanation. He addressed the woman directly. "You are Captain Erika Hernandez of the Earth starship *Columbia,* missing in action for more than two hundred years."

"Yes," Hernandez replied. "I was the captain of the *Columbia.* And I've been missing much longer than you think." She raised her voice to address the rest of the away team. "Welcome to New Erigol."

End of Book I

Star Trek Destiny
will continue in
Book II
Mere Mortals

APPENDIX I
2156
Featured Crew Members

Columbia NX-02

Captain Erika Hernandez
(human female) commanding officer

Commander Veronica Fletcher
(human female) executive officer

Lieutenant Commander Kalil el-Rashad
(human male) second officer/science officer

Lieutenant Karl Graylock
(human male) chief engineer

Lieutenant Johanna Metzger
(human female) chief medical officer

Lieutenant Kiona Thayer
(human female) senior weapons officer

Ensign Sidra Valerian
(human female) communications officer

Major Stephen Foyle
(human male) MACO commander

Lieutenant Vincenzo Yacavino
(human male) MACO second-in-command

Sergeant Gage Pembleton
(human male) MACO first sergeant

APPENDIX II
STARDATE 58100
(early February 2381)

Featured Crew Members

U.S.S. Enterprise NCC-1701-E

Captain Jean-Luc Picard
(human male) commanding officer

Commander Worf
(Klingon male) executive officer

Commander Miranda Kadohata
(human female) second officer/operations officer

Commander Geordi La Forge
(human male) chief engineer

Commander Beverly Crusher
(human female) chief medical officer

Lieutenant Hegol Den
(Bajoran male) senior counselor

Lieutenant Jasminder Choudhury
(human female) chief of security

Lieutenant Dina Elfiki
(human female) senior science officer

Lieutenant T'Ryssa Chen
(Vulcan-human female) contact specialist/flight controller

APPENDIX II

U.S.S. Titan NCC-80102

Captain William T. Riker
(human male) commanding officer

Commander Christine Vale
(human female) executive officer

Commander Tuvok
(Vulcan male) second officer/tactical officer

Commander Deanna Troi
(Betazoid-human female) diplomatic officer/senior
counselor

Commander Xin Ra-Havreii
(Efrosian male) chief engineer

Lieutenant Commander Shenti Yisec Eres Ree
(Pahkwa-thanh male) chief medical officer

Lieutenant Commander Ranul Keru
(Trill male) chief of security

Lieutenant Commander Melora Pazlar
(Elaysian female) senior science officer

Lieutenant Pral glasch Haaj
(Tellarite male) counselor

Lieutenant Huilan Sen'kara
(Sti'ach male) counselor

Ensign Torvig Bu-kar-nguv
(Choblik male) engineer

APPENDIX II

U.S.S. Aventine NCC-82602

Captain Ezri Dax
(Trill female) commanding officer

Commander Samaritan Bowers
(human male) executive officer

Lieutenant Commander Gruhn Helkara
(Zakdorn male) second officer/senior science officer

Lieutenant Lonnoc Kedair
(Takaran female) chief of security

Lieutenant Simon Tarses
(human-Romulan male) chief medical officer

Lieutenant Mikaela Leishman
(human female) chief engineer

Lieutenant Oliana Mirren
(human female) senior operations officer

ACKNOWLEDGMENTS

A trilogy is a large and complex undertaking, one that I knew from the outset would be greater in its scope and more demanding in its execution than any of my previous projects. I am, therefore, grateful for the support and encouragement of my lovely and loving wife, Kara, who is doing her best during this marathon endeavor to remind me why I do it in the first place.

As for where all this started, I guess we can thank (or blame) artist Pierre Drolet, whose painting of the crashed *Columbia* NX-02 in the book *Ships of the Line* planted the seed of this idea in the minds of my editors, Marco Palmieri and Margaret Clark. I am also enormously grateful that, of all the authors who Marco and Margaret could have invited to write this trilogy, they chose me.

As usual, my fellow *Star Trek* authors have been a godsend. In particular, I owe thanks to J.M. Dillard, Peter David, Keith R.A. DeCandido, and Christopher L. Bennett, who all helped set the literary stage for this trilogy, and to Kirsten Beyer, who has the Sisyphean task of mopping up after it.

Lastly, I'd like to extend my heartfelt thanks to those few, special people in Lynchburg, Tennessee, who do what they do so well, so that I can do what I do at all.

ABOUT THE AUTHOR

David Mack has written some books. He hopes to write more books. As of this writing, he is currently on Day 5,919 (and counting) of his corporate captivity in New York.